THE STORM LORD

TWILIGHT OF THE CELTS

BOOK II

By M. K. Hume and available from Headline Review

King Arthur Trilogy
Dragon's Child
Warrior of the West
The Bloody Cup

Prophecy Trilogy
Clash of Kings
Death of an Empire
Web of Deceit

Twilight of the Celts Trilogy
The Last·Dragon
The Storm Lord

M.K. HUME

THE STORM LORD

TWILIGHT OF THE CELTS

BOOK II

headline
review

First published in 2014 by HEADLINE REVIEW
An imprint of HEADLINE PUBLISHING GROUP

1

Cataloguing in Publication Data is available from the British Library

Hardback ISBN 978 0 7553 7960 6
Trade paperback ISBN 978 0 7553 7961 3

Typeset in Golden Cockerel by Avon DataSet Ltd,
Bidford-on-Avon, Warwickshire

Printed and bound in Australia by Griffin Press

Headline's policy is to use papers that are natural products and made
from wood grown in responsible forests. The logging and manufacturing
processes are expected to conform to the environmental
regulations of the country of origin.

HEADLINE PUBLISHING GROUP
An Hachette UK Company
338 Euston Road
London NW1 3BH

www.headline.co.uk
www.hachette.co.uk

This book is dedicated to my two sons, Damian Michael Hume and Brendan Niels Hume.

I take inordinate pride in both of these young men who have lived their lives with all the best qualities that I have recognised in the Arthuriad such as courage, generosity, patriotism, love of kin and the nobility of work.

I wish them love, happiness and a long life but, most of all, I wish them contentment.

M. K. Hume

2014

ACKNOWLEDGEMENTS

There are many people who deserve thanks whenever an author completes a literary work. In many cases, it's just *being there* at the times when the going is difficult and the author is lacking inspiration that we gain our greatest rewards from those around us. Others provide essential professional services.

My editor, Clare Foss, always offers positive and calm assistance, even when I'm puzzled and rushed off my feet over a myriad number of *undone* bits and pieces that remain outstanding. In fact, every staff member at Headline Review has this same helpful and encouraging approach to publishing so that I consider myself fortunate to be part of their family.

My agent, Dorie Simmonds, is a genius at what she does. I will always picture her in a March wind, with her cheeks flushed from the cold as she frog-marched into one of those interminable 5th Avenue department stores in New York City to buy an ever-so-essential lipstick. From trivialities like lipstick to working so hard that my dreams came to life, Dorie has more than earned a lifetime of my thanks. She is the ultimate example of the axiom that says: *The harder we work, the luckier we get!* Does she ever sleep?

The cover designs for my books from the Art Department at Headline are simply brilliant, and have been for all of eight of my novels. My congratulations must go to those brilliant artists who understand exactly what my work needs to stand out on the booksellers' shelves.

My thanks also must go to my friends and family who make my life much easier as I work away in my study at all times of the day and night. My husband, Michael, is very good at what he does and without the pushiness that goes with his nature, I doubt that my dreams would ever have come true. My sons, Damian and Brendan, also give me unfailing support and they make me so proud of them.

My final thanks should go to Rusty, my little 'rescue dog' whom I love to distraction. He provides the complete love that enriches me and makes every day special. Unconditional love is what all humans yearn for, so Rusty provides my little view of heaven. I'll repay you with the nicest of bones, sweet boy.

M. K. Hume

DRAMATIS PERSONAE

Aednetta Fridasdottar	The Witch-Woman. She is the paramour of King Hrolf Kraki.
Alfridda	The sister of Stormbringer. She lives at The Holding with her husband, Raudi.
Arthur	The illegitimate son of King Artor and Lady Elayne.
Artor	High King of the Britons. The son of Uther Pendragon and Ygerne (the widow of King Gorlois of Cornwall).
Barr	The young son of Master Bedwyr and Lady Elayne.
Bedwyr	Known as the Arden Knife, Bedwyr is the Master of Arden Forest.
Beowulf	Epic poem of a Geat warrior who helps King Hrogar, King of the Danes, against Grendel, a monster.
Bjornsen, Valdar	(See Stormbringer).
Blaise	The youngest daughter of King Bors Minor of the Dumnonii Tribe.
Bors Minor	King of Cornwall. Father of Eamonn and Blaise.
Bran	King of the Ordovice Tribe.
Cealine	Stableboy in an inn in Dubris.
Deuteria	Concubine of King Theudebert of Austrasia.
Eamonn pen Bors	Son of King Bors Minor and Queen Valda of Cornwall.
Egbert of Wurms	Innkeeper in Soissons.
Elayne	Wife of Bedwyr, Master of Arden.

Eta	Widow innkeeper in Dubris.
Freya	The wise woman at World's End.
Erikk	Son of Halver, Jarl of Halland.
Frodhi	The influential cousin of King Hrolf Kraki in Heorot and Stormbringer.
Gareth Minor	Son of Gareth Major. Raised at Aquae Sulis.
Germanus	A Frankish mercenary.
Gilchrist	The eldest grandson of King Gawayne and heir to the Otadini throne.
Gull	A young shepherd at World's End.
Heardred	King of Geats.
Hnaefssen, Ivar	Jarl of a small village near The Sound in Denmark.
Hoel Ship-Singer	Shipwright from Halland.
Hrolf Kraki	Also called Storm Crow. He is the King of the Dene.
Hubert	Servant of King Theudebert.
Ingrid	Wife of the camp commander at Lake Wener. Mother of Sigrid.
Lasair	The eldest son of Bedwyr and Elayne.
Leif	The commander of the Dene forces trapped by Geat attackers at the mouth of the Vagus River.
Lorcan ap Lugald	A Hibernian priest.
Maeve	Sister of Prince Arthur.
Myrddion Merlinus	Also known as Myrddion Emrys, he is named after the Sun.
Nimue	The Lady of the Lake.
Olaffsen, Rufus	Hrolf Kraki's champion who fights Eamonn.
Olaus Healfdene	Commander of the Geat army at Lake Wener.
Priscus	The innkeeper in Gesoriacum.
Rolf Sea-Shaper	The helmsman on *Loki's Eye*, Stormbringer's ship.
Sigurd	Headman of the village of World's End.
Sigrid	Daughter of Ingrid. She was captured at Lake Wener.

Stormbringer	His full name is Valdar Bjornsen (also called the Stormbringer). A member of the Danish (Dene) aristocracy.
Taliesin	Son of Myrddion Merlinus and Nimue.
Theudebert	King of Austrasia.
Thorketil	The Hammer of Thor. He is Hrolf Kraki's champion who fights Arthur.
Tominoe	Farmer in Austrasia.
Vermund Hnaefssen	The son of Ivar Hnaefssen. He fights at the Battle of Vagus River.
Wisigard	First wife of King Theudebert.

THE DENE KINGS – THE SCYLDINGS

Note: The details that follow are a representation of Dene kings in the fifth and sixth centuries. The kings shown below are those considered important to this novel. Records are sketchy, so information on personages and dates are approximate.

Skiold *(dates unknown)* — First of the Scylding kings. He led the Dene people down from Opland to the coast of Sweden.

Frodi I *(dates unknown)* — Danish king. The son of Skiold.

Havar *(dates unknown)* — Danish king.

Vermund the Sage *(dates unknown)* — Danish king.

Dan Mikillati the Magnificent *(dates unknown)* — The legendary founder of a new Danish dynasty.

Frodi IV *(dates unknown)* — The last of the ancient Scyldings.

Frodi V *(dates unknown)* — The start of a new order in the dynasty.

Hoc Healfdene *(dates unknown)* — Born to mixed parentage, he was half-Dene. He was a Scylding by marriage.

Hnaef Healfdene *(c420–c448)* — Probably the son of Hoc Healfdene. He was the sub-king of the Sae Dene. Hengist was his comrade in arms.

Healfdene Scylding *(?–c495)* — Nephew of Hnaef. First of the (new) Scylding kings.

Hrothgar Scylding *(c495–c525)* — Son of Halfdan II, he was married to Wealhtheow. He features in the Beowulf saga.

Sighere *(dates unknown)* — A king of the Sae Dene who is mentioned in the epic poem, *Widsith*.

Halga *(?–c530)* — Son of Healfdene, he was also called Hundingsbane.

Snaer Frodhi *(?–c530)* — Son of Frosti. He was a brutal and oppressive king who dishonestly usurped the throne by trickery.

Hrolf Kraki *(?–c530)* — Son of Halga, he was called Storm Crow by his subjects. He was the Dene king during the period of Arthur's captivity.

Frodi VII *(c530–c548)* — Danish king.

Halfdan III *(c548–c580)* — Danish king.

Myrddion's chart of
pre-Arthurian Roman Britain

Bremenium ●

Vallum
Hadriani   Onnum
                Magnis

                        Vinovia ●
Bravoniacum ●   Lavatrae ●
        Verterae ●
                    Caractonium ●

                        Eburacum ●

        Bremetennacum ●

OCEANUS HIBERNICUS

                Melandra ●
        Mamucium ●

Mona   OCEANUS
    Canovium   GERMANICUS
Segontium ●
        Deva   Aquae ● Lindum

                    Venta Icenorum
                    (Cerdicsand)
            Margidunum ●

    Letocetum Ratae ● Causennae ●
Viroconium ● FOREST   Durobrivae ●
            OF ● Venonae
            ARDEN
    Salinae ●   ● Bannaventa   Camulodunum ●
Moridunum ●
        Venta
Isca ● Silurum ● Glevum
                ● Corinium
SABRINA AEST ● Abone
                        Londinium ●
        Aquae Sulis   Calleva ●
                Atrebatum
    Lindinis ●
                        ● Venta Belgarum
    ● Glastonbury ● Sorviodunum
Tintagel ● Cadbury   Noviomagus ●
Isca Dumnoniorum ● Durnovaria   Anderida ●
                    Vectis

MYRDDION'S CHART OF
THE CELTIC TRIBAL AREAS

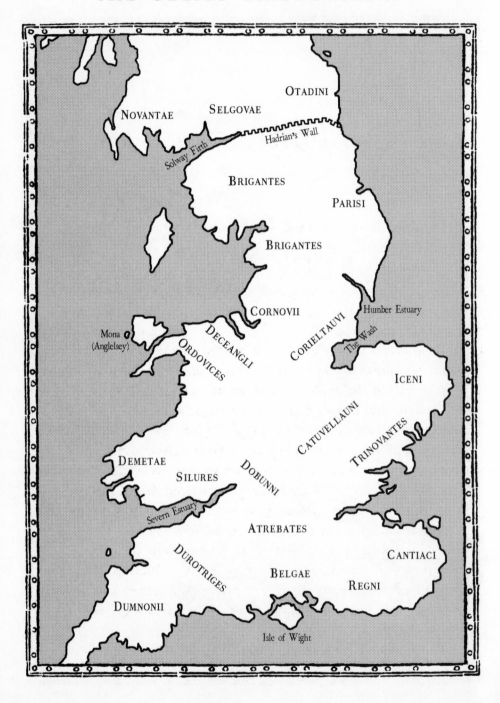

PROLOGUE

In nature there are neither rewards nor punishments – there are consequences.

Robert G. Ingersol, *Some Reasons Why*

The young man dreamed.

Deep below the keel of the leaf-shaped ship, where a pallid moon could not break through the blackness, he sank down and down. Strange fish lit the blackness with lights they carried in the flesh of their bodies, but no sound could pierce these silent waters. Within the strange dislocation of his dream, the young man could breathe the cold water and his body moved easily downwards without panic.

Just as he began to believe that this sea had no bottom, his naked toes sank into thick, fine mud. Strange elongated shapes, barely visible through the gloom, suggested great weeds with scalloped edges that strove to reach the light far above. As he moved through the water, stirring up small squalls of fine silt to further cloud his vision, he felt something smooth under the sole of his left heel. Rounded like a stone yet brittle in texture, the object had drawn his attention and he began to bend ... when a voice boomed out of the thick water and almost stopped his heart.

'Don't touch my treasures, earthworm, or I'll be forced to devour you.' The voice caused the water to shiver and drove a host of small sea creatures to swim, crawl and scuttle away from their hiding places nearby.

The young man would have fled himself, but fronds of weed wound themselves around his legs and anchored him to the ocean's floor. Terror gripped him as flames belched out of a vast, dim shape and a sanguine light bathed him with its bloody glare.

Now he could see the source of that thunderous sound.

The figure reposed on a bed of polished bones, worn to an ivory sheen by the many-coloured scales of her body. The she-dragon was long and seductively sinuous, with a head more serpentine than those of other dragons familiar to Arthur. Sculpted eye ridges rose out of a smoothly scaled forehead of a pale topaz colour and shadowed a pair of yellow eyes, slit with vertical pupils that were coldly venomous and wise beyond human understanding. The narrow nostrils still steamed gently in the cooling water. Only the mouth was frightening, for it was filled with carved fangs as long as the young man's arm. Yet her whole coiled and muscular length, elaborated with a web of delicate, transparent wings and powerful clawed feet, suggested might and the primal energy of water.

'Why do you disturb my sleep, earthworm? You could easily crush my treasured bones under your careless feet. I would become very angry if I were to lose the smallest rib or incur damage to the oldest vertebrae.'

Because the dragon seemed to expect it, Arthur bowed as deeply as the weed permitted. 'I don't know, Majesty. Perhaps I'm dreaming, but I have no intention of robbing you or of damaging your bones. Where did you find them?'

'Find them?' The she-dragon snickered and her mirth caused the water and her ossuary to shiver.

'I didn't *find* them – I *took* them! The sailors in my domain were hungry for life, but I am the only being who is permitted to live and breathe in my kingdom, along with those sea-creatures whom I permit to serve me – either as food or as amusement. Here, *you* are the trespasser. And if your bones are sufficiently perfect, earthworm, I will happily take them into my collection.'

The voice crooned out the threat with a hypnotic cadence that almost lulled Arthur into closing his eyes. How easy it would be to submit to those seductive suggestions that offered him eternity in exchange for his vital energy. With a herculean effort, Arthur wrenched his eyelids open and raised his head.

'Come to me,' the she-dragon ordered. Obediently, the waterweed lifted the young man off his feet so that he hung within an arm's length of her long pearly teeth. Her forked tongue explored his face with a sensuous knowledge.

Immediately, the she-dragon drew in her breath with a fearful hiss. The eyes flared with a sudden flame, lighting the rosy coral of the scales on her belly. 'Who are you, earthworm? I know the shape of your skull and the fine roundness of your hip bones. I have dreamed of the perfect alignment of your vertebrae – but though I would trade all my precious collection for you, I remember that my fore-dream forbade it. Yes, dragons can also dream. Who are you to deny me my desires?'

'I'm no one of importance, Majesty, other than an earthworm who longs for the sunlight,' Arthur pleaded with desperate honesty. 'I am called the Son of the Dragon by those who know me but at this moment I am a captive of northern seafarers. I have nothing that could cause harm to you.'

The dark waters shivered as the she-dragon stirred nervously on her bed of skulls. When she spoke, her voice was petulant and her hot breath caused Arthur to flinch away from the furnace that burned inside her.

'You shall become the King of Winter – whether you like it or not! You will renounce what you are, earthworm, so that you can survive in the bitter north and become what you once were – and more! But ask me nothing else, earthworm, for your strength lies with the sun and fire, and both elements would shrivel my scales and turn my beautiful bones to black dust.'

'No! I'll never renounce my ancestors, even to gain wealth and power. I'm no coward or turncoat,' Arthur howled with a sudden horror that is the way of dreams. 'I will return to Arden, I swear, and I will protect the legacy of my father.'

'What father, fool? Is it the king or the cuckold?'

The waters began to shiver and the reeds and waterweeds were torn away from his limbs by a sudden warm current that pulled him upward, away from the she-dragon and her ossuary of human bones. 'Leave me, earthworm, for you will bring misfortune to all souls who try to bar your way. Kings will perish because of you, and disease will dog your footsteps although you will remain unscathed. Your curse is to live for all time and to become part of a legend that no one credits, so leave me be!' Her voice followed him as he was thrown towards the light. 'Leave me to sleep until the oceans boil.'

The voice still shivered along Arthur's nerve-endings as his head broke the sea's surface. Water poured from his nostrils and mouth, and the young man discovered that he could scream – so he did.

As the sun burned his flesh and he felt his hair begin to smoke, Arthur woke to find himself in a cold, brutal morning.

A red sun tore free of a charcoal sea. Regardless of the hot colour, the cold ate into him like a knife of ice. The young man winced as a shaft of sunlight stabbed through his half-closed eyelids and forced him to open his eyes, until he groaned as a sudden pang lanced through his head. Already, the dream had receded, overtaken by the actuality of his captivity, the memory of the ambush on the northern road and the desperation of his party's situation. His breath steamed in the frozen air.

Barely awake, he sat upright with his back against the huge mast while a vast woollen sail snapped and soughed above him in the freshening morning breeze. For a moment the claws of the dragon, dyed into the wool, caught the dim rays of light and stretched down towards him, as if the she-dragon had animated the painted cloth.

'Lift me up and carry me away, Majesty,' he urged. 'To death if needs be – for I have failed in my appointed task. Lady Blaise will not wed Gilchrist of the Otadini and Maeve will never return to Arden; and it's my fault. My friends are held captive and I have managed to lose my father's knife. My sword is taken, but because Maeve and my charges are still alive I can't even throw myself into the sea. Do what you want with me, but send me no more dreams.'

A small hand snaked out of bundles of wool on the rough-cut deck to interrupt his brief indulgence in self-pity. Grimy fingers grasped his own with surprising strength and a tousled head appeared out of a nest of mangy furs. The girl shook herself vigorously and uncurled her body to rise and lean against his side.

'Don't be such an ass, Arthur! We're in enough trouble without our strongest warrior having fits of guilt and talking of killing himself.' The girl's hand and the comfort it brought mitigated the harshness of Blaise's irritated lecture. 'Grow up, you silly boy! You're years older than me and you're still complaining about honour and a lost knife. For heaven's sake, aren't we in enough trouble? Jesus alone knows where these savages are taking us! While you're going on about the dishonour of being captured, Maeve and I have to worry about rape by some hulking great giant.'

Arthur tried to remonstrate with Blaise, a girl who was little more than a child despite her brusque manner, but his words of protest caught in his throat. The child was right; he *was* being self-indulgent. 'We're depending on you to take care of us, Arthur. We need you to focus on our escape. Please ...' For the first time, Blaise's careful and courageous façade cracked at the edges and Arthur could hear the terrified tremor in her voice. He drew her close to him so that her wild curls tickled his chin.

'I'm sorry,' he whispered. 'I'll do better in the future. Just remind me of our real priorities if I should slip. Now go back to sleep, little one, while some darkness still remains. I'll keep watch for both of us till sunrise.'

Blaise snuggled her head into the hollow of Arthur's shoulder and ignored the generations of societal rules that forbade contact between the sexes. For his part, Arthur felt the shame and misery that had greeted him on waking dissipate slowly, to be replaced by something akin to hope. Despite his dreams Arthur was little more than a boy, still too young to be capable of visualising his own death. Therefore a new resolve made him sit a little straighter as he vowed silently to do everything a man could do to save Eamonn, Maeve and Blaise from harm. A lost knife could be found again, a sword could be won, and each new day would bring the promise of escape a little closer.

As the captives dozed, the sun began to rise higher to light the lower edges of wide cloudbanks with a line of scarlet and gold. The tops of the wavelets from the ship's wake to the eastern horizon were caught in flakes of gold so that the sea and the sky were a symphony of grey and black, gilded and embellished with vermilion, carmine and sanguine. The seascape was wild and beautiful, but Arthur was suddenly blinded with tears that trembled on the edges of his lashes. Stubbornly, he brushed them away.

His eyes ranged across the horizon, from the darkness that still blanketed the western sky on the far side of the vessel to where the white globe of incandescence was mounting through the clouds in the east.

In every direction, there was nothing except an endless expanse of water. No smudge of distant land; no seabirds squabbling over prey; no other vessels of any kind. Just the long slow swell of deep waters around them and below them. And only a frail vessel lay between him and the lightless depths beneath the planks of the hull. Arthur's dream returned to haunt the edges of his imagination, so he could almost hear the she-dragon of his dream snigger as if she waited for his clean white bones to sink down to grace her hellish bed.

The sky swung wildly for a moment and Arthur shook his head and dug his nails into his palms to quell his rising panic. The carved prow of the vessel and its terrifying dragon sail were only puny attempts by men to challenge the infinity of the ocean. He had seen the might of the waters in his dream when the she-dragon had berated him from her ossuary of drowned seamen. These Dene savages must be dauntless sailors to challenge the empty oceans with such daring.

But where *was* the land? Wiser sailors hugged the coastlines instead of sailing blindly through the wastes of water.

Just when the young man would have sobbed to give voice to his terror, Blaise stirred in her sleep and stiffened his backbone with her helplessness.

We may be sailing into the unknown, Arthur thought, but the Red Dragon leads the way. Perhaps I shouldn't be so fearful, for Father is with us. All will be well.

And then, against all reason, the snapping sail loaned him some of the dragon's mythic power. Arthur felt the shade of his father, and even the tainted spirit of his grandfather, as they settled behind him to protect his naked back. For the first time since the attack by the mercenaries had robbed the Britons of their freedom, he felt a renewed sense of purpose.

God still had a task for him to complete. He must have faith in his own abilities and, if he could only muster his courage, all would be well.

CHAPTER I

THE WRATH OF HEAVEN

To the gull's way and the whale's way where the wind's like a
whetted knife;

John Masefield, 'Sea Fever'

'Wake up and take the bowl, Briton.' The rich tenor voice with the
execrable accent attempted to speak Arthur's language with sufficient
clarity to be understood. While individual words were unclear, the
meaning was unmistakeable.

With his eyes squeezed tightly shut, Arthur attempted to take his
bearings. The pitch and roll of waves beneath the hull of the ship
reminded him that he was a prisoner of the Dene, while the smell of
salt on the wind explained more clearly than words that they were still
far from land. Although he strained to catch a faint scent of vegetation
or the distant shriek of seabirds, their lack mocked him for being a
wishful-thinking fool. He had slept past the dawn, and nothing had
changed during his slumbers.

Arthur opened his eyes as slowly as possible and acknowledged
Stormbringer, the captain of the vessel, when the Dene leaned over
him with a wooden bowl in his outstretched hand. Under close
examination, the Dene's skin was thick, smooth and golden-brown
where it wasn't covered with curly hair. When he glanced down at the

bowl, Arthur registered vaguely that it held an odd concoction of cold seafood. The food smelled pungent and fishy as it slopped inside the receptacle, so his appetite vanished.

Arthur accepted the proffered food, but his expression must have shown his lack of understanding of Stormbringer's mish-mash of language. The young Briton scoured his memory and tried a few hesitant words in the Frankish tongue, bolstered with Latin. He watched as Stormbringer nodded in surprised recognition.

So, Arthur thought, learning snatches of Germanus's language has proved useful.

When he was a boy, Arthur had laboured to speak Frankish and the languages of the Hibernian tribes, primarily to build a link with his tutors, Father Lorcan and Germanus. Unfortunately, the language of the Britons had no written form, but Arthur had become proficient in Latin during his childhood, especially when he had access to the scrolls that Taliesin had passed into his care on the explicit instructions of Nimue, the Lady of the Lake. These scrolls had opened young Arthur's mind to the art of healing, the stories of his father, the long wars to stabilise the British homeland and the nature of the Saxons who became their neighbours and their enemies.

Bedwyr, Elayne and even Maeve had read Myrddion's scrolls in those far-off days of peace and studious concentration, and all had learned much that was useful from that remarkable, well-travelled thinker. Arthur had found his own place in the world through the old healer's stories of Artor and had come to feel pride in his ancestry. As a by-product, he had also become proficient in written Latin.

Although the Roman Empire was now a distant memory, its language remained the one unifying factor in the West. Any man who spoke or wrote Latin could travel from Constantinople to Londinium or from Tolosa to Bremen, and still be understood by members of the local population. Arthur decided Stormbringer was a man of obvious intelligence, but he was unlikely to have had the need to master any written language, Latin or otherwise.

Then Arthur glimpsed the runes carved into a walrus-ivory tablet that hung on a thong around Stormbringer's neck. Stormbringer tucked the amulet away from Arthur's prying eyes, but the young Briton wondered at its significance.

'Thank you, Master Stormbringer.' Arthur spoke for his companions as he carefully framed each syllable. 'We're all hungry.'

'So . . . you speak the Frankish tongue,' Stormbringer answered, his blond eyebrows raised in surprise. 'You possess a host of talents and inconsistencies, young Dragonsen.'

This man has educated speech patterns for a barbarian, the young man thought. He was disconcerted, but made no comment. Lorcan had cautioned his student against such rash preconceptions, so Arthur decided he should watch and wait before deciding what type of man this Dene really was. Time enough in the future to learn everything he needed to know about his captor.

'Did you know that the Franks were originally a northern tribe, and neighbours of the Saxons?' Stormbringer asked; Arthur realised that he and his companions had fallen into the hands of a knowledgeable man. A moment of reflection convinced Arthur that only a highly respected leader would have been given the task of voyaging into the unknown on a mission of obvious importance. To jump to erroneous conclusions because Stormbringer and his crew were clad in hides and furs, and to decide that their culture was primitive because the Dene ship was held together with pegs rather than nails, would be a gravely wrong assessment of their technical ability.

'To underestimate an enemy is to be half-defeated before the battle commences,' Germanus had told him on many occasions.

'Is this the reason you speak my language, because it's so similar to the languages of Roman Gaul?'

The Dene captain shrugged. 'I have a gift with tongues, which is one of the reasons that my king sent me to your most pleasant island. We can speak Latin, if you prefer. As a boy, I was tutored in this language by a Roman priest who had come to our land, Dene Mark, to convert my people to the Christian faith.'

The Dene chuckled at a sudden recollection. When he spotted

Arthur's curiosity, he offered an explanation. 'The silly fool had almost convinced us that he wanted to be drained of blood – and then *eaten*.'

'I beg your pardon?' Arthur gulped.

'I can laugh at the humour of the situation because my people are now familiar with the Christian Mass. But when the priest first arrived, my father and his king thought the priest wanted them to drink his blood and eat his flesh. Of course, our king was revolted and insulted by the request. The priest almost lost his life for implying that we were cannibals.'

Arthur laughed lamely.

'I'll never forget Father Stephan's face when he realised how we had misunderstood his words. He almost fainted with shock.' Stormbringer shook his head contemplatively, a slight smile on his lips. One hand caressed his reddish-blond beard.

'The priest tarried in the Dene lands for many years and taught the sons and grandsons of Halga, the king of the Dene, and any other noble children whose fathers wanted their sons to benefit from a wider education. Latin enabled me to communicate with both enemies and friends from all the southern lands, regardless of their native languages. The peasants have embraced Christianity eagerly, so even our slaves remain peaceful and are well behaved. Christianity encourages both endurance and submission, however, so we aren't entirely Christian.'

Arthur learned much about the Dene and their attitudes towards the world through listening quietly to Stormbringer's conversation. His people had slaves; they had reached the Frankish lands by sea for trade; and they were able to grasp the importance of education. Stormbringer had also indicated that he was a nobleman, whatever the Dene interpretation of aristocracy might be. He might have learned far more from the captain if their attention had not been caught by a call from a tall, whipcord-thin warrior working as the ship's lookout. The crewman had climbed to the apex of the prow where a wooden serpent's head reared above the decks and spat eternal defiance at the waves. The lookout was now gesticulating furiously as he pointed towards the distant horizon.

'Master Valdar,' the lookout called, addressing the captain by his given name, a nomen which Arthur filed away for future use. The conversation that ensued was in a language that sounded deceptively like Saxon but was delivered far too quickly for the Briton to follow, although he caught an ominous reference to the word *storm*. Fortunately, the tall man was pointing to a line of black clouds scudding along the rim of the horizon.

'What's that?' Arthur asked, with one cold hand shielding his eyes from the glare reflecting off the slate-grey water.

'A winter gale,' Stormbringer snapped, before spitting out a list of crisp commands that set the Dene warriors scurrying to complete their foul-weather orders.

'The food in the bowl is for you and your friends to share. I'm sure you understand it's impossible to heat it,' he told Arthur over one shoulder. 'That storm might become dangerous very quickly, so we'll batten down in case it changes direction and crosses our path. We could turn and run towards Britain or Gaul but they're too far away to ensure our survival. We could be driven off course, and that would lead to worse problems. But for now, your companions must eat. Immediately, hungry or not, because there'll be no chance if we meet up with that little *kiss from the gods*.'

Blaise, Maeve and Eamonn were awake and listening to the hurried conversation with varying degrees of comprehension. Arthur nodded and hunkered down near the tiller, calling to his friends to join him and to remain out of the path of running warriors as they secured any loose items on board the vessel with ropes of plaited flax and hide, especially the large bladders of fresh water. As quickly as possible, Arthur explained the situation to his friends.

'What's in it?' Maeve asked suspiciously, as she sniffed the glistening brown and green slop. The crew and its captives had been at sea for over a week now, but the Dene had taken in a store of fresh food and water for the journey home, so the captives had a goodly supply of stale bread, cheese, cured meat and dried apples. To supplement these staples, Stormbringer's men were forced to subsist on what seafood they could catch as they travelled, and very unappetising it appeared to be.

'That bit looks like a baby octopus!' Blaise exclaimed with revulsion as she pushed with her forefinger at a tentacle that had risen to the oily surface of the stew. 'I'm prepared to eat cockles, fish – even oysters – but I can't look at those tiny legs with suckers all over them. Urgh! I could never eat them, even if I was starving.'

'I can!' Eamonn interrupted and plucked the tiny octopus out of the bowl and tossed it into his mouth. He chewed vigorously . . . and chewed . . . and chewed.

'It might be tough but it's still edible,' he pronounced as he made a valiant attempt to swallow. 'Just don't look at it when you put it into your mouth.'

Maeve and Arthur used their fingers to lift some unrecognisable pieces of dried fish and other seafood scraps out of the bowl. They ate tentatively but with determination, for they knew they would weaken and become ill if they failed to sustain themselves.

'You have to maintain your strength, Blaise, so don't be so stubborn!' Eamonn made no attempt to disguise his irritation with his recalcitrant and argumentative sister. Very little love was lost between the siblings, but Arthur was convinced that his excitable Dumnonii friend would die to preserve the life of his kinswoman. And so Arthur persisted and held the bowl under Blaise's nose until she fished through the meat and ate some large chunks of unrecognisable vegetables. Her face was a study in revulsion as she forced the food down and then gulped rainwater out of a leather flask that Stormbringer had left for them.

'It's seaweed!' she gasped, once she had caught her breath. 'I've eaten it before when I was sick and my nurse forced me to take it to build up my strength. And there's sand in the stew. Who'd willingly eat seaweed?'

'Anybody who had nothing else to keep them alive,' Stormbringer interrupted from his position beside the tiller. His expression was scathing. 'If the winter is very cold in my country and the harvest is poor, my people will eat seaweed when the sea is kind enough to deliver it up . . . and then thank God for his mercy. Otherwise the older people must go out into the snow when the food supplies run low.'

'But they'd . . . they'd die.' Blaise's voice trailed off as she looked at the iron expression on Stormbringer's face.

'You're right – they go out into the snow and they die! Now, enough! This is all the food that *anyone* will have today, and my own men will go hungry because the storm is likely to strip us of our supplies. Once you've eaten, you must tie each other together and lash yourselves to some part of the ship that is unlikely to be washed overboard. The base of the mast would be the safest place, perhaps? This gale that lies in our path is out of season and, as such, it will be dangerous and unpredictable. If we can't outrun it, we'll need every person on board to be at the oars.' He nodded towards Arthur and Eamonn. 'Are you prepared to row for me? I lost some of my men when we were taking you prisoner, so I'll need your help on the rowing benches.'

Arthur glanced across at his friend.

'I could manacle you to the oars and force your compliance, but I need men who are willing to row for their lives, not slaves who are terrified of death. And I don't need prisoners whose reluctance could fuck up our chances of survival. Do you understand?'

The crudity hung in the air to underline Stormbringer's urgency, so both young men nodded and rose to their feet.

'I meant what I said, girls! Lash yourselves down and cover yourselves with blankets or hides that will give you some protection when the waves start to batter us. The sleet and whatever else that Loki throws at us will freeze you rigid if you're exposed or washed overboard. Move quickly now, because I don't have time to watch out for you.'

As Arthur and Eamonn were pushed and shoved into their places in the oar stations, they took the opportunity to stare behind them at the advancing sky. An impossibly heavy mass of black, billowing cloud with a rolling straight edge at its head seemed to boil in the upper air. Although it was just past noon, the freshening wind was steering the storm towards them at an incredible rate as its centre continued to swell. The air currents around the ship were already gusting, causing the great sail to billow and snap until the forward momentum of the Dene vessel began to slow. The hull screamed and shuddered along every plank.

Stormbringer pointed upward and shouted something incomprehensible at two crewmen who began to climb the mast until they reached the spars holding the giant sail in place. Once they were hanging over empty air, they struggled to lash the sail into a long roll that they secured to the spar with lengths of rope and strips of hide. Freed now from the sail's drag, the ship swung sideway into a small trough that brought curses to Stormbringer's lips when a larger wave filled the scuppers with freezing, salty water. Then, almost magically, the prow of the ship turned directly into a wind that had now risen to gale force. The man at the tiller at the stern of the vessel put his back into the task of forcing the ship to remain head-on into the wind.

'To your oars,' Stormbringer bellowed, as another large wave broke over the prow of the vessel with a hard blow that caused the hull to shudder. 'Helmsman! Steer straight into this bitch or we'll founder! Put your backs into it! On my mark, bend your backs! If we have any hope of passing through the storm, we'll need you whoresons to row as if the Ice Dragons are lusting for your souls.'

He paused. The air was thrumming as if the gale was an angry insect.

'Row, you bastards, row!' The shrieking wind was already alive with noise as the moan of the sail's rigging, the howl of disturbed air and the dull thud from waves breaking over the prow gave Arthur a taste of the destruction that could be inflicted by the sea gods.

'Faster! Dig into the waves!' The helmsman cursed as the tiller was almost pulled from his arms by the ocean's force as it battled against the rudder. Stormbringer had to add his extra weight and strength against the straining blade of solid timber.

Bizarrely, the warriors began to shout a measured chant; Arthur thought they had all turned into madmen. Bearded faces were split with wide, manic grins and the song was a roared challenge to the might of the ocean. Then, after a few seconds, he realised the oarsmen were rowing to the beat of the chant. As loudly as he could, and inventing words in his own tongue, Arthur joined the refrain as his muscles dug into the task.

He soon learned why these tall men were so powerful in the shoulders, upper arms and thighs, while the rest of their bodies were lean and hard. The bite in his muscles as his long oar struck the water, dug in and then scooped itself free with flesh-tearing force sent a wave of hot pain screaming through his upper body. His thighs tensed as the power expended at the oar coursed from his toes to his groin.

He knew instinctively that only flesh and muscle could drive the ship through the face of this storm, and then only with luck. The forces of nature were so powerful that the combined efforts of thirty rowers would be barely sufficient to make the ship respond.

Maintaining a momentum in this chaotic weather seemed an impossible task at first. Soon, each rower found himself engaged in a solitary battle with the elements as he felt the long, slow swell of the ocean's sinews trying to tear the oar from his trembling hands. After ten strokes, Arthur could almost have imagined himself alone in the lung-tearing and bone-wrenching battle with his oar. Around him, the other warriors applied their strength to their own tasks in the same deadly isolation, while Stormbringer helped the helmsman at the rudder. The ship's commander threw his weight and his height against the wooden bar that hung above the deck. His powerful back bent like a great bow of bone and muscle, pitted against the might of the sea and the storm.

Because he had his back to the prow of the ship, Arthur had been obliged to turn his head painfully to one side to watch the advancing gale, but he still managed to keep one terrified eye on the captain. Stormbringer's expression remained unchanged throughout the inhuman struggle, but he showed no trace of fear, even when the waters boiled around his vessel and she began to take in water. He continued to shout his orders to the crew in a calm and controlled voice.

'Here she comes, brothers! Don't lose the beat! For your lives, drive the bitch down!'

The severity of the storm increased and the Dene vessel was hit with a sudden, crushing wave that rose over them like a mountain. Up went the prow until the serpent's head seemed to roar defiance at the storm gods above them.

Then the ship came down into the empty trough behind the wave with a crash that not only threatened to drag the oar out of Arthur's hands, but also jerked his body down to a sudden halt that sent a thrill of agony from the base of his spine to the muscles of his neck.

'Jesus Christ, save us!' Arthur screamed as he spat out a sudden gobbet of blood from where he had bitten his tongue. And now the air was full of sleet, blown horizontally by gale-force winds that shrieked like all the blue hags that had ever lived.

Objects tore loose from their bindings and flew through the air to strike warriors or the ship. The benches on which the warriors crouched were wet and freezing, while the oarsmen were soon ankle-deep in gelid salt water. Yet no man, Briton or Dene, would cease his defiance or falter with the steady beat of the oars. If they weakened, they would rot in an icy sea, unmourned and unsung.

By now, Arthur had caught the words of that chanted refrain, and he roared it out as fiercely and as furiously as the bearded madmen on the benches around him, even though he scarcely understood what he sang. In a world of wind, fiery ice and mountainous seas, the rowers alone were real in the maelstrom of the ocean's boundless strength.

Above them, the sun was extinguished and even the distant stars were blotted out, as if they had already fallen into the cataracts at the edge of the earth. Arthur was unafraid and his blood sang to the beat of his oar as if there was nothing else but this primal struggle against the forces of nature. If they were lost, the gods would know that they had risked their lives bravely in a gamble with eternity. All else was foolishness.

CHAPTER II

WHEN LOKI JESTS WITH MEN

There is one safeguard known generally to the wise, which is an advantage and security to all, but especially to democracies against despots – suspicion.

Demosthenes, *Philippics*

When Arthur came to his senses, the Dene vessel was bobbing on clearer water and he was bent over his oar like a drunken bar-room brawler. He was chilled to the bone and doubted that his legs would hold him if he attempted to stand.

From where he sat with his back to the prow, he could see the gale as it scudded away from them. As impossible as it seemed, the Dene ship had only experienced its edge, for Stormbringer had expertly steered the ship away from the worst of the storm. Had they experienced its full force, every soul on board would have perished. Now the Dene ship began to be lashed by squalls of driving sleet mixed with cold rain, so that Arthur thanked his own god and the Roman Mithras that he hadn't yet been called to join his ancestors in the shades.

Somehow, against the will of the gods, *Loki's Eye* was still afloat and under control. But the pace was much reduced by the sheer weight of the water that slopped around their legs and streamed from the scuppers.

When he straightened his aching spine, Arthur was conscious of the presence of every iron plate sewn onto his leather tunic for, when their weight was compounded with soaking wool and wet leather, his clothing seemed almost too heavy for his overstretched muscles to bear. Still, because he deemed himself a man and refused to be shamed by his bodily hurts, Arthur rested his oar and checked the safety and condition of the men around him.

The breathless Dene warriors leaned on their oars in various stages of exhaustion as normalcy returned to the ship. Stormbringer appeared above them on the upper deck and shouted orders with much laughter and a show of strong white teeth. From the few words he understood, Arthur deduced that Stormbringer was congratulating his men on their survival. Then, at a sharp order, the warriors began to draw their oars into the vessel. Arthur was happy to follow suit as he watched two of the sailors climb the mast to unfurl the dragon sail. With sighs, curses and winces of pain, most of the crew lay on the rowing benches, their chests still labouring as lungs and hearts returned to a normal pattern.

Loki's Eye wallowed under the accumulated weight of water that slowed her pace to a crawl. Using helmets, leather buckets or any of the variety of utensils floating around the warriors' legs, everyone on board began the dreary task of bailing water from the ship. This unpredictable storm could turn in its tracks and attack them from the rear. Carrying such weight of water, *Loki's Eye* could easily founder from the first great wave that crossed her bows.

Impossibly, and against every scream from their tortured bodies, the warriors bent their backs to the task. Arthur forced his shaking arms to dig the helmet he found into the swirling water and empty it over the side.

In a short space of time, the ship was made watertight and dry one more. Everyone and everything was sodden, but the gods of chaos would search in vain for the souls of these doughty seamen. The she-dragon must look elsewhere for bones for her ossuary on this particular day.

Freed once again to make use of the churning breezes that blew in the wake of the storm, the ship resumed its original course, a feat which only Stormbringer appeared to understand. On several occasions, he consulted an odd, circular piece of metal with strange runes carved into it, but Arthur had no idea what purpose the object served. The young Briton smiled ruefully. The Dene could do something that even the Romans had never mastered: they could sail beyond the sight of land.

Arthur dragged himself to his feet. Climbing over bladders of water, sodden rags of clothing, wooden boxes and other flotsam that lay in no more than a finger-joint of freezing water over the decking, he inched his way to the base of the mast and pulled a bundle of hides and wool away to reveal Blaise and Maeve huddled together with their arms around each other. A line of blood snaked out of Maeve's hairline where some flying object had struck her, but his sister was otherwise unhurt. Luckily, Blaise had suffered no harm either.

With unspoken thanks to God, Arthur slumped into his usual position against the mast and leaned back with a sigh.

'We're still alive,' Blaise murmured, then laughed shakily as she pulled the bowl holding the remains of the seafood stew out from the mess of blankets. An inch of viscous weed and vegetables still clung to the edges of the container. 'Look, I've saved my supper,' she chortled with a trace of hysteria. 'Master Stormbringer was wrong. We'll have something to eat after all.'

The captives fell asleep with the ease of young animals, but a strange sound woke Arthur with a rush.

A smiling Stormbringer stood above him. 'At last!' the commander said. 'I thought you and your friends planned to sleep all the way into harbour.'

'What's that?' Arthur asked. The faint light around them seemed to suggest that night was falling although common sense told him that the hour could scarcely be past mid-afternoon. Arthur's thoughts were scrambled, but his ears had been charmed to wakefulness by the mournful song of one of the warriors who was coiling a long piece of flaxen rope. As he sang, his shoulder and arm muscles flexed and relaxed in turn to the repetitive pattern of his labour.

'Ranalf sings of the birth of the Dene people and the long and perilous journey of the Scyldings to our first home,' Stormbringer told him. He sat at his ease on the half-deck that raised the helmsman up in order to control the great tiller. Even with extraordinarily long legs, clad in trews of leather for warmth and laced along the outside, Stormbringer was forced to swing them like a child on an overlarge stool because the half-deck was very high. Arthur had difficulty concealing a smirk of amusement.

'Who are these Scyldings? I presume we're to be taken to your king who'll determine our fates. I'm inclined to think that slavery will be the most likely outcome, so I'm anxious to know as much as possible about our future masters. I understand the fates of captives, although I'm upset that my sister and Blaise have been captured with me. If mercy can be granted to outlanders in our position, I'll happily beg for consideration for both of these young girls. They've done nothing to hurt anyone, so why should their lives be laid waste?'

Stormbringer shrugged with his usual enigmatic lack of expression, but Arthur thought he saw a shadow of regret pass through the Dene's startling blue eyes. Then it was gone.

'My lord, Hrolf Kraki, who is also known as the Crow King, is the king and my master. He alone will decide your fate and the separate destinies of your friends. Although I'll explain to my king that you were betrayed by a fellow Briton called Mareddyd, I will have no part in his decision. I might add that I refused to accept any coin from Mareddyd for his treachery because I considered that you might be of use to me if I were to take you to the Dene lands. In fact, Arthur Dragonsen, I gave three rings of pure silver to Mareddyd to have you lured into our ambush.'

Arthur shook his head, too angry to speak aloud of his frustration that Eamonn, Maeve and Blaise should suffer because of his feud with the traitorous prince of the Dobunni tribe.

'I will tell my king how well you assisted my warriors during the storm, so my lord may decide to be generous. He can be extremely fair when the mood takes him.'

Stormbringer paused as he considered his next words.

'In days gone by, the throne of Hrolf Kraki's father, Halga, was stolen by Snaer Frodhi, the son of Frosti, who used trickery to usurp Halga's crown. Snaer ruled our people in cruelty and oppression for the next fifteen years. During that time, many good Dene lords were forced to wander the earth else Snaer would have them murdered. Hrolf Kraki was one of these, banished after the assassination of his elder brothers. Ultimately, my master regained the throne and I returned from the Frankish lands where I had fled with my warriors. I know what it is to be a stranger in a foreign land who must prove himself with only the strength of his arms and the purity of his heart. Now, my king hates traitors and he might show mercy towards you, though only Loki or Jesus Christ can tell how he will respond to your pleas.'

'Any assistance you can provide to your king that will protect my companions will place me in your debt, Master Stormbringer.' Arthur rose to his feet and bowed his head to the Dene leader. In this obeisance the Briton lost no dignity, for Stormbringer judged correctly that Arthur asked for nothing for himself. He nodded to the younger man and extended his own sword hand in friendship.

'We're men, aren't we? I've been told by your friends that the British people call you the Last Dragon, and they believe you are the son and grandson of the ruler from the Red Dracos. Is that true? If so, I deem you to be a lucky man who's been blessed by the god of Father Stephan, for a sensible man hedges his wagers when it comes to recognition from the lords of Heaven. I'll help you all I can as long as you don't ask me to betray my own kin or my people, Arthur Dragonsen, for I have a feeling that you'll be a greater asset to our king as a warrior than as a slave.'

Stormbringer inclined his head in a gesture of respect as Arthur hastened to thank him.

'You asked about the Scyldings? Listen, Arthur Dragonsen, and I will tell you an ancient tale that will explain much about my people. Then you might understand what it means to be a Dene.'

And so Stormbringer told Arthur a story of Opland, the Dene's ancient homeland in the frozen wastes of the north, a place of mountains so high and bare that snow crowned their heads all year round like a cap of white hair; a place where strange lights blazed across the night sky like a gift from the gods of Asgaad; and huge deer came briefly in vast herds. The winter was long in these lands, so the ground was permanently frozen and no plough could break its crust of ice without a superhuman effort by those poor humans who dwelt there.

'In this land of deep fjords and long nights, where the sun is mostly a memory, the Dene people starved and suffered in silence, although they were good fishermen and clever farmers. In Opland, death stalked the people throughout the winter months if the harvests failed. My great-grandfather once told me of how children were forced to eat grass and leaves to still the agonies of hunger during times of famine. Despairing, the people decided to challenge the way that life and death afflicted them. They fought back against the will of Heaven.'

Shocked by the tale of children forced to eat grass, Arthur rejected it. Instead, he tried to picture a sky filled with many-coloured lights that flowed through the dark, velvet night in rivers of incredible beauty. The young man had never heard of this river of light. But Stormbringer swore he had seen its magic and Arthur was certain that Stormbringer never lied.

While the Dene leader spoke, several warriors paused in their assigned duties and hunkered down on the deck to listen to his tales with rapt attention. Not only was Stormbringer a gifted storyteller, but he used words and gesture to bring the ancient sagas to life. Arthur too became ensnared in Stormbringer's net of words and images, and was dragged into the world of the Dene.

'Eventually, a man called Skiold was born and grew to manhood in the tribe. Under his guidance, the first of the Dene people made their trek across treacherous rivers and glaciers of ice until they reached a softer land that was bounded on one side by the sea. Here, beyond the coastal dunes, the land was rich, flat and aching for the plough.

'In this land, fish seemed to leap into the coracles that those first Dene built, while cows stood belly-deep in green grass. The rivers were gentle and broad, and a great lake fed them with sweet water that flowed down from the mountains. The further south they travelled, the more blessed and hospitable were the lands that they took as their own.

'Sadly, the lands they settled were part of Vestra Gotland, whose king opposed the Dene invasion of his fiefdom. When his army came to kill the Scyldings who ventured onto his soil, Skiold led his desperate followers in a great massacre of the defenders. It was a time when brave men stood awash in blood and counted this land as a good reason to give up their lives, if their families could free themselves from the terrors of starvation.

'Vast rewards were won on that day of blood and courage, and when victory finally came, many songs were sung of the feats of Skiold's warriors, so those who survived were, forever after, proud to be called one of the Scyldings.'

Stormbringer paused for breath and a warrior pressed a fresh water bladder into his hands. The captain drank deeply before resuming his story.

'Many were the battles between the two tribes, but the Dene triumphed and held the coastal lands in their clenched fists. They set down their houses, built of flint, stone and timber which they found in abundance along the low hills. Skiold built his hall both tall and strong, and filled it with rich carvings that told the story of his exploits. These wooden panels were set into the lintels, so the Dene children would never forget the sacrifices made by the glorious dead for their safety.

'And so, the Scyldings came into being and Skiold's hall flouted the might of Vestra Gautland when our leader took the name of King of Reidgotaland so many years ago. His son, the first Frodi, followed Skiold and extended the lands of the Dene into the south. In Skania, Frodi called on his people to master the seas, so the Dene put aside their coracles and turned to those men who could sing the trees.'

Arthur had never heard of tree singers, although trees had always been sacred to his people. Stormbringer explained. 'Those of you who have grown to manhood in the halls of the Dene know that some women are gifted with the Sight and can sing the sea to gentleness. It's a pity we have no sea-wife with us on this voyage, but I am deemed to be Christian and few of the sighted ones choose to travel under the sail of the Christian God.'

'But your sail bears a red dragon,' Arthur said, with a quick glance to where the wool billowed in the wind.

'Aye, but I'm not just a Christian, you see. No Dene would ignore the dragons of ice or the serpents of Mother Sea. I'm a Dene, but I'm not a fool! A sensible man treads both paths.'

'I understand,' Arthur said. 'But I still don't comprehend tree singing.'

Stormbringer donned his storytelling face again; his voice deepened and became more authoritative.

'A man called Ragnarsen lived in Opland with many of those people who would become Dene. He had a talent. It was a strange, wild gift that allowed him to read and understand the secrets hidden within a tree. When a jarl needed a large beam that could hold a roof high above the chief's head, Ragnarsen would stare fixedly at a tree as if he could see through bark and foliage to its heart. He was rarely wrong and the trees gave up their hidden selves to his needs.

'Ragnarsen would beg the tree's forgiveness before he took his axe to its trunk, while he always promised that its timber would never be wasted. Every tree that Ragnarsen and his sons took from the forest was replaced by a number of seedlings, planted in open areas, while every part of the tree that was harvested was used for one purpose or another. Ragnarsen had always stood tall in the eyes of his tribe, for he gave succour to every family in his village. But even Ragnarsen suffered in the tree-poor hills of Opland and starvation had laid waste his family.

'And so, as a valuable member of the tribe, Ragnarsen travelled with the first Scyldings to a new home in the broad flatlands of the south.

'When Frodi, the son of Skiold, looked towards the islands that lay so close to the shore of his new realm, he understood that ships to carry his warriors into new lands would soon become necessary. And so Magnis Ragnarsen, the son of the first tree singer, was set to work on the great labour of building a ship. No Dene had ever needed seagoing vessels in past times, for Opland had been landlocked.

'Magnis Ragnarsen sat and thought for a very long time. Fridlief, who succeeded Frodi, grew impatient to see his father's dreams come into being, but Ragnarsen would not be hurried. Eventually, the first Dene to become a shipbuilder took his axe to a tall tree and used its one-sided blade to shape a long keel.

'Fridlief had heard that work had begun on the ship, so he travelled to the Ragnarsen home on a sunny morning in spring. The virginal forests of Vestra Gautland began a stone's throw from Ragnarsen's simple croft. The place where he was to build his ship had a roof put over it, and wooden walls were raised around it, because Ragnarsen built his workshop while the ship was under construction.

'What King Fridlief saw in that wooden structure became the stuff of legends, for he beheld a skeleton with great curved ribs rearing up as if to strike at the sky. Fridlief saw immediately that this rudimentary vessel demanded a tall figurehead on its prow for he could recognise in it the bones of an ice dragon. And so Ragnarsen promised to construct the head and wings of the magic beast that would carry his king across the waters in future conquests.

'When the king asked for the drawings of his ship, Ragnarsen smiled and shook his head. He explained that the plans lived within his head and there they would remain until the craft was completed. Even today, generations later, Ragnarsen's family are still our people's greatest shipwrights. No drawings were used to build our vessel, which has just survived the full force of the sea's fury. The drawings live on in the minds of those men who sing the trees.'

Arthur nodded his understanding and smiled. Even Stormbringer, accustomed as he was to praise for his storytelling skills, was gratified by the young man's appreciation.

'In the reigns of Havar, Frodi the Second and Vermund the Sage, trade began between the Dene and their neighbours, the Jutes and the people of Angeln. Within a century, the people of Skania grew rich and their influence spread inexorably into the islands close to the Sound. Sjaelland and Fyn, the largest islands, absorbed some of the Dene people, but most of the emigration was to Jutland, part of the mainland which the Romans called the Cimbric Peninsula. Many years of trade and migration by those Dene citizens followed, but the day inevitably came when the great king, Dan Mikillati the Magnificent, founded the Dene Mark by sending warriors to secure remote outposts in Jutland. Long was the rejoicing in Dan's Hall in the south, but the Jutes resisted the annexation.

'The kings of the Scyldings gradually became the masters of the islands, large and small, and the tribal lands of Jutland and the Angeln became Dene. Pitched battles were fought and the Sae-Dene came into existence to rove ever further at the bidding of their own kings who answered to the overlord of the Dene Mark. King Hnaef, who was the master of the mercenaries, Hengist and Horsa, was one such sea king. I'm sure you have heard of Hengist, Arthur Dragonsen, for it was he who became the first Saxon thane to carve a kingdom from the soil of your homeland. Yes, Arthur Dragonsen, the histories of the Dene and the Britons are intertwined like the tails of the ice dragons that rule the northern seas and skies.'

Arthur's face stiffened. Taliesin had told him the tale of how Hengist saved the child, Myrddion Emrys, from the malice of Vortigern, High King of the Britons. He recalled that Vortigern had also waged war against Arthur's grandfather, Uther Pendragon, and his brother, Ambrosius Imperator.

'The skeins of our histories are indeed tangled together, Master Stormbringer.' Arthur shook his head in perplexity and, out of long habit, his hand moved to stroke his lost knife. Although Stormbringer noticed his captive's confusion, he continued with the ending of his long tale.

'When Ranalf was singing, he mourned the death of the hero,

Beowulf. King Hrothgar Scylding, in his hall at Heorot, had called for the hero's assistance. The Dene people mourned the passing of the man who slew the traitorous Grendel and his kin for many years. But those who bear arms must risk a violent death. And so it was that Beowulf, the Geat, perished in battle against the mercenaries of the Angeln. I was a small child when Beowulf came to Hrothgar Scylding's hall, but I still remember the boom of his voice and the curling red beard that fanned out over his chest. I'm not surprised the harpists of the British Saxons are already singing his praises.

'The Scylding still rule the Dene and the Sae Dene. Now, with praises to Jesus and Odin, Hrolf Kraki rules, having sent that bastard Snaer to the depths of Udgaad where I hope he will trouble no other decent-living Dene. So the Scylding kings have won our country by right of conquest.'

Gradually at first, Arthur began to laugh, his laughter becoming harsher and very bitter.

'What is it that amuses you?' Stormbringer asked.

'Can't you see what the Dene have done, Stormbringer? Your people have inadvertently caused the destruction of the British homeland. The Dene drove the Jutes and Angles out of the Cimbric Peninsula and they moved southward. Like Hengist, they then crossed the Litus Saxonicus to Britain. The Angles displaced the Saxons, the Friesians and the Northern Franks. Then, as we know to our cost, the Saxons and the Angles have flooded into Britain in such numbers that our homeland is now called Angleland.

'And so my grand-uncle and grandfather, Ambrosius Imperator and Uther Pendragon, wasted their youth and their hearts' blood in a vain attempt to save the British people. My own father, King Artor, lived through sixty years of sacrifice while fighting for British survival. I have been used as a weapon against the invaders from the north for my entire life. In so doing, I was robbed of a father! How ironic it is that you should finish the task of my destruction by taking me into captivity.'

Maeve and Blaise had been listening quietly to Stormbringer's story, which they scarcely understood. But something of the tragedy of invasions must have become clear to them because they began to weep. Stormbringer looked from one child to the other and, like Arthur, he marvelled that one culture rose and became strong while another dwindled and was destroyed.

'Don't ask me to apologise for the deeds of my people, Dragonsen, for neither you nor I had any part in the decision-making that has laid waste to your lands. I am glad that the Dene tribes have thrived, although I regret that your people have been brought down into the mud.

'I once saw a boy throwing stones at a small dyke that lay beside one of the swiftly moving streams near my home. This dyke protected us from floods when the rains came in the spring.'

Arthur's attention was captured despite his despair.

'The boy eventually succeeded in dislodging a small rock halfway down the dyke wall. The rock was very small and, at first, only a small trickle of water breached the dam. Unbeknown to the boy, the water ate away other rocks alongside the first. Then another small rock fell, and the water turned from a trickle into a jetting flood and the pressure tore away a large section of the dyke. The boy's house was directly in the path of the resulting flood that roared down on his family, so a wall of water washed them all away. He and his kinfolk were drowned, because he had unwisely played a foolish game.'

At that moment, one of the crew asked a question of Stormbringer.

'The storm has blown us off course, but not so far that we'll be too late for Hrolf Kraki's audience,' Stormbringer answered. 'Fortunately, I know where we are and we can make up some of the lost time, if we row for part of each day.'

One of the sailors groaned at the prospect of rowing, but Stormbringer and his other companions fixed him with irritated eyes and the offender melted back into the crowd.

'The Skagerrak is nigh. We should enter the worst of the perilous waters that lie to the north of the Dene lands in three days at the most. If the breezes and currents are kind, we should reach harbour two days after that. My apologies, Arthur, but I must leave you now to consult with my helmsman.'

'So we're a week from harbour, wherever that is,' Blaise observed. Her eyes were almost black with fear. 'I'm concerned that we might be separated, and I might never see any of you again.'

Quietly, Blaise began to weep again at the thought of being enslaved in a land where she was ignorant of the language. Even Maeve, usually a placid girl, closed her eyes as if to hide from horrible thoughts.

'Don't be afraid, Blaise,' Arthur said. 'I intend to do everything that is necessary to keep you together. As God is my witness, I will find some way to save us. Fate seems to have chosen a decent man to take us into captivity. I really believe that we are on this ship, just as we were saved from the gale, for a special purpose. Everything will be well if we trust to God's mercy.'

Blaise dried her eyes with one grimy sleeve. 'So you believe that there's still hope?'

'Aye, my little sister! I also believe that Arthur is right,' Eamonn answered seriously. 'But I wouldn't plan on marrying Gilchrist of the Otadini at any time in the immediate future.'

Maeve was the first to giggle, struck by the ridiculousness of Eamonn's irony. Blaise had fought tooth and nail to avoid the arranged marriage, but had received her heart's desire in a most unexpected fashion. Then Eamonn began to laugh from the depths of his belly, great booming peals of mirth that caused the Dene warriors to turn their heads and acknowledge the madness of the captives. But as men who had seen the worst and the best of nature and human beings, the crew shrugged and quickly lost interest.

Finally, Arthur and Blaise joined in, until Arthur noticed a small, charcoal-coloured smudge on the horizon, partially visible in the gathering afternoon darkness.

'Land!' The Briton pointed. 'Stormbringer was right. Whatever comes, we'll know our fate soon enough. But I agree, Eamonn, Blaise won't be marrying Gilchrist – if he's still alive!'

In the hours that followed, Arthur searched for the itch at the back of his skull that had plagued him all his life. It had always warned him of approaching danger, but it had been silent since his capture.

How odd! Arthur thought. Even the onset of the gale didn't cause it to surface. Surely my gift can't have vanished.

But his inner voice stayed stubbornly silent, so Arthur suddenly felt bereft, as if a part of his essence had been torn away.

And, as the captives slept in their wet blankets, *Loki's Eye* sped northwards parallel to those tempting glimpses of land.

Gareth's Path through Central Britain

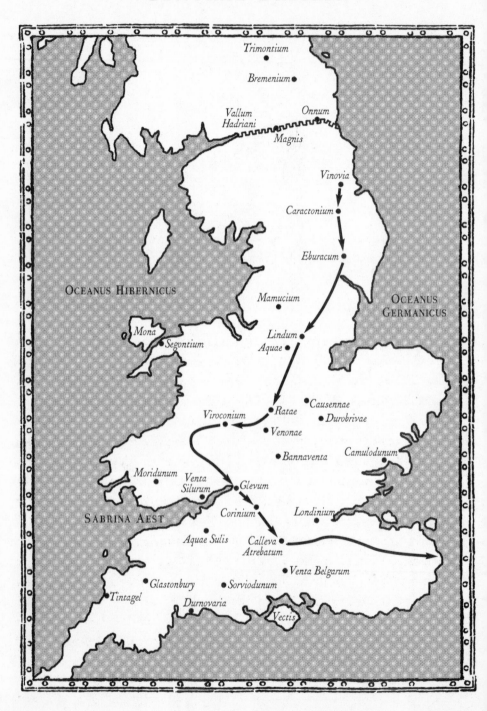

CHAPTER III

A BITTER SOLSTICE

A man is to be envied who has been fortunate in his children and has avoided dire calamity.

Euripides, *Orestes* 1

The solitary horseman rested in the saddle and gazed down the ill-kept Roman road towards the forest that loomed like a grey and charcoal smudge on the skyline. The trees hovered between the raw umber earth and an ashen sky. On the road that ran past Arden, there was no place to hide before the frowning, shivering trees, but nor did the empty road promise any greater safety. As the old year perished, winter gripped the forest in a frozen fist, so that the last patches of dried grasses beside an almost invisible pathway into Arden's depths snapped at the lightest touch. Even the poorest hunter could see the spoor of a stranger, for although many of the forest giants were wholly bare of leaves and their skeletal branches groaned ominously in the solstice winds, the forest was thick, still and primal. Unlike the flat farmland to the east, very little light filtered down to the frost-rimed floor of the ancient woods, even when the chilly sun stood directly overhead in the December sky. Now, at midnight, the pallid moon failed to reveal the narrow entry that led into the heart of Arden Forest.

Only a desperate man would ride at this time of night in such inclement weather. Sleet-sharp rain was falling, and even the hardiest of creatures would be seeking a burrow, a cave or an inn which could provide safety from the black ice and the Wilde Hunt. The rider was too pragmatic to be superstitious, but the thought of Cernunnos, huge, menacing and red-eyed, as he strode through the cloud-riven sky with the massive hounds and huntsmen of the gods reaping the souls of the unwary, was so grotesque that the young man shot a quick glance at the torn sky. Arden Forest was dangerous, because every tree might hide an archer, while desperate Cornovii tribesmen guarded the margins of the Wilde Woods. These embattled and encircled warriors were prone to killing anyone who ventured into one of the last strongholds of Britain. In addition to the obvious dangers for unwary travellers, every knowledgeable man knew that the Riders of the Hunt and other, more dreadful creatures stalked through the storm-torn nights before the solstice, eager to reap the souls of mortals for their warm blood during the dying weeks of an old year. Once the old king was dead and the boy king began to rule in the joy and laughter of the New Year, humankind would rediscover the pleasures of food, drink and warm, strong arms that promised ecstasy. So the gods had always decreed and even the Christian God could not quite stifle the lusts of the past.

Without any apparent fear, the solitary horseman had come out of the north and entered Arden Forest from Fosse Way. He had journeyed by the fastest possible route to reach the safety of the woods, so he only ventured from the road to bypass Saxon strongholds at Cataractonium, Eburacum, Calcaria and Lindum, sleeping during the day and riding during the hours of darkness. During his brief and guarded interludes with other travellers, the young warrior had managed to avoid questions and capture because his Jute features and sea-blue eyes suggested barbarian ancestry.

The weather had turned nasty a week earlier, so the hunched rider was wrapped in furs over his breastplate in order to protect and disguise the well-oiled Roman armour from rust and curiosity. He huddled within the shaggy pelts as the wind drove the rain under the hides. A steady stream of icy water ran down the back of his neck and pooled in the leather and wool that protected the flesh under his cuirasse at the base of his spine. Cold within and frozen without, the fur-clad figure allowed his beast to trudge its own way down the barely visible path that led to the thick blackness of the forest, while he slouched in the saddle and hugged his chilled arms to his body, permitting the horse to walk unguided.

The armed stranger, Gareth Minor, managed to penetrate the borders of Arden without incident, although his body was racked with hunger and weary to the point of collapse. During his trek into the south, he had been forced to steal provisions from richer travellers as he traversed the dangerous roads and avoided outlaws and hunting parties. Something in his nature forbade any theft that left poor families hungry, but traders who grew fat and wealthy from traitorous dealings with the Saxons were fair game in Gareth's personal code of conduct.

Although he had been careful to avoid the eastern settlements for the entire journey, Gareth was aware that the invaders had grown bolder over recent years. While the threat of ambush was ever-present, militant Saxon activity had mostly been confined to the warmer months of spring and summer during King Artor's reign. But the trickle of migrants across the Litus Saxonicum from the Cimbric Peninsula and Friesia had now become a flood, for these Jute and Angle settlers arrived daily in search of arable land. The pressure to extend their influence beyond Mercia and the eastern coastal lands sent armed families foraging further and further into Celtic-defended country, and Gareth had noticed that Saxon stockades had been built to control the roads leading towards Arden. With a pang of memory, he recalled his father's gravelly voice as he recited one of King Artor's maxims. *He who holds the Roman roads controls Britain!* How painfully accurate the long-dead High King had been. Now, Saxon farms lipped the edges of Arden Forest and the women labouring around their crofts were well-armed and watchful. The invaders from the north were here to stay. In fact, some parts of these isles had been populated by three generations of northerners who now considered this their homeland. They had fought to win a place here and had buried their kin in British soil, so they wouldn't be easily dislodged or rooted out.

The hordes of dispossessed migrants from the inhospitable northern wastes were now in control of at least half of the old British tribal territories and the Britons were retreating further and further into Western Cymru with every month that passed. The new Saxon kingdom of Mercia straddled the mountain spine and their warriors controlled much of the old kingdom where the Brigante tribe once reigned supreme. How Gareth's father would have mourned the loss of fair Melandra, now fallen into ruin. For their various treasons, as the old witch-woman had foretold, the mighty Brigante tribe had been reduced to an irrelevancy since the death of Modred the Matricide. Sadly, those Brigante who had not fled north across the Wall or travelled south into Cymru were clinging to the western coastline with little hope for a safe future as they faced the victorious Anglo-Saxons.

And so, in the many weary miles since leaving Hadrian's Wall, Gareth had had time to think carefully about the greater meaning of his misfortunes, as well as what he could do to salvage some honour from his defeats.

Arthur, who was his friend, his master and his companion of the road, had been taken prisoner by mercenaries and was now a captive of the northern seafarers. Dobunni treachery and the spite of that filthy creature, Mareddyd, had caused his friends to be spirited away in a strange ship, the like of which he had never seen. Maeve, Eamonn and Blaise, as well as his master, had disappeared from Britain; Gareth's dreams and expectations had vanished over the horizon with them.

As he rode under the dripping trees, Gareth's mind wandered back to the beginning of his journey when he had carried out a brief search for Mareddyd, the Dobunni prince. He suspected Mareddyd of treachery and would have happily killed the craven cur if he had been able to find him. But the treacherous young man had vanished from his lodgings. The innkeeper, Ossian, blandly professed to have no idea where the Dobunni heir had fled.

Gareth saw that the face of Ossian's daughter, Myfanwy, bore the marks of fists and she carried broken bones that caused her to move with great care. Nor did she meet Gareth's eyes directly, although Ossian was bluffly and guilelessly open. The young warrior was certain that every word that father and daughter uttered was a lie, but how could he prove they had some part in Mareddyd's disappearance?

Gareth's breast ached with the same hollow sickness that had almost crippled him when his ancient, half-crazed father had relinquished his hold on life with such relief. The only certainty in Gareth's rootless life was the need to travel to the north-east to rescue his friend, but no one had ever returned from those lost and barbarous places to tell of their adventures. Even the Romans had feared to face the northern barbarians, because their warriors stopped the inexorable Roman advances into the north at the Rhenus River. How much more terrible must be the lands that lay to the north of the Albus? How fearful were seas reported to freeze in winter or become studded with great mountains of ice that could smash a ceol into kindling?

Gareth felt a sense of relief once the bare frosty trees of Arden cocooned him as the intensity of the wind increased. He became one with the voices of the winter forest; trees creaked and groaned on the wind and the dry rattle of branches provided a warning refrain as he moved steadily towards his goal. Skeletal twigs clutched at Gareth's exposed hair and caught at his furs as if to prevent the young warrior from completing his mission. Every creak, every scream from an invisible hunting owl, warned Gareth that Arden wished to protect its old master from the dire news this young man was carrying.

'Only Bedwyr will know what I should do. The Master of Arden must be told,' Gareth whispered aloud to fill the aching melancholy of the winter forest. Under his fur hood, his face twisted as if he was on the brink of tears, for he had no idea where to go. Before he met Arthur, he had never left the fields that lay beyond Aquae Sulis.

Out of the heavy darkness ahead, a single lamp gleamed. 'It must be one of the lights from the fortress of Arden,' the young man said to himself. As a sentry called out a warning into the gloom, Gareth drew his exhausted steed and his packhorse to a halt. The spent beasts dropped their heads in resignation while they waited for the warm stable and sweet hay that might lie ahead in the darkness.

'May the Lord of Hosts make the decision for me, for I cannot decide where I must go,' Gareth whispered to the memory of his lost master and his God. 'Even if I don't know how, Arthur, I'll do my best to find you if you should still be alive. I can accept that task easily enough, but how do I tell your mother that you're lost, and that you have taken her youngest child with you? How can I bear to dash all Master Bedwyr's hopes of a future for the people of Arden? There will be no salvation for the Britons without you. Our people will disappear into the darkness like the Picts of old, and our children will be left with only vague memories of a lost way of life. We need you, just as we need the Lord High God to protect us from the heathen Saxon invaders.'

Suddenly, another voice broke through the darkness.

'State your name, stranger, and tell us why you trespass over Arden's borders in such vile weather. Stay where we can see you or you'll be dead before you move a single inch.' The rasping voice was flat and bland, so Gareth stayed perfectly still and ensured that neither hand strayed near his weapons.

'My name is Gareth ap Gareth of Aquae Sulis and I am the body servant and sworn guard of Lord Arthur of Arden. I bear news of his capture by a raiding party of barbarians to the north of Eburacum. Let me pass, for I must speak with Lord Bedwyr as soon as possible.'

An anatomically impossible curse was spat out and a lean, dark-clad man appeared as if by magic from a small cluster of bushes near the hooves of Gareth's horse. The sentry carried a longbow which had obviously been drawn and trained on Gareth until such time as the interloper made his presence known and explained himself.

'You bring dire news to our master,' the dour warrior replied without surprise. Gareth's bad news was only one more indicator of life in a society under siege. 'You're a storm crow, Master Gareth of Aquae Sulis, and you'll pardon me if I wish you'd never set foot inside our borders.'

'I have other news that will distress your master even more deeply, so I must speak with Lord Bedwyr and Lady Elayne urgently – before I lose my nerve.' In his distress, Gareth's voice was more brusque than he had intended, so the warrior took offence at once, clenching fists that itched to strike this stranger down and quieten his meddling tongue.

'Take me to your master at once!' Gareth insisted. He repeated the request again in a voice beginning to fray with frustrated impatience. 'I know the hour is late, but I have no time to waste on pointless gibble-gabble with servants.'

In affronted silence, other men appeared out of the woods to hem Gareth in before directing him along the dim track to a massive gate made from tree trunks. Soundlessly, as if in response to a mute instruction, the gate swung open so that the horseman, his packhorse and the sentries were able to enter the muddy forecourt just as the first flurries of a new snowfall began.

Gareth dismounted and handed over the horses' reins to a lad who ran to join them, rubbing his sleepy eyes. After issuing quick instructions for the care of his horses, Gareth turned to approach a dark building where two small figures stood waiting on the threshold. Behind them, the lamp from the king's hall surrounded them in a dim halo of light.

Before cock-crow, a grey and desolate winter's day began early.

In the hours before the arrival of Gareth, Bedwyr's dreams had been formless, like all his peculiar fits and starts. A small part of his brain wondered if blood called to blood, and if Maeve cried out for her father over the many miles that separated them. With resolution, the Master of Arden pushed these unsettling feelings behind him because he was unable to do anything to protect his youngest child. His hands were tied by the distance that lay between them and the Otadini court, so he struggled with horrible imaginings that kept him awake until the dead hours of the morning when word came to his door that a stranger was without.

'Join me, Elayne! Please?' Bedwyr's voice was ragged and pleading; his wife realised that her noble husband was deathly afraid of the tidings that had arrived at such an early hour of this cold winter's morning. Only the most pressing need would drive a messenger out into the freezing wind. Elayne's heart skittered with panic, but she climbed out of the warm nest of their old bed and stifled a little cry at the persistent ache of arthritis in one hip. Her dear old man had sufficient troubles without worrying about her, so she took his trembling hand and held it tightly against her warm breasts.

Elayne took two fur-lined cloaks from a clothes chest, including Bedwyr's wolf pelt, which she draped over his shoulders so that his hastily plaited grey hair mingled with the thick white fur. Elayne noticed suddenly that stiff white stubble covered her husband's chin. Uncharacteristically, Bedwyr bent over with a pathetic slump of his shoulders, but she refrained from any comment. Noble Bedwyr, the last of King Artor's legendary warriors, had lived beyond his time like an old hound that is determined to find his lost master before drawing one final breath. Men already marvelled that those warriors who had followed Artor seemed to live for decades beyond their allotted life-spans, as if the old dragon cursed those who loved him with unnatural reservoirs of strength. For over ten years, Bedwyr had been sustained by his ambitions for Arthur, the High King's bastard son, whom Bedwyr had raised as a cuckoo in his own nest.

Did this messenger bring news that would hasten Bedwyr's doom? Elayne would have liked to hide in her huge bed with the covers over her head, but she owed everything to her aged husband. She used a wisp of wool to wipe Bedwyr's streaming eyes. She couldn't tell if he was about to weep or not, but she could see an edge of panic in his enlarged pupils that was born out of the formless horrors of his frequent night terrors. Her man didn't want to face this unknown messenger alone, so she forced herself to find the courage buried deep in her heart since the time of Artor's death.

What if the messenger told them that Arthur was dead?

No! My children aren't dead, her mind protested vociferously. I'd know it.

'Come along then, old woman!' Bedwyr said as he rose to his

unsteady feet. 'Whatever comes in the dead hours of the morning will mean no good for either of us. If I'm honest, I'm afraid to hear this messenger's news without you. My water tells me neither of us will take any pleasure from this news.' His mouth twisted sadly and his age-spotted hand patted her shoulder as gently as a kiss.

'Of course, my dear, so we'll face it together. Has it not always been so for us?'

Then, hand in hand like little children, the old pair moved down the stairs and through the empty hall to where the servants were waiting to open the great oak doors. A gust of freezing air stirred Bedwyr's robes around his swollen ankles. At his gesture, the doors swung inward and the time of loss and mourning began.

In the house of oak, Gareth curled his long limbs into a woollen pallet and wished fervently that he had died in the ambush or had been carried off with Arthur and the girls. Any fate would be better than having to tell the Master of Arden and his lady that two of their children had been taken prisoner and their whereabouts were unknown. As soon as she had set her eyes upon him, Lady Elayne had called out his name in a horrified moan before fainting clean away.

'Perhaps I should learn to guard my face so no one can read it,' Gareth whispered into the soft wool. But what would be the good? When Lady Elayne saw Gareth was alone, she knew immediately that he would never willingly leave Arthur's side. A mother will always sense the full horror of a tragedy when only one member of the party returns at the end of a journey.

Bedwyr had seen to the care of Lady Elayne with a face as white as bleached linen, after which he had spent several hours questioning Gareth carefully, until the old man knew everything that had happened on the road to the north of Vinovia, including the possibility of Dobunni treachery. Gareth didn't spare himself, for he knew he had possessed a slim opportunity to attack the tall warriors with their bright iron weapons as they rode towards the sea. The chances of survival had been virtually nonexistent, but Gareth had opted to obey Arthur's orders, which were to look to his own safety. Gareth's oath to Arthur was paramount and his master's last order had been clear. Ultimately, he knew he couldn't save his master if he was dead.

Bedwyr had sucked on his few remaining teeth and looked through Gareth as if the young man was made entirely of clear water. The Master of Arden thought hard and considered his options.

'I understand your predicament, boy. By our lady, we can put ourselves in fiendish positions in order to protect our honour. Perhaps a warrior would be wiser to forego such senseless rules, but our foolish code is one of the few strategic weapons we can use against the Saxons. Even the Romans were prepared to die for the concept of honour, because a man's duty to hearth, home, master and gods is paramount. You did well to follow the raiding party to the place where they'd hidden their ship, so at least we know the fate of the children. But, for the moment, we must reflect and think of what can be done.'

Bedwyr had hunched over a cup of hot mulled wine brought to him by his eldest son, Lasair, who was now watching his father's face with anxious, proprietary eyes. Lasair was seventeen and a bonny, red-haired nugget of a lad, thick in the body like his father, but long in the shanks like his mother. Lady Elayne's features, made masculine, enlivened the face of the youth with an open and honest expression, but a hard brilliance lurked under the sweetness of his smile. As he waited, he stared at Gareth with a burning resentment for the troubles that the stranger had laid at his father's door.

Bedwyr's innate common sense reasserted itself with the heat of the wine in his belly. With open affection, Bedwyr patted Lasair's young hand in thanks and then caressed the boy's young face where his downy cheeks threatened the start of a beard. At that moment, Gareth missed his deceased father so intensely that he wanted to cry, although Gareth Major had rarely expressed any affection for his son.

'I beg your pardon, Gareth! I'm an old man now, so I lack the resilience of youth that allows us to think quickly in dangerous situations. But I have some more questions for you, if you can answer them. What happened to your guards?'

'All dead,' Gareth replied. 'The last man died of his wounds just before I left him to track the warriors.' Gareth hoped that Bedwyr would understand his predicament.

'The girls who served Lady Maeve and Mistress Blaise were sent back to Tintagel as soon as I was able to write a message to King Bors. To give this news in writing seemed cruel, but I owed you my personal explanation as soon as possible, and the servant girls were sick from fear and misery.'

'Don't fuss yourself, boy. I'll send word to Bors of everything that has transpired as soon as the roads are open. You have done your best. No blame for our losses should be attached to you.'

'My honour was torn when I followed the raiders, Lord Bedwyr. Perhaps I shouldn't have abandoned the corpses of our guard so far from their homes, but I didn't want Arthur taken away without any further blows being struck. I wanted to know where they were taking your children. Then, after I returned to the site of the ambush, I buried all five of our men before I started the return journey to Arden. I owed them all at least a deep grave where the scavengers couldn't reach them.'

Gareth had been alone for well over three weeks and his voice was beginning to sound rusty from lack of use. He was also finding it difficult to meet Bedwyr's deceptively gentle eyes.

'Try to answer me clearly, Gareth. What did the attackers look like? You described them earlier as outlanders because of the design of their ship. What was it about the warriors that made you believe they weren't Saxons or Jutes? Do you remember Odin? He was a Jute, and he was so large he could block out the sun.'

Gareth gazed sadly at Bedwyr. He realised that he was weeping: for his father, for Arthur and for himself. But mostly, he wept for this brave old man who was so gallant in his declining years. 'I never met Odin, my lord, but my father told me so much about him that I swear I can almost imagine his features. It was my father who knew the Jute – not I!'

Bedwyr winced. 'I forget sometimes that I'm no longer a young man, Gareth. It's your name, I suppose. It's odd, but I look at my hands and my soft belly, and I wonder who the old man is who has invaded my body. In my mind, I'm still the angry young man who first met King Artor at Moridunum. Ah, well! I'll see the High King soon enough – but I'd like to tell him that his son is well and happy.'

Gareth surreptitiously wiped his eyes while Bedwyr was reminded that this boy was only eighteen and younger than Arthur, his master. With infinite patience, Bedwyr waited until Gareth had regained his self-control.

'The outlanders were very tall, Lord Bedwyr, taller than Saxons or Jutes as a group and less burly around the chest. The leader was of a similar height to Arthur, if not an inch or so taller. Their skins were very fair, as if they had never felt a hot sun, yet they were weather-beaten and their eyes were narrowed like those of men who have spent many years on the northern seas. They were strange in appearance and dress, my lord, nothing like the Saxons or the Jutes. Some blond-haired warriors had red beards.'

Gareth paused as he remembered.

'The ship wasn't a ceol. I saw a Saxon ship up river near Venta Belgarum that had been taken in a raid. Saxon ceols are wider in the girth, although that's probably not the right word for the widest point of a sea vessel.'

'I'm no sailor either. I haven't been in a boat since I rode a runaway coracle down a flooded river many years ago,' Bedwyr grunted. He smiled as he thought of a long-past day when he had pursued Prince Galahad and a maddened pagan priest who had stolen the legendary Bloody Cup.

'This craft was narrow with a large prow at the front decorated with a long carving. I couldn't see the details. Once it was beyond the breakers, I saw the great sail unfurl in the moonlight, but until then, the warriors rowed the vessel themselves. What I remember most was the image on the sail.'

'What are you talking about, lad?'

'Their sail was decorated with the outline of a massive red dragon.' Gareth had been unprepared for the concept of such a ship.

'But the Saxons use the dragon symbol,' Bedwyr persisted.

'This dragon looked like a viciously toothed worm, or a serpent with huge teeth and great wings. But it had very short legs and was quite different from the Saxon version or the British varieties of dragon that I've seen. It's something new to me and I sense that it's very dangerous. Its tail is long and coiled like a serpent. I have dreamed of it every night since I watched it steal our own dragonlet and carry him over the darkened waters.'

A single rooster crowed shrilly to herald the beginning of an icy morning that would be dark with sleet and buffeting winds, even here in the living heart of Arden. As he thought furiously, Bedwyr's bones begged him to go back to his warm bed, but an itch of worry remained for Elayne's health. This boy was too exhausted to speak any further, so any more information buried within Gareth's memory would need to stay hidden until he had slept.

'Go to bed, boy. My servants and my son, Lasair, will show you the way. We'll speak again at noon, after you have had a few hours of sleep. Meanwhile, don't feel guilty, Gareth, because you can't be held responsible for what has happened. In fact, I'm fortunate that someone lived to explain the children's absence, else we might never have learned what became of them.'

So, shuffling wearily behind Lasair and his oil lamp, Gareth was led to a small room under the roof of the loft. Snug and warm on a clean pallet, Gareth could hear the howl of the wind as it roared through the trees, but it had no power to disturb him. Eventually, the exhausted youth fell into a deep and cleansing sleep that engulfed him like an ocean wave until the noise of serving maids woke him many hours later.

Another long day of greyness had begun.

CHAPTER IV

THE LAST OF ARDEN

Laugh no man to scorn in the bitterness of his soul.

The Bible, Ecclesiasticus 8: 10

Regnavit a ligno Deus. (God reigned from the wood.)

Venantius Fortunatus, *Vexilla Regis*

Lady Elayne stood beside her large marital bed that had always reminded her of the trust and friendship that existed in her marriage. Her chin was lifted and her remaining beauty was incandescent in the early-morning candlelight as she gathered her strength to bend her husband to her will.

Bedwyr felt his heart swell with pride in his wife. The flesh of her upper arms and her belly had been stretched by time and child-bearing, so that a network of jagged white scars covered her hips, her lower belly and her thighs. Her jawline was blurred with sagging flesh and the soft creeping of her eyelids gave her a permanently thoughtful and hooded expression. Yet, with her head lifted proudly and her faded hair tossed back defiantly, Bedwyr could understand why King Artor had turned to Elayne when his world had collapsed into chaos. While the Arden Knife had once been angry and jealous of Artor's attention to Elayne and had resented his wife's close friendship with the High King, Bedwyr could now accept that a man such as Artor needed a stalwart woman at his side who could offer advice and support. Lady Elayne was indomitable, more than capable of protecting her husband *and* her king. Any rage that Bedwyr had once felt had been washed away by Artor's sacrifice and guilt, so Bedwyr had learned to love the boy who had been foisted upon him.

'I would know if the children were dead,' Elayne stated flatly. 'I would feel it here in my heart, if they were in danger.' One hand tapped her breastbone, while her face was set in stubborn, uncompromising lines. 'Arthur's life skein is so strong that I would feel its lack in my world if he were dead, no matter how far away he was when he passed into the shades. I swear he's still living, Bedwyr! And what of Maeve, my strange little girl with her wild red hair and the largest eyes in a babe I've ever seen? Don't despair, Bedwyr. I'm her *mother*, and I felt her heart beating as she lay under my breast and kicked at my ribs. I would *know*, I swear!'

Bedwyr ran his hands over his face and tangled hair before kissing his wife's mutinous mouth. 'Perhaps you would, my only love, because we men know so little of the ways of women. What would we do to similar youngsters, if they were captured in our lands? We would turn them into slaves – or worse – so I despair for the safety of our children.'

Elayne made no attempt to argue. He had lived his entire life under the threat of Saxon invaders and had lost almost everyone he loved to their rapacious attacks. In the past, he had always faced the harsh facts of life. He had mourned for a little space, and then moved on steadfastly so he could make the Saxon hordes bleed for the pain he suffered.

'What can we do to find the children, Bedwyr? You're too old to raise an army, or to journey into the north to rescue them. At this moment, we hold Arden by our fingernails and a moment's inattention on your part will result in our people being overrun by the Saxon curs. They are already chopping down trees on our margins to build their halls and villages and, if they're allowed to continue their advances, we'll become a small circle of Britons inside a sea of barbarians. Will we perish when the Saxons drive us into the walls of our fortress, starve us and then burn us alive? I don't think so! I won't believe it, so I won't accept defeat.'

Bedwyr gazed into his wife's clear, golden eyes, the same eyes that Arthur wore during those times when he was happy and untroubled. He remembered small incidents from his foster-son's childhood, the little acts of courage and generosity that had made Bedwyr so proud. Even when the boy became an adult, Bedwyr treated Arthur as if he was his real son. Bedwyr's heart began to bleed when he considered that he might die before Arthur returned to Arden, if a return was possible.

Bedwyr recalled the special oak tree that Arthur had loved in his youth. And then he pictured the boy, wounded but still defiant when he returned from Crookback's farm after killing his first man. What a king the boy would have made! He'd been stronger than Artor and was more balanced and loving than his sire could ever be, for Artor had been shaped by tragedy during his youth. Now, when Arthur was most needed, he had been spirited away. Fortuna had turned her face from her people in their time of trouble. Perhaps the Celts would go down into the darkness without Arthur and they might never discover his fate. Something tore loose in Bedwyr's chest, and he clutched at his heart as a sudden pain took his breath away. Then he squared his shoulders and called for his remaining children to join them.

When Lasair and the others arrived in his room, they bowed to their parents with genuine respect. In turn, Bedwyr looked directly into their eyes and prepared himself for what he was about to tell them.

'I've made an irrevocable decision, children. In the spring, we'll send all our people to the Forest of Dean in the south. Every person in our homeland who is prepared to make the journey shall be invited to join us under our protection. Unfortunately, those who choose to stay here will be under threat from the Saxons.'

He paused to allow his audience to absorb the tenor of his words.

'I place no trust in the justice of those who rule the Britons, so we'll not relocate to Forden or any other likely refuge. We will travel further into the wildernesses to a place where I once ran mad while I expunged the blood of my murdered parents from my mind. I don't have any affection for these new lands, but the Forest of Dean is deep, dark and very ancient because the trees cluster around a great river that flows down from the mountains. Like Arden, it needs protection from those Saxons who'd cut down its trees to build their walls and make charcoal for their fires. And, like Arden, the Forest of Dean needs our husbandry.'

Bedwyr's expression softened as he gazed at Elayne.

'The forest is situated on the borders of Cymru in a position where we can guard the surrounding marches and keep the lands clean from Saxon vermin. We will also have the security of having strong allies at our backs. Dean will be hard for the invaders to approach. It has Sabrina Aest on one side and the mountains on the other, so it has a defensive advantage over Arden as a place we can protect. The Saxons fear the kingdom of the Silures, the Ordovice and the Deceangli with good reason, for they have consistently been driven out of Cymru, regardless of the many ceols that try to land along the shoreline. I will place my trust in Cymru and the Forest of Dean.'

'But it's so far away!' Elayne protested, although Bedwyr could tell that she was already assessing the problem of moving her entire household. Like any provident housewife, she knew every person who lived within the forest, and how willing they would be to tear up their roots and transplant their children to foreign soil.

The safety of their children was the only driving force that would persuade them to make a long and arduous journey to a new home.

As if he could read her mind, Bedwyr smiled before returning to the topic at hand.

'We must plan the movements to our new home very carefully. Lasair and Barr will supervise the movement of our people and will command the advance party. Lasair will find a site for a new fortress that will be built high above the river in the deepest part of the forest where it can be easily defended. His force will take as much of Arden's wealth as can be carried on horseback, so his party will consist of young folk who possess the strength to do the physical work necessary to prepare the fortifications and buildings. I want earth broken and made ready for spring planting so the first crops can be sown before we move our people into the forest. The boys will complete this task, Elayne, but you are the only person who can persuade the crofters to desert their familiar holdings. Their lives will be forfeit if they stay behind.'

Lasair and Barr bowed their heads obediently and left their parents to begin the preliminary planning. Soon, Elayne was alone with her husband and she sighed, for his tired body had begun to sag with weariness.

'Why now, Bedwyr? Why have you chosen to tear up our roots and move our people out of Arden?' Elayne asked tearfully.

'Please don't upset yourself, my dear. Your tears are harder to bear than the loss of Arden.'

'Then answer me fairly, my husband. Why now? If Arthur and Maeve do return, they won't be able to find us.' Elayne's eyes were so direct that Bedwyr winced.

'I've known that Arden has been lost to us for many months, my dearest one, but I was waiting until Arthur and Maeve returned from the Otadini lands before making my final decision. In doing so, I've placed us all at risk by trying to hold on to this isolated outpost.'

'So?' Elayne began. She could easily guess at his answer.

'Whether they are alive or enslaved, they'll not return before Arden is lost to the Saxons. Even Arthur cannot fly across the ocean in time to save us from our enemies, and I'm certain that he won't be home in the immediate future.'

Bedwyr refrained from adding *if ever* to his explanation, but Elayne could sense that the words weren't very far from his mind.

'What else can I do to help you then, Bedwyr?'

Elayne's hands were softly stroking the fine old bed. Her hands had stroked this same headboard every day for decades, and the honey-brown timber carried a patina of oil from her fingers and palms. 'How can I bear to leave this house where my children were born?'

Bedwyr knew she wasn't speaking to him, but to the deepest part of herself that had succoured her flagging spirits during dark and terrible times. He watched as she also came to the conclusion that Arden was lost and would never be hers again. 'I will visit the first crofts tomorrow,' she told her husband firmly. 'I will do what must be done.'

He embraced her, marvelling once more at the courage of women who can give up everything they cherish in order to follow their love.

'The last of our people don't have to leave until just before the end of winter, but they must be gone before the last of the winter snowfalls. After that time, the Saxons will anticipate our intentions and we could come under attack by Mercia. We will need every wagon we possess if we are to escape safely, and we'll probably have to construct more because I intend to leave nothing but empty holes for the Saxon pigs. If I could, I'd even burn down this lovely house where my heart resides, so the Saxons would lack a roof over their filthy heads, but to do so would be to warn them that we're moving. We'll take everything that can be moved, so our retreat will be relatively slow. I'll need every available man that Lasair can spare to protect the retreat of our wagon train.'

He watched the hypnotic movement of Elayne's hands as they stroked the wood of their bed as if it was a beloved child. 'What was put together can be taken apart, so your bed can be moved to our new home and our lives can continue untroubled in the Forest of Dean. I swear to you that you'll sleep snugly in your own bed when the summer weather comes.'

'I believe you, husband. But we cannot leave essential supplies behind on the journey to Dean just to make room for my bed in the wagons. I'd feel like a traitor to every crofter who gives up a snug home so they can accompany us on the journey. My bed should only be packed for removal once everything that must be taken on the journey is safely stored away in the wagons. Promise me this, Bedwyr, for I'd rather not be a burden on our people.'

'You could never be a burden, my dearest,' Bedwyr whispered as he kissed her work-callused hands, and then waved his hands around the comfortable room. 'I'm reluctant to leave all this, so you must leave this decision to me.'

'Are our sons old enough to carry such responsibilities? Lasair is little more than a boy. Only yesterday, he was a little red-haired baby toddling along after Arthur.'

Even as she smiled at her happy memory, Elayne's mood darkened. 'Of course, Lasair can do what must be done. Like all mothers, I would prefer to keep my babes in places where I can protect them from the world outside Arden. But the Saxons won't permit my children to grow in peace, and the outside world has come to Arden, even though all I want from life is to be left among the quiet of the trees. Lasair must do his part to save our people, for such is his duty.'

She squared her shoulders and Bedwyr took comfort from the steadfastness of her nature. 'I know that Lasair will do what must be done for the citizens of Arden.'

'Aye! His days are planned out for many years to come, but there are still some tasks for this old man to complete before I can lay down my head and rest.' Bedwyr grinned with the old, reckless devilry that had sustained him in the past. He planned to relish one last throw of the dice against fate, one last attack before he surrendered to the most challenging and fearful enemy of all, the journey into death. Bedwyr feared nothing that lived but his many dead weighed on his soul like small ingots of lead. He had avoided telling his devoted wife how deeply he feared the judgement of Heaven.

Bedwyr's ebullient mood fled, so his expression became dour, aged and patient.

'But Arthur and Maeve are still lost, and even if they return to Arden, they won't know where to find us. I may have to leave directions with those few of our people who remain behind. Perhaps I can leave a message in Latin if I can find someone to write it on a tree. Arthur will read that message and understand it – while Saxons won't be able to decipher it.'

'There must be something we can do to help the children, dear heart. Gareth thinks they were stolen into the distant north but he doesn't know where. Artor was right! It's difficult to rise each morning when you begin to lose all hope.'

Then Elayne began to weep again, quietly. Bedwyr longed to give her some shred of hope that Arthur and Maeve might return safely from their captivity with the northern barbarians. But Bedwyr had survived to such a great age because he was a realist. Wishes wouldn't bring his children home, so the old man must sacrifice Gareth by playing on the young man's honour.

'Gareth is our only hope, Elayne, because he's oath-bound to Arthur. I'll ask him to journey into the north and search throughout the barbarian kingdoms. I think he'll agree with me, because he's the trusted son of King Artor's most loyal bodyguard and the boy is loyal to the death.'

Elayne quailed to think of Gareth being used so ruthlessly. 'He's little more than a child! It's wrong to ask this boy to risk his own life in a vain search.'

So while Gareth was in a deep sleep, his future was being determined by kindly friends who meant him no harm, but who would expect him to travel to lonely and dangerous lands where the bravest of men would fear to journey.

When Gareth finally awoke, the sun was a watery yellow between layers of grey cloud cover. For a brief, halcyon moment, he thought that he was at home in the old villa outside Aquae Sulis. Soon, he would be called to feed his father and commence the daily routine of weapons training. His mother would pat his head as she paused in the task of collecting eggs, because she was a trusted house servant. Then the present returned like a sudden bucket of cold water thrown at his face.

Deep in the warm nest of his bed, Gareth pictured the icy paths that stretched out of Arden, and knew he must continue his journey as soon as possible. He shivered at the thought of the miles that lay before him. His horse was fully rested, so he had no other excuse to tarry. Far away in Cornwall, King Bors and Queen Valda had already received a message that Blaise and Eamonn had been captured by a group of foreign warriors. He had even mentioned his suspicion of Mareddyd's complicity in the kidnapping; decency demanded that he explain the situation in person. Gareth sighed at the thought of the families of the dead guards and the tidings he had sent to Tintagel.

While his courage was still strong, Gareth pushed aside the blankets and dressed quickly in the chill of the winter afternoon. But he needed to stay in Arden a little longer because his search must be thoroughly planned, and it was essential that he should elicit information from the Master of Arden that could speed his journey into the unknown.

The long winter nights in the fortress were warm, rich and filled with sensation, courtesy of a soft-bodied, sharp-minded servant girl called Kerryn, who had been placed at Gareth's disposal in the name of hospitality. She shared his bed and eased his night terrors by waking him before he said or did anything that would un-man him. In later years, his remembrances of Arden would always conjure up images of thick woollen pallets, hot wine in pottery mugs, the rich scent of dried rose leaves and the sensations of sexual fulfilment. But the most enduring memories only had beauty because they existed beside fragments of pain and suffering. In the aftermath of passion, Gareth had kissed the great veins in Kerryn's throat, her wrists, and in the secret places between her upper thighs. He felt the force of her, like the power of the Mother as it surged through him anew. He was her slave and her lover, but only for a week. Then, although she wept, Gareth left her easily and without thought. Such was the lot of women, even in idylls such as Arden.

As the fortress boiled with the imminent departure of Lasair and Barr in company with a large troop of young Britons of both sexes, Gareth Minor found he was being tied to Bedwyr's foster-son by the most potent ties of all, the iron-clad links of pity and responsibility. Manipulated by an expert, Gareth knew he must travel for the rest of his life, if need be, until Bedwyr's children were found. An old man's love bound the young warrior to an all-encompassing task, for Bedwyr was what Gareth had always desired above all things – a loving and loyal father.

Gareth had been engaged in a final conversation with Bedwyr when Lady Elayne had begged him to wait upon her in her winter garden. The canes of bare, thorny branches had rattled against the rough-hewn walls in an eerie echo of spring. She had stared down at her hands, embarrassed by her husband's presence.

Bedwyr had been giving the young warrior directions of the route to Caer Gai when Queen Elayne's message had reached them. Now, the old warrior used her presence to issue his last orders to Gareth, for he wanted his wife to understand his final demands on the young man.

'Whether successful or not, I charge you to search for my son for at least seven years. At that time, I free you from your oath – whether I'm alive or dead.' Bedwyr's face showed he was more than half-convinced that his son has been lost to him forever. 'After the passage of that amount of time, I will have become inured to the truth that my Arthur will surely have passed into the shades.'

Then Bedwyr stood and stepped forward to the tall young man with the pale hair and ice-blue eyes, and embraced him. At first, Gareth stood stiffly in the circlet of those once-strong arms. Raised from birth to be a weapon and an extension of his obsessed father's arm, he had known few affectionate moments, so he had no defences against Bedwyr's clever use of love. Gareth knew he would search for Arthur until death came for him so he hesitantly lowered his head onto the old man's shoulder like an exhausted child. Then he allowed himself to hold Bedwyr in his own muscular arms.

'The Forest of Dean will always be open to you, Gareth, and my sons will swear likewise. You've had a hard life, young man, but perhaps that harshness is what's made you so strong.'

Lady Elayne had raised her head once she was sure that her husband had no further advice to impart to young Gareth. 'My son is also strong and he is important to our people – but my daughter has been forgotten. So promise me, Gareth, that you won't forget little Maeve.'

With a silent oath to the Christian God, Gareth took Elayne's hand

and kissed it. 'I swear, my lady, that Maeve will be protected from anything or anyone who would cause her *any* harm! Fear nothing, for all will be well.'

The following day, Gareth was making his final preparations for departure when Lady Elayne stopped him as he was leaving the stables for the long journey to Caer Gai. He had hoped to make his escape from Arden without fanfare once the Master of Arden had suggested that the young man should seek assistance from Taliesin, the son of Nimue, who was considered to be wise beyond measure.

Lady Elayne intervened with one last request. Gareth was taken by surprise when she reached out to Gareth's destrier and gripped the saddle leathers, an action that caused him to pull back on the reins. The huge horse stamped and backed away with much snorting and bridling, while Gareth used hands and heels to keep the powerful beast in check. But Elayne ignored any personal danger as she reached into the capacious pocket tied around her still-trim waist.

A small box, the size of Elayne's palm, was pulled out and held up for Gareth to accept. 'Please take this, Gareth. I should have bequeathed this pearl to Arthur years ago, but I feared to relinquish my boy completely to his destiny. I've decided that the time has arrived when he will *need* it!'

With a deft flick of one thumb, he opened the beautifully crafted box. Inside, nestling in a twist of blue cloth, was an obviously valuable ring which caught the light serenely. Bedwyr joined them as Gareth opened the box, and the old man gasped to see Artor's thumb ring, remembering the time when Nimue had taken it from the High King's dead hand so many years earlier. Afterwards, on Artor's express orders, the Lady of the Lake had cleansed the ring of the last traces of Artor's blood with her own tears before presenting the jewel to the Master of Arden to give to Elayne. This ring was power, heritage and duty. This ring was Britain!

'This massive pearl was once inserted into the lid of a valuable jewel box owned by Uther Pendragon, a safe place in which the despot kept the secret spoils taken from those unfortunate citizens whom the tyrant murdered or ruined,' Elayne explained. 'After the bauble had come into Artor's possession, the High King met with Brother Isaac, a priest at Glastonbury Monastery who had once been a master jeweller. Isaac inserted the pearl into a fabulous ring that King Artor wore on his thumb.

'He told me it served as a reminder of his father's sins.' Elayne's flesh shrank with superstitious revulsion. 'My lord wore it in battle and often described how it resembled a blinded eye when it was awash with blood.

'King Artor bequeathed this ring to Arthur when my boy was only two months old,' Elayne went on. 'He told me on many occasions that he feared its power over any mortal who wore it. While the ring is very valuable, its true worth lies in the memories it excites. The pearl told Artor that power must be tempered with mercy – or else men become beasts!

'I feared to place such a cursed object on my son's innocent hand, but now I can accept the truth of Artor's intentions. The High King understood that this ring represented the nature of power and was a physical manifestation of the right to rule – and to choose. It can be bloody or it can be beautiful. Also, a man's intentions change its appearance, for pearls glow with refulgence that is a trick of the light. It all depends on what you choose to see!'

This fine old woman is an innocent, Gareth thought. All he saw was a plain golden ring, a simple object of considerable worth. Fortunately, Bedwyr joined them and gasped aloud, so Gareth revised his opinion. The bauble terrified Bedwyr, and the Arden Knife was a difficult man to frighten.

'Arthur must gain possession of this ring or he will never return to Britain,' Elayne said quietly. 'There is no other tie in existence that can tug at his heart and urge him to relinquish the life he constructs beyond the grey oceans. I doubt that I'll ever see my boy again, unless he receives this ring. It will remind him of Arden, the forest that he loved so well, and those people who love him. He will also understand that he was born to rule Britain. I haven't got the Sight and I'm not able to see beyond the veil. But I'm a mother, and I know my son better than anyone else ever could. Only the ring can remind him of where he belongs.'

Then, with a self-conscious smile, the Mistress of Arden stepped away from the warhorse and bowed her faded head. 'The Lord God of hosts will watch over you in the voyages to come, Lord Gareth, so know that you carry a grateful mother's hopes on your shoulders. Perhaps you were born to do this generous deed and bring Arthur home safely to Britain . . . and to me.'

I wonder! Gareth thought bitterly. My father saw me only as a small replica of himself. No doubt my mother was selected to bear me because she had the same colouring as Father had during his youth. If my father loved anyone, it was a dead man. Me? I'm just a joke played against mortality by a lunatic.

She had left him with little to say, so Gareth closed the box and slipped it inside his leather vest. He bowed to Bedwyr and dropped his hands so that his stallion was free to move. Buoyed with a sudden sensation of freedom the beast began to thrust forward, followed by the pack animal. The gates of Arden gaped widely before him.

The light was as dreary as the sky and the persistent cold reddened his nose. With an effort of will, Gareth chose not to look back, so he failed to see Elayne's legs begin to buckle in a faint. Bedwyr helped her to remain upright with his remaining strength and, together, the elderly parents held each other for comfort as their only hope disappeared into the charcoal trees.

After leaving the fortress of Arden, Gareth had only ridden for an hour and was feeling particularly discontented with his lot when he was overtaken by two older men. They were mounted on well-appointed steeds and were leading two packhorses piled high with armour, weapons, supplies and equipment of an indeterminate nature.

Gareth pulled his horses to a halt and waited for the two strangers to address him and pass him by. His hand automatically rested on the pommel of his sword, although Gareth could tell at a glance that these men had obviously lived for fifty summers or more. The facial hair of these strangers was liberally sprinkled with bristling white strands.

The elder of the two men sat very straight in his old-fashioned saddle with the terse watchfulness of an accomplished warrior. His blue eyes scanned Gareth's face, body, weapons and even the way he had loaded his packhorse and Gareth had the uncomfortable feeling that the older man disapproved of his organisation. The stranger's long plaits, fierce, grey-gold moustaches and bare chin proclaimed him to be a barbarian. He was also an extremely large and healthy specimen of manhood, so Gareth amended his assessment of the man's harmlessness.

The other traveller was disreputable, dirty and dressed in a coarse homespun robe that marked him as a Christian priest. Gareth's eyes opened very wide as this well-armed priest swore at his companion with a creative description of what he could do with his time. Then, almost as if he was surprised by Gareth's appearance in front of him, the priest pulled his mule to a stop.

'I suppose you must be Gareth? I've heard tales of your father when he was in the service of the High King. I always believed that most of those fabrications were designed to excite the imaginations of incredulous peasants, or to fuel the anger of the common folk against the Saxons. You're not your father, of course, but the seeds of Uther Pendragon seem to have a way with them. They trap us mere mortals so easily, that generation after generation of us are impelled to serve them. I recall—'

'Oh, for pity's sake, shut up,' the other warrior snapped at his friend, his eyes still fixed on Gareth's puzzled face. 'I'm Germanus, erstwhile armour-master to Arthur in all aspects of combat. This reprobate is *Father* Lorcan, if you can believe me. For his sins, this priest has been forced to teach Latin, history and natural science to his pupil. But Lorcan has one important talent that will be of use to you in your quest. He has a very capable tongue and is the master of many languages. Unfortunately, he exercises that tongue day and night at every possible opportunity.'

'Now, who's wasting time with shite?' Lorcan laughed gleefully, as if he'd won some form of contest. 'At any rate, we packed immediately when we were told of our pupil's little problem. It's perfectly obvious . . .'

'That you'll need our invaluable assistance once we leave Britain,' Germanus continued seamlessly. Clearly these two old men were affectionate friends, despite their constant bickering.

'I've spent a large part of my life in the north, but I was born in Gaul. I speak a number of barbarian languages and understand several more. Lorcan is highly educated, knowledgeable about geography and was a student of the Christian Church in Rome itself. We're both familiar with force of arms and we can look after ourselves,' Germanus explained.

'In short, you need us desperately,' Lorcan added with a cheerful grin.

'So we're volunteering to take you into the north,' Germanus continued. 'Don't bother to argue. If you think you can give us the slip, you're wrong. We'll follow you anyway and, eventually, we'll have to pull you out of some disaster caused by your ignorance of the barbarian kingdoms. It's up to you, of course, but it would be much easier if you agree to accept the inevitable.'

Germanus managed to grin without seeming too terrifying. 'He's right, you know,' Lorcan added smugly.

'But . . . you're so old!' Gareth protested with the first words that entered his head.

As he spoke, he wanted to kick himself, for both men bridled and puffed out their chests indignantly.

'I beg your pardon, but I doubt you'll be able to keep up with me.'

'You're an ignorant, bad-mannered boy!' Lorcan retorted irritably with an accompanying vile curse. 'I suppose we should tell you that Taliesin is returning to Caer Gai to meet with us, even as we speak. If we hurry, we'll find him there when we arrive. He'll be the first to tell you that we offer the only hope you have of finding Prince Arthur alive.'

'I'm going to Caer Gai anyway, so . . .' Gareth replied, feeling that he was trying to climb out of quicksand.

'I believe we'll just tag along with you for a while then,' Germanus added. And so the matter was settled.

Lorcan talked interminably throughout the first and second days of their journey as they slowly broke out of the thickly forested margins of Arden. While Gareth and Germanus watched the thinning trees for any sign of Saxons, especially those raiding parties from Mercia, Lorcan educated Gareth on every aspect of Arthur's early life that he could remember. As Germanus remained watchfully silent, the richly accented voice of the Hibernian droned on and on and, if Gareth hadn't found the stories of his master's youth so compelling, he would soon have grown weary of the endless gossip. Only sleep relieved the companions of the road from the chore of listening to the non-stop gabble.

Eventually, outside Viroconium, Germanus offered a friendly warning to Gareth. 'Avoid all questions about your destination or your links with Arthur, Bedwyr and Arden,' the Frank advised with a dour grimace. 'King Bran of the Ordovice tribe has no reason to love Arthur. If he discovers that Arthur has been captured by the northerners, he might decide that you're a danger. You could rescue the lad and return him to his home, giving Bran a reason to stop you. Silence on your part is essential.'

'I agree, boy! For your own sake, you must pass through Viroconium as quickly as you can.' Lorcan's clown face was uncharacteristically serious. 'We don't dare ride into King Bran's city with you. Oh, I don't believe that Artor's grandson would do any of us any deliberate harm, for he's an honourable man at bottom. But he's a jealous man as well, and he fears our boy as a divisive force that could weaken the position of his own son, Ector, whom he believes is destined to become the next High King of the Britons.'

'Yes,' Germanus added sarcastically. 'He wants his own child to become the High King of Nothing and No One.'

'Bran may have heard of the attack on Arthur's party already,' Lorcan explained. 'And his heart won't bleed if he discovers that Arthur has been lost. However, our presence in the town could let the cat out of the bag and he'd expect us to search to the ends of the earth for Arthur. So we'll make a deal with you. We'll go to Dubris and wait for you there, while you go to Caer Gai on your own. We'll expect to see you in Dubris after you've completed your business with Taliesin.'

And so Gareth had passed through Viroconium at speed and without incident. In the turmoil of a township that was bursting at the seams with refugees, he was just one more ragged, muffled man on horseback heading into the west. The fact that Gareth chose to be tight-lipped about his destination, or his plans, was hardly unusual. A blind man could see that the tall warrior was a seasoned fighter, so nobody cared to upset him by asking impudent questions.

The conical stone huts built by the Ordovice villagers were clustered together like shellfish on the rocks of the shoreline. In the town centre where all the crooked and muddy streets met, Gareth recognised a stone church, a hall where King Bran dispensed justice and a scatter of wood and stone buildings that had grown over the generations to shelter the tribal aristocracy. A large marketplace was busy with traders and farmers from both the local area and the more distant villages, hawking their wares on the muddy square, careless of the cold breezes and the threat of rain. Bright cloth was displayed on hastily prepared bench tables or flapped from tents where fruit, vegetables, dyed wools, metal wares and the gew-gaws and trinkets of a fair were touted in a cacophony of shouts and imprecations.

Regretfully, Gareth had skirted the edges of the colourful display to move to the outskirts of the town. A town fair promised laughter, good food and games of skill that excited the boy in him. An inn promised a bed for the night after days of sleeping on the uncomfortable earth, but his innate caution kept him moving.

The young man's spirits began to lighten once he reached the far side of the busy settlement and saw the mountains of the west as they rose in serried ranks.

Free of Lorcan's voice and Germanus's expertise in everything, Gareth rode in blessed isolation through Cymru with his thoughts ranging into the darkness to a riven tree around which an old villa had been built by Myrddion Merlinus many years before – or so the legends insisted. There, he would find the fabled Lady of the Lake and her son, Taliesin, reputed to be the wisest man in the isles of Britain. But Gareth Minor had lived with a legend and knew only too painfully that such men often had feet of clay.

At the mouth of a sooty cavern that was obviously used as temporary shelter by roaming shepherds, Gareth paid a local crofter for food and information. Over there was Caer Gai, according to the dour farmer, who saw no evil in the boy with the shining sword.

To pass the last hour of the late afternoon, the warrior cleaned and sharpened his sword by the waning light of a bloody sun. He sat cross-legged beside a sharp incline that overlooked the mountain valleys while, below him, a fast-flowing river boiled out from the mountains near Caer Gai and flowed down to Glevum where the soil was rich and deep. Gareth had never seen Glevum in her glory days, but he had been raised on the stories of the long-dead heroes of Britain. To look down on this narrow flood and understand that Vortigern had crossed this same river to take revenge on his son, Vortimer, was an experience that Gareth treasured. His father had spoken admiringly of the role played by Myrddion in the subsequent great victory, a tale that had been told to Gareth Major by the great healer himself. The boy Gareth had been transfixed by the heroism of the tale.

Gareth decided to rise before dawn the next morning, eager to reach his goal. He packed his few possessions onto his spare horse, saddled his destrier and prepared for the last push to the magical house at Caer Gai. Part of his heart quailed at the thought of explaining his failure at Vinovia once again, for he was aware that Taliesin considered Arthur to be one of the last hopes of the Romano-Britons. Gareth would be forced to disappoint a man of great power, sanctity and importance.

'On the other hand, horse, I'll get to meet the fabled Nimue,' Gareth told his destrier in a soft voice. 'Is she as fair as the songs promise? Perhaps no woman could be so beautiful, but I'll be honoured to meet someone who knew King Artor and was wed to Myrddion Merlinus, the great healer. Legends will have come to life for me, horse, and we'll be among them soon enough.'

Then, with a heart that was suddenly lighter, Gareth dug his heels into the belly of his horse and sent the flint stones flying under its hooves as he cantered down into the river valley. The rising sun stained the clouds with blood and washed the young man's face with a memory of guilt.

CHART OF THE LIMFJORD

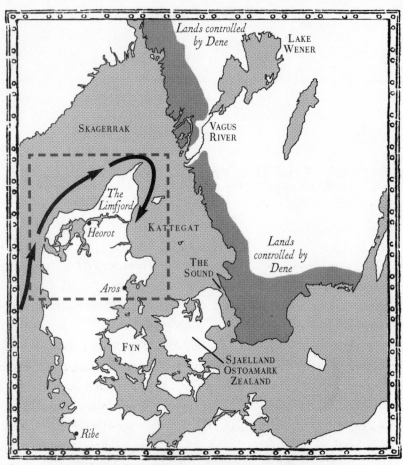

Lands controlled
by Dene

LAKE
WENER

SKAGERRAK

VAGUS
RIVER

The
Limfjord

KATTEGAT

Heorot

Lands
controlled by
Dene

THE
SOUND

Aros

FYN

SJAELLAND
OSTOAMARK
ZEALAND

Ribe

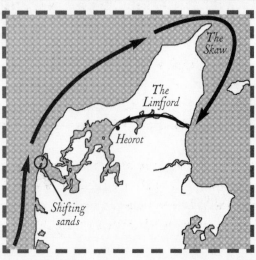

The
Skaw

The
Limfjord

Heorot

Shifting
sands

CHAPTER V

THE LIMFJORD

It is good for a man that he bears the yoke in his youth.

The Bible, Lamentations 3:27

The surface of the grey sea had no breaking waves, sea foam or iridescence, but the swell seemed to heave as if strange life forms twisted and turned beneath the surface. Huddled in coarse blankets, the four young captives looked to port and starboard ahead of them and saw the midnight-blue of land that lay like smudges of dark paint.

'Land!' Arthur breathed quietly, his heart in his mouth in the excitement of making landfall. Their fate hung in the balance and they would probably be enslaved once they arrived at Stormbringer's destination, but the companions were young and they had never travelled beyond the shores of Britain. Even the persistent ache of cold winds and colder brine failed to dull their high animal spirits.

'Captain!' Arthur called out to Stormbringer, who was standing with arms akimbo beside the helmsman. 'What land lies to either side of us? Where are we?'

Stormbringer shook his leonine head with amusement.

'You Britons always speak with long lists of questions. If curiosity was valued in gold, you'd be the richest people in our world.'

Then, with limber grace, he descended from his perch to face the four bedraggled young captives on the bare deck. They were full of questions, but Stormbringer was too busy to assuage their curiosity. So, to keep themselves occupied, they had eaten cold stew and had learned to chew their rations of raw fish while staring at the land beyond the grey sea and trying their best to keep warm. As a captive on this strange ship, Arthur began to feel like a true slave, for he was ignorant of their destination or where they were. His lack of knowledge and the enforced inactivity fed his growing temper.

Once land had been sighted, Stormbringer reverted to his role as a barbarian captain returning to his homeland, almost as if he feared to become too close to the Britons and the fate that awaited them. Arthur was alarmed, and this made him angry – both at himself and at Stormbringer.

'We aren't the ones who chose to sail across deep waters for weeks on end in order to find a strange landfall, yet you call *us* over-curious,' Arthur had responded. Stormbringer took offence at the younger man's bad-tempered jest. This young Briton sometimes forgot who was captor and who was captive.

'You're a fractious and arrogant young man, Master Dragonsen. I understand from your high-handedness that you have an inflated opinion of your importance and believe yourself to be the equal of any Dene. But you aren't a prince in *our* lands! Do you understand your position, boy? Your immediate future depends on the decisions my king makes when you appear before him, so you may become a slave and you'll have no status whatsoever among the Dene people.'

The captain's gaze was direct and confronting, so they stared at each other like two fighting dogs as they measured each other's strengths and searched for weaknesses that could be exploited. Eventually, Blaise stamped her foot forcefully on Arthur's instep because she knew it was the only way to force him to retreat from an unwinnable position. He yelped, his concentration was broken and sanity began to prevail.

He immediately got the point.

'I'm sorry if my manners and opinions have offended you, Captain, but no insult was intended,' Arthur said stiffly. As apologies went,

Arthur's response was grudging, but Stormbringer was a true leader of men and he knew what this half-hearted admission of regret had cost the young man. The captain felt a little foolish for taking offence at the immature attitudes of a stripling who was far younger than his size and martial skills suggested.

The Dene took a deep, steadying breath. 'To answer your questions, young man, the land to the north is Agder, part of the kingdom of Noroway. The land to the south was once called Jutland, or the land of the Jutes. But it's now the Mark of the Dene. We are about to experience those treacherous waters of the straits which are known as the Skagerrak.'

The word, *Skagerrak*, rose over the muted slapping sounds of the ship and the sea with a rasping noise that promised no good. Every syllable of the name was threatening.

'The skeletons of many men lie beneath our keel and their bones bleach in the ribs of the many ships that litter the ocean's floor. How many warriors have died here is impossible for a man like me to ascertain, but the dead are a vast throng trapped in the lightless under-sea. We Dene have learned to understand the waters that surround us. She is our mother now, even if some of the Dene tribes believe that the Ice Dragons were our first fathers, mothers and gods! We know we can never take the sea for granted, young man, even if she provides us with fish that fill our bellies and allows us to travel along her invisible roads to new vistas and wealth.'

Arthur tried not to be overawed by Stormbringer's passion for the sea and the heritage of his people. Belatedly, Arthur was grasping what Taliesin, Lorcan and Germanus had tried to teach him: that barbarians have souls too, and only a fool could believe them to be blights on the earth.

'Look to the north,' the Dene said, and Arthur followed the direction of Stormbringer's pointing hand. 'Can you see the current in that area that's closest to the shore line? In the Skagerrak the sea moves at great speed and many whirlpools are formed within the fjords. They've been known to drag a ship down if the captain isn't careful. The current runs close to the northern shore and the teeth of stone that lie in wait there. But we'll be safe, if we can stay in the southern waters where the seas are relatively calm.'

Arthur couldn't understand how one body of water could be divided into two very different stretches of sea, but he was prepared to believe the evidence of his own eyes. The wild current in the Skagerrak seemed to be moving at a greater pace than the waters under *Loki's Eye*, and this stretch of sea was darker in appearance than the grey-green flood beneath the hull of the ship. The leaden waves were more ominous than the white, swirling swells that indicated turbulent whirlpools; against his will, Arthur shivered with a sudden, visceral cold.

'Where do we go from here, Master Stormbringer?' Eamonn asked. He was standing, so he could gain a better view of the natural phenomena of the channels. Arthur noticed that his friend's lips were blue.

'You're a man of few words, Dumnonii! We'll sail through the straits and then turn to a southerly heading which will take us into the Kattegat. This stretches from the north-eastern tip of the Dene Mark to the land we call Skania. The sea here is much like the water in a large pot. If you stir the liquid forcefully with a wooden spoon, it will spill over in the same way as the Kattegat does.'

'So it's dangerous,' Blaise added cautiously, and Stormbringer looked uncomfortable. Arthur noted a flash of irritation in the captain's expression that a mere woman should address him directly. And Stormbringer knew that Arthur had seen this momentary lapse. Like most Celt aristocrats, Arthur respected those women who were his kin.

'The Kattegat is a cauldron of strange currents and deceptive winds, and it's always difficult to traverse,' Stormbringer continued. 'Some of the more superstitious of our seamen believe that a sea monster lies under the surface of the waves and this beast waits for unwary ships' crews to sail within its reach.'

Arthur recalled the she-dragon who still dominated his sleep patterns. In his dreams, her elegant, turquoise tail would stir the ocean, just like the turgid and deceptive waters that *Loki's Eye* was trying so hard to avoid.

The captain explained that he would turn *Loki's Eye* away from the Kattegat and its cruel history. 'While I don't subscribe to the sailors' beliefs about these waters, I'm not a fool so I'll always follow the safest course when I'm travelling through dangerous seas.'

Stormbringer dismissed superstition with an airy wave of one hand.

Given the superstition inherent in his own dreams, Arthur immediately felt like a complete fool, so he kept his mouth shut.

'Until better options present themselves, we'll avoid the Kattegat and sail due east before entering the deep channel of water called the Limfjord,' Stormbringer continued. 'A fjord is a narrow passage of water that separates two areas of land with high cliffs on both sides.'

Blaise was far from satisfied with this description, but she accepted it. She'd see a fjord soon enough if their voyage was fated to proceed to their final destination.

'Where does the Limfjord end, and what does it mean for us?' Eamonn asked slowly.

'The waters of the Limfjord flow across the width of Jutland from an inland lake to both coasts, but we'll be entering the fjord on the east coast – over there!' Stormbringer indicated a point on the eastern side of the peninsula that was sliding towards them. 'The Limfjord effectively cuts Jutland in two.'

Stormbringer's colour was high and Arthur noticed that the Dene was avoiding Maeve's eyes. Possessiveness flashed across the Briton's mind like a streak of Greek Fire.

'Are you saying that we'll sail through two dangerous bodies of water and enter a narrow fjord, when we could have saved days of travel and avoided considerable danger by simply sailing across the peninsula from the western coast?' Arthur snapped out each word like a mantrap closing on flesh. 'It seems a strange strategy to a landsman who is ignorant of your world.'

Arthur felt a weird triumph, as if he had caught Stormbringer out in a basic navigational error.

Blaise kicked him hard on the back of his calf, so Arthur knew he was being childish. The man had been decent to them, far more than was necessary. But, like two fighting tomcats, both men were circling each other as they searched for weaknesses.

'No, the western entry to the Limfjord is barred by shoals of shifting sand,' Stormbringer snapped back. '*Loki's Eye* is an ocean-going vessel with a deep draught. Can you understand *that*, Briton? This ship isn't suited to any part of the waters that lead into the Limfjord from the west, so we'd run aground in hundreds of places if we followed the path that you suggest. *Common sense* tells us to travel by the longer route around the tip of Jutland so that we enter the fjord from the east where the water is deep for the entire journey.'

'*Loki's Eye!*' Maeve interrupted. She had been silent for most of the exchange, but now she climbed gracefully to her feet and leaned on the beautifully smoothed wood of the ship's rail where adze marks from its construction gave it a simple grace and beauty. The hands of many seamen and the oil from their skins had polished the wood to the smooth beauty of old honey.

'Yes, the ship is named after the trickster god.' Stormbringer's voice was cool and polite, although everyone but Arthur could tell that the Dene was furiously angry. 'I once believed that challenging the sea in a frail ship was a joke worthy of Loki. I was foolish to challenge the god, but as I matured, I regretted my challenge to the gods and paid red gold and rings of silver to Loki as a penance for my stupidity.'

'Thank you, Captain. You've been very candid with us,' Maeve said, smiling at the Dene, whose face immediately softened. 'As captives, we could have expected to be chained, starved and beaten. Instead, you've treated us with courtesy and kindness, so you must forgive our endless, irritating questions.' Maeve's smile was ingenuous and frank, but Arthur knew that his sister was as manipulative as a cave spider – and just as patient. She toyed with Stormbringer in a flash of white teeth and innocence that completely disarmed him.

She'll soon have him eating out of her palm, Arthur thought. He was unable to fathom why he resented Maeve's success with Stormbringer, but when she smiled at the Dene and flattered him, something hot and angry coiled in Arthur's breast. Maeve was barely twelve, but she was speaking and acting like a woman twice her age. Her green eyes impaled Stormbringer and the captain blushed hotly, then moved back to his position beside the helmsman.

She's rattled him, Arthur thought with suppressed amusement, but he followed his sister's movements with eyes that were suddenly careful. What is she up to? And when did she learn so much about men?

Arthur and Eamonn were expected to relieve tired warriors on the oars, so the last part of the journey was divided between short periods of fierce physical exertion followed by longer stretches of intense boredom. Maeve had discovered a needle and some coarse thread in the small satchel that she had slung over her upper body when they were first captured. Since childhood, Maeve had always tried to carry her entire world with her whenever she travelled.

Some people are only content when, like turtles, their personal possessions are around them, no matter where they happen to be. A visit to her kinfolk in Viroconium had been the cause for a flood of quiet tears when five-year-old Maeve refused to travel unless she carried everything she owned on her person. The most casual of afternoon rides while she accompanied her mother on visits to sick crofters resulted in terrible inner conflicts because Maeve was torn over which of her favourite toys should also undertake the journey.

And so her mother had spent an entire winter weaving, curing and sewing a satchel of soft rabbit fur for her strange little daughter to take on their travels. There Maeve could keep all her small necessities of life. Now, on the verge of adulthood, the young woman still refused to stir from home without it. The only things that had changed over the years were the contents.

Despite their fingers being blue with cold, Maeve and Blaise forced themselves to mend their clothing so that the quartet of captives could present themselves as respectably as possible to the court of the Dene king. As members of the aristocracy, they represented Britain and the girls were determined that they would make a brave showing.

With grudging protests, Eamonn and Arthur handed over their

damaged items of clothing, although this concession left them to shiver in the cold, grey winds. Both men stripped to the waist and bundled themselves in their cloaks for warmth. Meanwhile, they were instructed to clean and polish the bronze plates on their studded jackets and put a shine on every piece of leather or metal that made up their dress. Above them, Stormbringer watched the youngsters with cynical amusement as they squabbled over their appearance.

On one of the planks normally used by the rowers, the four young people were able to watch the shoreline that passed on both sides of the vessel. The waters closest to the high cliffs of Noroway had a deep grey-green tinge in the occasional sunlight that indicated unfathomable depths. The Britons had already adjusted to the short northern days, so any snatches of sunlight and the resultant pretence of warmth were treasured. The Skagerrak was rumoured by some Dene to be a deep trench dug by sea monsters that gave the beasts an entrance into Udgaad, but the more pragmatic tribesmen believed that these super-stitions were nonsense. No Sae Dene had ever actually seen a sea monster, Stormbringer explained, and these intrepid masters of the sea were so important to the larger population that they were permitted to have their own king, a nobleman held to be secondary only to the High King who ruled the entire nation.

Stormbringer pointed out details of his land and culture with a strong sense of pride. The young Britons were accustomed to a society where tribal kings were subservient to a *Dux Bellorum*, or battle king, so the concept of a sea king seemed logical in a landscape where water was so important. For the first time, Arthur watched his captor with more careful eyes. What type of man would be entrusted with such an important mission by the High King of the Dene. Could Stormbringer be a Sae Dene lord?

No, Arthur decided. If Stormbringer was such an important personage, I'd be dead by now – killed for my impertinence!

Out of concern for the sea monsters or the treacherous currents, the superstitious helmsman steered *Loki's Eye* as close as possible to the coast of the land that had been known as Jutland. These pale waters were shaded to turquoise in some places, so the helmsman explained in execrable Saxon that the lighter colour warned of hidden sandbanks. 'The sea is a wild creature and she presents herself as a woman who can be soft, beautiful and seductive when she's in a mood to be loved. Then the sun and moon dance on her wavelets, when her warm arms and flanks look so soft that a man can believe that she'd hold him above the waves and preserve his life for love of him.'

Arthur nodded his appreciation and complimented the helmsman on his descriptive skills. The man blushed and continued his tale.

'Then, in an instant, the sea can turn nasty when she bares her claws. Ravenously, she tears the beaches into strips, carries away the sand and spews it into new places where the strongest ships can run aground, founder and sink. Aye, she can be a bitch, bless her, but we sailors love her, as do all Sae Dene who are forced to endure her moods. Where's the fun in a woman who's always smiling?'

Stormbringer laughed at the expression on Arthur's face that spoke more clearly than words that the Briton preferred his women to be compliant.

'You wonder why we travel around Vendsyssel-Thy rather than sail up the Limfjord Sound to Heorot? In a fit of temper, our mistress has closed the mouth of the fjord in the west and strangled the sea with sand.'

'Aye! I understand,' Arthur replied. 'You can tell your helmsman that he has a golden tongue, Captain.'

'Rolf Sea-Shaper will thank you for your kind words,' Stormbringer answered with a flash of white teeth. 'He sings the old tales well enough to stand in the drinking halls of Heorot if he was prepared to practise a little harder. But I'd regret his loss! Rolf keeps his head when the sea becomes angry and she tries to swat us like an insect.'

Arthur merely nodded. *Loki's Eye* was moving swiftly, powered by the full swelling of the great sail, but the warriors on board had no time to rest under Stormbringer's captaincy. The vessel must be checked from end to end, for every piece of hide or plaited rope must be examined in the daylight and replaced if worn or faulty. Every length of timber must be scrubbed and the inside of the hull must be checked for storm damage. Similarly, cargo must be kept secure to ensure that the ship stayed level and steady on the waves. Salt air and brine played havoc with weapons and armour, so even the youngest and most callow of the crew members took care when cleaning his fighting accoutrements when the weak light lasted and sea conditions were mild.

The warrior-sailors readily stripped to the waist to clean their leather shirts and plate armour. Arthur had noticed too that the Dene scrubbed their bodies in salt water when his own flesh shrank from any ablutions in the freezing conditions that turned their fresh water into ice. He wondered idly why fresh water froze much faster than brine and decided that salt must be the reason, then rejected any further distractions. They must be close to Heorot.

'I wish I knew who came into possession of my knife!' Arthur muttered to himself. He knew it had been taken when he was struck down, along with his sword, his shield and his helm. Gareth had carried his heavier armour on one of the spare horses, so Arthur knew that those items were safe. But what of the Dragon Knife? Even now, his palm itched to hold its shagreen hilt and watch the wings and tail of the dragon as they curved around his fist.

Since his capture, Arthur had concluded that the Dene sailors were intelligent and civilised warriors, especially after working so well with them during the storm and its aftermath.

And so it was that he found it difficult to remain angry with Stormbringer

He disarms me with his honesty when I question him but, ultimately, he remains my enemy. I wish I didn't admire him or feel such jealousy when he demonstrates his considerable talents, because I end up looking and feeling like a fool. He's taking us into slavery, so his kindness to us merely ensures that we don't cause him any trouble, as we could, quite easily, in a ship where all his warriors are fully occupied. Two determined warriors with nothing to lose could cause chaos on a fighting ship until such time as they were caught and killed. But Valdar

Bjornsen is a clever man, and he's far too knowledgeable to allow us to become a disruptive influence.

Arthur had listened to the Dene rowers talking late at night when all was quiet and the men were on the verge of sleep. During these discussions, Arthur had learned that Stormbringer's name was actually Valdar Bjornsen. The Sae Dene's father, Bjorn, was considered by these men to be one of the great heroes of the Dene people, although they were wary of disclosing certain oddities about the seafarer. The warriors spoke in awed whispers whenever they used Bjorn's name or spoke of his exploits.

'Your knife and your sword will be presented to the king, who is my master. Should he so wish, he can always give the knife back to you.' Stormbringer had heard Arthur's bitter complaint. Arthur responded by staring defiantly at the captain. Stormbringer could hardly miss the challenge in those feral eyes.

Has Stormbringer guessed that I'm considering my chances of escape? Arthur wondered. Does he think to calm me with empty promises? If so, he's mistaking my nature.

Under the pale moon, a small and very hard heel dug into Arthur's instep with surprising and painful force. He gasped and looked down into his sister's dimly flushed and furious face. Obviously, his youngest sibling had learned something from Blaise that had roused her slow temper.

'Are you moon-mad, you great lump? Or are your wits still wandering from that blow on the head? Master Stormbringer is our captor ... and he has treated us with consideration and generosity. What if he had chosen to be less kind? Do you fancy undertaking this journey tied up in the cargo hold at the bottom of the ship? Do you think you would enjoy the slap of foul, salty water from the bilges in your mouth and on your face? Do you long for the sight of your sister being ravished by a whole crew of hairy Dene? I can assure you that I don't. Every time you try to feel like a man rather than a prisoner, you're risking our safety. Blaise tried to tell you on a number of occasions, but you ... just ...

won't . . . listen!' Every word was punctuated by a sharp blow across the back of the head.

Maeve's face was twisted into a ferocious mask of anger while her green eyes crackled with energy. Arthur wondered how he had ever thought of her as an encumbrance. 'Just . . . don't . . . do . . . it . . . again!' she ordered.

Arthur nodded, dumbfounded by her passion.

As soon as the sun had set and the privacy of premature night had settled over *Loki's Eye*, Maeve separated Arthur from the Dumnonii siblings and beckoned him down into the scuppers. Her hissed words left Arthur in no doubt about her strong feelings.

Something of his regret must have flickered in Arthur's eyes, so Maeve's face changed as if by sleight-of-hand. Even in the deceptive half-light, brother and sister were accustomed to reading the language of each other's bodies. She was the maid again now, as harmless as a barn-mouse.

'Am I really so foolish, Maeve? It seems to me that Stormbringer welcomed my views and treated me as an equal, so I don't understand your anger!'

'Yes, you *are* a great lump,' Maeve said, but she laughed a little as she insulted him in her old affectionate way. 'Stormbringer is trying to suck you dry of any information he can gain about our homeland. When he enrages you, you talk! You've told him everything he's asked of you. Obliquely, it's true, but even a man bent on manipulating an enemy can be offended if they're insulted. Stormbringer is offended – and he's a bad man to cross! I think he's something other than a minor lordling, for why would *any* king entrust a nonentity with the exploration of fresh lands that could easily be filled with riches begging to be plundered?'

Arthur stared up at the enigmatic figure of Stormbringer as the captain stood beside the helmsman with his body loosely moving to the pitch and roll of the sea swell. Every detail of the huge Dene screamed that this man was a superb specimen of physicality. But what was the purpose of the expedition?

Yes, Arthur thought. At times, he had treated this voyage like an adventure rather than considering the horror and pain that threatened the captives. He had acted like a child, so he kissed Maeve's hand and watched her blush hotly.

'How else can I thank you, my speaker of necessary truths? You are always correct!'

Then Maeve swatted him on the shoulder with the full force of her hand.

'Ow! What was that for? I'm agreeing with you, aren't I?'

'Don't you realise you're our only hope, you idiot! Didn't Lorcan and Germanus teach you *anything* other than how to wield weapons? Eamonn, Blaise and I were just scooped up with the largest of large prizes, but we don't matter to the Dene in the greater scheme of things. You're the Last Dragon of Britain, and you're the one who will make or break the British people. Can't you feel it in your heart? Trust me, brother, for I know that Stormbringer understands your worth. I've seen him watching you, and he measures you to understand what it is about you that his instincts tell him is so important. I don't want you to beg my pardon, or to feel guilty that you might have been rude or impudent in your speech to the Dene captain. I want you to think *before* you speak – and to be careful of what you *say*.'

Arthur had always known that his little sister was strange.

In the dim light he examined her with eyes that were newly opened and aware. She was beautiful in an odd, Celtic fashion, with her wild red hair that defied her best efforts to plait it discreetly into a coronet around her head. Her eyes were the transparent green of water in sunlight, where tall trees lend colour to a clean river. A sooty ring of charcoal defined her irises and, depending on her mood, her eyes could burn or caress as easily as smiles came to her petal-pink mouth. He had ignored her or patronised her, but he could now feel the full force of her. His strength was trivial when compared with such power.

Then his sister giggled and the spell was broken. Maeve was his little sister and only a fond, twelve-year-old child. But Arthur wouldn't be deceived again.

'What about the itch at the back of your mind, Arthur? Does it still trouble you?' His odd gift had been a family joke for years.

Arthur shook his head regretfully. 'I haven't felt a trace of it since we were captured.'

'Perhaps it's only waiting until such time as it's needed. Be careful, Arthur! The sea is full of shadows and we weren't born to love these lands – or the waters around them. We belong to the forests, the rivers and ancient lakes that are deep, cold and filled with light. Your dragon is of the earth. Stormbringer loves a serpent wrought of ice and fire, so his dragon is mated to the cold seas. They are different! *We* are different – for all that we are alike in many ways.'

Then Maeve turned away to mend a pair of Eamonn's gloves. The moment of special communion was over, as she squinted in the fitful light of the flare above her and threaded her needle.

By daylight, *Loki's Eye* was surrounded by grey-blue smudges of land. The channel was narrow and the current ran strongly so that the rowers were forced to labour hard to keep to the courses that Stormbringer seemed to conjure out of thin air. Islands loomed around them and the coast to their right was wild, harsh and deeply slashed with the clefts that Stormbringer called fjords. Arthur could now understand why Britain was such a rich green prize. Here in the frozen north, the Dene lands were carved out of raw stone, the earth seemed sterile and the sea consisted of a series of stirred cauldrons, despite Stormbringer's assurance that the weather was very good.

In the night, just before daybreak, Arthur had been awakened to shouts and curses from Stormbringer and the sound of wood tearing along the sides of the ship from a drowned stone ridge. *Loki's Eye* bucked like a wild horse under the sting of the lash, so the helmsman threw the full weight of his body against the rudder, while the oars-men on the side closest to the hidden teeth of stone raised their oars to save themselves from disaster. The vessel turned the merest fraction, but the ugly, tearing sound ceased immediately. One of the more agile warriors leaped down into the bilges and its low hold, searching for damage to the ship's hull.

No water had penetrated the hull of *Loki's Eye*. The Kattegat had kissed the Dene ship with a lover's sharp teeth and an invasive tongue, but she had allowed the vessel to pull away skittishly from her embrace.

Nor, by even the flicker of an eyelash, did Stormbringer show any strain or nervousness. With newly alerted eyes, Arthur saw a thin bead of sweat glisten on the Dene's forehead and he knew then that they had been in great peril.

Now that Maeve had alerted him to his position on board the ship, Arthur began to watch Stormbringer more closely, while accepting that he was also being observed. He noted immediately that the crew treated the captain with all the camaraderie of the sea, but an extra layer of deference bowed their heads a fraction lower than was strictly necessary. Most crews contain at least one malcontent, slow to obey or a little insolent in his actions, but Arthur could find no recalcitrant sailors among this crew. In fact, Stormbringer's warriors worshipped him and hung upon his orders with an unusually ardent anticipation. Several hard-bitten warriors blushed when Stormbringer thanked them for exceptional efforts or congratulated them for work well done.

These men love Stormbringer like a father, Arthur thought, and they'd die for him in an instant, without regret. The Sae Dene captain is a very unusual man.

Once Arthur had been convinced to speak less and listen more, he quickly became aware that Eamonn had been struggling with a weight of misery invisible to the self-absorbed prince during the voyage. Eamonn had rarely spoken and was eating sparingly. During the day-light hours, he spent many hours staring out at the sea and was distant and vague when he responded to questions. Bad dreams caused Eamonn to be wakeful during the darkest hours of the night, while his sense of humour, previously his greatest strength, had gradually vanished.

Cursing his lack of sensitivity, Arthur approached his friend and ignored Eamonn's attempts to deflect the conversation away from his state of mind.

'Don't try to convince me that you're not feeling miserable about something because I won't believe you. I know you haven't been eating, and you've closed yourself off from the rest of us. It's my duty to protect the girls from the consequences of *my* failures, Eamonn. It's not your problem – because you're not at fault! We need you to be sharp and ready to fight if we're presented with even a faint chance to escape from our captivity.'

'Look at the barbarians, Arthur. Do you really think we have any chance against a nation of such huge warriors?' Eamonn's voice dragged with a desolation of the spirit that resisted Arthur's brisk pleas. The young prince tried to shake his friend out of his torpor once again.

'Some men can't bear to be constrained, Eamonn. Others feel that capture means failure. But you must believe me when I say that there's always hope. Sooner or later, the tallest and most intelligent of our jailers will make an error and we must be ready to capitalise on it. We only have to wait and trust to British luck. It saved us at the Battle of Calleva Atrebatum when we should have died. And it saved us from the storm. Ask yourself why we've survived so far, because I don't believe in chance.'

He smiled encouragingly at his friend. 'Meanwhile, I'm convinced that Stormbringer won't allow the girls to be despoiled. Oddly enough, I believe him to be a gentleman, despite being a barbarian!'

'Won't he?' Eamonn's voice was thick with sarcasm. 'You can't allow these bastards to fool you. He'll sell the girls for the highest price he can get, so we'll never see them again. I'll end my days chained to an oar until I drown on the rowers' bench. I should have killed my sister, and myself, before I surrendered our lives to the cursed Dene.'

'That's coward's talk!' Arthur exclaimed, before he could check his tongue. He paled, for the thought of Eamonn committing the sin of suicide had never occurred to Arthur before and he was appalled. If Eamonn had considered murdering Blaise, he must have been in torment for weeks.

'Please don't do anything stupid, Eamonn. I've discussed our likely fate with Blaise and I know she'd prefer to live as a slave rather than accept a watery grave in these seas. She'll gladly trust to Mistress Fortuna to determine her fate.' Arthur could see a gleam of red madness in Eamonn's usually dancing eyes, reminding him that his friend's ancestors were warriors of distinction. Eamonn would never surrender, as long as he knew he had no other honourable way out.

'There's always hope while we remain alive, Eamonn, so we may still be able to free ourselves in the future. I can think of no reason to succumb to death when every day gives some promise of a change for the better.'

Eamonn had been very successful in hiding his depression from his sister and Maeve. When the other captives had greeted each new day with smiles, regardless of privations, Eamonn had simply been convinced that their survival indicated a lack of moral fibre.

I'm an idiot, Arthur thought, for I missed all the warning signs.

'I can't afford to watch you every minute of the day, Eamonn. I need to be ready to find a way out of this cursed land and return to Arden. I am absolutely committed to our escape, one way or another. If you should throw your sister or yourself into the seas, you'll put an end to all my plans and make me very angry.'

That's right, Arthur, make Eamonn feel as guilty as you can. The voice in Arthur's brain was so clear he could have sworn that Eamonn heard it. Surprised, Arthur almost dropped the water-skin he was holding.

'I won't do anything untoward until I know the very worst fate that can be inflicted on us,' Eamonn promised wistfully. 'But if the worst comes to the worst, my oldest friend, you mustn't blame yourself for my actions. My mother would say our fates have brought us to this particular ship and the wild places through which we have sailed. I hunger for the smell of home – so to hell with fate, and to hell with the Dene!'

'Yes, Eamonn!' Arthur snatched at the sudden flare of rage in his friend's eyes. Anything was better than a blank submission to death. 'You must hate them, if that's what it takes to keep you alive. Just imagine how you'd kill them if they should give you the smallest opening. Believe in *anything*, but not in submission, for we are the people! We are kin to King Artor, and there's nothing we can't survive if we decide to endure. I ask only that you keep your promise, and do nothing to harm yourself until you speak to me first.'

Eamonn caught a spark of the fervour in Arthur's words and willingly gave an oath to do no harm to himself.

'Be warned that I'll hold you to your word, Eamonn.' Arthur had been holding his breath while he waited for Eamonn's decision.

'Aye, my friend! I know you will!'

Eamonn turned and wrapped himself in a blanket, ignoring the smell of fish and sweat that permeated the wool. Curled into a tight ball, he closed his eyes to declare to his friend that their conversation was over.

Arthur looked out over the rolling swell. As he watched the shoreline, he became increasingly aware that they were moving inexorably closer to the jagged cliffs marking the shores of Jutland.

Then, high on the mast, a warrior cried out a warning and the entire crew turned to look in the direction of his pointing hand.

'Look, Son of the Dragon, for yonder is Limfjord and our home.' Stormbringer's voice rang with triumph and the warriors at their oars broke into ragged cheering. They had dared to risk the impossibly dangerous seas, and the singers in Heorot would soon praise their exploits at the feet of the High King.

The Sae Dene crew were coming home at last.

The sun rose on what would be a perfect winter's day for these climes. The fjord was narrow and grim, with teeth of stone ready to snap shut on the keels of unwary ships. Only sailors of great skill would dare to sail through its gaping icy maw.

As if they smelled the woodsmoke that drifted from their homes, the warriors began to row with a will, and *Loki's Eye* slid into a current that carried them deep into the land until the open sea had completely vanished. Arthur began to fear that the speed of the slender vessel in the wild current would bring her to grief. Even Eamonn was wrenched out of his torpid sleep. Time scurried by on rats' feet as the ship rode the sweeping waters. Above them, the sky narrowed to a slit of pallid light as the jagged cliffs hemmed them in, leaving Arthur feeling dizzy as he stared skyward.

At the tiller, Stormbringer stood fearlessly and laughed as if he sought to challenge the combined might of wind, water and stone.

'Can you see into the distance, Arthur? Heorot is only a few hours away and, as I promised, the pleasure of the High King will reward us for our courage. See? Heorot is shining in the rising sun.' Stormbringer's voice rang out to the crew. 'Now is the time to prepare, my brave warriors, so we'll allow the sun to shimmer like fire on our shields. Make the sunlight bleed on our battle-axes so that the common folk of Heorot will know that heroes have returned with a tribute for their king.'

Us! Yes! We have become a tribute, Arthur thought drily, and forced himself to follow Maeve's instructions. Listen! Watch!

The warriors released their huge circular shields from the cradles on the outer planks of the hull where the shipbuilders had provided an extra layer of protection in case of attack or accident. In many ways, the shields were primitive, being made of an unusually light but dense wood. Huge bosses jutted out from the centre of the shields; their barbaric patterns caught any rays of sunlight and caused the metal to writhe and burn. The Dene artisans were obviously expert smiths, but heavy bull-hide was also used to supplement the metals. These shields were reinforced with hide from an auroch. The edges of all the shields were protected with this hide, except for Stormbringer's shield, which was edged with brass.

As soon as the shields were cleaned and polished, they were laid back into their cradles. Meanwhile, the current continued to drive the vessel on at breakneck speed.

Maeve's eyes were sad. 'When *Loki's Eye* rides at anchor, the women of the town will know who has returned and who has died.' Her eyes turned to a storage area near the bow of the ship where, for the first time, Arthur noticed that wrapped bodies lay in the darkness with their shields lashed to their corpses. Stormbringer had refused to leave a single warrior behind in the strange land of Britannia, so had brought their corpses home to their womenfolk. The corpses were still cold and seemed but newly dead within their shrouds.

Each warrior and crew member polished and sharpened his weapon and cleaned his helmet. The single-bladed axes had a wicked appearance, much more terrifying in their grim utility than the curved, two-bladed monstrosities used by the Saxons.

But it was the swords that made Arthur's heart stutter within his ribcage. The utilitarian Dene blades possessed a beauty superior to that of the gem-encrusted weapons used by British lordlings. When he was a young boy, Bedwyr had told him of *Caliburn*, the huge sword owned by King Artor that only a man of exceptional height and strength could hope to wield in combat. If Bedwyr spoke truthfully, this magical blade had been lost forever in the tarn at Caer Gai, but Caliburn would remain in the memories of all the men who had seen it.

Gods! Arthur thought blasphemously and invoked the curses of the Old Ones, as he often did when he was unsettled. We would stand no chance against an army of Dene warriors. Do they have armies? Pray God that they will be too disorganised to have a single, thinking head, else the ice-dragon will gobble us up entirely.

Stormbringer looked down with satisfaction at his men, who were now armed and seated in formal rows. He nodded once and lowered his twin-winged helmet over his head, until the long nose-guard turned his face into an enigmatic shadow. Then, reverently, he lifted a bag from a peg on the mast and drew out a huge bronze horn decorated with orange gold.

'Row now – by my count – and let's show our wives and sweethearts that they had best kick any soft bastards out of our beds. Their men have come home from the wild sea, and such warriors will not brook any interlopers at their hearths.'

Stormbringer lifted the great horn to his lips and drew in a mighty breath. The horn cried out in triumph with a raucous, brazen voice that shook the cliffs and the small coves that sheltered at their feet, sending the gulls into the air to flap and scream in fright. The cliffs sent the sound echoing along the narrow passage of the Limfjord, even as the dragon's prow of *Loki's Eye* turned and the vessel was driven at great speed across the terrible strength of the current.

Just when Arthur was sure that they would be dashed onto huge portals of rough stone that stood like graven sentries along the narrow passage, the vessel dived into a patch of still water. Beyond, the fjord opened up. Against the odds, the great lake on Limfjord, deep within the land mass, had been reached.

'Behold! We have arrived at Heorot!' Stormbringer shouted triumphantly and blew his horn once more until the echoes answered, causing the air to ring and thrum with brazen war cries. On the left hand, atop one of the stone portals, an indistinct figure raised his axe high into the new sun in welcome, while the winter light struck the edge of his blade with the sudden glitter of ice or iron.

Even in his anxious state, Eamonn felt his heart race with excitement as the sun struck a headland and a long hall that was gleaming in the weak sun. Arthur stood at his side and drew in his breath in wonder. Red blazed in the light like spilled blood. Gold, green, yellow and orange flared and danced with that crimson, while the great hall of legend seemed to coil with an unnatural life as if a serpent had raised its startled and angry head.

Their long voyage was over. Now, their fates would become clear and Arthur would learn what it was to be a slave.

CHAPTER VI

THE LAST OF HOME

Audentis Fortuna Iuvat!
(Fortune favours the brave!)

Virgil, *Aeneid*, Book 10

Nimue stood on a high knoll of land close to her crooked house with its ruined oaken shell. Along the steep slopes below her, her fields were filled with winter vegetables, sown grain sleeping under the mountain soil and grazing sheep that were neatly divided among cunning terraces carved out of the slopes of the Caer. With her usual pleasure, she sighed with satisfaction and marvelled at what her dead husband had coaxed from his unsleeping brain in a spring which burst from the earth and fed the terraces, so even stony ground became fecund and bore life.

During the night, she had talked with her phantom lover after they had embraced in the old way, hip to hip, thigh to thigh and mouth to eager mouth. She had wept then, and her black-haired ghost had kissed away her tears. 'I know I'm crazed, my love, because my grief has made me insane with the passage of the years I have lived without you. But if having you with me is madness, then I don't want to be sane. I wish I'd known you in those days when your body was like this strong, young shell your spirit now wears.'

Her black-eyed phantom had smiled at her from their warm nest while he had swept his black hair away from his eyes in the same old way of years gone by.

'You're not insane, my beloved. Time is a strange thing and I come to you as I once was so that you needn't remember the pain of my old, dying flesh. In my vanity, I wanted you to know me as I was when my world was young and green, and I was foolishly angry at my lot in life.'

They had often spoken of her man's childhood, both when he was living and now that he had passed into the shadows, so Nimue understood. Unafraid, she tried to name the troubles that most concerned her on this dark winter's night.

Taliesin had returned like the wight he was beginning to resemble as the white streak in his midnight-black hair began to widen. He had materialised at her door only hours after the arrival of Gareth, the strange young man who was now sleeping soundly in one of the old villa's storerooms.

'Will Taliesin go with Gareth to seek Arthur in the northern wastes?' Nimue asked her husband from the warmth of her bed. 'He's so tired that he can scarcely bear to sing, so I doubt that he possesses the strength to endure a long and arduous journey.' She frowned. 'I'm just being selfish, but I long to spoil my boy for a little time.'

Her husband looked down at her still-lovely face with affection and honesty. They had been hand-fasted at a time when spring had determined to cleave to winter, but they had been friends long before they became lovers, so the shared intensity of the mind was more precious by far than any momentary sexual relief.

'Have no fears for the boy, Nimue. Taliesin will make old bones, although his songs will live even longer. He's not destined to die in the northern wastes, but he must rest and regain his strength before he leaves your house. Our son is fated to follow the trials and tribulations of the Three Travellers of Yesteryear. Fortuna has brought the trine together again. They have been born anew as different souls, and they must journey into those places where the days are short in winter and the sun still shines at midnight during the endless northern summers. Your son will devise a way for Arthur to be released from his captivity, if that young man hasn't done it for himself, so that Arthur can return to his homeland. Unfortunately, despite his pleas, the British tribes will never be reunited, so no King Artor will ever return to these isles!'

'But I promised the people that Artor would return. Their songs already speak of a *King of Yesteryear* who will return to lead them at some future time. I've perpetrated a cruel lie!'

Nimue's face reflected her misery.

Such a long and weary time had passed since she had told Artor's bruised and battered army that the memory of their king would never die. Once again, she felt the fearsome weight of Caliburn's terrible blade when she had forced her woman's muscles to raise the sword high in order to catch the light while the sight of King Artor's body on Bedwyr's wagon had filled her heart with a bone-deep misery. With all her wild passion, she had made promises to give heart to her people without realising their need would translate her simple words of comfort into a paean of hope.

'Hush, sweet girl. You didn't deceive them, for Artor *will* return. His face will be legion, and his image will flicker on a wall without full form or substance other than to the eye. Don't ask me for explanations. I never understood my visions, even when I was alive. However, you can believe me that King Artor will appear in the flesh as Arthur, who is his natural son.'

Myrddion smiled down at her and kissed her throat. 'But his return will not be as you expect, even if you should live long enough to see it.'

'Will he become the Dragon King, like his father?' She recalled the first time how, as a young woman, she had knowingly met Artor, and how his bodyguards, Odin and Targo, had stood behind him to guard his back from potential threats.

The High King had seemed tall and strong enough to pluck the sun down from the heavens but, even then, his shark-grey eyes were disillusioned and tired. With a pang, Nimue felt her exultation begin to fray and fall apart like old grave shrouds. Did she really want Artor's son to suffer as he had?

'No, my Nimue! The tribal kings will never again have the guidance of a Dragon Lord and the Dragon's Lair will never again come alive to the sound of Artor's feasting warriors. Cadbury has already become an empty place of ghosts, wild beasts and dead hopes. The peasants drag away its stones, its timber and every small treasure they can steal, for they know that what is abandoned will eventually be taken by the Saxons. Cadbury won't fall to an enemy, but it will be ruined by time. No, Arthur will come again in the guise of an Ice Dragon and his own kin will not recognise him. On his return, the young man will rule in the northern lands where the Otadini bones lie rotting on the open fields of combat. Gawayne's spirit will be slaked in northern blood and it will drink its fill before Arthur is finished with Mercia.'

Nimue shuddered. The Saxons had spewed out of Mercia for several decades and had slain the British tribesmen without a care for what they burned and destroyed so wantonly. Bran and Ector had not ceded an inch of Ordovice soil, but the cost to the tribes in young lives had been catastrophic.

'Bran must retreat into the mountains and then make a determined stand in country that can be defended. He must build a shield wall around the remaining British lands in Cymru: a fortress so strong that the earth won't tolerate the touch of a Saxon foot. He must put away foolish thoughts of past glories, because there is no means by which he can hold the lands that his grandfather ruled. He isn't an Artor, for no one can fill those boots, no matter how they try.'

After Myrddion's spirit had left her bed, Nimue often wondered how her imagination had conjured him up in such detail. Perhaps she had been searching for an answer to King Bran's dilemma. Privately, she doubted that Bran possessed the dour stubbornness to do what must be done as an embattled ruler but, for now, she was content to lie in the remembered shelter of Myrddion's arms and drown herself in her own private delusions.

'Perhaps we should convince Taliesin to stay here while Gareth leaves for the continent. We should give Gareth the promise of a loving home which will welcome him on his return. The son of Gareth Major withers from within because his father, my old friend, turned selfish and half-crazed in his old age. To father a child in his dotage was unfair on any son and only served to retain the hope of glory from his long service to the High King. By insisting that his innocent son should dedicate his life to the service of Prince Arthur, Gareth Major attempted to keep his master, and himself, alive beyond their appointed time. Such a calculated plan of dedicated loyalty left no room for affection. As a consequence, Gareth's heart now aches for it. Give him yours, my sweetling. The boy will go into dark places on this quest and will lose himself in the shadows, unless he has the memory of the Lady of the Lake to draw him back by the ribbon of her love.'

'You're speaking in riddles, my love. But you always did,' Nimue had wailed plaintively. 'Speak plainly, so I can understand what I must do.'

'But you already know that,' her lover had answered. And then the time for words was over.

Now, with her tiny, self-sufficient kingdom spread out around her, Nimue acknowledged the accuracy of her husband's assessment. From the moment he had ridden into the villa's forecourt, leading a tired packhorse and seemingly oblivious to the driving rain, Gareth's loneliness had been a visible cloak of misery. She could feel his need, hot and desperate, but hesitant like the affections of a mongrel dog kicked away from a warm hearth on too many occasions.

When she returned to the separate kitchen, with its roaring fire and clay ovens, she was surprised to find the object of her concern deep in conversation with her dour serving woman, Gerda of the hill people. His blond head was bent attentively to hear every word of homely wisdom. Gerda was actually laughing at something that the boy had said, so he coloured with embarrassment at Nimue's sudden appearance. Oblivious to the presence of her mistress in the shadows, Gerda was joking with Gareth as if he had been one of Nimue's strong sons.

'Look at you, Master Gareth! I swear that you're blushing like a virgin. Hasn't anyone ever told you how pretty you are, and how all the young maids would spread their legs for you at your most casual glance? No? Heavens, boy, look at your reflection in the rainwater barrel on the next occasion you take a drink. God has made you comely and he has made you strong. I can't see any fau[...]

if a body notices how well you look.'

'I'm a fighting man, mistress. I'm not [...]

court that can be decked out in fancy-colou[...]

raised to serve the Dragon King and his kin.' Ga[...]

to control his blushes and the direction of the con[...]

'But what of fun, boy? Didn't your mother tell y[...]

you play with the other children? And didn't a willing[...]

teach you the nature of love in the hay?' She smiled. 'You[...]

again, Master Gareth.'

Many men would have taken offence at such banter, but [...]

could see the boy opening like a tight, winter-blighted bud under t[...]

warmth of Gerda's teasing.

'No!' Gareth replied sadly. 'My father planned out my days with education, exercise and weapons' training. Then I took care of his needs once I was free of my other duties. My mother was a simple village girl and wasn't permitted to share in my childhood.' This last statement was made softly, as if Gareth expected the servant to express some criticism of his dead father.

But Gerda persisted, until two spots of dull scarlet were visible on his cheeks.

She took a deep breath. 'How wicked . . . and how cruel! Your mother must have shed many tears if she was forced to be parted from you. Boys can't live on duty, education and weapons' practice. They need fattening up and must be encouraged to run wild – followed by a vigorous scrubbing when they're covered with dirt. But mostly, they need love.'

'My father was very old when I was born, so he didn't have time to let me play. I was required to perform my allotted duties and every moment of his life was dedicated to my training. But he did love me. Truly, he did!' Gareth's voice had risen in volume and stridency.

Gerda examined the boy's face as she slowly stirred the contents of a big pot of stew over the open fire.

'Why?' she asked abruptly.

lt in you, except that you colour up

bright-plumaged bird of the
ed ribbons like a pet. I was
eth was trying manfully
versation.
u stories? Didn't
girl decide to
re blushing
imue
he

an answer, but
is state of mind,
etence of youth,
father's lack of

. She rules this
nore sense than
l want to speak
ok famished so

Nimue . . . but I
y concentrated

the silver bells
i lands to the

south. Although she was elderly, he was already more than half in love with his beautiful and charming hostess.

'It's no trouble to me, Gareth, for Gerda presides over the preparation of all food in my kitchens. She does the sweating while I do the eating.'

With a wide grin, Gerda stirred a blackened pot of porridge with a curved spike of wood. 'In just a moment, young man, I'll have some porridge for you that will stick to your ribs.' With a wooden ladle she served a goodly portion into a beautifully shaped pottery bowl. Gareth marvelled at the natural beauty of the utilitarian objects scattered throughout this eccentric villa and treated so casually by their owners. The servant pressed honey upon him as a sweetener and, wonder of wonders, a whole box of crystalline salt.

'Porridge without salt is like going to bed with your boots on,' Gerda said with an easy, lecherous smile. 'Take as much as you want.'

Gape-mouthed, Gareth obeyed, stirring his porridge until it was flavoured exactly to his taste. Although he tried to eat slowly and courteously, he soon reverted to the eating habits of a greedy boy and almost licked the bowl clean in his enjoyment. Two bowls later, he was replete.

Unfortunately for Gareth's peace of mind, the young man was confused after spending several hours with Nimue and a further half-day with Taliesin as they discussed the complexities of his quest. His task had seemed so simple when he had left Arden. Gareth intended to persuade Taliesin to accompany him to the north and to use his magic to deliver Arthur from the hands of the barbarians. The rescuers would then transport the prince and his companions to Britain and the bosoms of their families.

But a blind man could recognise the harper's bone-deep exhaustion. Taliesin had burned out his energy selflessly as he travelled up and down the tribal lands to advise, cajole and threaten the aristocratic British leaders on ways and means of ensuring the survival of their tenant farmers. This task had been the last request asked of Taliesin by the High King, so the young poet had been prepared to squander his life to comply with Artor's wishes, hopeless as the undertaking appeared to be.

Taliesin could accept the urgent nature of the search for Arthur, despite his belief that Arthur had probably been lost forever. But the young poet's resolve had been weakened by the sight of burned villages and the dead innocents immolated within them. He had moved through the small, stone fortresses that the Celts inherited from the Roman masters of yesteryear, and he had shed tears over the bodies left to rot on the charred earth. Later, he had forced himself to enter the burned churches where he could sift through the ashes of their scriptoriums to find any scrolls that might have escaped the barbarian thoroughness. He had cried openly at the wanton destruction of libraries and had wept for the priests, monks and nuns murdered by the Saxons who believed that these pious men and women were cowards who refused to fight back.

Sickened by the Saxon hatred of learning, which they associated with the influence of Rome, Taliesin saved what knowledge he could.

Frequently, Taliesin called himself a fool for wasting so much effort for so little profit. Now, at his mother's home, his dead king was demanding more of his strength, although Taliesin had nothing left to give.

Taliesin had learned painfully that there was no nobility in dying pointlessly, so he was reluctant to chain the young Prince Arthur to an unwinnable war. But was the poet willing to leave Prince Arthur in slavery in the barbaric north? Ultimately, both Taliesin and Nimue concluded that that to sit in relative safety on their small caer would be sinful if Arthur was left in captivity.

'You must understand why you need to travel in company with Father Lorcan and Master Germanus and allow me to follow you into the north at a later time,' Taliesin explained to the earnest young man who stood before him. Such raw hero-worship was abhorrent to Taliesin, so his stomach roiled at the look of bitter disappointment on Gareth's face.

'I have been ill for some months, and I'm weary almost to my death. I must rest for a time, Gareth, or I'll sicken further and will be an additional burden to you while you are undertaking your journey.'

With some reluctance, Gareth nodded in agreement. He wasn't a fool, and he recognised the gauntness revealed in Taliesin's face, his expression drawn and lost, as if he had stretched his spirit so thinly that it was near to tearing apart.

'A man can only do what he can do. Still, we need your wise counsel, Taliesin, so I'll regret that you'll not be travelling with us.'

'I've no idea how long it will take before I'm fit to depart on the journey. But I swear by the oaths I made to Lord Artor as he lay dying that I will join you once I have recovered sufficient strength to undertake the journey. I won't desert Arthur in his time of need, nor will I fail to help you to find him.'

Taliesin smiled shakily at the young warrior.

'I suggest you maximise any skills you have that will ease your way into the north. If you are asked, you must claim to be a Roman-raised Briton who has been driven out of his homeland and is now attempting to sell his skills to the highest bidder. Thousands of other mercenaries have similar histories. I doubt that anyone will suspect you of having ulterior motives. I know from my own travels that innkeepers welcome singers and storytellers, just as villagers seek hardened warriors to assist them during times of threat. The larger inns also welcome toughs who are prepared to deal with troublemakers or to manhandle fractious drunkards. I suggest you call all men friends until they prove they're enemies, but always watch their eyes and hands carefully. Words are cheap in the lands you'll traverse and few men speak with total honesty. Expect treachery, even while you hope for generosity.'

'You give wise advice, my lord. But I have no knowledge of the arts of storytelling or music, so I'll have to rely on my skills with my sword and my bow.'

'You can profit from your skills with weapons, Gareth. Your sword-craft and knife-throwing can be used for entertainment or for the education of young lordlings. You can also hire your services out as a bodyguard, if you choose to tie yourself down for a time. Your need for coin will ultimately influence your decisions, but try not to hand-fast yourself to any single king or lordling, for Arthur could be forced to languish in the north for years. No master will cheerfully relinquish a good fighting man who enters his employment. If God is kind to us sinners, I'll be arriving in the Saxon lands in about a year and a half, so you can expect to hear of me in the north around then. I'll ensure I become known as the Harper of the Britons; listen at inns for some word of me.'

Gareth's throat felt constricted. 'A year and a half?' he gasped. 'That's such a long time!' He thought of the quiet halls of Arden Forest and the sweet scent of Nimue's home, and he felt a sudden yearning for a home of his own that might eventually give his life some purpose.

But a year or more would seem like a lifetime if he was forced to survive in hostile places.

'The road you must take is long and dangerous, Gareth. The north is an alien place filled with dangerous enemies, so you must be brave if you hope to complete your quest and fulfil your oath. No man will blame you if you decide to leave Arthur to whatever fate Fortuna has planned for him. Your father made you swear your life away to Prince Arthur before you'd even met the boy, but such an oath cannot be totally binding on you. You're still too young to throw your life away on pointless dreams of glory.'

Gareth sighed, so Taliesin was certain that his advice would be ignored.

'That isn't so, Taliesin! Arthur treated me like a man and as an *equal*, and he never saw me as a pale imitation of my father, even if that's all I have become. I must honour an oath to my friend.'

Gareth felt no compulsion to explain to Taliesin why Arthur was his *first* and *only* friend.

The harper clicked his tongue in growing irritation, for he'd become tired of the demands of pointless loyalty over the long years.

He recalled a story recounted by Myrddion Merlinus about one good and faithful servant who possessed marked similarities to Gareth Minor. Botha, the arms master of Uther Pendragon, had been oath-bound to that monster in the years before that terrible man had gained the throne. Again and again, Botha tried to protect his honour without breaking his oath. Ultimately, he had died when the task proved impossible.

Taliesin vowed to himself that he'd never put Gareth in the same untenable position that had killed Botha.

'You're nothing like your sire, Gareth. I knew him well and spoke to him often, so I can swear that my words are true and aren't offered out of pity. Your father couldn't accept that his master and hero had died from his wounds. He wouldn't face up to the inexorable march of the years or the strength of our enemies. I'd hope that you're far too clever to blindly accept such nonsense. From our brief acquaintance, I can tell that you're a man who sets great store by the truth. Remember what I say, my young friend, for Taliesin offers his hand to *you* as a warrior – and not as the reflection of a dead man.'

Then Taliesin offered Gareth his hand in the old Roman fashion. In the warmth of those strong fingers, Gareth felt the constriction in his chest begin to loosen. He wept like a child for the man his father had ultimately become.

And, for the first time, he also mourned for the boy he should have been.

THE VILLAGE BELOW HEOROT

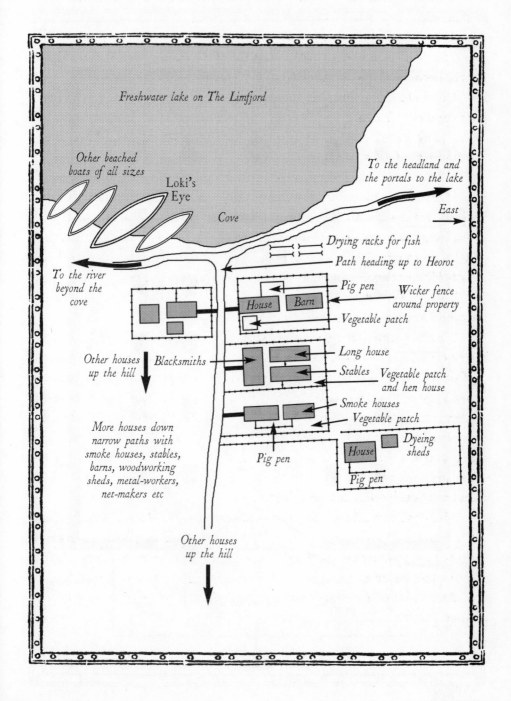

Freshwater lake on The Limfjord

Other beached
boats of all sizes

Loki's
Eye

Cove

To the headland and
the portals to the lake

East

Drying racks for fish

Path heading up to Heorot

To the river
beyond the
cove

Pig pen

Wicker fence
around property

House   Barn

Vegetable patch

Other houses
up the hill

Blacksmiths

Long house

Stables   Vegetable patch
and hen house

Smoke houses

More houses down
narrow paths with
smoke houses, stables,
barns, woodworking
sheds, metal-workers,
net-makers etc

Vegetable patch

Pig pen

Dyeing
sheds

House

Pig pen

Other houses
up the hill

THE HALL OF HEOROT

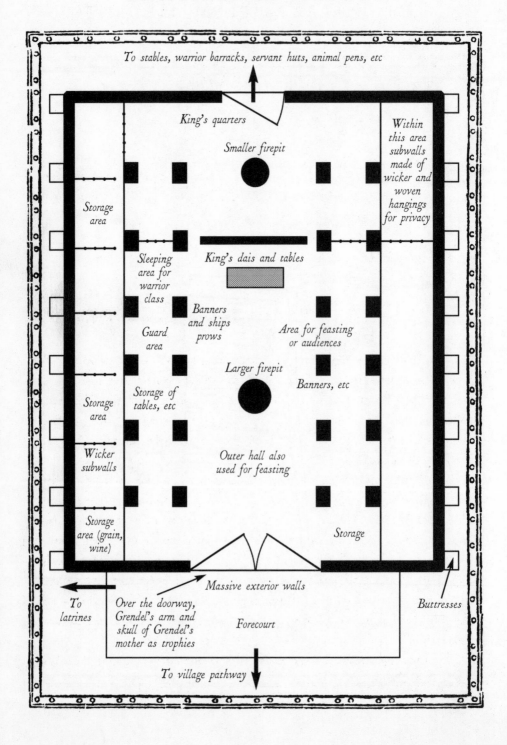

To stables, warrior barracks, servant huts, animal pens, etc

King's quarters

Smaller firepit

Within this area subwalls made of wicker and woven hangings for privacy

Storage area

Sleeping area for warrior class

King's dais and tables

Guard area

Banners and ships prows

Area for feasting or audiences

Storage area

Larger firepit

Banners, etc

Storage of tables, etc

Wicker subwalls

Outer hall also used for feasting

Storage area (grain, wine)

Storage

Massive exterior walls

To latrines

Over the doorway, Grendel's arm and skull of Grendel's mother as trophies

Forecourt

Buttresses

To village pathway

CHAPTER VII

THE HALL OF THE DENE KING

Per Ardua ad Astra.
(Through struggle and adversity to the stars.)

The motto of the Royal Air Force

The captives were made aware of their real status in the Dene world from the moment that *Loki's Eye* made its swooping dive towards a pebbled beach below the hillside crowned by the great hall of Heorot. With a small grimace of apology, Stormbringer asked each of the Britons to extend their arms so their hands could be bound tightly in front of their bodies.

The consternation of the warriors around him put Arthur on his guard, for these strong and clever men seemed nervous and seemed almost shy. Arthur distrusted any court where the ruler was feared by his own aristocrats, so his eyes searched for his sister's cool, clean gaze.

'Aye, brother! Perhaps this Dene king isn't cut from the same cloth as Stormbringer, so you'll have to be careful,' Maeve hissed, while her guard was engaged with polishing finger prints from the metal boss of his shield. 'That means keeping your mouth shut, Arthur. Think before you speak!'

Stormbringer leaned over Arthur's shoulder and whispered in his ear.

'You mustn't show any fear when you stand before the king. Our people put a high price on courage and fortitude, so any pleas or tears will only heap scorn upon you. For my part, I'd prefer to leave you unbound, but my master expects you to be in chains and he'll think more highly of you if he believes you are too dangerous to be left loose.'

'All I ask is that you look to the safety of the girls, Stormbringer. They are children and they're still too young to be raped by grown men. We both know what happens to pretty slave girls...' Arthur's voice contained a raw edge of distress.

'Their value lies in their youth and purity, so no man will touch them until our king gives his consent,' Stormbringer promised, but Arthur could see a shadow on the brow of his captor.

'What aren't you saying, Captain? Do you doubt your king's capacity for mercy?'

The Sae Dene shook his head fiercely. 'I've told you repeatedly that our king, Hrolf Kraki, will decide your separate fates. My king is a warrior. He took his father's throne back from Snaer through force of arms, so the tyrant was fed to Hrolf Kraki's pigs while he still breathed. Be careful what you do, or say. I have no part in his decisions. Because I have captured you, I might be able to intervene to some extent, but the king would be angered if I attempted to dictate to him on any matter which is rightly his province. I won't anger him unless my honour is compromised through my silence.'

The message was clear: Stormbringer doubted his king's capacity for mercy – and he was upset by what *might* happen to the British girls.

The captain paused and mitigated his words carefully. 'Our king is not unkind, but his experience has made him hard and untrusting. And he has sometimes been known to consider advice which is... unfortunate. He survived banishment during Snaer's reign after that tyrant stole the throne. Traitorously, Snaer received assistance from the Hundings, the Germanic tribes who swore vengeance against the Dene kings after the leaders of that tribe were crushed in battle. Such hatreds are the normal pattern of life in northern lands. This land cannot support two peoples, two kings and two cultures, so only one can be permitted to prevail. Hrolf ensured that many of the Hundings perished for their various treasons.'

He smiled grimly. 'Snaer blighted my master's youth, ensuring that our king hates slavery on principle – although ours continues to be a slave society. I've found that he won't normally punish a man he believes is deserving of mercy. For my part, I'll do everything I can to speak kindly of you and your friends.'

After living in close contact with the Dene captain on *Loki's Eye*, Arthur had observed the Sae Dene's worth in situations of danger and imminent death, so he knew that Stormbringer wasn't easily frightened. Hrolf Kraki must be a formidable and unpredictable man if Stormbringer was wary of endangering his own position.

There's something wrong about this king – something that Stormbringer isn't prepared to voice aloud. And what does he mean when he refers to *unfortunate advice*?

Before Arthur could voice his concerns to Maeve, strong hands gripped his shoulders and lifted him bodily out of *Loki's Eye* as if he weighed no more than a child. The vessel had been run aground on the shingle, so the Britons stayed dry as they were herded along a narrow path that wound upwards to the king's hall. Arthur heard the jeers and laughter of a crowd of bucolics, staring at the outlanders with curiosity and amusement. Men, women and children had gathered in their gaily dyed wools and sturdy leather boots to view the strangers at close quarters.

Over the chatter and noise, one stentorian voice could be heard. The crowd scattered like chaff before a strong wind, while Arthur's mouth gaped.

'Valdar, you bastard! You've survived again and, no doubt, you've returned weighed down with gold and slaves. You've got Loki's luck, you son-of-a-whore . . . and you're still a good-looking bugger to boot. As usual, you return with beautiful women.'

A large leonine man strode down the path from Heorot, his arms spread widely to lift Stormbringer off his feet as he embraced him. If

Arthur had been asked to describe what a Dene king should look like, this man would be a perfect example.

'Frod?' Stormbringer's voice was incredulous and, yes, excited at the arrival of this man with such an odd name. 'Frodhi! You turn up in the damnedest of places at the most opportune times – but look at you! You've gained weight!'

'I'll have you know, you half-arsed Sae Dene, that everyone else but you tells me that I'm a fine figure of a man.'

Stormbringer snorted, then his humour evaporated and his usual lack of expression returned. Frodhi continued to grin amiably.

'How's Hrolf Kraki? He's your cousin – so if you don't know, who does? We're all kinsmen, but you're in the line of succession, not me, since my mother is the Crow King's blood relative. You've always managed to keep Hrolf sweet and malleable, even when he's half-crazed with his woman.'

'He's his usual curmudgeonly self and spends his entire day looking for traitors in the corners of his hall and thinking of new ways to wring the last pieces of gold from our farmers.' Frodhi evidently had a healthy lack of respect for the king – or was in the fortunate position of being a favourite in the royal court.

He was an exceptionally handsome, strong and vigorous man, aged somewhere in his thirties if the white, wire-like lines at the corners of his eyes were any indication. His white-gold moustache was both ferocious and luxurious, while the chin that he kept shaved was cleft and strong. His thick hair curled to his shoulder blades, a perfect foil for his golden-tanned skin.

Both Maeve and Blaise reacted to his animal magnetism, shown in their heightened colour and bright eyes. Arthur felt at a total disadvantage in the company of this handsome, witty barbarian, so he searched avidly for any sign of weaknesses in Stormbringer's cousin.

His eyes are too close together, Arthur decided. And he's obviously too interested in joking and foolery. Stormbringer is the better man!

All thoughts of the coming meeting with the Dene king disappeared in the excitement of the moment.

'And who are these captives? Damn me, Valdar, you always manage to find the pretty ones.' Frodhi bowed courteously at the waist to both girls and when Stormbringer introduced him, he took their bound hands in his and kissed their knuckles.

In turn, the girls giggled and blushed attractively.

'And what of these young roosters? The big one looks like a Jute!'

Arthur bristled with insult, so Stormbringer explained the ancestry and reputations of Eamonn and Arthur.

'So you are the Last Dragon! The title has a nice sound, doesn't it? But it's also a little too final for my liking. It implies that someone is going to end your career rather abruptly.'

Frodhi laughed uproariously and then apologised. But Arthur sensed a scratching deep in his consciousness, faint as the stirring of a mouse's tiny claws. He was instantly on his guard.

This man isn't a true jester – and he isn't as mild as he'd have everyone believe. But even when Frodhi said his farewells to Stormbringer, with a promise to drink beer with him later, Arthur attempted to keep his facial expression blank and his thoughts to himself.

With a cheerful wave, Frodhi bounded upwards towards Heorot, his long hair flowing in the light breeze.

Arthur squinted upwards at the dim sun. By his estimation, the hour must have been close to noon, but sunrise had only arrived an hour or so earlier. The inhabitants treated sunny days as unofficial festivals and the crowd was in the mood to be entertained.

At the epicentre of the crowd, the Britons blinked in the fitful sunlight with bowed heads and tied hands. They shared feelings of failure and trepidation, for they had been taken alive, a shameful thing.

Do we look so strange to them? Arthur wondered and, with deliberation, rose to his full height and stared arrogantly at the crowd around him. When his gaze caught the eyes of a watchful commoner, the peasant became embarrassed by the contact and eventually looked away.

Taking Arthur's lead, Eamonn followed suit, while Maeve tossed her scarlet head and tilted her chin proudly as if no bonds restrained her. Blaise pulled her skirts out of the mud on the roadway and straightened her tunic. Then she stared at the mob to show her contempt. We must act as if *we* are the masters and Britons rule the known world that lies beyond the Dene lands, thought Arthur. Our arrogance and pride must be the armour that demands respect from Dene society.

But the Dene common-folk had cause to be proud as well. Arthur made an instant comparison between these strong, athletic bodies and their smaller British counterparts. Again, most of the Dene women were taller than Eamonn, who was much the same size as the immature and beardless youths of this strange land. Similarly, the Dene girls stood taller by far than many warriors in Britain and their fair colouring made the captives seem exotic and dark by comparison. The darkest hair colour among the Dene villagers was pale brown and most of the people present seemed to possess blue eyes of a shade which was rare in Britain.

'Their feet are *huge*,' Arthur muttered to Eamonn under his breath. 'In fact, they're like big hairy animals. We mustn't act as if we're beaten before we begin. Stormbringer told me that his people came from a land of deep snows. People of small stature would die in the snowdrifts and the lack of sunlight seems to have leached the colour from their skins. Only the tall and the strong lived long enough to breed.'

'But the king's cousin seems quite reasonable,' Eamonn muttered. If Hrolf Kraki is like him . . .'

Then Blaise broke into the men's conversation to hiss out her opinion. 'I don't believe we have anything to fear if Frodhi and Hrolf Kraki are alike.'

'I'm not so sure,' Arthur grumbled darkly while scuffing his toes on the muddy roadway.

'It's all right for you, Arthur. You're tall enough to look directly into the eyes of these man mountains,' Eamonn retorted with a flash of his old humour.

Now that the journey had been completed, Eamonn was freed from the long, despairing greyness of the voyage. He grinned like the boy he still was. 'I get a good view of Dene bellies, and I can tell whether they're flat or paunchy. Unfortunately, most seem to be flat.'

From the Dene perspective, these four outlanders were very strange in appearance because their colouring was so dark as to be almost fabulous. Arthur spied a number of grizzled warriors who wore grey-streaked red beards, but not a soul among the noisy and curious throng seemed to have red hair on their heads. Maeve's red-gold coronet of curls was a source of great wonder to the Dene. Several daring women reached out to touch the rich, glossy curls when she came within reach, although Maeve drew back from their impudent fingers. Similarly, Arthur's mane, rather than his great height, was a source of interest. Only Stormbringer's intervention prevented some of the more advent-urous members of the crowd from snatching a souvenir and, in the melee, one crude young man pulled the pins from Maeve's coronet so that the russet-blond locks unravelled and tumbled past her knees. The crowd gasped at the marvellous sight, while the youth relinquished the hairpins to Stormbringer with good humour and the crowd's applause.

In Dene terms, Arthur was still tall, but not unusually so. However, his pale, changeable eyes were rare in these lands and the heaviness of muscle that covered his long bones was much greater than the general lankiness of most northern youths. It seemed to Arthur that Dene warriors became heavier in the body as they aged, or so he determined from the many older folk around him.

'There doesn't seem to be any fat Dene among the peasantry,' Arthur hissed at Eamonn.

Eamonn shrugged. 'Nothing would surprise me with this lot. Rowing would add bulk to their upper bodies, and we've seen how proficient they are when they're at the oars of their ships. They seem civilised in the way they live and speak, yet I believe we'll discover that they're a merciless race when forced into a corner. They seem to view us as beasts, as if the luck of being born a Dene raises them above the stature of all other tribes. Such pride and arrogance can be exploited.'

'You're right, Eamonn,' Arthur said with a broad grin. 'You're beginning to think clearly again!' Eamonn had found a chink in the Dene armour, so his heart leaped in fierce joy to discover that these warriors mightn't be invincible.

'At least I hope so,' Arthur added to himself.

But the greatest curiosity of the Dene villagers was reserved for Eamonn and Blaise, whose tempers were soon tested by the rude stares and comments that came from the crowd. Eamonn put his own interpretation on their discourteous gestures and interpreted their comments regarding his short stature as mortal insults. Blaise slapped away one intemperate hand that snaked out of the crowd and sought to fondle her breast. The warrior guards sniggered, but they made no move to chastise the peasant.

For his part, Eamonn fell into a fighting crouch despite being un-armed. With gritted teeth, Eamonn responded to the curiosity of the crowd by growling and straining against his bonds until the Dene villagers recognised a berserker redness forming behind the stranger's eyes.

With an unexpected sensibility, they ceased to torment him.

Meanwhile, Blaise could feel the eyes of the Dene males mentally caressing the curves of her small, beautiful body while they imagined what lay beneath the dark-blue robes she had donned on the morning of their capture. She felt dirtied by the lustful gloating in those eyes.

The blue dye of her dress served to hide the grime of their long voyage, so that the girl looked like a princess forced to walk amid common citizens. Her proud face spoke of her scorn, so the crowd respected her for hating them, even as they were amused by her pointless defiance.

Although Blaise's outer robes were salt-stained from seawater, the tarnished gold thread that decorated her tunic at the neck, hem and wrists spoke eloquently of the wealth of her family. The raven hair that had come loose from her plaits tumbled down her back. Sword-straight and strange in this northern world of fair-haired women, its blue-black gloss was so fabulous that many of the Dene women reached out their hands to see if it was real. But her eyes snapped with fire, so no man present doubted that she was a highly spirited young lady.

Dene women were beautiful and seemed to enjoy extraordinary good health, but they weren't voluptuous in form. In these lands, a smallish and lush-bodied girl like Blaise was a rarity from her rounded breasts to her womanly hips. 'I reckon she'd be a hellcat,' one warrior whispered to his friend, but Arthur was able to understand their conversation. As usual, his speed and skill with languages had brought him a rudimentary understanding of the northern tongue.

'This lady isn't for a pig like you,' Arthur spat out in rudimentary Dene. The warrior would have responded with his own insults, but Stormbringer slapped the man across his cheek and issued orders so quickly that Arthur was unable to keep up with the flow of words. Then, before any further trouble could develop, the Dene captain led his men in orderly ranks up the cobbled path towards Heorot and the king's hall. He ensured that the captives were enclosed within the ranks of his warriors, more for their protection than to stress their status as prisoners.

The reaction of the common folk towards Blaise and Maeve served to underscore Arthur's misgivings. Blaise's marked difference to most Dene women, coupled with her rarity and her voluptuousness, indicated that the young girl would soon become a rape victim if she was enslaved. Her master would own her – body and soul!

While not as softly curved, Maeve's hair colour alone made her a valuable asset and therefore a source of status for any man fortunate enough to possess her.

Arthur felt ill at the very thought of the grim life that stretched out before them.

Although his heart was heavy with foreboding, Arthur's eyes were hard at work as the prisoners were escorted up the cobbled road. Alert to the possibility of escape at some time in the future, he was determined to become familiar with his surroundings by absorbing everything he saw around him.

The village of Heorot seemed to be well planned and efficiently constructed. The rectangular walls of the cottages were quite foreign to Arthur's eyes, for they were only three feet high on the outside edges. But each roof was steeply pitched in an unusual design whereby the apex of each structure was at least four times a man's height under a central pole. Arthur realised that snow would easily slide down. Smoke was allowed to escape from a central gap in the wooden, split-timber roof partially sealed with a hide flap, and a riot of decorations had been painted all over each simple construction.

A tall, thin shutter high up near the roof suggested that a second storey existed inside each building. Used to the simple, round homes of ordinary Britons, Arthur was fascinated.

The ends of rafters, doorways and roof supports were heavily carved with complex curving designs superficially like Celtic interlace, with a strange resemblance to decorated serpent forms reduced to linear patterns. To add to the overall effect, the houses were also lime-washed in vivid hues.

Light snow covered every detail of the village and harbour, although the narrow paths between dwellings were cleared of snow. Wicker structures such as cow byres, smoke houses, pig pens and well-kept gardens were also clean and tidy, necessities in these climes where the snowdrifts were often as deep, or deeper, than the height of a tall man. Such deep snow was unheard of in Britannia, except in the far north, but the Dene peasantry seemed unconcerned by the cold. The snow lay deeply on the slopes behind the village; Arthur looked at the rosy cheeks of the peasants with new respect, because they seemed to take such snowfalls in their stride.

No wonder they're so tall and so ruggedly built, he thought. You'd need long legs to plough through these snowdrifts.

Vegetable gardens were laid out in cheerful coverlets of straw in shades of beige and chocolate-brown where the soil and tentative shoots of green showed through the light dusting of snow that hadn't been cleared away by hand.

Braziers were burning in a few places where some plants had grown taller, although judging by the strong traces of blue above him and the melting snow beside the roadway, spring was advancing towards Heorot on green-shod feet.

Occasionally, Arthur observed the flash of metal ornaments worn on Dene shoulders in great pins made of brass, bronze or even tin, but it was obvious that gold was a prized metal in this town. It was almost as if the Dene population was poor. Yet the pelts of small, furred animals were staked and stiffening on drying racks behind the domestic houses, while strings of fish were hung out and threaded onto sharpened sticks to cure. Smoke rose in the gelid air from small huts. Evidently the Dene had no lack of physical comforts.

The cobbled road suggested that the Dene were scrupulous about the cleanliness of their environment. Rough channels running parallel to the cobbled surfaces were designed to carry away the deluges of water from driving rain or the floods from the spring thaws, thereby minimising the sticky, brown mud in the tangle of pathways between the rectangular cottages.

The huge king's hall at Heorot was soon looming above them and the captives were halted on a stone platform in the forecourt of the impressive building. Arthur shuddered at the sight of a skeletal arm nailed onto a large cross plank of oak above the door. Amazed at such a barbaric decoration, he peered upwards at the delicate bones of a hand that should have separated and fallen away with the first thaw. But golden wire held the delicate finger-bones together. The nails that secured the arm at wrist, elbow and where the shoulder should have been were gleaming with the same ruddy colour of precious metal.

'That's Grendel's arm,' Stormbringer stated. 'And above that trophy is the skull of Grendel's mother. All enemies of the Scyldings are doomed to perish in this way, so their bones now decorate our halls. Any man or woman planning treason should see these bones and beware of the king's punishments.'

The captives looked at the space under the painted eaves of the hall and saw a skull nailed into place by its long bony forehead and lower jaw. The delicate teeth, elegant cheekbones and smooth ovals of the empty eye sockets suggested that this grisly trophy was, indeed, the skull of a woman.

We considered the Dene to be civilised because we were captured by a sweet-talking, cultured and educated man, Arthur decided with a jolt of despair. Now, after seeing these grisly trophies, I realise that I don't understand the Dene and their violence at all.

Then Arthur remembered what the king of the Ordovice tribe, his own kinsman, had done at Calleva Atrebatum. Bran had unleashed Greek Fire, the flammable weapon far more barbaric than anything the Dene could imagine. The memory of men burning within their armour in a fire that couldn't be extinguished continued to haunt Arthur. Even worse, the knowledge that his kinsman had killed so many men through such barbarism ate at his vitals whenever his thoughts dwelled on the destruction of that venerable Romano-British city.

The two guards at the great timber entrance to the hall bowed their heads respectfully to Stormbringer and then used their combined strength to open the two doors that were easily the height of two men. Automatically, Arthur noticed that the massive structures were almost five inches thick and made from heavy slabs of tree trunk heavily carved to decorate the entrance and to create an overall pattern in which the winged worm was prominent. He was reminded of the great doors leading into Uther Pendragon's hall at Venta Belgarum; these Dene doors had the same brutal power. Arthur wondered if he might be able to use the Dene superstitions to his advantage.

Inside, the gloom blinded the captives for a moment after the weak sunlight outside, but the details of the room's contents gradually became clear. The low sides of the huge hall were shrouded in darkness. Huge tree trunks supported the steep roof, brightly painted with scenes from mythical and historical tales with repeated use of the motifs of tree, moon, dragon, wolf and sword.

Arthur had expected the hall to be filled with a gloom that matched the dark and snowy landscape surrounding the town. Yet the interior of the hall blazed with scenes filled with light and colour. Huge bronze sconces were attached to the columns where torches soaked in pitch and fat were blazing fiercely with an intense white-gold light. Holes cut in the steep roof permitted the smoke to be drawn away so that the air remained relatively sweet close to the floor, although the rafters were black with soot. Beneath his feet, Arthur could feel crudely sawn floorboards.

Generations of feet had worn the wood until it was smooth and honey-coloured, while the inevitable spillages of food and drink and countless bones and shells had created an oily patina on the porous wood. The refuse had created a gleaming polish that no man or woman could duplicate. Arthur raised his eyes across the brick fire pit that was so large it could roast several whole bullocks on its elevated spit. Then his eyes followed an avenue of shields and the figureheads of ships forming a trophy wall that showed the spoils and exploits of war. Beyond, a raised dais and a throne permitted the seated man to see everything and everyone within the confines of his hall.

A single closed door behind the dais indicated that other quarters used by the king existed behind this imposing space while above the door large shutters stood in rows leading up to the roof.

Someone coughed and Arthur saw warriors, old and young, assembled in rows stretching from one large set of pillars to the other. Frodhi stood in a prominent position in the front row. As Arthur watched him through narrowed eyes, Frodhi turned and winked at Stormbringer.

In darkened corners beyond the pillars, small rooms provided space for warriors to use as barracks when they were called upon to serve the king inside his hall. Further rooms had obviously been designed as storage space for weapons and equipment. Arthur imagined that some-where in this maze, Hrolf Kraki's treasure was also stored under guard.

Most of this detail had been revealed to Arthur by Stormbringer in a whisper as they waited behind the Dene warriors and their lords. The air was charged with reverence and something less tangible. Caution – or was it fear?

Arthur could smell a heavy aroma composed equally of woodsmoke, fish oil and wet fur. He also thought he recognised the scent of burning aromatic herbs. So the air of Heorot contrived to smell of green and growing things and of the deep forest, as it cleansed away the stink of men's bodies.

'Stormbringer! Valdar Bjornsen – Hero of the Sae Dene! What have you brought me from across the icy seas?'

The voice that boomed out into the open spaces of the hall was a strong, hoarse baritone, damaged during years of shouted instructions over the tumult of battle and efforts to overcome the noise of howling gales at sea.

As Stormbringer's warriors moved forward, the gentle hubbub that flowed through the hall was stilled by that same impatient voice.

'Don't keep me waiting, Stormbringer. I want to see these Britons you've caught for me.'

Arthur looked up and there, in restrained splendour on Heorot's dais, sat Hrolf Kraki, Lord of the Dene. Arthur's confidence dissipated like smoke in a gale. The time of testing had come.

Somehow, he must keep his friends safe.

Somehow, he must win the trust of the owner of that harsh, unlovely voice.

Somehow, he must survive in a world so alien that he felt like a child among giants.

In the silence that followed the king's command, the sound of their booted feet could be heard as they clicked on the dense wooden floor. In his head, Arthur could hear his inner voice shrieking sharply at him and he knew, beyond doubting, that they were all in terrible trouble.

CHAPTER VIII

BLOOD PRICE AND DANGEROUS LIAISONS

Ignorantie, quem portum, petat, nullus suus ventus est.
(If one does not know to which port one is sailing, no wind is favourable.)

Seneca the Younger, *Epistulae ad Lucilium* 71:3

A silence charged with danger and imminent threat settled over the massed warriors in Hrolf Kraki's guard. Arthur glanced at the backs of the men of Heorot and was disconcerted to see how many of them were standing at attention with their hands tightly clenched. Every line of their bodies indicated stress and fear, hardly the emotions one would expect from the king's lords and allies. Who was this Hrolf Kraki? Only Frodhi seemed unmoved, but even that equable man's fingers were twitching.

As if on a signal, the rows of warriors moved to the left and to the right in unison, leaving a corridor some five men wide that allowed Stormbringer and his warriors to stride forward and approach the dais. The Sae Dene inclined his head, and ordered his warriors to march in disciplined ranks ahead of him till they reached a space below the throne where they kneeled and lowered their proud heads in obeisance.

Feeling awkward and nervous, the captives remained standing and Arthur could feel his body assessed and analysed by dozens of pairs of curious eyes.

But only one man's opinion really mattered among this throng, so Arthur felt the chill of a particularly cold evaluation. Our time has come, Arthur thought, his heart beating wildly. Our doom or our fortune is in the hands of God or Fortuna.

Stormbringer kneeled on the wooden floor and bowed his whole body in homage. 'Hail to Hrolf Kraki, true master of the lands of the Dene, lord of the Sae Dene and ruler of the wide seas. Hail to the king, lord of the Scyldings and master of Midgard.' His voice carried to the extremities of the hall as it reverberated through the still air.

As Stormbringer rose to his feet, the strong voices of his warriors repeated their greeting to the king until the rafters seemed to shake under the power of their reverence.

'Hail to Hrolf Kraki, master and king. Hail!'

Then, as one, the warriors beat their shields on the wooden planks of the floor in a rumble of powerful sound, until the man on the throne raised his right hand and ordered silence.

The stillness, when it came, was immediate and complete.

'You may speak, Stormbringer, kinsman and Sae Dene beyond compare.'

Arthur was amazed at how the inscrutable, unflappable leader blushed like a girl at praise from the man on the dais. Not for the first time, Arthur wondered how Hrolf Kraki could command such homage from such men. He reassessed his plan of action. It was obvious that truth would best serve the interests of the British prisoners.

'We journeyed into the western seas last spring on your orders, my lord. When we made landfall, we sailed through the islands to the north of Britannia and learned that they were green with grass and deep, untouched forests. The land holds great bounty, the seas are filled with large schools of fish and the hills are alive with game. We sailed further south and learned that these lands are so soft and bountiful that cows seem to produce cream rather than milk and the earth gives the farmers such pleasure that they cannot eat all they grow. Britannia has metal aplenty and the people grow fat from the pleasant conditions in which they live.'

Hrolf Kraki leaned his bearded chin on the back of his hand and examined Stormbringer, his warriors and the captives through his eager, bright-blue eyes. Hrolf, the Crow King, was an extremely tall Dene who stood at six feet six inches in his bare feet, but he was also heavy-set from good living. Arthur caught a glimpse of a family similarity with Frodhi. Hrolf Kraki was also striking in appearance, and ruddy with good health. The only hint of age or weakness was a small paunch that strained against the waistline of his long belted robe. With eyes made attentive by necessity, the captives recognised that the king's face was craggily handsome while his complexion was so browned that the wrinkles at the corners of his eyes were white scars against his tanned, wind-blown face. Hrolf Kraki was clearly a man of action.

The king was blessed with long, blond eyelashes that softened the hardness of his eyes. His wide mouth was cleanly shaped, although his lips were partially hidden by sweeping white-gold moustaches and a curling beard of a slightly darker shade. Side braids kept his long hair out of his eyes and, although silver strands glittered in that hair, Arthur was hard-pressed to determine the king's age.

'How much of these lands did you see, Stormbringer?'

'We sailed south in a direct line to the channel that separates Britannia from the land of the Salian Franks. Britannia is now called Angle Land by the Saxon population, so we were able to explore the coastline with only minimal difficulty. Saxons have occupied the whole east coast and south of Britain but, as you know, their ceols are no match for our vessels.

'After a time, we reversed our course and headed back towards the north of the island. We stopped periodically and made forays into the countryside where we discovered the incredible natural wealth of Angle Land that seems to be consistent across the whole country. No one in this land starves or freezes during their winters. Ordinary Saxon and Jute farmers utilise iron hoes and hay forks with casual familiarity, and they do not lack food, regardless of the weather conditions which are gentle and ideal for livestock. The greatest problem appears to be the continuing struggle between the Romanised Britons who originally inhabited the land and the Angle, Saxon and Jute warriors who migrated into Britannia from their northern and eastern homelands. They have overrun the lands, except for a few enclaves in the west and the far north where the native Britons manage to survive. I saw some famine and desolation in places where there was no need for conflict except frail, human pride. I took trophies to bring as a tribute to you, my lord, so that you could see for yourself what this new land promises to deliver to our people – if we are bold enough to claim these lands as our own.'

Arthur sighed aloud as Hrolf Kraki rose to stand before the gilded throne. What treasures had Stormbringer taken from his lands during their raids, and would these trophies tempt the Crow King to invade? Weakened as they had been by decades of war, the remnants of the British warrior force had little chance of survival.

Arthur caught Frodhi's eye. Of all the nobles and warriors in Heorot, only Frodhi seemed totally at ease and fearless. That cool, fleeting glance was followed by a broad and impudent wink from the older man.

Arthur turned his attention back to the king. With that small, insolent glance, Frodhi was promising Arthur that Britain would know the Dene as masters. Suddenly, Frodhi was no longer a jokester. Hrolf Kraki and Frodhi were formidable opponents as individuals but, together, as masters of the Dene fighting force, they were well-nigh unbeatable.

Arthur struggled to keep his face cold and impassive. Fortunately, Eamonn and Blaise had no understanding of the Dene language, but Maeve's eyes were wide and deep wells of concern.

So my little sister understands more Dene than she admits, Arthur thought. Pray God she keeps her face blank and uncomprehending so these devils don't learn what she is, or knows.

At a single gesture from their master, two of Stormbringer's warriors bowed and backed out of the long hall. When they returned some moments later, they were accompanied by two guards who helped them to carry several large wooden trunks and heavy bundles of sheep's hide.

Stormbringer took the hides and carried them to the lowest step of the dais on which Hrolf Kraki was standing. Then, with a flourish, he unfurled their contents. 'Behold some of the weapons we found in Angle Land.'

The air hummed with the energy of men concentrating on the array spread out before them. Rust-free because of the greasy wool, the weaponry included long Celtic swords, a gladius, Roman stabbing spears, daggers of antique and modern designs, the double-headed axes of the Jutes, and even several narrow eating knives that glittered and threatened from their nest in the fleece. In other bundles, more weapons were accompanied by simple domestic tools such as shovels, rakes and digging implements, all heavy with iron and tin.

'You say that even the poorest farmers have access to these iron tools?' Hrolf's voice grated harshly, but Arthur was unable to tell from the king's expression whether he was surprised, envious or angry.

'Aye! The Roman invaders taught the Britons how to smelt ore and work their metals with great skill, so that only the very poorest citizens use wooden tools. The Saxons have in turn learned many new skills from the Britons. Some of the recent migrants from the northern lands still make wooden tools, but this choice is mainly dictated by the materials that were available to them in their own homelands – or by foolish sentiment!' Stormbringer added derisively.

'What do you mean by sentiment?' the king asked in a low, aggressive rumble.

'Many of the Saxons have chosen to live much as their forebears did when their tribes lived in northern climes. On many occasions, I saw how they destroyed the ancient rock and stone fortresses built by the Romans and Britons, for they prefer their own wooden palisades. I cannot fully understand the ways of the Saxons in Britain, my king, although not all Saxons are foolish. But familiarity causes some of the newer Saxon settlers to follow the ways of their ancestors, whether they are sensible or not.'

Having said very little in as many words as possible, Stormbringer waited quietly for the king's response.

'Humph!' Hrolf Kraki rumbled. Arthur could read nothing from his closed face.

The captain stepped aside from the weapons and tools at the foot at the dais because the implements required no elaboration on his part.

'Other metals are plentiful as well,' Stormbringer added casually and flipped back the lid of the nearest trunk. Bowls, cups, chalices, bits for horses, scabbards, platters, necklaces and cloak pins rioted among the contents of the heavy case. The bronze, brass and silver plate was heavily decorated and embellished, with complex interlace set into the embossing, and beautified with cabochon gems, pearls and skilful examples of scraffito designs. A sigh of jealousy, or of greed, whispered through the hall as if Heorot itself had exhaled.

'There also seems to be no lack of gold in the British lands.'

Stormbringer threw open the last container, a little larger than the first, and exposed crosses, jewellery, goblets and torcs of that buttery metal. The objects were sometimes set with gems, sometimes embellished with silver or electrum, while other pieces depended only on the beauty of the gold itself to compensate for any lack of ornamentation.

Hrolf rose to his feet and descended the few steps of the dais with the grace of a younger man. He plucked a torc from the tangle of beautiful objects and examined the precious insignia of aristocratic power with intent and controlled eyes. The torc consisted of three thick strands of gold plaited into a gilded length of rope. At each end, a large pearl from the land of the Scots shimmered with a strange grey lustre.

Arthur knew that torc! He had seen it many years earlier at a time when Gawayne paid a visit to Arden fortress. Then, the torc had graced the throat of Gawayne's eldest grandson, Gilchrist, who had accompanied the great man to Arden. The boy would never relinquish that torc until his father died, at which time he would assume the torc that graced Gawayne's old-man's throat. Only death would part him from the mark of his destiny.

The warning voice in Arthur's head, silent for so long, screamed shrilly. Arthur knew he must be silent, but the knowledge that he had travelled with that torc and that Stormbringer might have killed his kinsman overrode any thoughts of caution.

'Don't touch that torc, my lord,' Arthur interrupted curtly, and the king's fair brows rose in anger.

'My kinsman wore that torc to indicate his position as the heir to the throne of the Otadini tribe. Such an emblem is guaranteed to bring bad fortune to anyone who has stolen it, for it once belonged to Prince Gawayne, the greatest warrior in the isles of Britain. Gawayne was the nephew of Artor, the High King of the Britons, and no man other than his direct heir was permitted to touch it. The fact that the torc lies in this chest indicates that my kinsman is murdered, and the object is part of a stolen treasure! Beware, King of the Dene, for Gawayne's aunt was the witch-woman, Morgan the Fey, who will have cursed the insignia of that noble house before she fled to Hibernia. This torc will kill anyone who claims it.'

Then Arthur raised his bound hands and ripped his under-tunic from neck to hem in the age-old Roman gesture of mourning and sorrow.

'My kinsman has been killed and I pray that God has borne his shade to Paradise,' he stated in his strongest voice. 'Lady Blaise was promised to a man who is now dead, so we must mourn for his shade and ensure that his curse doesn't follow us into these distant lands.'

Given their cue and Arthur's translation, Eamonn and the two girls tore at their tunics and Blaise ripped at the flesh on her arms with her sharp nails. Only the intervention of Stormbringer stopped her from scarring herself as she gave a long ululating moan of grief for a man she had never wished to meet – and a wedding that would never have happened if she had any choice in the matter.

A heavy fist struck Arthur behind the right ear. Dazed, he shook his head, but he managed to keep his footing, despite losing his sight for a brief moment. Strong arms forced his hands behind his back and tried to bring him to his knees, but Arthur fought back, spread his legs and centred his weight to use it against his captors. A well-placed kick behind the knee felled him. Even then Arthur forced himself to raise his chin and hold the king's eyes with his own arctic gaze.

'How dare you threaten me!' the Crow King snapped.

'I spoke nothing but the truth, your Highness. Whether Stormbringer killed my cousin or took the torc from my kinsman's murderer doesn't matter a jot. You may kill me if you wish, but I won't submit to force, even under threat of death.'

The knowledge that Gilchrist had been killed before they were captured made Arthur feel sick. Worse still, he was shamed to realise he couldn't remember the face of the Otadini prince.

A blow across the mouth caused a rush of blood to pour from a bitten tongue and a salty taste filled Arthur's mouth. Rather than swallow it, he spat deliberately onto Hrolf Kraki's polished floor, earning another heavy blow across the back of the head.

Now that he was committed, Arthur scrambled for a solution that would save the other Britons. Hrolf Kraki would kill him for his insults.

Unfortunately, only one idea came to mind.

'I claim blood price, your Highness. I am owed justice!'

He gazed directly at the king. Then, against his volition, his eyes were dragged across the room to the blue, amused gaze of Frodhi who grinned openly in a room full of angry or puzzled men.

'Explain yourself!' the king demanded coldly. 'Before I take out your tongue.'

'I am not a slave, or a peasant, and I've been educated in the northern laws of revenge by Odin, a Jute bodyguard of King Artor, my father. If you follow the same customs as the Jutes, you are obliged to accede to those ancient laws of justice. I demand blood or gold as reparation for the murder of my kinsman and for Blaise's betrothed. I claim the right to the life of your heir or a compensating sum in gold. As the son of Artor, I claim my right to this revenge. I am the Last Dragon, and the only one who can speak for my murdered kin.'

The hall was unnaturally silent. Only a single indrawn breath indicated that someone was very afraid.

'What is this idiot raving about?' the king demanded of Stormbringer in a voice that boded trouble for the Sae Dene. 'I refuse to be threatened by a slave, so explain to me what this bauble means, and where you found it.'

Stormbringer glanced at Arthur with all his anger, disappointment and disgust compressed into his expression. If he had known the meaning of the torc, he would have removed it from the king's cache to avoid a scene such as this.

'I took the torc from a warrior whose name was Deorsa, a man who claimed to be in the employ of King Bran of the Ordovice tribe. He told me that he'd been instructed to murder the heir to the Otadini tribe in the north of Britain. We put Deorsa and his bodyguard to the sword, so I can swear to this prisoner that Deorsa died like a woman, begging for mercy like a coward. If any blood price is required, then our prisoner should consider that it has already been paid.'

'It's refreshing to discover that the Britons are just as venal as the rest of humanity,' Frodhi interrupted. 'If we were to judge all Britons on the example of Arthur and his moral rectitude, we would be making a serious error of judgement.'

Frodhi continued to smile. Some of the lords were amused as well, but Stormbringer frowned in irritation at his cousin's sarcastic interference.

'Bran?' The incredulous young Briton spoke aloud without realising that others were listening. 'Why would Bran sink so low as to kill one of his own kinsmen? Would he have sought to prevent Blaise's marriage for fear of such a powerful alliance? Surely not! He knew that I was taking Blaise into the north, so he must have hoped that we'd be caught up in any mess of succession to the northern throne.'

Arthur shook his head with frustration and confusion.

Of course, Bran would hate the thought of Blaise's marriage to Gilchrist because it would have brought two powerful families into a strong alliance. The descendants of Morgause, Bors and Ygerne would all become threats to Bran's plans for his own heir, Ector. But how could Bran fall so low as to hire an assassin?

'It can't be true,' Arthur muttered to himself. Only one pair of wise, amused eyes really watched him. More and more, Arthur was fearful of his reaction to Frodhi.

A cuff on the head stilled Arthur's rambling diatribe, but the young man paid no mind to the blow. He turned to face Maeve. 'I can't believe that the ever-cautious Bran would risk his reputation by such a cowardly murder,' he whispered to his sister in Celt. 'Would Bran fear and hate me so much?'

Maeve reached out her bound hands and stroked her brother's face. Her answer was clear in her pellucid eyes.

'Yes, he does, Arthur.'

'Then I must live to revenge this treacherous murder,' Arthur swore to her. 'Bran must account for his actions.'

During the hubbub, as his jarls argued over precedents and whether Arthur merited any access to justice, Hrolf Kraki strode towards the prisoner and thrust his bearded chin into Arthur's face. 'You talk like a king, Briton! You act as if you *are* a king! But in truth, you are less important to me than the meanest servant in this hall – so why should I treat you as a person who merits any consideration? What do *you* matter? You're a slave and even less important than my servants for, at the very least, they are northerners by birth. You are nothing but impertinence, impudence, arrogance and ingratitude!'

'I am the Last Dragon of the Britons, your Majesty, as Stormbringer will tell you. The people of Britain believe me to be the last of the bloodline of King Artor, the ruler who was their hope for the future. Perhaps I am less than the dust beneath your feet, but I come from a line of kings, including Romans, so I was born to the purple. Also, I have won personal honour in desperate battles against superior forces, and have prevailed. I killed my first man before I was ten years old, so my body bears the scars of engagements with adversaries who were much older and much stronger than I was. Look at my scars if you doubt my word. I insist I have the right to stand before you and affirm the honour of my house, although I release you from my demand for the ritual of blood price, because you and yours had no part in Gilchrist's death.'

Hrolf Kraki was struck dumb for a moment by Arthur's effrontery and his eyes crackled with the energy of ungovernable rage.

'You don't have the authority to release me from anything, mongrel dog.' The insult was hissed, although Stormbringer whitened at the king's viciousness.

'Perhaps this young man feels a need to prove himself, Majesty,' Frodhi interrupted from the front line of the jarls in the audience. 'You know me, cousin! I'm always ready to be entertained. This young man is touted as a warrior of distinction, worthy of carrying the name of the Last Dragon. Why should he have a nomen even more imperious than yours, noble king, for he hasn't been required to lift a sword to prove his right to the title?'

The name Crow King ranked several steps in prestige below that held by the captive. Crows were vermin and scavengers, so Hrolf Kraki bridled visibly.

Arthur lifted his chin. Equally matched in height and breadth of shoulder, they stood toe to toe as equals, until Hrolf Kraki snorted with an impatient gesture, then turned away from his youthful opponent.

'Strip him!' Hrolf Kraki ordered. 'Let's see if this young whelp speaks the truth or is merely an idle boaster. You do the honours, Stormbringer. After all, you brought him here. Is he an imposter, a fool or a king's son? He's a damned nuisance, if nothing else.'

The king allowed himself a secretive smile. 'You can help Stormbringer, Frodhi, since you've seen fit to stick your nose into my affairs.'

Frodhi bowed his head contritely and stepped forward.

'Shut up, you idiot!' Frodhi hissed under his breath to Stormbringer as the Sae Dene began to protest. 'You'll only make him worse.'

The king returned to the throne and sat down casually, as the two strong warriors began to cut Arthur's clothes away from his body with their razor-sharp knives.

'Let me undress myself,' Arthur insisted, but his captors refused to listen. The king wanted Arthur humiliated and, as Arthur had caused Stormbringer, his benefactor, to suffer Hrolf Kraki's anger, humiliation was the least punishment Arthur merited.

'Frodhi's right, you idiot,' Stormbringer hissed, his mouth close to Arthur's ear. 'Perhaps it's possible to salvage something out of this fiasco you've created.'

Arthur stood passively under their ministrations, lifted his arms above his head and turned in a circle so every man present could see the white seams of deadly scars across his torso.

Once he was stripped naked to the waist, his years of battle training showed in the slabs of muscle that overlaid his powerful arms. The golden tan on his face, his forearms and his legs below the knees threw the whiteness of his tall and graceful body into sharp focus, and even the angry Dene king could see that this particular Briton was a warrior in both musculature and strength.

'Your scars are impressive,' Hrolf Kraki stated evenly. 'They're old scars and they're all on the front of your body!'

'I congratulate you for having the good sense to play fair in your battles,' Frodhi murmured, so his respective kinsmen were unable to hear him. 'Every wound is very sensibly on the front of your torso. I do approve of a clever man!'

'Fuck off!' Arthur hissed, but his voice was so low that his comment went unheard. However, Frodhi stopped his annoying whispers.

Something stirred in the darkness behind the king, while Arthur's mind suddenly screamed shrilly in alarm. At the same time, Frodhi cursed and quickly stepped back into the watching line of Dene warriors. Hrolf Kraki heard the small movement as well, but he raised his hand in a beckoning gesture, although his eyes never shifted from the outlander.

'Aednetta! Come forward and tell me what you think of this young man. Should I treat him like a Dene, or order him to be chained to Stormbringer's longboat to row until he rots?'

The warning voice in Arthur's mind rose higher and higher in a scream that was primal, urgent and infused with danger. *Don't trust this witch and her evil words*, it roared.

This woman plans treason. Then, as if it had never existed, the warning voice was silenced.

'I know you're there, Aednetta, so don't keep me waiting,' Hrolf Kraki's voice was impatient but a whine underlay its force. The Dene king oscillated from brutal tyrant to careful assembler of information. Who was he?

Conscious of his nakedness in front of a woman, Arthur dragged his torn tunic over his head and awkwardly straightened his leather trews, while struggling with the laces because of his bound hands. Around him, the warriors paid no mind because their eyes were fixed on the dais and the small figure standing in the shadows. Surreptitiously, Maeve passed her brother a strip of cloth from her battered skirt to wipe his bleeding mouth.

From those pools of darkness behind the throne where the light of the sconces failed to reach, a darker puddle began to coalesce into the form of a woman of indeterminate age. She glided forward as if her feet were hovering several inches above the wooden floor, so her felt slippers were eerily soundless.

Maeve stiffened and her head swivelled towards the newcomer as if she smelled something vile. Her green eyes glowed oddly, and their amber flecks darkened as if a flare had been lit inside her skull. Arthur could feel his sister's sudden intensity and shot a warning glance at her as she stood with her gaze fixed glassily on the coalescing form of this wise woman who was Hrolf Kraki's most respected adviser.

'I'm coming, my lord, so there's no need to shout or to be disturbed. Your Aednetta will always be standing at your side, to protect you and advise you in times of threat.'

Untrue! Arthur's warning voice whispered inside his brain. *Look at her hands.*

Arthur's eyes slid away from his sister to the woman whose pale hands were half-concealed in the folds of her robe. Flickering torchlight shone on her knuckles, polishing them to the whiteness of bone as they clenched into fists that revealed her irritation and repressed dislike. Yet what was visible of her face was as smooth as the complexion of a new-born babe. She showed no appreciable emotion, but the tell-tale fingers were busy pulling at the hems of her sleeves with sharply destructive nails.

'I can't see your face, Aednetta, so come into the light where I can talk to you properly.'

The king's orders were uttered reasonably and courteously, but the witch's hands convulsed in the folds of black material as if he had been cursing her. As she moved to obey her master, her eyes smiled obligingly while her lips repeated that shallow emotion, but her guilty hands were busy saying something quite different.

Aednetta was neither young nor old; and she was neither beautiful nor plain. This wise woman was so self-contained that her features appeared to have been forced into a mould, like the ceramic funerary masks that Arthur had seen in the house of King Bran. His mind skittered away from Heorot and for a brief moment, he was a boy again in his kinsman's house.

What wonders I've seen, he thought sadly, and what horrors! His muscles twitched with the memory of the Dragon Knife that had lain in his left hand since he was a boy.

The wise woman came fully into the light now, and those tell-tale hands rose to touch the king lightly on the forearm with the ease of long custom.

See? The voice in his head was almost too loud to bear. *Beware! The witch is no adviser, for she has seduced the king. Does no one else notice? No, they're accustomed to her, so her actions are invisible to anyone but a stranger. Or they think she's negligible.* Arthur had learned to rely on his inner voice since childhood, so he decided that this woman was an even greater danger to his friends and himself than the Dene king was likely to be. That Maeve was also on her guard was more than enough reason for Arthur to distrust Aednetta on sight.

The wise woman raised the cowl of her robe to reveal her full face to the light of the sconces. Her face was smooth, egg-shaped and lacked clear definition, but she could be beautiful and ugly by turn, depending on her emotions and the quality of the light.

'What do you require of me, my lord? You know you need only ask.' Aednetta's voice was a deep, husky contralto that was drenched with sexual promise.

At last, Arthur could see the attraction that she possessed. Her voice, if Arthur closed his eyes, promised silken flanks, breasts that pillowed a man's head perfectly and an innocent lasciviousness that suggested subtlety and any number of exotic and erotic sins that would be available at his command. Such a voice seduced the listener by its timbre, its warmth and its ancient femininity. Even now, Arthur's body was responding.

Now that he recognised their closeness was something more than master and servant, Arthur could read the intimacy in the king's eyes. The young man groaned, for this relationship between a lord and his adviser was highly dangerous to the four captives. When sex was added to such an explosive mix, his dealings with Hrolf Kraki were doubly unpredictable. The king already disliked the captives because of Arthur's inability to control his tongue.

Aednetta's brows were thin and highly arched so her expression was one of perpetual surprise. Her eyes were blue, but the colour was so pale that they seemed to be transparent. Likewise, Aednetta's skin was so thin and smooth that Arthur swore he could see the blood pulsing in her veins, rosy or blue by turns. In fact, her unlined flesh had an unearthly blue blush, creating an exotic aura. Maeve was quick to notice that the warriors closest to the wise woman avoided her gaze as if her eyes could blight them – or suck away their wits.

Maeve had never possessed any special intuitive qualities, but the girl had scented wrongness in this woman from the moment that Aednetta appeared in the hall. She had smelled a reek of wickedness in the king's woman, much like the faint sourness of tainted fruit. The woman was obviously a witch of some kind, or thought she was, although Maeve had never previously believed in such nonsense. Now, as Aednetta's eyes drifted lightly over the four captives, Maeve felt her stomach begin to revolt and only a concerted effort of will prevented her from vomiting uncontrollably onto the smooth floor of Heorot.

Yet the face that gazed so lightly and disinterestedly at the outlanders seemed harmless. Perhaps the woman's cold and passive calm was what disconcerted Maeve and Arthur so profoundly. The mouth that smiled so delicately was both seductive and ugly, a rare combination. The top lip was thin and pale, suggestive of a cold and secretive nature, while the bottom lip was full and rich. This contrast of cruelty and voluptuousness was compelling.

While Arthur struggled to thrust lascivious thoughts of that full bottom lip out of his mind, the king explained Arthur's insults to his wise woman. Aednetta smiled at Arthur and the young man's tumescence deflated with a suddenness that spoke of his instinctive understanding of her.

'This boy may be of royal blood, my lord, but he is of little importance to us.'

The wise woman smiled beatifically and exposed a pale tongue, serpentine in its unnatural length. Carnality was her promise as she slowly licked her lips, but Arthur grimaced as he noticed that her canine teeth were both much longer than normal and appeared to be very sharp. She must file them, Arthur decided with a sick feeling of dread. He had been told how his aunt Morgan had done the same to all her teeth.

A picture of Morgan's face, with her shark-like teeth, swam into his mind. It was a face he'd never seen, but could imagine from the many descriptions he had heard as a child. His aunt Morgan had searched for power and collected fear like coin. Some women who search for earthly domination through the dark arts are prepared to deface themselves. He knew in his bones that this creature, Aednetta, would kill without mercy if she could arrange such a fate for him. But why?

Perhaps she was curious about the outlanders? Perhaps she wanted something of him before she had his life snuffed out?

'Blood price is for the Dene alone and, perhaps, for those Jutes who haven't forgotten their ancestors,' Aednetta stated baldly. 'This boy –

regardless of his antecedents – doesn't merit your generosity. He claims to be a man who has been touched by the gods, so we should allow him to prove his power. Words are cheap, master, as you learned when you had to resist the treachery of Snaer and his minions.'

The slightest mention of his predecessor, Snaer, filled Hrolf Kraki with fury, so that his keen mind was blunted by old resentments. Hrolf Kraki's fear of potential traitors was always paramount above all others.

'Aye! Words are cheap and only actions will impress the Dene people,' Aednetta continued gently. 'He is as tall as our warriors, but can he fight? Can he earn our respect?'

'The wise woman seeks to blind you, Lord Hrolf,' Maeve called out from the press of warriors. 'Perhaps you should ask her why she would have the Last Dragon put to death! Ask her why she wants loyal warriors like Stormbringer to be kept away from your court? And then, ask yourself why she seeks to bend you to her counsel with silken ropes of sexual desire, so that you seek her in your bed by day and by night.'

The room erupted with a rumble of voices, until Hrolf Kraki rose angrily to his feet.

Maeve had no idea why she had spoken in such an inappropriate fashion for a young maiden. The warriors around her were shocked, and instinctively drew away, leaving her alone inside a small cone of superstition. Arthur deliberately stepped back to stand at her side. 'Do you truly believe that spring cleaves to autumn? Or does Aednetta desire something else rather than love?' Maeve spoke out so clearly that her voice carried into the darkest recesses of Heorot.

'Your insinuations are lies and insults,' Aednetta whispered so softly that the king had to strain to hear her, while Arthur was forced to admire how the wise woman could adroitly play the victim. Single tears snaked down from her colourless eyes and she allowed them to fall onto the dull black cloth of her robe. Maeve appeared to be shrill and self-serving by comparison.

'They seek to save themselves by driving a wedge between the king and his most loyal subject,' Aednetta stated blandly, her face expressing hurt, as if she was genuinely upset by such perfidy. Her hands tore at the hem of her sleeve, unravelling and shredding the coarse black wool.

Puzzled and suspicious, Stormbringer frowned at his liege lord's reaction to the words of the witch-woman. He had never liked or trusted Aednetta, although she had once breathed an invitation into his ear that had both excited and repelled his younger self. Fortunately for all concerned, the wide seas had kept him out of her sphere of influence, but he was uneasy to see the light of affection that glowed in Hrolf Kraki's eyes whenever she was in the king's presence.

The common people read Aednetta's character unkindly. The women who spent their time at the wells frightened each other with tales of her spells, her curses used to garner power over foolish men and her use of the pleasures of the bed as a trap and as an illusion. Stormbringer had always been immune to sexual blandishments, something that made him a rarity in the halls of Heorot. He spoke out bravely now, but he remained very careful, for any criticism of Aednetta was an implied attack on Hrolf Kraki himself.

'I was the servant who brought these captives to you as a personal gift, my lord. They were purchased with my own rings of silver from a man who vouched for the quality and value of all four. Before any decisions are made concerning their fates, I ask that you hear more of their pedigrees so you can judge for yourself if they have been raised in an honourable court, a place where warriors are required to conduct themselves in the same way that Dene men are expected to behave.'

'For honourably raised persons, they have destructive, boastful and divisive tongues. Perhaps I should order those tongues to be removed immediately.' The king's face was sullen and angry, while Aednetta seated herself on the top step of the dais and leaned against his right leg.

'Perhaps,' the witch-woman echoed the words of her master.

'But such actions would destroy a valuable source of information that could be of use to the Dene people, my lord. Britannia is rich beyond our understanding and their tribes are in turmoil as war ravages their lands. We can profit from their misfortune by sending suitable families to settle on the coastal areas where our forces can gain in strength until, as with Jutland, we have sufficient power to claim huge tracts of their tribal territories. It will be invasion by stealth! Such action would require minimum force and could be achieved at virtually no cost to the Dene nation. The captives I have given you hold valuable information that meets the needs of our people, because these prisoners come from the greatest families in that rich and verdant land. Your prisoners also hate those Saxons who control the east coast of Britannia, the very part of the country that would be of most use to us. I beg you to consider the practical uses to which these prisoners could be put. Their unintended insults are as nothing when compared with the information and influence that they possess.'

Stormbringer's impassioned speech stirred the warriors to voice their approval behind their hands, but Hrolf Kraki was further angered by this swelling wave of low muttering.

The Sae Dene's heartfelt words had weakened Hrolf Kraki's position, although the king never doubted the loyalty of his vassal. Weeks earlier, Aednetta had warned Hrolf Kraki that he would be safer if Stormbringer vanished under the distant seas forever. But the long duty and comfort provided by the captain's father, the legendary Bjorn, prevented such a permanent solution. At heart, Hrolf Kraki was an honourable man. As he had listened to Stormbringer's words, his face had darkened with irritation and the desire for thwarted violence, but the calm and logical centre of his brain urged caution. The open, puzzled faces of the Dumnonii siblings revealed that they had little understanding of what their captors had said. Only Arthur, the young warrior, had revealed by the furrowing of his brows that he knew and understood.

That is one young man who must be watched closely, the king thought. If he survives the night!

Hrolf Kraki felt the impatient, insistent pressure of Aednetta's hand which had been caressing the soft, unprotected skin behind his knee. The king closed his eyes for a moment, because he was caught between common sense and obsessive suspicion as he felt his lover's nails bruise the tender flesh.

'I have heard your words, Stormbringer,' Hrolf Kraki began, although

Aednetta's hand continued to explore the back of his knee. He almost gave the order to kill the captives out of hand, but something inexplicable twisted and changed the words in his mouth.

The king shook his head, as if to clear the webs of his lust from his mind.

'Very well! I can't decide whether these Britons are speaking the truth or are crafting cunning lies to mislead our people. The prisoner's purpose in invoking blood price made me doubt his motives, but he has since relented and called back the demand – a concession which I accept. He appears to be a young man of education and he certainly possesses physical gifts. I must also consider the word and worth of my greatest Sae Dene captain, Bjornsen, who vouches for these Britons. They seem so helpless while they are surrounded by my warriors but, yet, they have dared to attack the motives of my adviser, the lady Aednetta, who is dear to me for her continuing advice and loyalty.'

He gazed directly at Arthur and smiled. The curve of his mouth had no trace of mercy in it, and Arthur was immediately on guard.

'Therefore, we will let God make the final decision, as Father Stephan would have urged us to do. I have decided that open, single combat alone can reveal the fate of these prisoners. Both men will face suitable adversaries, and we shall let the truth of their words be proven by the strength of their bodies. The men will fight Dene champions of our choosing, and I will think deeply on how the honour of the young girls can be tested.'

A buzz of noise from the crowd followed the king's decision.

Even Frodhi's smile was wavering and the meaningful stare he shot in Stormbringer's direction was pregnant with warning. Had Frodhi been closer, Arthur knew the Dene would have begged Stormbringer to be silent to save his reputation and his life.

Some of the Crow King's warriors looked forward to the spectacle of combat, while others were concerned that politics could threaten the safety of young girls who had barely reached marriageable age. Some white-haired old men shook their heads in disapproval at the lowered standards of modern times. Predictably, the audience blamed the witch-woman for the king's decision, but wisely refrained from saying so.

Regardless of the voice in his head that warned him his decision was flawed, Hrolf Kraki ploughed on, pleasing no one, and causing several of the more influential Dene jarls to become concerned for his sanity.

'And so it shall be!' Hrolf Kraki stated fretfully. He was wise enough to know that discord was already dividing his subjects, so he pushed Aednetta's insistent fingers away and continued. 'Let us discover the truth about these captives tomorrow during a contest where God and the Dene people can judge them. Until then, Stormbringer, you are ordered to care for your gifts assiduously within the walls of Heorot. If they are false, they must have no opportunity to infect my people with their poisons. Since you have chosen to champion the captives over the wishes of my most loyal adviser, your fate now rests on what they can achieve. For now, that is quite enough!'

The king's face was frozen and adamant. Stormbringer was aware that the views of the Crow King couldn't be shaken.

'God help us all,' Stormbringer said softly so that only his warriors could hear him. 'Tomorrow might see the end of all our dreams and plans.'

The king stalked down from the dais and retreated to his apartments in the rear of the building, while Aednetta followed in his wake with a barely controlled smile of satisfaction. One hand was toying with a soft woven pouch containing small, white fragments of bone with black runes burned into them. They clicked together ominously. As master and adviser left the hall, the hearts of Eamonn and Arthur sank at the magnitude of the task – and their slim chances of survival.

Breathlessly, Arthur told the other captives what the king had decided, but Maeve was unperturbed. She continued to stare at the back of the retreating witch-woman and a world of malevolence was contained in her long, flat glare of hatred.

The young prince would have chided her, but he lacked the words or the will.

CHAPTER IX

A VERY NASTY NIGHT

Nowhere can a man find a quieter or more untroubled retreat than in his own soul.

Marcus Aurelius, *Meditations*, Book 4

Even before the audience had ended and the witnesses had departed, Stormbringer gripped Arthur by his bound hands and dragged him back the way they had come, followed by three of his warriors escorting the other young captives. Frodhi surreptitiously brought up the rear. Around them, the curious bystanders took one look at the Sae Dene's furious face and disappeared like smoke. Stormbringer yanked Arthur to his full height. Arthur was disturbed to see a flicker of fear in Stormbringer's furious eyes.

'Are you a complete idiot, Arthur? It is one thing to make a ridiculous claim for blood price, for I can understand your rage when you discovered your kinsman was dead. I suppose I might have reacted much as you did, if I were in your shoes. But why did you and your sister attack the king's adviser? What possessed you? I wouldn't have dared to criticise the witch-woman, and my mother was his father's sister.'

'She's false, Stormbringer . . . I swear to you that she's a creature of wickedness.' Arthur used his entire weight to halt the Sae Dene's headlong rush. Then he brought his face close to the captain's and hissed back at him as he tried to explain what he and his sister had clearly recognised – that the witch-woman was a danger to all their lives.

'Could we possibly talk treason somewhere a little more private?' Frodhi added his opinion in a drawled whisper.

'I'm not playing games, Stormbringer, and I can swear that I never meant to say anything to insult the king. My sister reacted without thought when she was faced by a creature from the darkness. I'm afraid that neither of us is used to holding our tongues, and we could clearly see that the bitch oozes danger and seduction from every pore of her body.'

'That's as may be, Arthur, but Aednetta is unassailable. Do you hear me? She can't be touched!' Stormbringer's voice was heavy with regret.

Frodhi attacked the Briton immediately in a thunderous voice from which all humour had vanished. 'My cousin has treated you well, yet you've persisted in dragging him towards disaster. Do you want to see him executed as a traitor? You can believe me when I say that the Crow King is quite capable of ordering such an extreme punishment.'

'You've no need to explain Stormbringer's position because I under-stand the situation,' Arthur snapped back. 'The king is unreasonable to blame a loyal servant for the actions of strangers. Is he such a tyrant then?'

'Here you go again, trying to have all our heads separated from our shoulders,' Frodhi replied seriously. His normally amiable expression was sharp and angry. 'The witch-woman has eyes and ears everywhere and she feeds on my cousin's fear of treachery. If he had even a hint of what you just said, I would be also be deemed guilty by association – even though I've taken pains to stay on his right side. Gods, Stormbringer, you've brought us trouble with this little lot. The girls are pretty, but that Maeve is near as crazy as the witch-woman.'

'Where did she come from?' Arthur asked, careful to keep his voice down. He was displeased that Frodhi had insulted his sister by such an obscene comparison, but in truth Maeve and he had made a bad situation a hundred times worse, and, now that his blood had cooled, he felt sorry that he had involved his benefactor in so much trouble.

'What's her relationship with Snaer – or the Hundings? I smell a connection,' Arthur added. 'If you discovered a link with Hrolf Kraki's enemies, she'd have to be vulnerable.'

Stormbringer agreed. 'I'll try to discover what I can of her life before she came to the Dene court. But I'm also aware that better men than I have attempted to chase down Aednetta's antecedents. They failed . . . and they died.'

He smiled awkwardly.

'My men and I must act with great care now that our king has intertwined our fates with yours. I doubt that I and my warriors will survive his anger if you fail to rise to his challenge.'

'If it makes life easier for you, Valdar, I'll be the one to dig into the witch-woman's past before she came to Heorot.' At long last, Frodhi seemed to be talking in deadly earnest, and Arthur liked him the better for it. 'I am far better placed to act in this sensitive matter, kinsman, and my search won't cause the gossip that questions from you would start.'

'You're being generous,' Arthur said quietly.

'I'm being realistic, Briton, and I'm used to cleaning up messes not of my making, which is probably why I play the part of a jokester. Admittedly, it's the Crow King who usually needs my help, rather than my big hairy cousin.'

'Thank you, Frod! I think!'

'In all good conscience, I can't allow my captives to be murdered, even if they've brought it on themselves. But I'm not prepared to act dishonourably – even if I lose my master's trust.'

A small hand reached out to touch Stormbringer's forearm and he looked down into Maeve's transparent face.

'I've brought trouble to you, my lord, and I'm truly sorry. But the witch-woman appeared to me like a black serpent. I saw her forked tongue beneath the normal features of her face – and I was afraid! I know that she saw me for what I am too, and she hates me with every fibre of her being. She isn't a witch, and she has no spells or curses that can harm any of us. But she has the *knowing*, which is more dangerous than false spells, because this woman's heart is black, through and through, and it's filled with her hatred and malice. Cold freezes her and I sense only one dark passion, one overriding love that weakens the chill self-interest of her nature. I swear she's no true woman – just lust, envy and vengeance in the likeness of a female form. Still, I beg your pardon because I've managed to bring harm to you and yours. I wish I didn't have the *knowing*. Sometimes ignorance is better and safer than knowledge.'

Frodhi gazed at Maeve as if this girl-woman had suddenly sprouted black wings. 'Have you always seen through to the hearts of people, little one? It must be very difficult at times for your kin and your friends.'

Maeve blushed to the hairline, but her brother was unable to tell whether it was through anger or embarrassment. 'Never before, so I suppose that's why I blurted out my reactions to the witch-woman.'

Frodhi crossed himself surreptitiously while Arthur tried to explain.

'Our whole family has odd traits, especially on my father's side. But Maeve was born early and it's said she had the caul over her face. The old women in our household swear that my sister is fated to become a great queen and a priestess.'

Frodhi bowed ironically in acknowledgement. Then we must ensure that this novice sea-wife survives the next few days. I'll help in any way I can, Stormbringer, but I've spent too much time with you tonight. I don't want any awkward tales to be passed back to Hrolf Kraki if I can help it.'

'Thank you, Frod. I'll do my best to make certain that you're not dragged into this mess.'

Frodhi inclined his head and stepped backward into the shadows.

Although he was watching carefully, Arthur was amazed at how such a large man could vanish like a puff of smoke in a high wind.

I don't want you to suffer on our account either, Frodhi, Arthur thought as he patted Maeve encouragingly on the shoulder. But there was no denying that he felt more comfortable now that Frodhi had left them to their own devices.

'It's time for Eamonn and me to decide how we can fight Hrolf Kraki's warriors when we haven't practised or even held a weapon for weeks. Aednetta believes we'll fail and become so much bloody meat. If she's correct, you'll also be harmed by our failure, which would, at best, be unjust.'

Arthur was beginning to feel much better, now that his anger and frustrations had been expressed.

'Have you considered the possibility that Aednetta is seeking to crush you, and that our presence simply provides her with another weapon that she can use against you? I've fallen into her hands, but I believe you're the real target.'

'I've had time now to consider what happened tonight, and I've concluded that the witch-woman came to tonight's audience with one aim in mind: to reduce your influence within the king's court. Your spoils from the raid into Britain, your gifts to the king and the heroism of your successful journey could be expected to win Hrolf Kraki's praise. You must be careful! Very, very careful! My friends are just an extra amusement that allows her to flex her claws in the background. And, yes . . . I played directly into her hands like the fool that I am.'

'Not a fool – just young!' Stormbringer replied, but his mind was obviously distracted.

He reacted to Arthur's proposition by pulling the young man forward again so that the small party continued into the darker recesses of Heorot's unlit flanks. Arthur permitted himself to be led to a place where half-walls enclosed small storage areas.

Maeve's skirts made a gentle susurration on the planks. She slowed Stormbringer's steps with one white hand.

'You have the solution to one of Arthur's problems, master. You're still in possession of the Dragon Knife and the sword that was gifted to Arthur by our father. You also hold Eamonn's weapons. I noticed that they weren't among the tribute weapons that you gave to your king, so you seem to have the *knowing* yourself.'

Stormbringer snorted, but said nothing. He simply lengthened his stride so that the party was dragged along in his wake towards one of the storerooms in the buildings adjacent to the king's hall.

The captain led Arthur to the right of the central hall where the low outer wall met the floor under a steeply pitched roof. The height of this space was barely sufficient for a woman to stand upright and Arthur noted how the low roof had created a storage area. It had been turned into a room by the placement of wooden barrels and large pottery containers. More stored foodstuffs hung from the roof where rodents couldn't pillage them.

Coils of rope, heavy bales of wool and wooden tubs were packed tightly against the outer wall. The space was warmer than Arthur had expected because the stored articles provided heavy insulation against the bitter cold of the outside air. Stormbringer explained that surplus grain, mead and dried meat were stored in Heorot to protect the Dene food supplies within the most easily defendable structure in the town.

'Food supplies are of enormous importance to our people in times when nature's generosity is limited. Some of the populace might be asked to give up their lives for the good of the rest. Can you imagine the misery a man feels when he permits his parents to walk out into the snow, stark naked, so that his children can live?'

Arthur shook his head, certain he could never ask for such a sacrifice, even if his own life depended on it.

'Our kings make provision for times of hardship, so you can understand why they are greatly honoured. We're fortunate here in Heorot because we have ample space to store excess food; our king takes food from some of his subjects in lieu of coin, so those supplies are also available in times of famine. Despite what you have seen of him today, Hrolf Kraki has always been a good king who understands the basic needs of his people.'

Arthur admired the Sae Dene's defence of his king, considering Hrolf Kraki had been so unkind to him; Stormbringer was a decent man attempting to understand the motivations of a confused and morally compromised ruler.

Stormbringer unbound the four captives and explained that they would be protected by his personal guard during the night. Food and water would be brought to them, and no poisons would bring them to an untimely death. In the meantime, they would be able to practise with wooden weapons as much as they chose, although they would need to wait until the morning to receive their fighting blades.

They listened carefully, while Arthur asked patiently if water for washing would be made available. 'I will be shamed if I'm forced to stand before your king and risk death while I'm dirty and unkempt. I can't do anything about my torn clothing, but I can ensure that I'm clean. If I'm going to die tomorrow, I'd hate to perish with dirty hands, feet and hair.'

'Aye!' Eamonn agreed, only partly understanding the conversation, but recognising the words for water and washing. 'I'm not as fastidious as my friend here, but I'm aware that I smell as bad as a spavined old mule.'

'You underestimate your stink, brother, because you smell like an old, *dead* mule,' Blaise added. 'Please, Captain, we all long for a chance to be clean and neat. Maeve and I don't even have a comb to untangle our hair. We must look like scarecrows.'

Stormbringer promised to find some way to accede to their needs. Unfortunately, the captain was distracted and his eyes kept darting towards the lighted regions of the hall, as if he had business elsewhere and needed to absent himself quickly.

'You can tell your friends about my king's demands after I've gone, Arthur. In the meantime, you and Eamonn need some basic combat practice and then you should eat and get a good night's sleep. Much will hang upon your skill tomorrow, not least your lives. I'll do my part to prepare you for battle in the morning.'

Stormbringer took two rapid steps away from the small group of bedraggled Britons. Suddenly, a further thought occurred to him and he turned back, with regret clearly written on his face. 'I will also act on your concerns about the witch-woman's confederates. My cousin, Frodhi, will keep his word in this regard, but his investigations will take a great deal of time – several weeks, even months. If Aednetta has been indiscreet, which I doubt, we'll need proof of what we intend to say. In the meantime, you should depend only on each other! These islands are like the rest of the world, and respond to strong rule. It's sad, but it's true.'

Stormbringer stared off into the distance. 'I'm totally loyal to the Dene people, so I risk much by acting on your suggestions. One thing is for certain, Arthur. I won't betray my country or my king for you or your womenfolk, even if you're correct in your assumptions about Aednetta. Unless I find firm evidence that I can use against her, I'll be keeping my tongue between my teeth. I have the welfare of my daughters and my two sisters to consider. They shouldn't be made to suffer because I placed my trust in you and yours.'

'That's quite reasonable,' Arthur replied as Stormbringer retreated into the darkness with long strides, leaving three guards behind him and a single lamp to light the uncomfortable gloom.

After he had gone, Arthur had the leisure to consider what Stormbringer had said. The tall Sae Dene had never mentioned children before and had made no reference to a wife during the discussion that had just taken place. He wondered if Stormbringer's woman might have been exposed to the elements at some time in the past, shuddering at the thought of having to carry out such a task.

'If I were in his shoes, I wouldn't risk anything for four strangers from foreign lands,' Arthur decided. 'After all, we've caused him a great deal of trouble – not to mention expense!'

'Aye, brother,' Maeve answered softly. 'And he's too good a man to be destroyed by a woman who wishes to place herself on the throne of the Dene.'

'You sound certain about this witch-woman, Maeve. Is it possible that you're wrong, and we've made a big mistake?'

'You don't think I'm wrong, do you?' Maeve answered, her eyes far wiser than her years. 'I must pray now, for only God can protect us from the king and his paramour. I'll pray for Stormbringer as well, and Frodhi, because they deserve better than to be killed for the criticisms we made of that bitch. Even now, she's wheedling the king to finish Stormbringer off for good.'

'Yes, even now,' Arthur agreed.

A number of slow hours passed while Arthur and Eamonn attempted to kill each other in simulated combat with the aid of wooden practice swords. The guards had handed over these children's weapons with several demeaning jokes, but Arthur had refused to rise to the bait and respond to their good-natured banter. The three guards had watched the mock battles with amusement, even laying modest wagers on who would win each bout.

'These contests aren't realistic,' Eamonn panted as he blew a lock of dark hair out of his eyes. In the close, dark confines of the storage area their bodies were slick and shiny with sweat and the wooden hilts of their makeshift swords became difficult to grip. Even as he spoke, Eamonn was crouching over his wooden sword with his eyes glued on Arthur's face.

'You're far too tall for any equal contest to take place between us because you've almost a foot longer reach than me,' Eamonn added, before laughing at the self-evident complaint. 'You've always beaten me, anyway, so I'm wasting my time by whining.'

'Your opponent tomorrow will also have a height and reach advantage, so you'll have to cope with it. Practise on me! I doubt, somehow, that my opponent will be short. The king has ruled that we must both win tomorrow, or we both lose. I'll try to think of some way that we can gain an edge. All opponents have some weakness, regardless of how skilful they are. I can recall Bedwyr telling me that only one man could beat King Artor when the High King was young and almost invincible.'

Arthur was panting for, while Eamonn was smaller, he was an active and elusive target who used his speed to counteract Arthur's power. Eamonn forced himself to save his breath and responded by raising one dark eyebrow.

'Artor's sword master, old Targo, was barely five feet four inches in height, if Bedwyr is to be believed. When my father was twelve, they were the same height, proving that length of leg and reach of arms isn't everything. Artor was growing at a phenomenal rate. Yet, time and time again, Targo would sit Artor on his arse. The years spent fighting for his bread in the legions had given Targo special skills, so he was a perfect example of how good technique can make a small man into a deadly opponent.'

Men of Arthur's size were usually slow, but the prince was un-naturally quick and his reflexes were excellent. Still, battling against Eamonn was always a difficult proposition.

As they continued, Eamonn's breathing remained loud in the quiet of the room. Meanwhile, the girls were employed in sewing torn tunics and robes back together, using most of the light while the men were forced to practise in virtual darkness.

'At least we'll be able to see in the daylight,' Arthur said. His mind kept drifting back to those years when Taliesin had gathered the noble youths of Britain to build a defensive dyke and develop lasting loyalties among the fledgling young warriors from the British tribes.

Suddenly, Arthur swore as Eamonn broke through his guard and slammed his wooden sword onto the prince's left hand.

'Ouch! That hurt!'

Arthur cursed his own stupidity. Only a fool allowed his mind to wander when they fought Eamonn, son of King Bors.

'Good! If my weapon had an edge, you'd be minus a hand.' Eamonn sounded gleeful at his winning stroke. 'You've got something to learn about fighting a smaller man as well, so perhaps we're even.'

He grinned with a flash of white teeth in his darkened face made even swarthier by his stubble of dark beard. Arthur imagined that his own face was also furred and quickly determined to find some way to shave, no matter how difficult it might be.

Eventually, Arthur managed to drive Eamonn into a corner and 'despatched' him. 'You'll have to work on that defence, my friend, or you'll perish for sure. I haven't enough friends to be able to afford to lose you.'

'Don't fret, Arthur. I'm working on an idea or two, although I wouldn't say they were very honourable.' Arthur presumed that his friend planned to tire his opponent out and then use a low blow to further his advantage.

'Who's this Frodhi?' Eamonn asked once they'd allowed their muscles to cool. 'I gather he's Stormbringer's cousin but he's also the Crow King's cousin. And I thought the ancestry of the British tribal families was complicated.'

Arthur flexed the fingers of the hand that Eamonn had caught with his wooden sword. Fortunately, there was no swelling and just enough of an ache to remind him to take care on the morrow.

'I've no real idea, Eamonn – none! He's irritating when he's amusing himself at our expense, but I think he really has Stormbringer's best interests at heart. Frankly, I don't know what to make of him.'

'He's too clever by half,' Eamonn retorted. 'He's the sort of man who makes me wonder about his motives. On the one hand he seems as open as the wide blue sky, but I've noticed that he's careful to guard his feelings with everyone.'

'If all goes well tomorrow, I'll ask Stormbringer about him,' Arthur promised, although he was sure that Valdar Bjornsen would be insulted by any implied criticism of his kinsman.

At that moment, both young men turned as their noses and stomachs reacted to the wonderful aroma of a hot stew. Arthur had yearned for a hot meal during their weeks at sea. Then, during the past day, they had missed breakfast in the urgency of mooring *Loki's Eye* and keeping their appointment with Hrolf Kraki. Consequently, four healthy young animals greeted Stormbringer's warriors with the excitement that hot food merited.

'Bless him, hot stew!' Maeve said gleefully as she lifted the lid of a large container. She breathed in the aroma of the food as if it had been the finest perfume. 'You're a lovely, lovely man, Stormbringer!'

'And there's hot water,' Blaise added, as she dipped one finger into a lidded leather bucket that a second warrior set down onto the floor. 'We can bathe, Eamonn. I believe he presented us with this just for you to get rid of your smell.'

'At long last – we can shave!' Arthur added his own enthusiastic mite to the general air of celebration. 'That is, if one of these fine fellows will lend us a blade that's sharp enough to remove these beards.'

This final comment was spoken in rough Dene, a suggestion which almost caused the warrior carrying the food to drop the containers in surprise. Eamonn and Arthur quickly helped him to retrieve his burdens, while the girls continued to exclaim over the basket of bread brought in by two more warriors who appeared out of the gloom.

'Look at this, Arthur, he's found us some armour!' Eamonn exclaimed. 'Most of it is metal-reinforced oxhide, but it's better than nothing at all. And there're some clean tunics and soft boots.'

Blaise was ecstatic at her discoveries, although she examined the huge second pair of footwear with doubt.

'I don't think you've much chance of fitting into these boots, Eamonn, but perhaps we can stuff the toes with padding.' She caused her friends to laugh by raising one large boot and putting it on her head. Its leather thongs were then tied into a bow under her chin.

'And here's some mead, and more cold water and . . . heavens!' an incredulous Maeve exclaimed. 'It's milk! Stormbringer has found us some milk!'

'Our captain is a marvel,' Blaise added.

Blaise was aglow with joy, as if she had been given a fine, new Samhain dress. She had never been half so appreciative of much finer gifts in the past.

The young companions set about gorging themselves on beef stew flavoured and thickened with turnips, swedes and carrots. Leafy vegetables of some kind provided welcome bulk.

'And there's no seaweed!' Blaise crowed with pleasure.

With greasy faces, the captives used thick slabs of black bread to sop up the remains of the gravy, leaving the whole pot of stew scoured clean. Their guards were also wolfing down another pot of stew, so Arthur saluted his captors with a gravy-soaked hunk of bread. With much laughter, the guards returned the salute; these brave men too had been surviving on a diet of cold fish soup for months.

As they ate, the men gulped down drafts of mead, while the girls merely sipped on the sweet, potent alcohol and used a little of their precious hot water to dilute its strength. Finally, replete and contented, they surveyed each other, their quarters and the work that still had to be done before they could devote some time to sleep.

'We have no lengths of cloth to hang that will guarantee the girls some privacy while they bathe, but I'm damned if our sisters should be exposed to the gaze of our guards,' Eamonn said with a smouldering determination in his voice that Arthur found heartening.

Arthur beckoned to one of the guardsmen who possessed a smattering of Saxon to ask if the warriors would be prepared to move to a distant corner of the storage area so the ladies could wash their bodies in private. After some ribald comments in Dene, the warriors agreed and allowed Eamonn and Arthur to join them. The two young Britons used the opportunity to borrow a pair of rather blunt knives for the purpose of shaving.

'We're finished – so you can come back now,' Maeve eventually called. The men traipsed back to the circle of light created by the pitch torch. The girls sat primly, wrapped tightly in their cloaks. They had used some of the rope that had been neatly coiled atop a barrel in order to create a makeshift clothesline, so their shifts and underclothes of linen were now hanging discreetly from rafter to rafter, creating a temporary division in their living space.

Maeve unbound her wet hair so Blaise could carefully comb the superb abundance of red tresses with a battered comb, another example of Stormbringer's largesse.

Eamonn and Arthur used the last of the warm water to scrub at two weeks of accumulated salt and grime before sluicing their whole bodies. With a little of the conserved hot water, they used their borrowed knives to scrape away at the remaining stubble on their chins. Very little blood was spilled, although the blades were blunt. Finally, both men took the opportunity to wash some of their more intimate clothing with the very last of the shaving water. Clean now, and with their cloaks wrapped around them for modesty's sake, they soaked their dirty feet and did what they could to trim their toenails.

Embarrassed, Arthur allowed Blaise to untangle his mane of hair. This intensely private action was embarrassing for both parties, but Blaise persisted. Arthur's riotous curls disguised the true length of his hair which had grown almost to his waist. With patience and a little pain, Blaise managed to force it into some kind of order and then carefully plaited his forelocks. Then, once she was satisfied with her efforts, Blaise turned towards her brother with the battered wooden comb in one hand.

'Don't think you're coming near me with that thing. I'll untangle my own hair, thank you very much,' Eamonn complained with a mulish expression on his face.

'You'll have a painful time of it, judging by the state of that birds' nest on top of your head,' observed Arthur.

'Humff!'

As Arthur and the girls settled themselves to sleep, they were entertained by the spectacle of Eamonn tearing his hair out at the roots as he fought his way through three weeks of neglect.

Eventually, the captives and their guards slept, for who can escape from the halls of Heorot where the malign spirits of Grendel and his mother keep guard over all those souls who enter its dark and secretive corners?

CHAPTER X

BY THE TRUTH OF
THEIR BODIES

For the Lord seeth not as man seeth: for man looketh on the outward appearance, but the Lord looketh on the heart.

The Bible, 1 Samuel 16:7

Arthur felt sick. He flexed his muscles and began a series of exercises designed to warm his body and prepare him for the day that was about to begin.

He had awoken in pitch darkness and, during a moment of panic, had wondered where he was. The floor was still, so he knew he was no longer aboard *Loki's Eye*. As the tide of panic gradually subsided, his agile mind began to work and he remembered the disastrous audience with Hrolf Kraki. He stirred and forced himself to his feet, naked under his tangle of cloak, recalling the coming contest when he would be forced to prove his skills as a warrior.

The faint touch of a damp cloth on his face reminded Arthur that his clothes had been left to hang on the makeshift clothes line and would be stiff from the cold morning air. With fumbling hands, he searched along the line for his trews and a tunic, but such was the drug of good food and clean bodies that his companions didn't stir from their sleep. Then, with a heart heavy for the day ahead, Arthur picked his way towards the faint glow of light that came from the gaps between the closed doors of the hall.

Had he not tripped over one of the sleeping guards in the impenetrable darkness, Arthur might have reached the door without being challenged. But the Dene warrior sprang to his feet with his sword drawn and the blade against Arthur's throat in an instant. Only by hissing his name had Arthur prevented the guard from splitting his neck from ear to ear.

'I need the latrines,' Arthur stated truthfully.

Fortunately, the warrior knew Arthur well and remembered his contribution during the storm at sea, so he grumbled, hawked and spat before sheathing his sword and leading his charge out into the dark and damp morning.

With some difficulty, both men had hauled one of the great doors of Heorot open, a movement that alerted Hrolf Kraki's guards who had been on picket duty around the building throughout the long night. In a light drizzle, they were sheltering in the lee of the hall as they tried to keep warm. While the warriors' speech was far too rapid for Arthur's limited understanding, the young man lost his concentration and looked around him from his vantage point on the cobbled forecourt of Heorot.

At first glance, the village below seemed to be asleep. Then Arthur saw lights in the narrow windows and signs of workers abroad in the outbuildings as they milked cows, collected eggs and fed the pigs and other livestock.

Mist and fog boiled up to the steps of Heorot from the fjord where only the top of the mast of *Loki's Eye* was visible. The mist dissipated slightly as it rose through the narrow streets of the town but, from the flat forecourt, Arthur felt as if he was standing high in the sky in Stormbringer's Asgaad and was gazing downwards, god-like, on the small ants of humanity labouring below.

The mists not only concealed, but they deadened the sounds of human activity within a rolling blanket of whiteness. The rasping of the guards' feet on the cobbles sounded unnaturally loud and intrusive in this dripping-wet world.

A feeling of intense loss swept over Arthur. He hungered for the close and misty skies of Britain and homesickness struck with such suddenness that his eyes filled with tears. Below him and to his right, half-seen trees reminded him of Arden where he had climbed into the tree tops and seen the crowns of great oaks rise out of autumnal mists like heavy green and gold clouds. Then, as he bent to touch the slick, wet cobbles of this foreign land, he swore that he would return to his homeland one day. He would once more climb his tree and carve his own place in the world now owned by the Saxons, who would forever be his mortal enemies.

And, once ensconced again in the bosom of his homeland, he would discuss the fate of Gilchrist with Bran, although neither man would gain any satisfaction from such a conversation.

The common latrine was relatively clean and discreet but the smell drew Arthur's attention long before he saw it. With a brief nod to his guard, he relieved himself without embarrassment while the hall's warriors examined him closely to see if he possessed marked physical differences to them.

'Just when I credit the Dene with good common sense, they prove themselves to be backward in such surprising ways,' Arthur said aloud in his own language, his voice heavy with irony. 'Ah, well. Perhaps it's time to dress and prepare myself for what is coming.'

Although the Green Dragon of the Deep had promised him that he would prevail, he was aware that he stood on a knife's edge where the slightest error could cost him his life and jeopardise the girls' safety. Besides, what power could a dream possess? And how could Eamonn hope to succeed if he sensed Arthur had doubts for the success of the trials that lay ahead of him?

'If you want my bones in your fine ossuary, Beast of the Boneyard, you'll need to wait until the oceans boil and turn you into so much cooked meat,' he added. His voice was so clipped and aggressive that the guards shifted carefully with their hands on the hilts of their swords.

'Can you point me to clean water to wash my face and hands?' Arthur asked his guard in stumbling Dene. 'I apologise for causing concern to your friends this morning, but I was very nervous – as I'm sure you understand. But you can be sure that I'm determined to perform at my best, regardless of the strength of the warrior that your king selects as my opponent.'

The warrior pointed laconically at a large butt of rainwater against a wall at the back of the hall. Meanwhile, he repeated the explanation given by Arthur to his compatriots. The hall guards laughed and Arthur heard one name spoken with awe and a certain degree of reverence – *Thorketil, the hammer of Thor.*

So Thorketil is my opponent, Arthur thought, while breaking a thin skin of ice from the top of the water. He forced himself to display a feigned nonchalance as he doused his face, hair and hands in the freezing liquid.

As he strode back to his companions with the guardsmen trailing in his wake, Arthur's face was stinging, but glowing. The cool breeze on the droplets of water in his eyebrows and hair chased the last of the night from his brain and he felt wholly alive, even if he was about to face death. Back in the area where the prisoners had been con-fined, he discovered that Stormbringer had arranged for food to be delivered. A large, wrapped bundle of sheepskin accompanied the food containers.

His companions were fully awake and eating with gusto, while making jokes about Arthur's tardiness. 'I told you he'd smell the food, no matter how far away he was. He'd rather lose a toe than miss a meal.' Maeve's remark caused more laughter than it merited, telling Arthur that everyone was a little on edge by what the coming day promised.

'I've kept some of this muck . . . I think it's meant to be porridge.' Blaise spoke without her customary snap, as if she, too, understood how their separate fates rested with the fighting skills and courage of their brothers.

'There are herrings, boiled eggs and a large hunk of cheese as well. An odd breakfast, but it's very tasty,' Eamonn added as he bit into a herring. He chewed vigorously and swallowed. 'Join us! There's warm milk too!'

Arthur seated himself within the makeshift circle and accepted a wooden bowl of honey-sweetened porridge from his sister. Ravenous, he then devoured a number of herrings, two boiled eggs and half of the pungent cheese. The others watched him as he ate, their eyes dancing with amusement.

The moment that Arthur finished eating, Maeve unwrapped the parcel that had been delivered with their meal. She'd been desperate to discover what Stormbringer had sent them and her fingers had itched to slake her curiosity. From its weight, she had reasoned that it concealed weapons.

But which swords and knives had been sent by the Sae Dene?

'Look, Arthur! Stormbringer has returned all your weapons!'

'Is my Dragon Knife among them?' Arthur felt his heart leap.

Yes! There it was! As perfect and as beautiful as on the day it was first forged by a humble blacksmith with a heart full of gratitude for the young Artor, Arthur's father, more than sixty years earlier. The dragon appeared to be asleep on the hilt while it lay curled up and quiescent in its fine-gold plating. But if turned just a little the garnet eye stared up, filled with purpose and malevolence.

Beside the Dragon Knife was Bedwyr's gift to the young man, the sword wrought with much thought and many prayers by a master metalsmith trained by the Romans. The very long gladius was both power and art. Eamonn's sword had also been wrapped in the sheepskin, and the pristine condition of both indicated that they had been lovingly cleaned and prepared for the task they were about to undertake.

'We have our weapons at last,' Arthur declared reverently. 'Everything will be different now. No matter how large or how tall our enemies are, or how skilled they might be, Hrolf Kraki's best men will underestimate us because of our youth. They can't know that Britain has tempered most of her true sons in the crucible of warfare by the time they are old enough to lift their weapons. We can win, Eamonn, I *know* we can win, and all we need to do is to have faith in our abilities.'

He picked up the Dragon Knife with his left hand and felt it vibrate under his fingers as if it had returned to life once it recognised the touch of its master. In Arthur's other hand, Bedwyr's gift of love, his own sword, snuggled into his fist with a deep, vibrating purr when he swung it. Point and counterpoint, knife and sword were complementary, for one weapon was forged out of gratitude and the other was hammered out of love. 'There's nothing I cannot do – now that this knife has been returned to me,' he vowed.

'The sun is rising,' one of the Stormbringer's guards interrupted. 'Our masters have sent word that the contest will begin shortly, so you must ready yourselves to be called to the arena.'

Maeve turned towards one of the guards.

'Do you care who wins?' Maeve asked in Saxon with a veneer of calm. 'I know your master is doing everything in his power to help us, but do you and the other guards have any thoughts about what will happen today?'

The man shuffled his feet and lowered his eyes under the girl's uncompromising stare. 'Yes, we do! All Stormbringer's men are concerned for what might happen. Our master is brave and he's a true leader of men who has taken us through many battles. He's won booty aplenty for us, so his leadership allows us to stand tall in Heorot. I'd do anything short of treason for my lord Valdar! I've wagered on the blond lad, but I haven't decided whether to lay coin on his dark friend. Regardless of what I think, my comrades are certain that the king and the witch-woman intend to kill you.' He smiled bashfully. 'Wodin knows it isn't right – but many good men have been sent to their graves before their time simply because a king didn't like their faces. The blond boy knows how to rub the king's fur the wrong way. Begging your pardon, miss, you fair upset the witch with your home truths. I would have cheered, except you and your brother had landed my master right in it, if you know what I mean. But the boy has Loki's own luck, so I figure he'll take out the Troll King – although he's so much smaller.'

The guard paused for breath.

'I hope I've chosen the right words to explain how we feel, mistress, but the Saxon tongue doesn't come easily to my mouth.'

'I understand what you mean . . . only too well! I hope you win your wager on my brother, but you would also be wise to set coin down on his friend.' She smiled at the guardsman. 'I can assure you that my companions will both win their contests, regardless of who is sent against them.'

She paused and the warrior had to strain to hear the last words. 'As will I,' she sighed.

Arthur was dressed in the armoured tunic and boots that Stormbringer had sent, and had completed his warm-up exercises by the time Stormbringer and Frodhi arrived. The Sae Dene captain, beautifully armed and dressed, was carrying a large bag over one shoulder.

Surprisingly, Stormbringer's cousin was clad in rather nondescript clothing, as if he sought anonymity within the crowd. Fat chance of that! Arthur thought. Frodhi will stand out regardless of how he dresses.

With a flourish, the Sae Dene opened the drawstring of his bag and exposed three helmets for selection by the two combatants. One helmet in the Dene style bore heavy embossing and the long, curving horns of a steer. Arthur's fingers only stroked it briefly before he rejected it. 'It's too ornate, Eamonn. There are too many decorations that can catch a blade and turn it downwards towards the wearer's face and body. This thing is only fit for ceremonial occasions.'

'Well! So much for your father's old ceremonial helmet, Valdar. I told you any man of sense would reject it. No self-respecting warrior would ever wear such a thing in battle, so you now owe me a finger of silver.' Frodhi's voice was triumphant and, somehow, his irreverence gave a festive air to what was a serious and dangerous occasion.

'Then which one would you choose?' Stormbringer asked as he held out the others.

'You should choose first, Eamonn, because your size puts you at a greater disadvantage.' Arthur waved his friend forward. 'Either of these helmets will serve my needs.'

'I'll take the one with the wide nose guard.' Eamonn smiled. 'My sister never tires of telling me how big that part of my face is, so it needs special protection.' He picked up a shining helmet that was almost bare of decoration except for an exaggerated nose and cheek guard that protected the top half of the face.

'Consider your visibility with this one, Eamonn. It's a very good helmet, but I'll wager it has a blind spot that could bring you to grief. I'd be happier if you practise with it now, while we still have time to reconsider our choices.'

'So you'd choose to use this Sae Dene helmet?' Stormbringer asked, holding the conical headpiece up for Arthur to admire the wings that gave the helmet an arcane beauty. However, although the bronzed gull wings could have caught a sword blade and inflicted harm on the wearer, the accoutrements had been finished with an upward slant designed to hug the head of a warrior. An attacking blade would be deflected away from the wearer, regardless of where the blow fell.

'I'll gladly wear a Sae Dene helmet because I've never met warriors who use the sea as well as you and the other Sae Dene do. I'll think of the gulls as I fight, and how they steal what they can't kill. Like them, I must be brave and brazen when I go about my own hunting today. Now isn't the time for posturing or arrogance!'

Frodhi laughed and slapped Arthur hard on the back, a blow that caused the Briton to stumble. 'Gods, but I like you, lad! You've got that arrogant, spit-in-their-eye view of the world that I admire. And it's a good helmet, Arthur. When did you first use it, Valdar?'

'My father gave it to me on my majority when I was sixteen. I thought myself a true man at the time. How we live and learn, cousin.'

Stormbringer spoke with a nostalgic regret that dampened the optimistic mood in an instant. Wisely, Frodhi changed the subject.

'Do you want to know anything about Thorketil, the Hammer of Thor, who is your opponent? I can give you some of his background, if you want it.'

'Yes, please, Master Frodhi. Any information you can provide might help me to obtain a useful edge.' Arthur asked his sister to plait his hair

159

to form a cushioning coronet that would sit under the heavy helmet, while Frodhi chose how best to describe Thorketil.

'Clever!' Stormbringer said reflectively as Maeve eased the winged helmet into place on Arthur's head. 'Look, Frod! Rather than use lamb's wool, Arthur's long hair makes an effective layer of resistance between his skull and the iron of his helmet.'

'I'd heard that King Artor was reputed to do the same.'

'Aye, cuz!' Frodhi nodded seriously. 'It's a subject that's worth thinking about. Have you noticed how many men suffer from brain fever after battle, having taken a blow on the helmet that doesn't immediately kill them? They seem to die later, almost as if the brain has been damaged by the invisible force of the blow.'

'Yes, I have. It's like the effect on your skull when you accidentally hit your head on a tree branch. I remember being chased by you when we were youngsters and having just such an accident.'

'One of many,' Frodhi joked while both Eamonn and Arthur looked at each other quizzically, surprised at the frivolous direction the conversation had taken.

Arthur wanted to shout out his need for an explanation of the strengths and weaknesses of Thorketil, but his debts to Stormbringer stopped the rude rejoinder in his throat.

'I've cleft the odd skull in my time and found the brain to be a wet, grey slop,' Frodhi commented without warning. Maeve almost retched, so he apologised immediately. 'I forgot that girls have weaker stomachs than men.'

'Perhaps if you are hit on the front of the head, the brain moves to strike the skull bone at the back,' Arthur interrupted with mounting impatience. 'I'm sorry to be rude, Stormbringer, but what has this anatomy lesson to do with my battle against Thorketil?'

'The name of Hammer of Thor is evocative,' put in Eamonn tactfully. 'I imagine him to be a large and skilled warrior.'

'True,' Frodhi replied. 'Thorketil is a giant of a man who stands at least four inches taller than any of us. He's a freak of nature in more ways than one and he's also heavily muscled. As a man-mountain, he destroys his opponents by sheer physical force. Of course, his reputation as a warrior and harbinger of death precedes him, so most of his opponents are terrified before he even unsheathes his sword. Further, he is also amazingly fast for such a huge creature. You must remember what I say, young Arthur. We call him *Troll* behind his back, because he looks as if he would be at home in the deep forests, in caves or in those dark places where trolls are protected from the sun. But Thorketil won't turn to stone in the morning light. Nor is he stupid.

'His face looks unfinished . . . almost as if he's wanting in his wits,' the Dene nobleman added. 'He had a hard time of it as a boy because most of us thought he was one of those unfortunate giants who are slow-witted. He is no beauty, but he's clever and far more intelligent than he appears.'

'Oh, that poor little boy must have suffered terribly,' Blaise said.

'Uh! Well, I suppose he did.' It was obvious that Frodhi had never before considered the effects of relentless bullying on the child that Thorketil had been.

'You speak of my opponent as if he's invincible,' Arthur interrupted slowly, his mind already probing for any weaknesses that might be used against his enemy.

'Yes! At least he has proved to be invincible in the past,' Frodi continued. 'In his youth, the boy had reason to hate more handsome warriors and was teased for being an ugly monster so often that he gradually became more and more bitter and enraged. If he does have a weakness, you'll find it in his temper, something that he usually keeps firmly leashed. A resourceful opponent could use words to harm Thorketil more effectively than any weapon.'

'That's not a very heroic plan,' Arthur objected, his sense of fairness affronted.

'And there's no guarantee it'll work anyway,' Frodhi added. 'Thorketil's been chosen by Hrolf Kraki because he's a devastating warrior. Gods, Briton! My royal cousin has eyes to see for himself. He's seen how strong you are and he has a fair idea that you're likely to be very well trained. We Dene aren't stupid, you know! We realise that you've had the benefit of trade and communication with the wise ones of the Middle Sea, and we're quite aware that you consider us to be barbarians. Don't you understand that the Crow King will throw his most invincible warrior against you? He's determined to prove that you Britons are inferior to us, because he's a little afraid that you might be superior. Do you follow my reasoning?'

'I think so,' Arthur replied slowly. 'Hrolf Kraki knows that Britain and the other countries of the south have more knowledge and a higher standard of living than the Dene, so he has to demonstrate his superiority by killing me.'

'That's it in a nutshell,' Stormbringer replied for his cousin. 'I'd suggest you wait until you see Thorketil before you decide how to mount your defence against the man. Most of our information will make sense when you eventually see him in the flesh.'

'As always, the Crow King seeks to crack a walnut with a battle-axe,' Frodhi went on. 'He's shown his fear so clearly that every fool at the contest was able to see it.' Frodhi was obviously scornful of his kinsman's strategy, further sparking Arthur's curiosity about his opponent.

'Oh – there is one thing that hasn't been mentioned,' Stormbringer continued. 'Our king has now decided that you are to fight Thorketil in the second bout, and Eamonn will provide a tasty prelude to the main event. I think he hopes to demoralise you, because your cause will be irretrievably lost if Eamonn should fail in the first bout.'

'I suppose that Maeve and Blaise are considered to be the honeyed sweetmeats.' Arthur's voice was thickly laced with grim sarcasm.

'Exactly! My king expects this afternoon's entertainment to amuse the people and reinforce their belief that Dene warriors are unbeatable. With this prospect in mind, Hrolf Kraki can afford to be generous in his choice of an opponent for Eamonn to confront. Besides, like many Dene, he judges Eamonn to be less powerful because he's short in stature.'

'Which is stupidity again on Hrolf Kraki's part,' Frodhi said. 'The first thing a successful warrior learns is that appearance is only a part of what makes a dangerous opponent. It's typical of him, but our kinsman has always been impressed by size.'

Then Frodhi winked broadly, so that even Arthur smiled at the double meaning. The girls giggled demurely behind their hands and Eamonn laughed naturally for the first time since they had left Britain. Only Stormbringer remained glum and thoughtful.

Once the moment had passed, Eamonn and Arthur looked expectant and nervous by turn, eager to discover the details of Eamonn's opponent. But neither man spoke.

'Your opponent is Rufus Olaffsen, Eamonn, and he is one of our most competent warriors,' Stormbringer stated in a firm voice. More importantly, he is a man of unquestioning obedience and is oath-bound to Hrolf Kraki personally, as well as to the Scyldings and the ruling class. He will obey his king without question and will sacrifice his life for his master without a second thought.'

'Lovely!' Eamonn muttered. 'I'm to fight a mindless savage who is determined to protect his king from my threatening presence – no matter what!'

'He's not quite as tall as the other bodyguards, which is no disadvantage for you. I know little about him, so I can't speak for his intelligence.'

'A capacity for blind obedience doesn't speak well for his thinking processes,' Arthur said.

'I can say without fear of contradiction that Rufus is a man of honour,' Frodhi told him. 'It is true that he's not a superior warrior. But he's extremely skilled and has survived battles beyond count. Don't rule him out because he's the kind of man who has a great admiration for Hrolf Kraki and has dedicated himself to his king's interests.'

'We'll find out for ourselves once the combat begins,' Eamonn concluded.

'Aye! I hope that you're the darlings of the gods of Asgaad and the Christus, because I happen to like you, both as persons and as warriors! Whatever happens today, you can trust in my personal regard. I'll champion you as far as I can.'

Stormbringer straightened his body armour with his customary efficiency. 'The hour marches towards noon and my king is waiting impatiently for his entertainment to reach its climax.' He turned to face the two young girls. 'There is one important matter for you to consider, young ladies. The Dene place a high value on stoicism, so you mustn't show any weakness, no matter how terrible the contests may prove to be. Present calm faces to the witch-woman and show no fear, because she'll feast on your terror.'

'I'll also be leaving now,' Frodhi said emphatically. 'Good luck. I've wagered on you both, so I'll be very disappointed if you should lose. I'll stay away from Stormbringer and his warriors during the contest because I don't want to remind Hrolf Kraki of our connection through kinship. I've also sent a trusted servant to Ribe, the town which Aednetta claims as her home, so you can be assured that I haven't forgotten my undertaking to you.'

He paused delicately and looked down at his feet.

'If I seem to deny any links with you, Valdar, please understand that I'm firmly in support of you and yours, but I'm also looking after my own skin by keeping the Crow King convinced that I'm his faithful servant and his kinsman. I'd never betray the Dene people – never! But I'll have to support you in secret.'

'I understand.' Stormbringer embraced his cousin warmly. Then Frodhi disappeared into the dark corridors of Heorot.

I don't understand, Arthur thought. I don't see how you can play two kinsmen against each other. Charming as he is, I don't think I'll place all my trust in the hands of Master Frodhi of the Scyldings.

And now to more important matters, such as our lives!

'By the proof of our bodies!' he said flatly, as if raising a toast to something of trivial importance. 'Whatever will happen, will happen, but I don't intend to die at the hands of a troll. My father would be disappointed in me.'

Then, with a final affectionate pat on the hilt of the Dragon Knife, Arthur ushered the girls ahead of him and followed Stormbringer into the gloom.

CHAPTER XI

THE TRINE

Never break a covenant, whether you make it with a false man or
a just man of good conscience. The covenant holds for both, the
false and the just.

The Avestan Hymn to Mithras, Verse 2

The port of Dubris was smelly and thick with the abandoned garbage
of careless humans. The town's inns were doing a roaring business,
while eager traders and passengers bound for the continent were
forced to wait for the first ships of the spring to make the crossing of
the passage that was now being called the Channel. Landlocked sailors
drank, whored and gambled for their shrinking supply of coin to last
until the next berth came their way. Meanwhile, the town's prostitutes
continued to ply their ancient trade among the dregs of the waterfront.
Nothing much had changed for them and the spring sailing simply
changed the faces of the men who degraded them in dirty alleys or in
filthy whorehouses.

Two men stood out starkly in this throng, not because they were
clean, but because neither was as bedraggled as the other denizens of
Dubris's slums. Nor were these two men any less threatening than the
sailors and displaced mercenaries who were seeking new masters in

this crowded seaport. What set them apart in this godless and violent cesspit was the way they were dressed.

One man wore the robes of a priest, a novelty in Dubris where men of the cloth rarely ventured, because Saxons had a particular contempt for priests and Dubris was a largely Saxon town. He was the shorter of the two and possessed an unembarrassed elan, especially since his scarred leather belt carried a sharp sword. One servant girl insisted that she had seen the priest hiding several throwing knives inside his boots in a very unpriestly manner.

The priest had attracted the attention of a group of Saxon warriors when he and his companion had arrived in Dubris. The two men were drinking beakers of beer in a stinking inn on the outskirts of the town when a young oaf knocked the horn cup out of the priest's hand, a blow that sent the muddy-coloured liquid flying and splashing onto the priest's boots.

'Are you always so clumsy, son?' the man asked with an oath.

'Nah! I just don't drink with cowardly priests! Off with you, dung-eater, or I'll kick you in the slats for your trouble.'

The young man glanced at his grinning cronies for their approval, so he never saw the priest's hard fist coming until he found himself lying, dazed, on the greasy floor. Before he could gather his wits and protect himself, the priest took aim and kicked the Saxon squarely on the jaw.

The priest dusted his hands theatrically and allowed his gaze to wander over the group of shuffling young men who surrounded him. Then, ostentatiously, he bared the long sword that hung from a worn belt around his paunch.

'Next?' Wisely, the young men decided to drift away, leaving their unfortunate friend to recover amidst the sawdust, spilled beer and scattered food scraps.

After that altercation, the denizens of Dubris gave the two companions a wide berth.

The taller of the two men, who was obviously a Frankish warrior, was even more ferociously armed than the priest, while his calm manner was in direct contrast to the varied array of weapons he wore with aplomb. He donned his red cloak with pride and his accoutrements were shining, well kept and sharp. Although the Frank seemed amiable, no one dared to anger this mature warrior after seeing the penchant for violence displayed by his priestly friend. How much more savage would the Frank be if he was angered? They were so evidently men who had served in violent conflicts that at least one wise patron of the inn was heard to whisper that careful men permitted sleeping dogs to lie in peace.

'They'd be good men to avoid,' Grod the helmsman declared after his first glimpse of the pair. 'They've got the stink of professional killers about them, even if they are a bit long in the tooth. Perhaps they're waiting for another victim to send to the shades!'

'I don't know about that,' his younger Saxon companion scowled, sneering at the abilities of any warrior who had reached middle age, 'I reckon I could take them both on.'

'More fool you then, Heinie,' Grod snapped. The sailor was irritated, because he would never again see his fortieth summer. 'You'll end up with your tongue cut out and your manhood stuffed into that noisy hole you call your mouth if you challenge either of them. Don't let their devilish accents fool you! Hibernian he may be and priest he may be, but don't expect this churchman to fall to his knees and pray while you cut his throat. I've known men with eyes like his and he's not like other Christians in this godforsaken country.'

Heinie grumbled, but when the priest spun a dainty eating knife between his fingers with the sleight-of-hand usually reserved for mountebanks and jugglers, Heinie's face paled at the warrior's expert touch.

Shortly thereafter, when a drunken seaman attempted to slap the priest after tripping over his own feet, the Frank nailed the drunk's hand to the rough bench with a wicked stabbing blade.

'I hope you saw that?' Grod admonished his friend. 'These are two men who need a wide space around them.'

Heinie shrugged, but when Germanus turned his bland gaze in the

Saxon's direction, the younger man found his grubby toes had suddenly become very interesting.

And so Lorcan and Germanus were allowed to idle away the dreary hours, days and weeks in old Dubris, a town which men called by many names, few of which were complimentary. The weeks passed slowly and the two old companions were beginning to despair that Gareth would ever rejoin them when Lorcan sighted him riding down to the docks with a spare horse plodding along behind his destrier.

The priest had risen early and was emptying his bladder when he saw Gareth trot past the latrines. Scarcely pausing to straighten his robe, Lorcan ran into the middle of the muddy street after Gareth while shouting the young man's name.

'Hoi! Gareth! Stop, you big lug! I can't keep up with your sodding horse.'

Gareth was treated to the spectacle of a priest hopping along on one muddy foot after extricating a lost boot from a particularly sticky mud-hole in the roadway. After a miserable journey through dripping forests to avoid Saxon enclaves, Gareth was weary, cold and hungry. But even an empty stomach was unable to crush a boyish peal of laughter at the ludicrous vision of the priest as he hopped, flapped his arms and tried to put his wet boot back on. 'Don't you laugh at me, you shite! We've been awaiting your pleasure for weeks and we'd have missed the first sailing if you'd delayed much longer. For the sin of tardiness, you can buy me a drink.'

'The sun has barely risen above the horizon, priest, so it's far too early to drink,' Gareth retorted with unusual good humour. Against his better judgement, Gareth was glad to see the priest again.

'Come, come, Gareth, me boyo! Morning food is calling, even if you don't want a drink. With any luck, the Widow Eta will prepare something delicious for us. But Germanus will miss out, because he's an idle old man and is overfond of his bed.'

Still grinning, Gareth followed the limping Lorcan back to their inn. The ramshackle establishment was only slightly cleaner than its fellow buildings that lined the main road leading down to the docks.

The inn sported a crudely painted sign of a rooster, its mouth agape and its head thrown back as it looked up at a bright yellow globe which Gareth assumed correctly was meant to represent the sun. Of two-storey construction, it possessed a rickety outside staircase that seemed in danger of collapse.

Surprisingly, a well-polished brass bell with a stout rope attached to the clapper took pride of place on the door frame. Gareth raised one eyebrow at this garish decoration and then dismounted and stared around in search of the stables.

'The horses are quartered at the rear of the main building,' Lorcan explained. 'Our beasts have been stabled there for weeks and the buggers have been eating us out of drinking money while we waited for you. Ask for a red-headed man called Cealine who bears a very grand name for a squinty-eyed Saxon bastard who actually likes horses. You can trust him with your stallion, but bring your packs into the inn. Poor Cealine might be tempted to stab you from behind and steal your possessions. He's a heathen, but I like him and I'd hate to have to kill him because he acted as his nature dictated. We'll have our meal once you've brought your packs inside.

'Oh, and don't pay any coin to the ostler in advance,' Lorcan offered in a final, sardonic warning. 'The bastard might get ideas!'

Gareth asked why the brass bell seemed to be the cleanest and most-loved object in the whole street.

'Why, lad, Widow Eta owns this establishment and she's awaiting the return of her husband, a man who went off to sail the seas and make his fortune near to ten years ago. Whenever a ship enters the port, Widow Eta rings the bell in welcome as she used to do in those days before her man vanished. We all know he's drowned and his bones lie scattered on the sea bed, but Widow Eta will have no truck with common sense.'

'So you haven't bedded her yet? You're slipping, Lorcan! From all I've heard from Germanus, your vows don't extend to celibacy.'

'God wouldn't have given me the equipment to disobey him if He truly expected abstinence from me. The poor woman is only human, while ten years is far too long to remain virtuous. Perhaps I've helped her halo to slip a trifle, but a gentleman never tells.'

Gareth nodded to Lorcan, who was lost in his own lecherous reverie, then walked his horses towards the rear of the inn where a withy and mud building, complete with a thatched roof of reeds, hunkered down in a frosty hollow. A fenced pasture, now mere mud that sported a light fuzz of green, indicated that Cealine had grazing land for his beasts. The primitive structure was a long, uneven rectangle with a number of open doors that led into dark, interior horse boxes.

'Hello?' Gareth's voice seemed unnaturally loud in the early-morning silence, although a clutch of chickens began to squawk out warnings to their fellows from the safety of the rafters.

A red-haired man with an ugly face and a ferocious squint strode out of the furthest door and blinked in the weak morning light.

'I'm Gareth from Aquae Sulis. My horses need rest and feed before my friends and I make the crossing to the Frankish kingdoms,' the young warrior explained pleasantly. 'I'll pay for their upkeep with good coin.'

The stable-master looked up into Gareth's face with open admiration for, superficially, Gareth was everything in face, form and height that Cealine desired to be. But then the ginger-haired ostler shrugged, shook his head regretfully at his lack of height, and stood away from the half-door leading into the stables.

'Of course, Master Gareth from Aquae Sulis! There's always room for a fine animal like your stallion. I swear it's been many months since I've seen a horse of such quality, so it'll be a pleasure to care for him.'

Cealine patted the nose of the destrier with obvious affection and rubbed the stiff hair under the stallion's chin. The horse stamped and blew air out of his nostrils in ecstatic pleasure, while the ostler regarded the beast with a sly, speculative eye. Gareth wondered if Cealine had mares in need of servicing.

'Aye, he's a lovely fellow and I'll wager that he'd be as sweet as a nut in temperament. I can tell by the softness of his mouth that you've had no occasion to discipline this beauty by the use of one of them murderous straight bits that some warriors prefer to use. I'll tell you true, master, that I have no patience with them men who break the spirit of a good horse.'

Scarcely pausing for breath, Cealine continued to talk as he coaxed the stallion into the cosy dimness of the stables. The stalls were welcoming, with bales of fresh hay and deep butts of clean water within easy reach of the tethered horses. Ropes secured coarse flaxen bags of grain that smelled sweet and fresh, even to Gareth's sensitive nose. These stables might have been crudely built, but the horses within were glossy with good health from the daily brushing of their shaggy winter coats.

Once the stallion had been led into a stall, Cealine turned his attention to the packhorse that was patted just as enthusiastically as its more aristocratic brother. Somehow, Cealine's ugliness seemed to disappear as he caressed the horses, while his amber eyes turned soft and gentle.

Ignoring Lorcan's warning, Gareth took three pieces of silver from his purse. It was an over-generous payment, but such care warranted worthy recompense. Cealine attempted to protest, but Gareth waved any refusals aside.

'My horses are valuable to me. I'm happy they've found a sympathetic man who'll treat them well,' Gareth explained to Cealine as he took his packs and slung them over his shoulders. He was obliged to make two trips to the inn and, mindful of Lorcan's warning, he trotted there and back to save Cealine from temptation.

Once inside the dim taproom, Gareth paused to get his bearings. The first thing he noticed was the smell. The pungent mix of human sweat, stale beer, spilled wine and cheap perfume seemed to ooze out of the floorboards and the crude furniture to slap him across the face. As his eyes adjusted to the gloom Gareth observed that this inn was cleaner than most of its kind and that its floor-space had been freshly swept. Although nothing could mask the tell-tale reek of an inn that had been in business for many years, bunches of mint and sage had been hung from the raw oak rafters. Even withered bunches of pungent marigold and strongly scented bay leaves masked the worst of the stink, an effect that demonstrated a woman's husbandry. Fortunately the host of this establishment had rejected the use of thick straw or sawdust on the floor to hide the unpleasant droppings that caked the floors during the long winter months. As the weather warmed, the stench of such inns was beyond description.

Gareth breathed a genuine sigh of relief. This inn appeared to be moderately acceptable, especially as the floorboards felt damp. Someone had sluiced the floors with warm water, thereby washing away the worst of the unsanitary habits of its customers. Whether Gareth was prepared to eat there was another matter.

Some customers were obviously regulars who kept their own pottery mugs on a rough shelf above the primitive bar. These drinking vessels showed all the individuality of men who came from a variety of backgrounds. Some cups were made of coarsely fired clay, others bore the distinction of coloured glazes or simple embossed designs. One wooden goblet, beautifully carved and sealed with beeswax, shone with distinction in the gloom, while a base metal cup boasted a scratched representation of the horned god of the hunt. Gareth was a Christian, but the servants employed at the Poppinidii Villa during his youth were inclined to hedge their bets with eternity by giving the old gods their due in blood, deference and offerings.

'Oi, Gareth, where have you got to, boy? Your food's waiting.' Father Lorcan's voice boomed from the nether regions of the building, so Gareth dropped his packs on the floor inside the door and trusted to the earliness of the hour to keep them safe from thieves. Then he followed his nose towards the smell of prepared food.

The inn consisted of one large downstairs bar with an attached storeroom and another small room which the mistress of the house utilised as a sleeping chamber. Above this floor, four small cubicles were kept for accommodation, with barely enough room for a crude bed or a stuffed pallet of greasy wool. Because of the threat of fire in the wooden buildings along the road, the kitchen was located in a shed linked to the main structure by a paved courtyard and a woodpile that was much depleted after a cold winter.

Although the smell of food sizzling on an iron plate made Gareth's mouth water, he took a little time to examine his temporary home. Someone at the hostelry had some imagination and a much-damaged sculpture of a laughing child, similar to a cupid, had been placed on a purloined plinth in the middle of this courtyard. Hardy shrubs and herbs grew beside a small path that ran parallel to the walls of the inn, while a vegetable patch had been planted behind the kitchen and along the front wall of the stables. Even now, sturdy green seedlings were breaking through the thick loam.

A row of poplars served as a windbreak behind the kitchens and stables, so Gareth could see that spear-heads of green and gold rose above the reed-thatched roof like a living hedge. An apple tree budded enthusiastically in an area of crazy paving near the back door, and the courtyard had recently been swept using a birch broom that leaned neatly against the wall. From the faint smell of horse dung, Gareth assumed that Cealine added his mite to food production at the inn as his horses' copious manure was stored in a simple covered pit. The aroma was homely, rich and comforting to any young man who had been raised on a farm.

'Hurry up, Gareth. Your share of the food is starting to burn!' Lorcan's bellow was urgent, so Gareth found the open entrance to the kitchen on the side furthest from the manure pit.

Gareth recognised signs of sweeping inside this room where a broom leaned against the open entrance. This spoke well of the landlady, although Gareth wondered that any woman in this filthy port would battle dirt so obstinately. Perhaps, like her lost husband, she had memories of an earlier and cleaner existence where she had once been happy.

Lorcan was seated at a rough table on one of several uneven bench seats, as he ate with his usual voracious appetite. Oddly fastidious for a man whose feet were so dirty, the priest used the point of his eating knife to scoop up meat rather than use his fingers.

'Come in, lad. Come in and meet our hostess. This is Widow Eta, a lady who is, without doubt, the best cook in this whole benightedly heathen pit of iniquity.'

Lorcan indicated a plump woman who was wielding a double-pronged wire fork to turn over some slabs of salted bacon sizzling vigorously on a long plate of iron that rested over the glowing coals of the fire. Periodically, spilled fat flared as it struck the ruddy coals with small explosions of flame. With innate courtesy, Gareth bowed and the woman flushed at the compliment. Eta raised a perspiring face, surrounded by curling tendrils of sweat-dampened hair. She curtseyed sketchily and grinned as she exposed a missing front tooth from her upper gums.

Despite this small flaw, the widow was a very attractive woman who wore her obvious Saxon ancestry in her face and her figure. Tall for a woman, she was well over five feet ten inches in her bare feet, and very broad in the shoulder and hips. Her hair, kept in order under a crimson scarf, was golden blond and inclined to curl; most men would have described her as pretty, with her small, rosy mouth, ruddy cheeks, blue eyes and large, pillowy breasts.

'Welcome, Master Gareth. I've heard much of you from this sorry excuse for a man of learning, but I can see with my own eyes that Lorcan hasn't exaggerated.'

Eta turned and spoke directly to the priest. 'He's a good-looking young man, Lorcan, and I can tell he drives the girls fair crazy with them muscles and that long white-blond hair he sports. Bless me, but I'd tumble him myself if I weren't hand-fasted to my dear Odo. But, as you well know, Lorcan, I remain a faithful wife.'

'Yes, my dear! Your Odo is a very lucky man, wherever he is,' Lorcan replied tactfully and winked at Gareth.

Mistress Eta had seen the wink and clouted the priest over the knuckles with the flat of her fork, a blow which caused the joker to yelp in mock pain.

'Sit yourself down, lad, and I'll fetch you some porridge with berries and honey. And then we shall give you some of our fresh bacon. What country did your parents call home, young master? I can tell you're not from the land of the Britons.'

Eta fetched a bowl of porridge from a black pot hanging over the fire, while Gareth seated himself carefully on the lop-sided seat. Among the many treats on the table, the young man immediately noted a honeycomb that was lying on a platter, oozing amber honey. But this bustling, grubby port was no Caer Gai and Gareth would search in vain for any salt, an expensive item that only the wealthy could afford.

The lad excused himself for a moment and returned to the inn with his pack. In it Gareth found a twist of parchment in which he had stored one of Lady Nimue's parting gifts, a large packet of rock salt in an oilskin container.

When he gave his gift to Eta, she looked delighted.

'Is this for me, Master Gareth? You do me far too much honour, sir, for this rock salt is worth nearly as much as this whole kitchen. Truly, this gift is too valuable for a lowly innkeeper in this flyblown port.'

With trembling fingers, Eta took only a quarter of the salt from the oilskin, before transferring her treasure into a small pot with a tight lid. The bulk of the salt was re-wrapped and pushed across the table towards Gareth.

'This is rock salt, not the muck that Paidraig, the herbalist, palms off on us from his sea-water vats. I am not greedy, Master Gareth, so I must insist you take the rest of your gift back. I thank you for what I have taken because it is beyond value to me. You can be sure, young man, that this house is yours whenever you wish to stay here.'

Gareth was touched by her gratitude. Belatedly, he realised he had embarrassed the innkeeper with his generosity and cursed himself for his lack of tact.

Silent now and fully engaged in eating his first real food in three days, Gareth devoured two plates of porridge, a large slab of bacon and three thick slices of fresh bread to sop up the last of the juices, all of which was washed down with passable mugs of beer. Replete and content, Gareth leaned back and thanked his hostess with complete honesty.

'I've rarely enjoyed a meal like this, Mistress Eta. I must say too that it tasted even better for being prepared by your own fair hands.'

Then Gareth rose gracefully, bowed and kissed Eta's free hand. Her palm was faintly scented with lavender and Gareth found her cleanliness pleasing in this town of filth and ordure. The journey ahead would be much more tolerable if Lorcan could conjure up more inns of quality like this one in Dubris.

For his own part, he would now cherish Nimue's gift of rock salt as it deserved.

A sore and sorry Germanus joined them shortly before noon. He was nursing a painful head and an irritable temper, but the three companions began to talk seriously once the tall Frank had drunk several mugs of beer and eaten an amazing amount of bacon.

'Well, where do we start?' asked Gareth. 'I have no idea, so I depend on your superior knowledge of the landscape.'

'Finally!' Germanus noted. 'I was almost certain that you'd try to avoid us and hare off into the continent on your own. Where's Taliesin?'

'He's ill and weary, and halfway down the stairs that lead to death. He's going to rest for the time being and will join us in Saxony once he has recovered his strength. It may take as long as a year for him to catch up with us. How far would we travel in that time?'

Both men stared incredulously at Gareth. Germanus understood that the young warrior was ignorant of the countries that lay beyond Britannia, and considered the whole jaunt to be a simple ride into the north. He tried to explain the magnitude of the task ahead of them.

'While we were waiting here, we decided to ask the local Saxons about the Dene warriors that made up the raiding party. At first, we gained the impression that no one at this port had ever heard of them.'

Lorcan nodded his agreement. 'We thought that you'd got the tribal name wrong, but then we were fortunate enough to meet up with a Jute seaman who answered all our questions. He almost took our heads off out of sheer hatred for the Dene nation.

'The man's name is Erikk Eanwulf and it seems that his father had lost all their possessions when the Dene drove his family southward into the land of the Angles, a secure haven where they survived on the bare bones of family charity until Eanwulf was in his teens and had taken a wife. At any road, the poor bitch was killed by a Dene hunting party and the invaders seem to have infiltrated the last of the Angle and Jute strongholds and driven the defenders into the south. Erikk eventually arrived in Dubris, accompanied by the last of his kin and a hostile attitude towards every Dene inhabitant of the northern lands.'

Lorcan paused for breath and Germanus took over. Drawing a lump of charcoal from the fireplace, the Frank began to sketch a primitive chart on the pale stone of the hearth. Britannia was depicted as a rectangular shape separated from the mainland by a narrow stretch of water. Then Germanus quickly roughed in the outline of the coastal mainland, right up to the northern climes where a small peninsula thrust its way out into the sea.

'Pretend that the peninsula I've just drawn is Jutland – and that's the land which is now inhabited by the Dene.'

'That?' Gareth gasped. 'It's too small! The whole country would fit at least four times into our lands. How could such a fleabite be responsible for so much trouble?'

Lorcan and Germanus remained mute.

'Anyway, how do I know this scrawl is correct?' Gareth asked with a suspicious stare.

'You don't!' Germanus was curt with irritation. 'You have a knack for rubbing everyone the wrong way, Gareth, especially people who are trying to help you. I've seen a number of small fragments of maps detailing parts of our world during the time when I served with the Franks some twenty years ago. I'm working from memory now, for there are very few charts in this world. Taliesin is a fortunate man, for he has access to a complete collection of rare maps drawn by Myrddion Merlinus.'

Lorcan cut in over his friend's attempt to explain. 'What studies have you done, *boy*? When did you last travel through distant lands, *boy*? Your quibbling is an insult to those men who wish you well. You cast shame on this fine man who should be at home with his wife and sons rather than gallivanting over the countryside assisting such an ingrate as you.'

It was Gareth's turn to hang his head in regret now, so Germanus continued with his lesson. 'The Romans left the Britons a treasure trove of very good charts. And before you ask, the journey we are proposing could take us nine or ten months, even if the circumstances under which we travel are uneventful.'

Gareth became increasingly glum. 'But why would such a simple journey take so long?'

'We will be forced to travel through the lands of many foreign kings.' Lorcan raised one hand and proceeded to tick off each tribal group as he named them. 'The Salian Franks, the Alemanni, the Neustrians, the Austrasians, the Thuringians, the Frisians, the Saxons, the Angles, the Jutes and, if we're really unlucky, the Sorbs lie between us and our eventual destination. You can also add the Pomeranians, the Obotrites or the Lotharingians to these tribes, for we will pass by their borders. None of these tribes likes each other very much, so the only time they agree on anything is in their hatred of outsiders. In case you haven't noticed, that's us!'

Gareth tried to imagine how so many tribes were competing for the richest lands, the deepest mines and the best rivers.

'The Dene tribes are moving further and further into the south,' Germanus added, and then drew a line with his charcoal that stretched downwards from the north into Jutland. 'Their initial invasion displaced the Jutes who, in turn, displaced the Angles and they displaced the Saxons and the Frisians, etcetera and etcetera.' The thin black line of charcoal spread southwards, and then into the east and the west to intrude into the east coast of Britannia as a reference point. 'Much of the present flood of Saxons migrating to Britain was initiated by the early expansions of the Dene people.'

'Oh!' Gareth gulped. A world of regret was obvious in that simple sound.

'Yes!' Lorcan agreed. 'If we survive all those competing tribal groups, it will take us at least a year to get through Saxony in one piece.'

'So ... when do we begin? Arthur and his companions are waiting for us, and God alone knows what the Dene will do to them while we're trying to reach Jutland.'

'The first ship will dock within the next couple of weeks, so we should begin our preparations immediately,' Germanus warned. 'But now that we know you're serious about this journey, we can make our plans. Firstly, are you well supplied with coin that will sustain us during our travels?'

'Arthur made sure that I carried all our funds as we travelled along the roads leading into the Otadini lands. My master realised that I'm frugal to a fault.' Gareth grinned crookedly, and both older men saw the sheen of tears in his eyes. 'At any road, I also have coin given to me by Bedwyr and his family, prior to my departure from Arden, plus more coin advanced by Nimue and Taliesin.'

'By the bare breasts of Venus, boy,' Lorcan swore with very unpriestly imagery. 'There's five pieces of gold here.' He continued to sift through the coins, many of which were stamped with the likeness of the long-dead Valentinian, one of the last of the Roman emperors. 'Fifteen silver coins and a pile of bronze, copper and tin pieces of various worth. And look, Germanus, there's a pearl ring – a real pearl – and a small ingot of green Cymru gold. And there's a brooch here that is ...' His voice trailed away in wonder.

Words failed the older man as he picked up a huge breast pin of gold, cut gems and electrum. 'The workmanship in this piece is beautiful, but I can't place the style.'

'Lady Nimue gave this piece to me. She assured me that Myrddion Merlinus received it from a kinglet from Babylon when he lived in Constantinople, wherever that is. I protested that we were unworthy of such a princely gift, but she swore that Master Myrddion would have gladly given us this bauble, and more, to save his master's only son from harm. Only the greatest need will induce me to part with it.'

'Give us the base coin and two pieces of silver,' Germanus said softly. 'That amount of coin will be more than enough to purchase our passage, including our horses, although we should consider selling them and gamble that we can find better mounts on landfall. The remainder will buy us provisions that will last for a month or more after we reach the mainland. We may have to purchase extra space on the vessel, because it would be better to outfit ourselves here rather than gamble on what we can obtain in Gesoriacum.'

'Meanwhile you must keep that pouch directly over your heart, boyo. You mustn't show it to anyone, even to a lover.' Lorcan's face was extremely serious. 'Men here will kill for a copper, let alone coins of real worth. And the ladies are worse! There's no limit on what they'd do to us if they became aware we were holding a large store of gold and valuables.'

Mutely, Gareth obeyed and tucked the pouch away inside his undershirt.

'And then we must practise our martial skills,' Germanus continued. 'And yes, you're included, old man. I'll admit that I'm rusty and you've been carousing and whoring for a year or more to my knowledge. As for Gareth, I've no idea how skilful he is, so he needs to impress us with his ability to use his weapons. Also, we should practise in public so that we can dissuade any cutthroats who have designs on our possessions. After your very public arrival, the ostler will have told all and sundry about the quality of your stallion. Once our practice begins, we'll be as ready as we can be when the first vessel arrives to take us to the continent.'

In the weeks that followed, the thaw continued to release the earth from its winter fist and buttercups, snowdrops and daffodils made the muddy verges of the road bright with their massed blossoms. A festive air overlaid the filth of the town and even the cracks in ruined buildings and broken mosaic floors were softened by cascades of weeds and clumps of hardy flowers. Dandelions made a bold showing, and Eta's vegetables flourished.

Each morning, the three men went through a disciplined ritual of exercises, using swords, shields, knives and bows. The rigorous training had all the grace and elegance of a complex, deadly dance as the companions worked on honing their skills and hardening the muscles that had weakened during the long winter. The two older men laboured hard to maintain their flexibility.

'I've rarely seen a better swordsman than you, Gareth,' Germanus told the young warrior without emotion. 'Arthur is better, but he was born with extraordinary physical attributes that surpass yours. I can tell you that your father must have been a master swordsman, because he has trained you to perfection. One thing I'm sure of is that skill and will, if you'll pardon the rhyme, are not always enough. Listen to your instincts, Gareth, for that feeling in the gut is sometimes more reliable than the hardest muscles or the fastest arm.'

'My father taught me that combat can often be meticulously planned out. He was trained by Targo, the great sword master who trained Artor, the High King. I've been told that some veterans still pray to Targo and ask him to intercede for them with God, an odd belief when we consider that Targo was a pagan. Targo believed that you can determine the course of any engagement if you approach an enemy directly and force him to fight on your terms.'

Germanus bit his thumbnail. 'Your father's methods certainly work on nine occasions out of ten, but it's the one exception to the rule that will get you killed. For starters, your enemy might have been trained to take the initiative back from his opponent, after previously having relinquished it. This warrior won't respond as you want him to because he uses his senses and his instincts to guide his strategy. Such a warrior has no obvious flaws. You can't really anticipate what he'll do next, because he doesn't know himself. He is the most dangerous of all.'

'Think about what Germanus is saying because he's usually right!' Lorcan gasped, as he raised his sword in a series of painful, complex moves. 'But don't take too long, for there's a ship approaching the port even as we play our little games. We'll be on the *Litus Saxonicus* within hours.'

Gareth stared seawards at the harbour and was rewarded by the sight of a sail on the far horizon.

Several hours elapsed before this vessel made landfall, allowing the process of unloading passengers and cargo to begin. Barrels, boxes and packs of goods that would soon be on sale in the town were the first items of cargo to be taken off, while wine was transported in the old way, in huge terracotta amphorae sealed with beeswax. Even as the ship emptied, the captain was hard at work accepting passengers and cargo destined for the land of the Franks. Tablets of wax and a stylus recorded all transactions.

Fine wood in bales, pigs of lead, tin and copper, iron weapons, cloth, dried meat and fine leather goods were all stacked high on the wharf before being stowed in the hold to earn a handsome dividend for the owners of the vessel. The world still moved as trade flooded through her arteries.

While the sailors took the opportunity to drink themselves into stupors or sample the whores who frequented the ale houses, the captain happily accepted Germanus's coin in payment for the passage.

Germanus discovered that this trade ship had made the long journey from Constantinople and had zigzagged its way across the Middle Sea while trading with Greece, Ravenna, Palermo and Massilia, before passing through the Pillars of Hercules and continuing its journey to Brigantium and Gesoriacum. Here, sailors jumped ship cheerfully, for who would willingly be away from home for over two years?

During the night before embarkation, Gareth found that he was incapable of sleep. Try as he might, the gentle anodyne of oblivion refused to come, even when the young man swallowed a large draft of plum brandy. The possible privations that might lie ahead were terrifying, because he had no idea what the future might hold once he left the familiarity of his homeland. For one sickening moment, Gareth thought about running, but then his oath burned away his fear, leaving a memory of his unmanliness in its wake. Shamed, Gareth dropped to his knees and prayed, invoking the courage of his father, the spirit of the High King and the steadfastness of Old Frith, his family's most respected and revered ancestor.

Out of the past, to a great-grandson she had never known, Mistress Frith seemed to whisper the words of comfort that called to him from their shared blood.

'Without fear there can be no courage, Gareth. You must stand straight and tall, while trusting in your God and your strong right arm to carry you safely into the land of the Dene. You will meet your fate there – and you will find your purpose in life.'

'I'm afraid of failure.' Gareth spoke to the empty darkness. He knew that Frith was long dead and powerless to help him, but he could almost feel an invisible hand that smoothed back the fine hair disarranged by his nervous fingers. He was being forced to trust the expertise of other men at a time when he was far from sure that this honour was deserved.

'You'll not fail, son of my grandson, not if you lay down your pride and learn to trust other persons during the darkest of nights. You must risk everything and hope to win.'

The young man should have been confused by the riddles conjured out of his tired brain, but the scent of clean wool and lavender seemed to drive all scepticism from his heart. Suddenly weary, Gareth lay down on the prickly straw pallet and submitted to his exhaustion.

In his dreams, a seamed old-woman's face smiled down on him and Frith's ancient arms rocked him and caressed him throughout the night.

CHAPTER XII

THE FORTUNES OF
THE SWORD

Whatever befalls you was prepared for you before-hand from eternity, and the thread of causes was spinning from everlasting both your existence and this which befalls you.

Marcus Aurelius, *Meditations*, Book 12, Section 5

According to the old Romans and their stoic concepts of fate, Fortuna always displayed a sense of humour as she spun her dreadful wheel that they believed brought failure, as well as good fortune, to every individual under heaven. So Arthur looked for a sign to give him guidance. He would prefer this spiritual aid to come from his mother's Christianity, but Fortuna would do if she saw fit to smile upon four lost Britons who were far from their homes.

As if in answer to Arthur's earnest prayers, a shaft of brilliant sunlight penetrated Heorot through the wide-flung portals. After the mists and rain of the dawn, the sun had risen to bring a day filled with golden sunshine. The air was crisp and cold, but the sun gave the illusion of warmth. The hall was exposed in all its violent glory, as was the king, so the Britons were left dazzled by an alien splendour.

Hrolf Kraki had dressed for this auspicious occasion and the light caught at a blood-red garnet on his thumb and found the blazing hearts from the cabochons in his crown. Blue, green, purple and scarlet rioted in his greying hair, while the display invested the occasion with a holiday mood of celebration completely at odds with the blood that was about to be spilled by the combatants.

'You've come, Stormbringer, albeit tardily! I see that your charges are clean, armed and well rested, so I expect they are eager to prove their worth.'

'Aye, your Highness! Prince Arthur and Master Eamonn are ready to prove their innocence and their mettle in combat with your champions.'

Hrolf Kraki's voice was jovial and avuncular in manner, although he was glaring suspiciously at his Sae Dene captain. Stormbringer recognised the obvious loss of royal favour, as did the observers present, while Arthur noted that many of the assembled warriors leaned away from the captain as if he were suffering from a contagious disease.

Frodhi had warned Arthur how it would be, although he was one of the few lords who stood firmly and refused to shun his cousin.

'Ave, Frodhi,' Arthur whispered to Eamonn, although the scratching of the voice in the back of his mind still bothered him.

'I've decided to give our loyal townsfolk a Spring celebration,' Hrolf Kraki announced to the assembled crowd. 'The contests will take place in the forecourt of Heorot, so all folk who wish to see the trial by combat are free to attend.

'I've been told the townspeople are already ten deep around the area prepared for the contests, mainly because they are curious to see how long these Britons will last against our champions. I hear that wagers are being laid on just how long your friends will stand upright and how proficient they are in the manly arts of war,' he stated blandly as he waved a negligent hand towards Maeve.

The king smiled wolfishly.

Stormbringer felt Maeve stiffen and he wondered at how well she understood the king's rapid-fire speech. Like her brother, she had the irritating habit of being far more acute than her composed, flower-like face suggested. For some reason that Stormbringer barely understood, the fate of little Maeve mattered to him. Impatient at his sentimentality, he pushed the conflicting thoughts away.

'It's time to go, my loyal subjects, for the townsfolk are waiting patiently,' the king decided with mock solemnity. Arthur wondered momentarily if Hrolf Kraki was quite sane.

'I've no doubt that my loyal Rufus grows tired of practice at a time when his sword hungers for red work,' Hrolf Kraki added, with such enjoyment that Eamonn knew the king expected that Rufus would emerge victorious.

But Eamonn swore that he would win, even if he had to cheat to do it.

The king rose to his feet with boyish vigour. Then, with a warrior's briskness, he gestured for the witch-woman to follow him before striding through the mass of warriors towards Heorot's open doors.

The witch-woman had dressed with care and had exchanged her widow's garb for a robe of heavily bleached wool. With her pale hair and skin, she seemed innocent and very young, except for something scaly and ancient that Arthur imagined he saw slithering behind her pale, secretive eyes. In the rays of sunshine passing through the great doors of Heorot, she appeared to be an incandescent column of light.

This is superstitious nonsense, Arthur thought, and shook his head vigorously to banish any thought of failure. I don't believe in magic and those who do are fools, charlatans or worse.

The king has underestimated us, especially Eamonn, so it's likely that our opponents are over-confident as well. That certainty of victory will make them careless. Only careful men survive mortal combat with battle-hardened veterans.

At that moment, Arthur longed to wipe the supercilious sneer from the king's lips. As for Aednetta, he would have given a great deal to shake her out of her preternatural calm.

Across the room, Frodhi nodded in the direction of Stormbringer. His salute also included the four Britons and Arthur turned back to the dais in time to see a sudden frown cross the Crow King's face.

Standing directly in front of the captives, the Sae Dene whispered haltingly over his shoulder. Arthur had to strain to hear the words, but the substance of the Sae Dene's message warmed them all. 'My cousin, Frodhi, has asked me to inform you that he has placed a large wager on Eamonn on principle. He'll be obliged if you were to win him a large sum of gold.'

'We shall try, my lord,' Arthur hissed back. 'But I must say that while I find our huge friend to be an object of trepidation, I am even more terrified of Hrolf Kraki's woman.'

Aednetta had been staring fixedly at the Sae Dene's profile with an expression that was most chilling because it said nothing in particular. The Crow King was seated above her in the throne room, as was appropriate, but her status was still far above everyone else's in Heorot.

'Look at her feet!' Maeve urged and Arthur felt a genuine shudder of horror as he saw something he had never experienced before, even in the heat of battle. Aednetta's near-naked feet in their gilded sandals were sensuously caressing each other. Her largest prehensile toes ran along the inner side of each foot, while the hennaed nails were scoring her own flesh hard enough to draw thin streaks of blood.

Another quick glance revealed that Aednetta's big toenails had been tipped with narrow sheaths of gilded metal sharpened to points. At the same time, her tongue was darting in and out of her mouth as she moistened her pale lips.

To further enhance her appearance, Aednetta had cinched her slender waist with a scaled belt of rosy gold. The complex pattern seemed to coil around her narrow body like a serpent. More gold glittered from her ears on rings so heavy that her earlobes were dragged downwards. Her braided hair was partly loosened and fell almost to her calves in attractive waves and curls so thick and voluptuous that even Arthur and Stormbringer felt her seductive pull. Only the image of those deadly nails as they drew blood from her own flesh stopped the rise of heat in the Briton's mind and body. Almost every red-blooded man in the audience wondered what it would feel like to run his hands through that cloak of pale hair. Yet few could fail to recognise the cold, knowing triumph that lay under her cloak of innocence. After looking deeply into Aednetta's pale-blue eyes, Arthur knew that she would remain an implacable foe until one of them was dead. He had no idea *how* he had offended her, but the reasons mattered little. She had primed the king all night, so the ruler would follow her instructions implicitly.

The entire royal party moved through the central aisle of Heorot with the captives and Stormbringer close behind them. The assembled warriors, landowners, aristocrats and citizens hurried behind them to find vantage points where they could watch the combat in relative comfort. In the undignified scramble behind them, Arthur gained some insight into how cheerless and bare of amusement winter must be in the Dene lands.

The spring sunlight hit the captive's eyes with the force of a bright, white blow. On any other day, Arthur's thoughts would have winged away with the gulls to distant and exciting shores.

But today was for death, not for possibilities and promises.

A large circle was constructed by an eager press of bodies against a ring of fully armed warriors. High-born or low, the Dene had come to this contest of arms as if to a celebration.

The noise from the excited crowd was deafening. As the king approached, the crowd roared and chanted words of worship, although Eamonn said quietly to his friend that the witch-woman was ignored in the frenzied acclamation. The warriors beat the hilts of their swords against their shields, creating a crazy cacophony of noise that lasted until Hrolf Kraki seated himself on a temporary dais above the crowd where he would sit and watch the violent proceedings. That blood would be spilled was beyond question and Arthur recognised the crowd's demands for death and pain.

I will not die, Arthur vowed silently. I will not!

Then the voice in his mind screamed out a warning as he saw the size of their opponents.

A grizzled warrior introduced Rufus Olaffsen to the expectant crowd who roared their approval as the heavily armed man crossed his sword over his shield in salute. He was well over six feet and towered over Eamonn. Under an embossed ceremonial helmet Rufus's face was weather-beaten, tanned and handsome, although his features were bisected by a long scar across his face that almost reached his right ear.

'I think your enemy was scarred by a left-handed warrior at some time in the past,' Arthur told his friend. 'You must change hands if you get the chance, because it just might confuse him. Watch his eyes also, for he becomes vulnerable if his thinking is announced in advance.'

Eamonn nodded his understanding. 'I see it!' The nearest Dene cuffed Arthur to silence him and the young man's sight dimmed for a moment with the force of the blow.

Eamonn had already recognised his opponent's flaws as soon as he had taken his first glance at the king's champion. Rufus Olaffsen's eyes were grimly determined, but his hazel stare was shallow. While he would obey his masters until death, did this particular warrior have the originality, the capacity or the experience to defeat an enemy who refused to fight by the rules?

And then Thorketil was introduced to the crowd and the response was almost hysterical.

Stormbringer had told the Britons that Thorketil was perceived by many to be a warrior out of legend, so Arthur expected the crowd's approval. What was unusual was the way the densely packed bodies of the audience heaved away from the tall figure that approached the circle, bare-headed and threatening from head to foot.

Arthur estimated that the giant must top seven feet in his bare feet. Unlike most Dene, this warrior was heavy with slabs of muscle so large and bulging that at first glance the warrior's frame appeared to be deformed. His hair was the colour of driftwood, partly bleached by salt seas and hot suns, and partly darkened by long immersion below pounding waves. Even his thick mane was somehow inhuman, like the ruff of a monster out of legend.

If I can grab some of that hair, he'll discover that it's unwise to take an enemy for granted, Arthur thought. I'll drag his head back and cut his throat in an instant. I can't give any chances to a monster like this man.

Thorketil had bright-blue eyes that protruded a little from his skull. His odd appearance was accentuated by a bulging forehead and a thick, heavy jaw. As Arthur had been warned, the coarser bones of the warrior's face suggested the stupidity of a malformed child, but the protuberant eyes were quick and calculating. How many men must have perished because they assumed that Thorketil was only a mindless hulk?

I won't be making that mistake. Let's hope that Thorketil is accustomed to frightening his opponents to their deaths before he strikes an actual blow! Arthur examined his opponent from head to heel and realised, belatedly, that he was being coldly examined in turn.

Then the Britons were placed into a position below the dais where they were forced to stand like suppliants or slaves. As Rufus began to enact a series of simple exercises to warm up his muscles, Stormbringer bowed to the king and offered Eamonn the use of a large Dene shield.

'Rufus will be using a shield, as will Thorketil. You can't afford for a single blow to fall on either of you, so I hope you've reconsidered your use of this defensive weapon, my friends.'

'I agree,' Eamonn responded quickly. 'I'm prepared to use a shield, but I'd prefer to use a smaller one. I don't want to be hampered by any extra weight.'

Stormbringer was surprised by the young man's composure, for all traces of nervousness had vanished. Had the Dene captain known Eamonn a little better, he would have understood that Eamonn suffered from a vivid imagination and the longer he had to wait, the more nervous he became. By being in the first contest, Eamonn had been spared the anxiety of having to wait for his moment of truth.

Arthur nodded his approval when a child-sized shield was brought by one of the Dene warriors. Although small, the shield possessed the same heavy metal boss and wooden armour of a full-sized protector. Eamonn would certainly need to wear his enemy down, so this shield would become essential against his taller opponent. As for himself, a shield would make his Dragon Knife useless if it remained in its scabbard. Arthur was sure his knife would be a key factor in his contest against Thorketil, although he had no idea how it could best be used.

Arthur rejected Stormbringer's offer of a shield, then watched as impatience mounted in the eyes of his patron. The use of two blades in personal combat wasn't a familiar concept to Stormbringer, although he was personally adept in the use of axe and sword as dual weapons of choice. For the Sae Dene, a knife was too paltry a weapon to harm an enemy.

'You must understand, Stormbringer, that British warriors are under attack from childhood,' Arthur explained to his mentor. 'I know your people are raised in a cruel and unpredictable environment, but we Britons have been at war for nearly one hundred years. As I told you, I was forced to kill my first man and take my first wounds before I was ten years of age. I must be allowed to fight Hrolf Kraki's champion in my own way.'

Stormbringer nodded slowly. He understood the nerve-stretching agony of waiting for trouble that may or may not come, compared with the self-control that a man can exert once the danger is clear and immediate.

A grizzled master of ceremonies proceeded to introduce Eamonn to the crowd as a British prince. Eamonn bowed towards the king, his opponent and the onlookers with irony written in every line of his body, but his courtesy effectively stilled the noisier ruffians. Silence fell as both men entered the killing circle.

Predictably, Rufus Olaffsen struck the first blow as he charged at Eamonn with a bloodthirsty roar of challenge. His upraised sword was brought down to cleave Eamonn's head in two, if the Briton had been so foolish as to wait for the blow to fall. The younger man skipped to Rufus's left and his sword struck sparks on the cobbles.

Muttering an insult under his breath, Rufus turned to slash at Eamonn's legs, giving an immediate indication of the speed of his reactions. Once again, Eamonn sidestepped the blow, while Rufus tapped his sword against his shield in the universal signal that the young man should be prepared to go onto the attack.

With minimal pressure being exerted on him by his young opponent, the Dene warrior decided to taunt the young Briton into making an inopportune move. Rufus hissed under his breath and spoke slowly and loudly so that the first ranks of the audience could clearly hear him.

'Come and fight me, little man! Or are you still such a boy that you can only use a child's shield? I'll have to tan your backside with the flat of my sword if you don't stop dancing around like a girl.'

Eamonn gritted his teeth and closed his mind against the half-understood insult.

Fortunately he had no real idea what Rufus had said. Even so, Rufus punctuated his insults with several rude gestures and swung his hips in a parody of a girl, an insult which any fool could interpret.

Arthur had warned him that Rufus would use offensive words and insults if Eamonn should prove difficult to catch, but the contempt in Rufus's voice and his demeanour stung Eamonn's personal pride.

Keep your head, Eamonn, Arthur prayed silently.

Blaise watched her brother square his shoulders and ignore a pointed insult aimed directly at her. For her part, she didn't really care what the Dene called her. This clod could call her a slut all day and into the night, as long as her brother remained safe. Sometimes, it was useful to be ignorant of a language. She recalled her complaints on the roads leading into the north and felt a pang of shame for her whining.

Somehow, Eamonn had managed to keep his head under the barrage of invective, until shortness of breath eventually brought Rufus's insults to a stop. The younger man continued to dance around his opponent, while Rufus attempted to find a gap in the defences of the Briton. The Dene began to feel the heat of irritation rise like bitter curd in his mouth.

Although the sun lacked any sting in its brilliance, both men were soon sweating heavily from their exertions. Again and again, Eamonn circled his larger opponent in such a manner that Rufus had to look towards the light that dazzled off the boss of his shield and the metal plates of the young man's armoured vest. On at least three occasions,

Eamonn noticed that Rufus's eyes squinted from the reflected sunlight. Good! I might be able to capitalise on a brief moment of sun-blindness, the Briton thought with savage pleasure.

'Stand still and fight like a man, you coward,' someone in the crowd shouted loudly.

Still others began the chant of '*Fight! Fight! Stand and fight!*', so that the air was thick with a cacophony of catcalls and abuse that Eamonn struggled to ignore.

Then, as Rufus managed to manoeuvre the Briton towards a corner, several arms snaked out from the crowd and around the guards to grasp at Eamonn. As Rufus charged in to take advantage of this new development, Eamonn managed to tear his body free and avoid the savage thrust designed to gut him. However, the blow was impossible to avoid entirely, so the British captives watched, aghast, as a fine line of blood began to seep from a cut along Eamonn's breast. Although the sweep of the sword slice was almost spent by the time it split his skin, the cut was almost twelve inches long and would soon begin to weep profusely. As he danced away, a red stain began to widen along the edges of the protective leather tunic.

Eamonn had no time to staunch the flesh wound and control the dangerous flow of blood, so realised he was in dire straits. He must even the score now, or he would lose this bout! The Dene had been the first to cheat, or benefit from cheating, so Eamonn felt free to fight with every dirty trick he had ever learned.

For his part, Rufus was certain the contest was all but over, and Eamonn was at his mercy. Strutting like a cockerel on his dung-heap while dragging out the moment of victory to savour it, the Dene swung his sword in a shining parabola for the delight of the crowd, all of whom stamped and cheered until the hard-packed earth and cobbles vibrated under their enthusiasm.

Flamboyant with confidence, Rufus stepped in close to finish Eamonn off but, carelessly, he lowered his guard for the first time. Using the reflection from his shield to dazzle the Dene's eyes, Eamonn capitalised on the Dene's error. As Rufus was momentarily blinded, the younger man used the sharpened edge of his shield to strike at Rufus's face directly under the warrior's noseguard. At the same time, Eamonn took the enormous risk of leaving the inviting target of his own body exposed to Rufus's sword. His own blow caught the Dene squarely on the sinew under the nostrils, causing Rufus to squeal with pain. An immediate rush of tears further blocked off Rufus's vision and the warrior almost made the fundamental error of lowering his shield. Then, as the Dene castigated himself, Eamonn kicked Rufus in the balls before his opponent could re-gather his wits.

The low blow dropped Rufus like a stone, while every man in the crowd groaned as their hands inched towards their own groins.

With eyes reddened by bloodlust, Eamonn swung his sword in a precise sweeping motion that opened Rufus's arm to the bone from shoulder to elbow. The razor-sharp blade clove through flesh, muscle and sinews with ease, and only the discipline and precision of Eamonn's swordplay saved Rufus's arm from amputation.

As Rufus dropped his shield and gripped his suddenly nerveless and useless arm, pain and shock brought the Dene warrior to his knees. The crowd howled in fury and disappointment.

'Stand up and fight, you coward!' Hrolf Kraki shouted at his defeated and unresponsive champion, while Arthur watched with disgust as every word struck deeply into the heart of the king's loyal retainer. Rufus Olaffsen was bereft as the strong rock of his honour crumbled under his shambling feet.

With a superhuman effort, Rufus used his shield to support his agonised body as he attempted to clamber painfully upright. Eamonn waited courteously, choosing to give Rufus a chance to continue the bout if he was capable of doing so. Staggering and weaving, but with his feet widespread to support his weight, Rufus tried manfully to over-come the agony of his arm and groin wounds. But Eamonn was now a misty, wavering figure that he couldn't keep in focus.

Like a wounded bull, Rufus shook his head to clear his vision. Slowly, far too slowly, he forced himself to raise his sword. Arthur swore under his breath, for Eamonn would be guilt-ridden for the rest of his life if he had to kill this man who had shown such determination in this combat.

'Another good man who's been ruined by a bad master,' Arthur exclaimed to himself.

Beside him, Stormbringer shot a surprised glance in the young man's direction when he realised that Arthur was serious. It's a pity that this fine young fellow must die at Thorketil's hands, the Sae Dene thought. But, wisely, he kept his opinion to himself.

From a vantage point at the back of the crowd where he was perched on the roof of an outbuilding, Frodhi called Eamonn's name. When both Eamonn and Arthur looked towards the sound, Frodhi raised his thumb in a gesture of approval. Unfortunately, Hrolf Kraki also saw the movement of Eamonn's head. As quick as a snake strike, the Crow King turned to discover the object of Eamonn's attention and watched Frodhi's gesture.

Hrolf Kraki knew instinctively that he was being gulled; he realised instantly that his jokester cousin had been mocking him in some way; and he was angry and enraged by Rufus's failure and his own loss of face in the crowd's esteem. He would have acted precipitately if Aednetta hadn't pinched the soft skin on the underside of his forearm to remind him that he was in open view of the population of Heorot. Her warm little hand burrowed into the arm of his robe, an intoxicating and deliciously wicked distraction.

'At least the Troll King will finish off the other Briton,' the Crow King insisted savagely, while savouring his pet name for his champion. 'Thorketil will devour the British upstart, and then spit out the bones for my amusement.'

Stormbringer turned in the king's direction and inclined his head in deference, but Hrolf Kraki could see something closely akin to contempt in the action. 'I'll chew your bones as well before this year is done, you bastard,' the king vowed as he irritably shook off Aednetta's restraining hand. Stormbringer seemed to sense the enmity as he glanced at his king before returning his gaze to what was happening in the arena.

Stormbringer was unaccountably excited by Rufus's loss to Eamonn because there was now some hope that the Britons could win but his innate common sense told him that the sheer strength in Thorketil's bulk would favour him during Arthur's bout. Even so, the Sae Dene was sure that the young Briton would be difficult to kill.

'What a fucking waste,' Stormbringer swore under his breath; Arthur, unable to tell whose fate was under consideration, would have been surprised to know that it was his own.

Predictably, Eamonn knocked Rufus off his feet with the same lack of triumph that had soured Arthur's pleasure in the victory. The Dene fell to the ground but, like a true warrior, he tried desperately to roll over and hoist himself to his feet once again.

'Stay down, Rufus Olaffsen,' Eamonn hissed at the Dene. 'No man will judge you to be a coward, for you've already proved your courage in this contest.'

The Briton had already forgotten the barely understood insults that Rufus had hurled at him. Such ploys were the way of all personal battles. But Rufus was unable to accept his loss. Once again, racked by pain and with blood streaming from his wounds, he forced himself to stagger to his feet and charge blindly towards Eamonn's hazy form. Regretfully, Eamonn used his sword hilt to strike Rufus behind the ear as the pain-blinded man stumbled past him.

The contest was over and Rufus was dragged away with scant concern for his wounds. His bleeding head thudded sickeningly on the first step of the forecourt.

Without preamble and without waiting for any introduction to the crowd, Thorketil strode into the circle and rammed a plain helmet over his mane of hair. Staring implacably in Arthur's general direction, the Hammer of Thor made the universal beckoning gesture that invited Arthur to join him in the centre of the makeshift arena.

Arthur turned to see if there was any reaction on Hrolf Kraki's intent face and noticed that the witch-woman had moved so that she was standing behind the king with one long-fingered hand resting in a proprietorial fashion on his shoulder. With the attention to detail of a man about to face death, Arthur noticed that her nails had been stained dark blue with woad, a strange affectation that suggested her fingers had once been frozen by terrible cold. The oddity registered strongly in Arthur's consciousness.

'It's time!' Arthur said to his friends. 'Thorketil might be a troll, but he's a great troll. So pray for me to prevail in this trial of strength!'

Maeve threw herself into her brother's arms, and whispered a few brief words of advice into his ear before Stormbringer pulled her away, allowing Arthur to enter the circle with his Dragon Knife in one hand and his sword in the other.

'Briton! You! Briton! Where is your shield?' the king demanded.

'I don't use a shield, Lord King, but I use my long knife as my second weapon. If your champion comes within my guard, one of us will die and no shield will change that truth! I will keep my knife, and your champion may use whatever protection he prefers.'

Arthur ignored Hrolf Kraki's baffled face and kneeled on the edge of the killing circle where he could compose himself by sinking down into that cavern in his mind where instinct lived within a cool and narrow focus. When he could no longer feel the cold of the earth through his knees, he rose to his feet. His eyes were now as calm and as grey as the empty seas.

'I'm glad you've prayed to your gods, Briton, for you'll be joining them soon enough,' Thorketil sneered as he hefted his inhumanly large shield with its boss shaped like a bull's head.

'May Mithras continue to protect you from harm,' Arthur replied. A bull was often sacrificed to this Roman deity, so Thorketil's choice of emblem, whether conscious or not, was very appropriate. But Arthur's salute thoroughly confused the giant warrior, for the Dene weren't very familiar with Roman customs.

Thorketil responded to his embarrassment by snarling deep in his throat in the mistaken belief that Arthur was mocking him.

For one short moment, the giant was frozen in anger, but then he brought his red temper under control with a practised discipline that Arthur recognised and admired as the mark of a gifted warrior.

The young man dropped into a fighting crouch then, and the twin blades began to weave patterns in the air that seemed like bands of silver light in the sunshine. The tips of the weapons circled like spools of thread, an effect which seemed to distract Thorketil's eyes and hypnotise him with their steady, even tempo. Then, without further warning, Arthur moved forward at lightning speed and the tip of his knife tore its way through Thorketil's leather tunic as if the sturdy armour was made of smoke. The suddenness of this attack was the only reason that Arthur managed to breach the Dene's guard.

A faint line of blood was left in the Dragon Knife's wake but, like all its victims, the great troll imagined that the blade had bucked in its master's hand, as if it was hungry for blood. Thorketil shook his head to kill a sudden rush of superstition, while the crowd howled in mingled amazement and horror.

Then rage filled Thorketil's vision with a red mist. No man had ever breached his guard so easily; Thorketil was humiliated and furious with his enemy and with himself. His pride could not permit another blow to drag his reputation for invincibility into the dust, so he slammed his naked blade upon his shield to show that his arm was unharmed.

An ugly, half-formed smile appeared on his face – one that few living men had ever seen.

'Well done, little man. You can boast in Hell that you managed to shed some of Thorketil's blood before he killed you.'

'You talk too much,' Arthur answered from the coldest spaces of his brain.

Thorketil chose to make a dramatic charge to restore his status in the eyes of the crowd. Rushing at Arthur, he raised his shield like a battering ram to drive the younger man down into the dirt where the Briton could be despatched with a simple stabbing blow from above.

The ploy had worked repeatedly in the past, for most enemies never expected such explosive speed from so huge a man.

The trick would have worked again, except for Maeve's final message given to her brother at the commencement of the bout. 'Watch his eyes,' she had warned Arthur before the bout commenced. 'He's never learned to disguise his thoughts, because he's never had to learn how to use guile. His physical strength has always been enough to win.'

Clever Maeve! Arthur thought as he allowed his body to take over the tactical considerations of the bout that stretched out before him.

It was only Arthur's exceptional speed that saved him from a crushing blow from the shield's deadly boss as he threw himself to the right, and away from Thorketil's monstrous sword. The many years of practising swordplay with Germanus, who had seemed at the time to be a veritable giant, saved the young man from an ignominious death. On his feet in an instant, Arthur used his acrobatic grace to tumble behind the man-mountain while swinging his own sword to one side. As he fell, the tip of his sword touched Thorketil's ankle. The strike was solid enough to raise blood, but not enough to cut directly through the tendon and bring the troll to his knees.

On his feet at once and on guard, Arthur and Thorketil struggled for mastery for a long time, far past the point of exhaustion for any normal warrior. Thorketil was slick with sweat, so the dampened curls along his hairline were the colour of stained old bones. But Arthur was carrying bloodied injuries from a dozen small scrapes and cuts in places where the monster had almost caught him, so each small wound was draining him as they sucked away at his icy calm.

Now is the time for courage, the voice of his beloved Bedwyr whispered in his ear and Arthur repeated the words aloud for comfort. For the very first time, the young man could taste the bitterness of defeat in his mouth, because he had tried every trick he knew against Thorketil and each attempt to gain the ascendancy had failed.

For his part, Thorketil had that same unpalatable taste in his mouth. Again and again, he had pitted his unnatural strength and speed against an elusive target and had failed to finish off this irritating opponent, one who should have been crushed with that very first blow. For the first time since he had been a tormented boy, teased and tortured because of his size, Thorketil began to consider the possibility of failure. Although he refused to show this fear of defeat by even a single slumped muscle, each attack was becoming a little more difficult to mount than the last. Thorketil longed to be done with this Briton and his dangerous little knife.

'Will you finish with this irritating Briton, Thorketil? I had hoped for better from you.'

For one moment, Hrolf Kraki's unjust words clouded the giant's brain. But his ire was clearly aimed at the Crow King, so the young prince readied himself for an inevitable attack.

'You've shamed me before my king, little man. I'll crush your skull with my own two hands and feed on your liver for your sins,' Thorketil promised, and made a further rush at Arthur, his courage bolstered by his fear and humiliation.

For once, Arthur chose not to retreat but allowed his knife and sword to block the blow from Thorketil's huge sword above his head. The metal in the crossed blades screamed, but the two craftsmen who forged the weapons were master metalsmiths and they had wrought each edge with love. The sword and the knife never wavered, while Arthur's muscles cracked and strained with the effort of holding the troll's huge weapon at bay.

A flash in Thorketil's eyes warned Arthur that the Troll King was about to use his shield to smash him to the ground. From somewhere unknown within himself, Arthur dredged up enough strength to defy the combined forces of Thorketil, gravity and Fortuna herself.

'Words!' Arthur whispered into Thorketil's ear. 'I am the Last Dragon, so the gods will never allow you to kill me! No troll can put me under the ground, not even one who lives in the sunlight.'

Even as Thorketil swung the huge shield to strike Arthur on the back, Arthur's reflexes took over and he made his move. Quickly, so fast that the onlookers could barely anticipate his sudden disengagement, Arthur allowed his torso to slide away from the close body-to-body contact. The weight of Thorketil's huge sword, too heavy for any normal Dene to lift, forced it to fall downwards towards the ground while pulling the surprised Dene warrior off-balance.

Arthur acted instinctively. He rolled away on the uneven ground and leaped to his feet with renewed strength. Skipping behind the giant, who had taken longer to regain his balance than the lighter Briton, Arthur slashed just once with the Dragon Knife and felt the blade bite deep into the tendons behind Thorketil's outstretched knee.

Thorketil knew instantly that he was finished. His hamstring was severed and he would never stand on the field of combat again, nor hear the acclaim of the crowd as it washed over him. He realised that the boats would sail in the spring without him and the red work which had given his life purpose and respect had been stolen from him forever.

On his knees, Thorketil bared his throat, screamed once in unbearable anguish and then begged for death as his blood began to turn the packed brown earth into red slurry.

'Kill me! You've beaten me – so cut my throat and have done with it. I am nothing without two good legs, and I won't crawl in the dirt like a back-broken lizard or beg in the marketplace for the amusement of the crowd. Please, Briton? Allow me some pride!'

Arthur looked towards Hrolf Kraki, who was slouching on his throne in obvious irritation. With some effort, the king hid his chagrin in an outward show of boredom.

'Kill the bastard and we'll get this whole mess over and done with.'

Arthur felt a surge of revulsion at Hrolf Kraki's callousness, because the king seemed untouched by Thorketil's tears and the obvious loss of everything that mattered to the warrior.

The Crow King's eyes were hard and dry.

'This man has been crippled to advance *your* interests, master,' Arthur asked with real concern. 'You are the king, my lord, but Thorketil is owed something more than a casual rejection. Why should I stain my soul with the blood of an honourable warrior?'

Hrolf Kraki's malignant frown would have melted glacial ice, but Arthur stood his ground and faced down the king's obvious hatred.

'If you want to claim the life of an honourable servant, then you must use another man to carry out such an ignoble task. We honour such men as the Hammer of Thor in my homeland, so I must suppose that the Dene people place no value in valour, sacrifice and nobility. I'll not kill your champion – for he is a true man, a remarkable warrior and a loyal servant to his king. If you want him dead, then you'll have to kill him yourself.'

The growl from the crowd was low and deep, as if a wild beast had turned its hungry eyes upon the king. Hrolf Kraki shifted in his seat as he recognised their change of mood, but Aednetta's fingers dug into the large muscles across his shoulder as she encouraged him to regain control over the disastrous train of events.

Arthur joined the other captives below the throne. Unfortunately for Hrolf Kraki, Arthur had spoken in Dene and, while his pronunciation had been execrable, the closest townsfolk had heard and understood every word. Those who hadn't heard Arthur's response demanded a précis of his words of defiance from their more fortunate fellows, so the young man's rejection of the king's ignoble order was speedily passed back through the audience. Ordinary Dene folk were observing their king through newly opened eyes, while nodding their heads respectfully towards both Arthur and his erstwhile enemy.

With a sudden surge of fury and blind to the harm he was doing to his own reputation, Hrolf Kraki demanded that his guards should drag Thorketil away. The crowd groaned and Arthur saw two spots of redness appear on Hrolf Kraki's wind-burned face.

Aware that any loyal Dene was obligated to save the king from the consequences of his callousness, Stormbringer hurried to provide an alternative solution before the guard obeyed Hrolf Kraki's orders. The warriors' faces were frozen and expressionless as they tried to hide their repugnance for the task they had been allotted.

'As your loyal servant, my king, I would ask a boon of you. I ask that you give Thorketil and Rufus to the Sae Dene in recognition of the many services they have given the Dene during your reign. Thorketil doesn't need two strong legs to serve in your ships, not when he is such a powerful and knowledgeable warrior. Rufus would also be invaluable to us, and I believe his wounds will heal in time. If you are in agreement, I will find many opportunities for these heroes to continue in your service.'

Only too conscious of the mood of the crowd, Hrolf Kraki considered the diplomatic and strategic advantages of complying with Stormbringer's request. He realised immediately that the Sae Dene's offer was an excellent means of saving face and defusing a possibly dangerous outcome. Still, resentment towards Stormbringer bloomed in the king's heart like a poisonous flower.

Still begging for death, Thorketil was carried away by four of Stormbringer's warriors, so Arthur breathed a sigh of relief. He might have won his bout with Thorketil, but he had been lucky; lucky to withstand the feelings of defeat that had almost overwhelmed him; fortunate that Thorketil had tried to browbeat him with words at a crucial stage of their contest and, most importantly, lucky that years of training had prepared him for a risky manoeuvre whereby he disengaged his own weapon from its place of safety below Thorketil's heavy sword.

Arthur thanked God that the Hammer of Thor's shade would not join those dead who already came to his bedside in the minutes before sleep overtook him. Those long-dead visitors implored him or cursed him with empty eyes.

'This contest is over, Stormbringer. I expect you to bring your captives to my hall to face my judgement as soon as the forecourt is clear,' the king ordered. His voice was perfectly steady and composed now, although Hrolf Kraki's hands suggested that he desperately wanted to kill someone.

With sinking hearts, Eamonn and Arthur limped after Stormbringer, who had taken the precaution of removing their weapons which were spirited away by one of his warriors. Arthur hated to lose both of his blades, while his left hand still itched for the feel of the Dragon Knife in his palm. But, for safety's sake, he accepted that his weapons should be kept as far as possible from Hrolf Kraki's reach.

Instinctively, Maeve understood that the next turn of the sun would be crucial to the salvation of the Britons and the position of Stormbringer, who was now their patron. She had watched Aednetta's features as Arthur's contest of strength had played out before her and, although the witch-woman's face had remained impassive, her tell-tale blue claws had displayed her growing impatience more clearly than any words. Even Aednetta's exultation when Hrolf Kraki had ordered Thorketil's death had been obvious to Maeve's observant gaze.

The real struggle with the witch-woman was yet to come.

Stormbringer, the captives and a slew of warriors waited within the long, echoing vastness of Heorot for the king to explain his wishes. All the witnesses showed some signs of trepidation as Hrolf Kraki settled himself onto his ornate throne with Aednetta seated gracefully at his knee.

A heavy silence fell when Hrolf Kraki raised one hand to impose order on the throng.

'You! Arthur pen Artor, or whatever heathen name you give yourself. You and your friends have won the trials of strength by the truth of your bodies. I am forced to accept the wishes of Heaven and the laws of this kingdom, but I am most displeased. I've lost the services of two good men because of your impudent and insulting ideas, expressed openly, concerning my adviser, Aednetta Fridasdottar.'

Hrolf Kraki paused and Maeve watched as Aednetta's nails traced patterns on his knee in encouragement.

'Your disparaging comments were unwarranted and unwelcome. You sought to ruin the reputation of my counsellor and bring my rule into disrepute. You may have avoided earthly punishment in combat on this occasion, but your sister has yet to answer for her inflammatory insults.'

'Lord King, my sister—'

Arthur tried to interrupt, but Hrolf Kraki cut across him.

'Be silent! Your sister claims my counsellor is in league with my father's murderers. There's no excuse for such slurs and, while Aednetta Fridasdottar doesn't choose to vent her revenge on a child, I'm not so generous.'

Gesturing to her brother to maintain his silence, Maeve moved forward to stand below the king's dais in a pool of light from the setting sun. She appeared to be small and slender, with beautiful red hair that hung to her knees like a curtain of the rarest silk from Constantinople. No man present was impervious to that wonderful hair, regardless of his age or his contentment with his wife or his family. Maeve's beauty turned the witch-woman's obvious charms into a tawdry counterfeit of innocence that was blatant and contrived. Each man yearned to touch Maeve's hair and feel the river of vibrant life that coursed through every strand. Each man longed to protect her and win regard from her direct green eyes. Even Hrolf Kraki had felt her charm and Aednetta's claws almost drew blood from his knee as she sank the nails of jealousy into his flesh.

'Lord King and master of the Dene,' Maeve began to speak in the Dene language in a clear, bell-like voice. 'I regret any pain that I may have caused you. But I will be forced to repeat my words again, because the only excuse for such impudence is the truth of what is said. I had an inspiration yesterday, suddenly and without warning, so I spoke of my beliefs with complete truth. But if I was wrong, I must be prepared to suffer for my actions.'

Maeve's eyes never wavered from the king's face. He felt the truth in her words, like ribbons of gold thread, and, for a moment, he was ashamed of his callous actions during the noon-time combats. More importantly, he felt regret for his treatment of Thorketil and wondered, irrationally, why he had acted with such arrogance and cruelty. For a single pivotal moment, it seemed to Hrolf Kraki that he hadn't always been a man with such a capricious temper that led to frequent fits of rage. Impaled by the young girl's clear and innocent regard, he saw Stormbringer behind her, the same Valdar Bjornsen who had always been his friend. How had he become such a tyrant? Why had he changed, both as a king and as a man?

Then Aednetta startled the king out of his reverie as he turned to look at his counsellor. All unmanly thoughts were swept away.

Maeve felt the king lose interest in her and his body changed subtly as he became rigid and predatory once more. But she knew she had reached him – if only for a few moments.

'Even now, my lord, you have placed yourself in the power of

Aednetta Fridasdottar. She encourages you to act in ways that were once foreign to your nature. What do you truly know about your *wise* counsellor, and how strong have your relationships been with your allies in the months since the witch-woman came to Heorot? You must remember, Hrolf Kraki, that there are greater threats to your people than Grendel's mother. You've been led astray through the lure and power of a woman's eyes.'

Maeve saw a redness flare in the king's expression as he lumbered to his feet. Quick as a young deer, she turned to the assembled nobles and spread her arms to beg for their support.

'Answer me then, loyal jarls and warriors of Heorot. Has your king shown his usual wisdom since the witch-woman first warmed his bed? Do the men of the Noroways stand firmly at your backs while they defend Dene interests? Will your allies in Skandia come to your aid when the Hundings begin their attacks on the outer settlements? Answer me fairly! Is Hrolf Kraki as he once was – a wise and generous king?'

The Dene warriors shuffled their feet and tried to avoid each other's eyes lest they should be accused of conspiring to act in a treasonous manner.

And so Maeve turned away from their cowardice with a shy smile. 'I can see how it is, my lord. It appears that the Dene have forgotten how to think and act like men.'

'Enough, woman, of your lies.' Hrolf Kraki's voice was shrill and almost womanish in his anger.

'Then you should cast your gaze on those loyal warriors who refuse to meet my eyes, or yours! I'm only a girl who is sorely lacking in knowledge of the world, but I saw into your soul only a moment ago and recognised a man who had dreamed for many long years how he would take back what had been stolen from him through blood and death. I saw *you*, late at night, as you hungered for the death of Snaer, the man who usurped what was truly yours by right of birth. No coward convinced the Dene to rise up and smite the tyrant. For many good years, a true and strong man has ruled them with generosity and hope while caring for his people, for that is his duty.'

She paused to draw in a rasping breath.

'Look at them. Look at your warriors! And then look at yourself! How far have the Dene fallen? Even Stormbringer, the Sae Dene, is now mute under the power of this wicked woman.'

Hrolf Kraki snarled, but he was busy assessing the faces of those men who refused to meet his adamantine gaze.

'Your allies will desert you if you don't cast her off. Or they will attack you, for they will deem you to be ensorcelled. Even as I speak, word comes by ship that your end approaches if you don't begin to act like a man. You may kill me if you wish, my lord, but my words are true. The Dene will perish and Aednetta Fridasdottar will dance upon your splintered bones.'

Just as Hrolf Kraki rose to his feet, with spittle darkening his beard and one pointing finger shaking under the force of his passion, a messenger stumbled into the hall, clutching a torn and burned banner to his breast. The dyed cloth with its rampant dragon was thick with dried blood, while the man who carried it bore serious wounds that stretched from his hairline to his jaw. They were still bleeding sluggishly, leaving the courier pallid from loss of blood.

He fell to his knees in an untidy puddle of torn clothing, ruined armour and tangled hair, while the dragon banner was humbled as it lay on the wooden floor of Heorot.

'See, Lord King?' Maeve shouted over the hubbub of consternation that rose towards the rafters. 'This messenger has come to your palace, bringing word of the treachery that will soon spell out your doom.'

'Let the courier speak,' Stormbringer demanded. 'By his wounds, he bears a message of trouble. By the Lord High Jesus, let the courier speak!'

'I bear a terrible tale of treason and murder, my lord,' the courier managed to rasp in a voice almost destroyed by the tumult of the battle that he had survived. Every man present was silent and shamed.

'The King of Gothland has attacked Skania and many towns and villages have been laid waste. Traitors bearing your name told us that you ordered the towns to be opened to the enemy because you had signed a treaty with the Goth ruler. When our elders were so foolish as to believe these lies and opened the gates of our towns to the enemy, they were all put to the sword. My master, Leif, has sent me to beg aid because he *still* holds on to much of our lands and awaits the arrival of your warriors. We have placed all our trust in receiving assistance from you and your warriors, my lord.'

The wounded man sat bolt upright in distress. His breathing was laboured and he seemed to be on the point of collapse. Then his eyes rolled back into his head and he fell forwards.

'Who has committed this treason? Who has betrayed my people through the misuse of my name?' Hrolf Kraki roared, and Heorot's rafters shook with his anger. Aednetta tried to soothe him with her blue-tipped hand, but he shook her off impatiently. 'Who has conspired to destroy the Dene?'

Maeve spoke so quietly that her bell-like voice shouldn't have been heard. But it was.

'You have, my lord! You and Aednetta Fridasdottar have betrayed the Dene!'

Her brows drew together in puzzlement, as if the king's questions had surprised her. 'I was sure that you understood me.'

CHAPTER XIII

WHEN KINGS FALL OUT

Each man is the smith of his own fortune.

Appius Claudius Caecus, Proverbs, 599: 34

'So this is Gesoriacum! What a shithole!'

Gareth kicked a bale of wool with a particularly savage swipe of his booted foot. Unfortunately for Gareth's toes, the wool was densely packed and had been laid on a base of crude wooden slabs to protect it from seawater. His foot struck the inserts with a sharp crack.

'Shite!' He hopped on one foot and glared at Germanus, daring the older man to even consider smiling over his foolishness.

'I've thrown up for a whole night and shared the ship's deck with horses that liked the voyage even less than I did, while they defecated over my cloak. Oh, yes, you may laugh, you doddering old bastards! But I hate the ocean, if that voyage is anything to judge it by.'

Lorcan snorted with his usual irony. 'A cloak can be brushed clean, even by a spoiled brat like you. Any other man would be grateful if he was gifted with the opportunity you've been given to see strange and wonderful places.'

'Shut your mouth! Please?' Gareth snapped in his sulkiest manner.

'Can't take the heat, eh?' Germanus observed. 'Good heavens, boy! You'll feel like your old self after a day and a night without a deck moving under your feet. We've much to be grateful for! The horses made the crossing successfully – even Lorcan's mule – and we've come to this port during a period of relative quiet. The ship wasn't too verminous and the voyage took very little time. No princelings appear to be killing any of their enemies – or their own subjects – and neither has the Byzantine army moved out of northern Italy to conquer the Frankish lands. All told, things seem to be very quiet in the land of the Franks.'

Lorcan scanned the long, grimy road that linked the decaying wharves with the town on the higher ground. The muddy verges were churned by the feet of men and livestock, while prostitutes plied their trade as openly and as briskly as at any seafaring port. Workers carried the ship's cargo from the vessel to the warehouses on the shore with the same phlegmatic stoicism of dumb beasts, yet there was an expectant, anxious stillness about this mundane scene that made the priest's nerves quiver.

'It's too quiet!'

In retrospect, Gesoriacum seemed to be waiting for something unpleasant to happen. Lorcan narrowed his eyes at Gareth and the younger man recognised that the usual jocularity in Lorcan's manner had vanished like woodsmoke in a breeze.

'What is this place?' Gareth looked out at a precariously balanced town that seemed to be trapped between the sullen sea on one side and a line of ill-defined tidal marshes on the other. The town itself was built on a set of low hills above flatter land where trade and industry fed the town with coin. That this port was ancient was beyond doubt, for the splintered wooden structures on the wharves and the much-damaged remains of Roman roads spoke mutely of centuries of occupation by foreign powers.

Gesoriacum still bustled, but it was tired and she was deciding how to change her clothing from the Roman peplum to a fabric that was newer and more tawdry.

'This *shithole*, as you call it, has been used as a port for many centuries. It's been called Portus Itius and Bononia at various times, names that have been used as often as its Roman title of Gesoriacum. Whatever you choose to call it, the world comes to Britain through this port.' Germanus spoke with his customary calm, so the explanation helped to settle Gareth's nerves.

The young man had been vilely ill during the night with *mal de mer*, as the locals called seasickness. The vessel in which the party had travelled to Gesoriacum, the *Golden Nymph*, had a name that was far finer than its actuality, and the vessel had nothing to recommend it other than its cargo-carrying capacity and surprising speed.

From the moment that Gareth had eaten a hearty breakfast in Dubris on the morning of departure, he had been harried and hurried to collect the horses, take them to the dock, drag them onto the deck where they were to be secured, and help the older men to store their possessions.

The ship had then set sail on its return journey to Gesoriacum.

Their quarters below decks were verminous, stuffy and dark, although Germanus seemed quite comfortable with their accommodation. Gareth had stayed on deck until the pitching of the vessel eventually nauseated him. From then on, below-decks vomiting had convinced him to remain in the open air where he could curl up in a ball of misery and curse the sea and all who sailed in ships.

Harassed and confused, Gareth's excitement at finally setting forth on the quest to save Arthur was mitigated by his illness, his anger at his own weakness and his confusion at the speed that two older men could muster when they were finally in a position to act.

Unable to relax, and aware that every word that left his mouth was discourteous to his companions, the young man's temper became badly frayed.

Something of Gareth's sense of confusion and frustration was evident in his troubled face. Both Germanus and Lorcan had left the boy to his own devices during the Channel crossing for they understood how Gareth must have hated being seasick when every other man on the *Golden Nymph* had been untouched by the illness. With his usual sensitivity, Germanus reminded himself that Gareth was still well short of his twentieth birthday and was ignorant of many of the important things in life – except for the trade of killing.

'We need to find somewhere clean to stay until we're ready to continue the journey into the north. I'm already missing Dubris and the cooking that Eta did so well, but we won't find an inn of that quality in Gesoriacum.'

Lorcan's proposal was practical, but Gareth remained sullen and argumentative.

'I don't see why we can't start on our journey into the north immediately. God only knows what problems will beset Arthur and his friends while we dilly-dally and gorge ourselves on bacon and sweetmeats.'

Germanus sighed. He could see that Gareth was in a mood for argument and Lorcan was becoming restive at the boy's aggressive attitude. Germanus was almost prepared to oblige the young man, for he knew that Gareth would be impossible to live with if Lorcan lost his temper and sat the boy on his arse.

'Where will we go? And what route should we take, Gareth? It's important that we know the terrain and the political situations *before* we move into new territory. Besides, our horses need rest! They don't like sea travel any more than you do, so several days will elapse before they're ready to continue our journey.'

Gareth was forced to agree, but he was far from happy. The constant grumbling forced Germanus to wish that he could shut him up by boxing the young man's ears. Understanding bad behaviour and living with it were two very different propositions.

Finally, the boy agreed to assist Lorcan by settling the horses, while Germanus commenced a search for accommodation at a suitable inn.

The establishment chosen by the Frank mercenary was situated on a side street at the edge of the port district and it appeared to be unusually clean. The hostelry was a little way from the main thoroughfares, so it should have been less popular than other public houses situated close to the wharf area. Yet its prices were slightly higher than those of its competition, an inconsistency that surprised Germanus.

The owner of the inn, Priscus, was a rail-thin man who obviously had a good eye for the main chance. When asked why he had chosen to set his tariff so high, the glibly tongued innkeeper explained that patrons were unlikely to walk in off the street in a location as remote as this, so he concluded that a reputation for good beer and wine, clean rooms and excellent food could win him a good share of the travelling custom in an area of Gesoriacum that wasn't famed for quality inns. Wealthier passengers had to wait somewhere for ships to set sail, or to find a place to rest after a long voyage.

What better place to stay than Priscus's inn?

Once he had inspected the kitchens, Germanus decided that several days' rest at the Green Man would benefit all three travellers – and their horses.

The name of the inn worried Lorcan a little because, despite his best efforts, a streak of Hibernian superstition ran through his thinking and he wondered whether the use of a hostelry with such an evocative name could bring bad luck to the party. Even ardent Christians were wary of the legendary Green Man of the Woods. But Germanus and Gareth, more pragmatic, banded together to override Lorcan's formless reservations.

Although Gareth's bad temper led him to doubt the wisdom of Germanus's choice, his first sight of the well-maintained stables with the sweet, clean smell of fresh straw and rows of well-treated beasts convinced him that he was being uncharitable. The innkeeper talked incessantly, but the rabbit pie made by his silent woman was rich with gravy and Gareth almost wept at the memory of plain country food. With mugs of fresh ale in front of them, the trine ate voraciously before settling down to discuss their plans for the next stage of their journey.

Lorcan asked the innkeeper to join them. With a conspiratorial wink, the priest produced a silver coin from his purse to purchase a jug of Frisian beer. Priscus bit on the coin to check its purity, and then grinned at the profile of Valentinian which indicated that this small piece of Roman workmanship was nearly a century old.

'You've not seen our master's new gold coins then?' Priscus asked with a greasy, knowing expression on his thin face. He returned a handful of silver coins to Lorcan in change, and then placed brimming jugs of warm beer on the table.

'What master would that be, good Priscus?' I seem to recall that it's against the law for any person, other than the Emperor Justinian, to have his likeness on coins of the empire.' Lorcan's voice was cool and unthreatening.

'The king of Austrasia is Theudebert, who's the hero of a hundred battles, if we believe half of the stories that we've been told of his fighting prowess.' Priscus smirked with a most unpleasant expression that made Gareth long to kick the innkeeper savagely in the backside. Something about Priscus raised the hair on Gareth's arms.

'Theudebert was victorious in the Dene Wars twenty years ago, when his father ordered him to kill Hygelac of the Geats. I know that Theudebert was little more than a boy when he defeated the Dene and Geat forces, so I can assure you that our king is a man to be reckoned with.'

Priscus tapped the side of his nose and then winked broadly.

'Was Hygelac the king of the Geats – or the Dene? I always seem to get those tribes mixed up. Their warriors are all so large, and they grow too much hair on their bodies. It seems to be all over them,' Lorcan added guilelessly, before grinning at the innkeeper as if he was sharing confidences with an old friend.

'Aye, sir! It's all too true!' I've heard that the Dene carved out the coastal areas to the west of Gothland as their own by claiming Geat lands as their own, but heaven knows where their people came from originally. The Geats and the Dene are allies of a kind now, but they're a hardy and a prickly people who are known to take offence at trifles. Wars between the peoples of Skania, Halland and the other states are a regular fact, and not just a possibility.'

'For a cynical man, friend Priscus, you're quite aware,' Germanus replied drily.

'I try to give my customers the best service I can, but after many years at my trade, I don't have much faith in the nature of the great ones that I serve. I know them too well!'

As Germanus and Priscus conversed and laughed together, Gareth felt his impatience rise again, even though he was basking in a mellow glow after drinking two mugs of strong beer.

'Will your presumptuous King Theudebert allow us to pass through his lands if we want to travel into the north?' Gareth's voice was sharp, leaving Priscus to stiffen with affront.

'What this rude young cub is trying to ask is whether we're likely to encounter any obstacles if we decide to pass through Reims on our way into the north,' Lorcan interrupted. 'Reims is a major city ruled by Theudebert, isn't it? And it's also on the most direct route leading into the north. We can travel through Tournai, Cologne and then up the River Rhin to either Friesia or Saxony, but I'm a little nervous about making an incursion into Saxony. They'll never forgive the Dene for their humbling of the Jutes and the Angles, or for the flood of refugees who weakened Saxony. There are too many possible problems if we choose to follow that route.'

'Is that so?' Priscus said conversationally. He shot a jaundiced glance towards Gareth. 'Your problems in the north will be more easily solved if you can convince your young friend to explain himself in a civilised manner. If he should speak to Saxons with such a lordly and condescending tone as he used with me . . . Well, he'll not have a tongue in his head for long.'

Gareth opened his mouth to argue, but Lorcan kicked hard at the young man's ankle under the table.

'Gareth has spent his whole life in a provincial Roman villa outside Aquae Sulis in Britain, a place where he was denied a suitable education,' Lorcan added politely. 'He's ignorant of the ways of your civilised world, but he'll soon be schooled. I apologise for any lack in our young friend's manners.'

'Then your apology is accepted, my friend!' Priscus rubbed his long palms together to show his lack of offence.

Affronted and sullen because his companions had apologised to a common innkeeper on his account, Gareth believed that the apology placed the three travellers at a disadvantage, in spirit if not in fact, despite Germanus's later explanation that they had little choice other than to ask Priscus's advice.

'To answer your question, young man, our king is famed as a warrior and as a leader of other fighting men. He's been playing ducks and drakes with the emperor of Constantinople for years. He's taken the emperor's coin to keep the peace, but . . .' The innkeeper's voice trailed off and he laughed sardonically. 'But you'd have to be naïve, or another emperor, to consider that Theudebert would rise up and strike a treasonous blow against his kin who rule in Neustria. It won't happen, because Theudebert is far too astute to be pinned down by an unworkable alliance. Yes, he'd happily take Justinian's coin. Who wouldn't? But when the time came to strike a blow against his fellow Franks? Well, I'm sure that Theudebert would simply ignore Justinian.'

'Then what route would you suggest we follow?' Germanus asked with a raised eyebrow.

'I'd travel through Reims and Metz, although you'll be heading south for a short distance during your journey into the east. Our king is distracted and has turned his eyes to Thuringia in the north to settle an old and bitter debt for wrongs done to his kin in times past. If I stood in your boots, I would use the military advances of our king to safely clear your way. Given that the armies involved in the conflicts are trying to destroy each other and aren't over-interested in the movement of small groups of outlanders, you should be able to reach the towns of southern Jutland with relative ease, if you're fortunate enough to pass through the Saxon and Thuringian borders without too much difficulty.'

'So we'll be riding through several armies who are actually at war with each other?' Lorcan asked. 'Shite, I suppose it's better to know the worst straight away.'

His last comment was directed at Gareth.

'But most of the threats posed by the lesser kings will be removed by the presence of Theudebert's army, so you won't have to worry too much about ambush. Being impressed into Theudebert's army might be your biggest problem, because his officers are always on the lookout for trained fighting men.' Priscus laughed with an edge of malice.

Gareth might be an innocent in many ways, but life in the villa had been a microcosm of the world. He recognised Priscus's salacious cynicism because he had seen it often enough in his youth. Men like Priscus were always for sale and they always thought they were more intelligent than anyone else around them.

'Thank you for your advice, Priscus. Your local knowledge will keep us safe during our journey into the north.' Germanus was always the soul of tact and his skills hadn't deserted him, although the man was far too oily and self-satisfied for the Frank's taste.

For his part, Priscus glowed with approval at Germanus's generous compliments. He never doubted that he was more worldly than most of his customers.

'And what news has arrived from the east?' Lorcan asked. 'Is Italy still in Justinian's hands? And does he still plan to advance into Gaul? We've heard rumours that he has big dreams and wishes to rebuild the collapsed Roman Empire in the west under his own rule. Another madman with huge plans!'

'Justinian will be the lord of all he surveys, another Alexander if he lives so long. The last ship from Ravenna brought news that our esteemed emperor has had a narrow escape from death. We also heard that Theudebert cursed God for permitting Justinian to live.'

'Was it an attempt at murder? An accident? Or an illness?' Germanus asked bluntly. His face expressed his concern, because Justinian was perfectly capable of gobbling up the west, and Germanus remained a good and loyal Frank.

'As a matter of fact, it was a rather nasty disease. Several other persons are rumoured to have contracted the same illness and died from it, so Justinian was lucky and we were unlucky.'

The three travellers absorbed the astonishing news.

The disease, which had since killed a number of citizens in Constantinople, was now being referred to as Justinian's Disease. Sadly, the physicians had no idea how the illness was transmitted from person to person, nor why some people lived when so many more died.

'So a new disease has appeared in the Eastern Empire,' Germanus mused. 'With luck, Justinian will stay put until he's fully recovered, while we'll have passed into the north by the time he organises his armies. We should be in Jutland by winter, or else we'll freeze to death on the road. Thank you, Priscus, for you've been an enormous help. We'll show our appreciation before we leave!'

Gareth was pleased to receive the innkeeper's information, but Priscus sensed the young man's antagonism from across the table. At the same time, Gareth realised that Lorcan's nostrils were flaring as if Priscus reeked of a sickening smell. It's not just me, the young man thought, for Lorcan dislikes the innkeeper as much as I do! He knows the bastard would sell us out for a few copper coins – so why is he so pleasant towards him?

The conversation continued in desultory fashion while Priscus slaked his thirst at the travellers' expense. Deft in his questioning, he learned a great deal about the three mismatched men who had come to his establishment from across the Channel, but less than he thought he had, because Germanus and Lorcan were men of vast experience, while any loose words from Gareth had been silenced by his dislike for the innkeeper.

Once Priscus had left them to finish the remaining beer, Gareth attacked Lorcan. 'You can't stand that string-bean turd, so why were you so respectful to him?'

'You're such a child sometimes, Gareth, and you're in need of a loin-cloth. Of course I can't stand the shite! He'd rob us blind in a moment, if we were worth any coin to him.'

Lorcan examined Gareth carefully and incredulously, as did Germanus.

'Did you really think that Priscus fooled us, laddie?' Germanus asked. 'He's a crooked snake, but his beer's good and the information we gleamed from him is excellent.'

'And just because Germanus and Priscus are both Franks doesn't mean that Germanus would sell us out, boyo. You're not a particularly wise young man, and you must learn to think before you open your mouth.'

Gareth forced himself to remain silent so he could consider Lorcan's words. Perhaps dissembling was acceptable if men used it to discover what they needed to know?

'Word of these men will be worth a gold piece or two from the king's officers,' Priscus told his downtrodden woman later in the evening as she hurried to place a hot brick wrapped in lamb's wool at the foot of his sumptuous bed. The guests might sleep on flaxen pallets of clean straw, but Priscus enjoyed the comfort of a large and ornate Roman divan piled high with wool-stuffed cushions.

She nodded in her master's direction to indicate she was listening alertly to his every word.

'Yes, Delia. I think our king will pay for these skilled warriors, now that he's so eager to put down any insurrection in Thuringia. He is a man bedevilled by two women, so he looks to a war beyond his borders as a means of bringing some peace into his life.' Priscus snickered with amusement at the cleverness of his own joke. 'I have a small task for the horse master tomorrow, woman, so make sure he's here first thing in the morning. Now, get into bed and warm my blanket – and try to make your face more cheerful.'

Delia eased herself under the covers obediently and star-fished her body to cover as large an area as possible. If she thought of anything other than the need for her own sleep, her concern dwelled on an ulcer that she had found under her tongue. Anything her master had said to her was washed away by Delia's weariness and her desire to stay, snug and warm, in this thoroughly comfortable bed.

All too soon, her master kicked her out of his bed and left her to lie on the flat pallet on the floor. She fell asleep to the chorus of snores that resonated from Priscus's aquiline nose.

The three travellers spent three days in Gesoriacum. Gareth slept for much of that time. In the many weeks that had elapsed since Arthur had entered captivity, Gareth had spent the bulk of his days travelling constantly to deliver bad news, robbed of rest so regularly that he

219

scarcely realised how exhausted he'd become. So, for now, he was happy to catch up on his long-lost sleep, waking only to eat and drink or to discuss possible changes of plans with Lorcan and Germanus. Fortunately Priscus was otherwise occupied, so the travellers rarely saw him.

On the morning of the fourth day, Gareth arose before sunrise. He'd been tossing and turning restlessly for some hours. As quietly as possible, he rose and struggled into his trews in the thick darkness.

His companions were deeply asleep and Lorcan's steady buzz of snoring suggested that he had enjoyed a little too much beer or mead during the preceding night. A dark mound close to the door revealed Germanus who, although he was fast asleep, had positioned himself so that any interloper would fall over his sleeping body. As Gareth pulled on his boots, he realised that his movements could wake his companions. Holding his breath, he crept towards a shuttered window. Then, with extreme care and praying that the catches of the shutters had been recently oiled, he pushed them open and allowed the fresh early-morning breeze to enter the small room.

A barn owl shrieked shrilly in the darkness and Gareth almost cursed aloud from fright. Beating wings and a tiny cry told Gareth that something small had perished, impaled on cruel, curved claws, and now the large bird was tearing its prey to pieces.

Death is a part of life, Gareth mused. Young men died before their time; other hale young men and women were killed because of the greed of kings or nobles; chance brought accident or illness to knock at the doors of both adults and children, rich and poor, while some infants never even took their first breath. Even the most gifted philosophers were unable to explain why some good people were taken, while some less worthy souls prospered into old age.

Gareth looked out into the night and saw a line of white fire along the hills to the east.

'The sun is rising to announce the day of our departure. Oh, God, please let everything go well.'

The young man had seen that Gesoriacum was an ugly town by day, and the docks were even more grimy and dilapidated than the residential areas. But now the parts of town that lay on the higher ground were invested with an otherworldly beauty as the sun sent out tendrils of light that moved upward through thick cloud or mist to reveal low towers, the grace of ruined temples and the edges of houses that clung to the high ground like limpets.

As the first strong light reached the window, Lorcan opened one eye and stirred on his straw pallet, but Gareth remained transfixed by the changing landscape revealed by the emerging dawn.

As he stretched carefully, Lorcan felt a twinge of pity for the boy who was sitting so still and so serene at the window. The boy's hair became a nimbus of intense and blazing fire in the chiaroscuro light. While most of his face was hidden by darkness, his profile was thrown into sharp focus; Lorcan was amazed at the delicacy and cleanliness of line that dominated the boy's features. As Lorcan knew to his cost, such beauty was dangerous.

Gareth had a sad face, far too old for a lad who wasn't yet twenty, but the slight furrowing of the boy's brow seemed to symbolise his emerging development of self. For the first time, Gareth was rejecting the thinking of his father and, in the process, was casting off the unnatural burdens laid on him so unfairly.

Lorcan remembered his time in Rome and a fresco he had seen, painted by an anonymous genius. On one side of the painting, angels with great, flaming swords rose triumphant to the feet of God while black-clad, armoured angels fell towards a desolate plain on the other side. One angel in particular had caught Lorcan's attention, a beautiful creature with such a fair face that his heart was touched by such outward loveliness.

But Lorcan's heart had been torn by the expression on that distant, inhuman face. Such loss and such sorrow could only be felt when a creature of might was separated forever from the love of God.

So Lorcan looked at the profile of Gareth and saw the ruined angel anew, while he began to pray for the boy in silence and in true repentance.

At that moment, a sound must have reached Gareth and he turned away from his reverie at the window.

'How goes the day?' Lorcan asked, after clearing his throat to cover his lapse and warn Gareth that another soul was awake and watchful.

'Have you ever noticed how darkness creates beauty where none usually exists? I've seen so many dawns since this quest began, and I'm beginning to view them differently now to the way I saw the dawns of Aquae Sulis. This place is still a shithole, but even an ugly and vile place like Gesoriacum can have its moments of loveliness for us to enjoy. The trick is to avoid being seduced by beauty at the expense of reality.'

'It seems there might be a poet under all that hair, boyo,' Lorcan replied as a lump began to form in his throat. He had last wept when his wife was killed, so until now he had believed he had used all the tears that were allotted to his body.

The boy is growing up at last, Lorcan thought, but the realisation came with a pang of regret. He has so little to sustain him that I can admire his determination even while he infuriates me with his single-mindedness. He'll become a fine man once he learns to bend a little with the ebb and flow of life.

Then Germanus woke with a rush, thrust into wakefulness by a half-remembered night horror. He scratched vaguely at an insect bite on his left arm and cursed when he moved suddenly and felt the sharp stab of a headache on the side of his head.

Lorcan felt the pangs of an overfull bladder and stumbled off to find the latrines, while Germanus slowly grumbled his way into his clothing. From his perch beside the window, Gareth felt the day continue to stir and waken.

The three travellers had made their farewells to Priscus before full light. They had packed their saddle bags, eaten a hearty breakfast served by Priscus's nervous woman, paid for their room and then ridden off into a new day where anything seemed possible.

The roadway that the three men travelled was broad and flat, and had obviously been constructed by Roman engineers at the height of the empire. Despite the damage caused by a century of neglect, heavy carts and the pillaging of stone trim, the travellers found themselves well into the countryside before they took their noontime meal.

Farms carved the landscape into a patchwork of agriculture. Like scraps of precious cloth that had been stitched together by a provident housewife, much of the productive land seemed to be green with young cabbages or the fronds of carrots. Still more fields were golden with growing pasture where cows grazed in the new spring grasses, while sheep nibbled delicately at juicy thistles on the sloping ground behind the low walls of fieldstone.

Gareth felt his heart lift at this bucolic landscape, one which he understood and loved.

'You look almost happy, boy!' Germanus grumbled. His thudding headache had refused to budge, even after he had eaten a full meal to break his night fast and had placed several wet, cooling cloths on his brow. Like most men who enjoy rude good health, he was impatient and bad tempered when he was unwell. Now, slumped low in the saddle, he was still sufficiently familiar with these lands to advance the small group in the direction they needed to follow.

'I put no trust in kings!' he declared. 'It has been my experience that they'll *even* impress young boys and toothless old men into their armies if they need the manpower. Give an old man a pike, sharp or not, and the killing of him takes time and eliminates the need for one more able-bodied warrior on the defensive line. Of course, the untrained men will be killed because they have no martial skills. So ordinary folk, and even the most valued warriors, exist as fodder to fill the battle lines of the ruler's armies. I know that Master Bedwyr is different to most rulers but, then again, Bedwyr isn't a true king.'

Lorcan felt concern for the man whom he had known so well for more than a decade.

'I'm worried about your health, Germanus, regardless of these untrustworthy kings who seem to be causing you so many bad dreams and an even worse bad temper,' Lorcan said softly to his friend. 'Your skin is pale and clammy, so you'll need to rest before we go much further.'

'We'll rest once we've passed through Reims,' Germanus snapped back. 'There are at least three rivers to cross between us and Reims and, if my memory serves me rightly, they run strong and deep. The hills where the tributaries rise will slow us down a little, but the Romans built good roads and the local kings have kept them in good repair. I can't remember whether they're bridged or not.'

Germanus might have been in some pain, but his mind was still working efficiently. He managed to grit his teeth and drive his large horse onward. Lorcan pushed away his reservations and followed in the big Frank's wake, while Gareth scanned the view ahead to assess the line of distant hills which must be crossed before they could reach the ancient city.

Uncharacteristically, Germanus barely ate during the evening that followed, and his two worried companions began to eye him with genuine concern. Lorcan examined his friend closely and realised that Germanus's forehead was hot and the man was sweating profusely within his armour.

'You'll find some rags from an old shirt in my saddle bags, Gareth. Can you fetch them for me? I'll also need fresh water from the stream so we can cool our friend's body.'

As Gareth moved off with alacrity to obey Lorcan's instructions, he felt a few scattered raindrops fall through the large alder tree which was providing shelter for the weary travellers. More raindrops, fat and heavy, began to fall on his forearm and he shook his head with concern as he returned with the rags.

'We need to find some shelter for Germanus. The sky is even darker than usual and no stars are visible. I can smell heavy rain coming, which will make him worse, given the severity of his temperature.'

Lorcan nodded absently as he soaked the rags, and then helped Germanus out of his mailed shirt. Gareth stowed the vest away in his friend's pack, knowing that the Frank would fret if his precious armour was allowed to rust.

Concerned over the whole situation, Gareth went to find his hobbled horse. Once the stallion was saddled, he rode back into the clearing where Lorcan was bathing Germanus's head and shoulders beside the warmth of the fire.

'Where are you going, boy? I need your help to undress this big lump. He's far too heavy for me to do it myself.'

'I can undress myself,' Germanus retorted tetchily, but fell back on his folded saddle blanket when he tried to sit upright. He panted a little from the pain, and then closed his eyes against a stab of agony that passed through his temples.

'See!' Lorcan hissed at Gareth. The priest's face was flushed with worry and exertion. Gareth patted his shoulder in sympathy.

'I thought I saw some cultivation from the top of the hill when we first decided to set up camp under this copse. If there's a farm yonder, I'll try to locate a barn or some kind of cover where we can care for Germanus. It could rain for a week or more at this time of the year, and a man of Germanus's age would have difficulty surviving seven days of illness if he's wet and unprotected. The local peasants might be frightened of us, but one of the farmers might accept payment for shelter and some of our basic needs.'

'But you don't know the terrain,' Lorcan grumbled.

'Why do you think I'm so weak that I'll die from a little rain?' Germanus added shakily from his makeshift bed.

Gareth waved away their arguments and kneed his horse into movement. The sounds of its hooves were quickly lost in the thick darkness.

When Gareth returned about two hours later, Lorcan was attempting to feed his large friend. The priest looked up as Gareth dismounted and tied his reins to a nearby bush. His face was strained and pale in the firelight.

'I found a farm about a mile away. The old couple who live there can't do much to keep their acres cultivated. We couldn't really understand each other, but I gathered that their four sons have been taken from them by officers from Theudebert's army. They are very angry at their king, but they'll allow us to use their barn if we're prepared to pay for the privilege. Rain is falling heavily down the road and it'll be here quickly, so we must hurry or we'll be caught in the open.'

Lorcan was naturally suspicious. 'Are they likely to rob us when we're asleep? Are you sure their kin weren't in hiding and a son or two won't reappear as soon as we lower our guard?'

'No! I'm not sure! But the old man seemed genuine and he was keen to have my assistance with their planting. I had to promise to help with his spring ploughing, or anything else that needs doing. Anyway, what choice do we have? Germanus needs to be kept warm and dry, and he needs to sleep in a comfortable bed if one can be found for him.'

Lorcan's gaze moved from Gareth's irritated face to the taut, pain-filled countenance of his friend. He was certain that Germanus was suffering from something far more dangerous than a headache. The heat rising from Germanus's skin was unusual and, despite his vast experience, Lorcan was totally unfamiliar with this type of illness.

'Very well then, young man. We'll go to your farmhouse and its barn, but you'll be doing the planting for the farmer, not me! I have to look after Germanus.'

Lorcan rose to his feet, creaking a little at the knees, and threw the last of the water onto the fire which hissed like a broken snake as the flames died in a cloud of steam.

'Lead the way, lad,' he croaked to Gareth. 'And if your plan goes wrong, I'll be the first to remind you that Germanus will pay for your mistake.'

Without further argument, Lorcan packed away their few possessions and Germanus's remaining armour while Gareth prepared the horses and pack animals for the short journey and loaded the important bags of food and trade goods purchased in Gesoriacum. Within ten minutes, Germanus was lying over the neck of his horse and they were ready to move. Gareth took the reins of both horses, the pack animal and Germanus's spare horse. With Lorcan bringing up the rear on his mule and holding the reins of the remaining pack animals, the small party picked their way through the darkness to rejoin the Roman road.

How can everything go so wrong so quickly? Gareth thought. Germanus only had a headache when we set out from Gesoriacum. He's really ill now, and we're miles from a healer or even a herb woman. Fortuna has turned her face away from us!

In a silence broken only by the noise of their stolid, patient beasts and the stillness of a night that was hovering on the brink of a storm, Lorcan found himself praying wordlessly to God. Germanus had pushed himself to reach the shelter of the alder tree, but then his pain had doubled once he was able to rest. Spent now, he was as weak as a child. Lorcan knew that only God could provide salvation and his heart quailed at the chance that the Almighty might find his prayers to be unworthy. After all, he had fought, whored and blasphemed his way around Gaul for years with only scant respect for his Maker.

'I swear I'll do your works until I die if you decide to save my friend,' Lorcan swore to God as lightning began to split the sky with the beginnings of an unseasonal storm. 'I swear it, Lord, and Lorcan always keeps his word.'

Thunder rumbled and the horses neighed in fright and skittered in the gravel surface of the roadway. Germanus was almost unseated, but Gareth stopped his fall with a steadying hand.

Another flash of lightning lit the landscape with an unearthly, incandescent blue. Only in the return to darkness after the flash were the travellers able to see their destination, a light that glowed in the blackness through the curtains of rain. With shoulders bowed by the weight of the sudden deluge, the small party plodded towards their goal and its promise of dry beds, warm hay and, hopefully, the warmth and comfort of a fire.

Around them, the pyrotechnics of the storm continued. It was almost as if God was venting his anger on foolish humans who only called on Him when their needs were greatest.

THE VILLAGE OF WORLD'S END

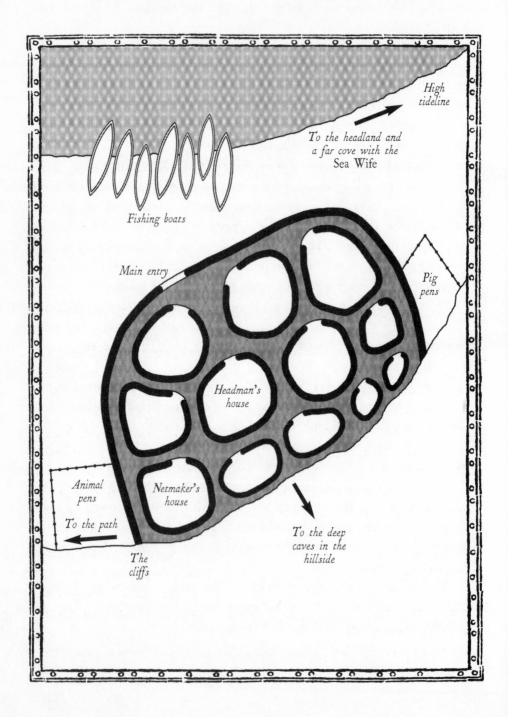

High
tideline

To the headland and
a far cove with the
Sea Wife

Fishing boats

Main entry

Pig
pens

Headman's
house

Animal
pens

Netmaker's
house

To the path

To the deep
caves in the
hillside

The
cliffs

CHAPTER XIV

REFUGE AT WORLD'S END

Justice is the constant and perpetual wish to render to everyone
his due.

Justinian, *Institutes*

Arthur could have sworn they had run for hours, but Stormbringer still
urged his men to greater effort. No ropes constrained the prisoners,
only the knowledge that they must be far away by the fall of darkness,
the time when Hrolf Kraki intended to unleash the warriors.

'Why didn't we take *Loki's Eye*?' Eamonn panted, as he helped Blaise
to her feet. She had tripped over her long skirts and fallen hard onto
the muddy roadway.

'You heard what Stormbringer said,' Arthur snapped as he ripped
away the entire skirt from Blaise's offending dress. With a few appropriate knots, Blaise was soon standing with her legs half-bared, and her
useless skirts had been turned into a facsimile of the tightly laced trews
worn by men. 'You'll be able to run faster now.'

Before he could give his sister the same freedom of movement,
Stormbringer materialised from behind them and began to rip at
Maeve's skirts.

'Yes, we could have taken *Loki's Eye*, but the king was expecting
that we'd try to flee in that direction.' Stormbringer grinned wryly and

his handsome face twisted with regret for the loss of his vessel. 'I knew the ship would be well guarded because that's what I'd normally do. But it's just a ship, carved from wood, and fitted with a woollen sail. It has no soul and I still have access to other vessels. We must reach the sea and the fishing village that calls itself World's End. My uncle's ship, *Sea Wife*, has been beached there for near to twenty years. My uncle went to the fires of the gods when I was still a boy, so I don't even know if she's seaworthy. I can only pray that the Lord, Jesus, is with us.'

He rose to his feet and Maeve discovered that Stormbringer had created comfortable leggings from the rags of her skirt. She bent and flexed her legs experimentally, then her face split into a wide, delighted smile. Watching her, Arthur recalled a private conversation the girls had enjoyed as they travelled along the north road that led into the Otadini lands. They had listed all the traditional constraints of their lives caused by their sex. Skirts had been high on their list of rabid hatreds, because they restricted movement and tied them to the home. At the time, Arthur had resented their desires to be free and to break away from women's accepted roles. Now? He wasn't so certain of anything.

'Now you know what it's like to dress like a man – but we've rested long enough. It's time to run for our lives!' Stormbringer's long legs led the way, while his warriors and the captives followed in his wake.

The yards lengthened into miles until Arthur's shoulders ached from the contusions incurred in the battle in the forecourt of Heorot. After the bout, there had been no time to bind his injuries or to bathe and soak away the weariness of abused muscles or the pain from bruises.

The miles unravelled under the desperate beat of running feet. And Stormbringer was still driving them on to further and greater efforts.

Run! Run! Run for your life!

The situation in Hrolf Kraki's hall had deteriorated rapidly after Maeve had blamed the king's lack of foresight for the invasion of Skania in the north-east. The king's carelessness and distraction was clearly a cause of unrest in the south of the Cimbric Peninsula, a region that had once been under the rule of the Angles. Enemy tribes waited for such carelessness, so the whole frontier, to the south and to the east, teetered on the brink of open warfare. In his heart, Hrolf Kraki knew how much trouble he had caused, so he was incensed that lips other than his own had commented on his many omissions.

Nor would he willingly admit that Aednetta had reminded him of the oracle's curse. Angry at his theft of Geat gold, Woden had withdrawn his favour and, if the Crow King went to war again, the gods had promised that they would surely crush him. In the middle of the night, Aednetta whispered to him of how Stormbringer desired Hrolf Kraki's destruction by arranging for war to be declared on the Geat king.

'Let Skania take care of itself. Why should you always have to rescue incompetent warriors from their own ineptitude?' Trapped between her warm thighs, he had agreed with her appraisal. But the arrival of the courier had made the king appear cowardly, so his rage had festered and grown.

For her part, Aednetta was very angry with Maeve and her accusations. Any chance to punish the red-haired bitch had been lost with the arrival of the wounded courier, but Aednetta had other fish to fry. Maeve had not kept her silence!

'I tell you, King of the Dene, that your woman will bring the people of these lands to ruin. Disease will come, and it will be potent and killing. Your strength will leach away like snow in the hot sunshine, while many years will come and go before the Dene are strong enough to extend their borders. Near to half the Dene will die, but you will still remain lost in the seduction of her arms while your lands and your people perish around you. Believe me or not, as you wish! I care for nothing that is yours to give, but your people will curse your name if you don't cast the witch-woman off.'

'Cast her off? You claim to see into the future, so try to read your own destiny.'

'There's no need to be a soothsayer to read my fate, my lord. You intend to kill me! And my brother and any other Briton who comes within your grasp. Even now, Aednetta has filled your mind with poison so that the death of that poor man who brought news from Skania has not deflected you from your immediate purpose. You are wasting time by dithering and taking your petty revenge out on us. You have forgotten how to be a king, my lord!'

Hrolf Kraki rose to his feet in a deadly rage. His large head turned and flexed like that of an enraged bull that intended to impale its enemy upon its spreading horns. His eyes were reddened and burning in the afternoon light, while his hands opened and closed into fists, as if relishing the thought of snapping the girl's neck with his thumbs.

'I order that you and yours will henceforth be outcast! You, Stormbringer, brought these creatures to Heorot, so you and yours will also pay for their impertinence. You and all thirty members of your crew must run for your lives! Your family won't become outcasts, but they will be taken as slaves and will await my pleasure, every one of them. You have until nightfall to quit this place, by which time my guards will be free to pursue you. They will not delay for bad weather or to rest until such time as I give them permission to stop, and they will be my dogs until their deaths – every one of them. When they catch you, your lives are forfeit and you will be killed without mercy.'

'Lord,' Stormbringer tried to interrupt. 'You're wasting time while Skania—'

The king's face was twisted with excess emotion. 'Be silent, traitor. I have given my orders, so Skania can wait!'

'Lord—' Stormbringer appealed again, but Hrolf Kraki ignored him.

'If you should escape from my justice, then you should consider how best to save yourselves. I suggest you run far and fast, for nothing else will succeed.'

'Lord, your kingdom is under attack from traitors. Surely you need all the help you can get,' Stormbringer tried to protest once more. 'Hundreds of warriors would be prepared to follow my standard and join an attack on Skania if you permit me to act.'

Without a thought for his own safety, Arthur protested that Stormbringer could hardly be held accountable for the sins of the Britons.

But Hrolf Kraki was too incensed to listen to explanations or excuses. 'You're wasting time when you should be running! Meanwhile, I'll send fleet horsemen throughout the countryside to declare you and your men as outlaws, so you needn't think that your precious reputation will secure any assistance from the common folk. They'll be warned what will happen to anyone who gives succour to you or your warriors.'

On the outskirts of Heorot, Frodhi openly approached Stormbringer with a face that was bleak, angry and frustrated.

'I'll not say anything about my kinsman's decision or the part played by your captives in the development of this fiasco,' Frodhi said pointedly. 'Incidentally, I won a tidy sum of red gold on them both, so I feel I'm in a position to offer advice and assistance to you and your men – and to your captives.'

He pressed a purse into Stormbringer's hand. 'Don't bother to refuse, cuz, for there mightn't be anyone else who's prepared to help you. I must add that I'm prepared to use my winnings, and more, to hire mercenaries who can relieve the situation in Skania if you manage to escape and you're prepared to lead an expedition into the lands under threat. For my part, I'll send ten fully manned ships to The Holding, and I'll spread the word about the peril that menaces our people. The Crow King might be too besotted with his whore to act, but there are many Dene warriors who are willing to stand and be counted.'

Stormbringer embraced Frodhi briefly and Arthur could tell, by the slump of the captain's shoulders, that he was deeply troubled by the apparent hopelessness of their position. His cousin patted Valdar's cheek affectionately once, and then again, just hard enough to leave a flush-mark.

'You're dwelling on defeat, Stormbringer. Don't be a fool, cuz, because if you make it to *Sea Wife*, there's every chance we can overcome the trials that lie before us. If you can take the place of the Crow King in the coming battles with the Gothlanders, I'd expect you to lead the Skanian people to victory. There's never been a Gothlander king born who could beat the Dene in battle.'

Arthur had no idea what The Holding was, although he vaguely recalled hearing that *Sea Wife* was a ship. Nor did he dare to ask any questions in this intensely private moment between the two kinsmen. As always, Frodhi was careful to guard his tongue and Arthur wondered at the number of years that the Dene nobleman had been forced to filter his language and control his every action for the sake of self-protection.

'The victory will be yours *if* I live to reach The Holding, and *if* I can raise a force that will relieve the Skanian lords. I swear to you that I won't forget the gamble you are taking by helping me, Frod, for anyone watching today could sell you out to Hrolf Kraki for a few coins.'

Frodhi laughed, but there was very little humour in his voice. Arthur wondered how he could have suspected such a brave man, even if the Dene lord did play so many games. But his inner voice continued its warnings by whispering in his head whenever Frodhi was close at hand.

He still took the opportunity to thank the Dene lord before he left them at a brisk trot.

Finally, with the sun beginning to descend through the sky towards the western horizon, Stormbringer realised the hopelessness of their position and gave the order that those who had been outlawed should run for their lives.

And so all thirty-one Dene warriors and their four captives ran.

The townsfolk of Heorot had heard the news of the king's justice with remarkable speed, so Stormbringer expected that they might be stoned or pelted with ordure as they fled from the town. But, to his surprise, women pressed wrapped food into the hands of his warriors and maidens looped chains of flowers around Stormbringer's neck. Nor were Arthur and Eamonn ignored. One wizened old woman pressed a curiously carved walrus tusk into Arthur's hand while Eamonn was given half a cheese wrapped in cabbage leaves. The crowd was mostly silent, but the mood was sullen and pregnant with anger, as if their king had betrayed them in some fundamental matter.

Almost to the last man, woman and child, they offered gifts and support in direct disobedience to Hrolf Kraki's edicts. These simple people knew that they could be executed or punished in various

234

unpleasant ways, but they still offered what they had to the Sae Dene's warriors in a time of need.

'Don't these people realise the risks they're taking?' Arthur asked Stormbringer, gasping slightly as he skidded on the slick cobbles.

Stormbringer laughed sardonically.

'How could the Crow King kill them all? Who would clean Heorot, pander to his needs, guard his hall and grow the food that is cooked for his table? The people know that if they all disobey, it is difficult for Hrolf Kraki's lackeys to single out individuals for punishment.'

Arthur nodded, but he thought long and hard about civil disobedience as the group of outlaws ran on into the sunset.

The fugitives had followed a path that ran parallel to the fjord. Then, as darkness and fog began to surround them like a thick blanket that muffled all sound, Stormbringer accepted the necessity to construct a torch out of driftwood, dried moss and the remains of Maeve's skirt. With a light of sorts to guide them, he continued to run ahead of the party with the makeshift torch held close to the ground so any pitfalls could be spotted before the fugitives fell and injured themselves.

Arthur worried that Hrolf Kraki's warriors could be in close pursuit and might see the bobbing light of the torch, but he also realised that Stormbringer had set a wicked pace, even by Dene standards. Perhaps Hrolf Kraki's warriors weren't even in the vicinity. At any rate, they needed to see if they were to run – and run they did, long into the night.

Against his will, Arthur considered the likely fate of Thorketil, the wounded giant who had been his opponent. His concerns also extended to Rufus, the warrior humbled by Eamonn. Stormbringer had taken both men under his protection, for what it was worth, but both men lacked the capacity to run, so citizens loyal to Stormbringer had agreed to take them to a safe house in Heorot where they could recuperate in relative safety until such time as horses could take them on the long journey to The Holding. Both men had sworn to rejoin Stormbringer's troop when they were healed, and were bound by their honour to keep their individual oaths, or to risk damnation.

Why are we taking untrustworthy men into our party? Arthur thought angrily. Rufus was a defeated man whose pride had been dragged in the mud. *What would he do to earn the Crow King's gratitude? He must be closely watched!*

'There are times when we have to gamble.' Arthur felt impelled to speak aloud to break the brain-numbing rhythm of running feet. 'Sometimes Fortuna curses us, only to bless us in the next instant. Dear God, let it be so on this occasion!'

Like his birth-father before him, Arthur saw no oddity or hypocrisy on those occasions when he invoked the good wishes of the Christian God and the pagan Fortuna in the same breath. He put no faith in Fortuna, but she was a useful parable for fate and all its inconsistencies. On the other hand, Arthur believed in the majesty of God; Lorcan had been a wise and knowledgeable spiritual adviser. Arthur's mother, Elayne, had been ardent in her faith, but she would never believe that her God could turn His face away from those tempted to follow false gods.

So Arthur could invoke both pagan and Christian faiths without any feelings of guilt or dread. As he loped along in a steady rhythm, the various philosophies of religion skittered through his head like disoriented frogs in search of pond water. Above these mental meanderings, his mother's voice remained a constant, leaving him so full of love and loss that he wanted to cry like a desperate child.

After several hours of traversing difficult terrain, Stormbringer halted the troop and seemed to scent the air like a hunting dog. Changing direction, he led the party down a wider path towards the south-east, although the Sae Dene slowed the pace to conserve their energy. The Britons had no choice but to follow where Stormbringer led them and to enjoy this opportunity to summon their reserves of strength.

One foot in front of the other!

If you fall, rise quickly and continue to run!

Even the powerful Dene warriors were beginning to flag from their exertions and the girls were staggering with weariness by the time

Stormbringer halted, spoke briefly to his second-in-command, then ordered the party to move off the pathway.

'We'll sleep here in the bracken for the rest of the night. There'll be no fires! Two sentries must be on watch at all times, and we'll draw straws for that duty. Eat what you have in your pouches, for there'll be no comforts on this night. Hrolf Kraki's dogs could be hot on our heels, so I only hope that they're less motivated to run as far and as fast as we've been travelling. Sleep now, for we need every man to be awake and at his best when the dawn arrives.'

Arthur gazed up at the moon. Its white face was extremely clear and odd shapes seemed to shade and pock its surface like old scars. He led Maeve and Blaise off the roadway and told them that they should seek shelter in the darkness of the trees where bracken grew lushly in deep shadows. Once they were cocooned in their cloaks, the dry ferns made comfortable nests.

The girls were too tired to protest and had to be forced to swallow the remnants of some black bread from the morning meal and the pungent cheese given to Eamonn by his elderly benefactor. Arthur even devoured the raw cabbage leaves that had wrapped the bread and cheese after his friends had refused to touch such bland fare. The Britons fell asleep, comforted by the fact that Stormbringer's warriors were nesting around them.

Later in the evening, the moon disappeared behind a thick bank of cloud and cold rain began to fall. The captives had no rest during the downpour but sleep came almost immediately once the rain had eased to a soft drizzle, and even the thick mud under their cloaks was no real impediment to the healing rest their bodies craved.

Then, roused by Stormbringer's large and horny hand shortly before dawn, Arthur actually enjoyed the first rays of sunlight that edged their way over the horizon.

'We must go, Arthur. If you've any food left, we'll eat on the run because we've remained here for as long as I dare. Rumours of our banishment will spread through the countryside and while many men dislike the ruler that Hrolf Kraki has become, some of the more remote farmers will be seduced by the promise of coin. My uncle's boat is still three days away so, by my reckoning, we must move as far and as fast as we can while we are under the protection of this half-light. We can rest later, or when we've been killed by Kraki's warriors!'

Several nearby warriors snickered; humour could be important when disaster loomed at them from behind every tree and in every farmhouse.

The Dene fugitives set off at a steady, mind-numbing pace that left a little energy for a fast burst of speed if such a desperate pace became necessary. The girls' feet developed blisters, and Arthur carefully wrapped the injuries with rags from their skirts to minimise the pain. Fortunately, Maeve's pouch held a small container of salve among her odds and ends, so the girls were once again able to don their shoes. They begged for permission to run barefoot, but Arthur was as obdurate as stone. He knew that bared feet would swell, split and eventually cripple them. Soft moss was used to pack any gaps in their shoes where it could cushion their wounds without contaminating the blisters.

Food supplies for the fugitives seemed to magically appear as they followed the path to their destination. The local populace ignored the danger of punishment by death for aiding the outlaws and contrived to leave dried fish or bread near barn doors, while new milk appeared in large earthenware jugs alongside baskets of fresh eggs. Never given openly, this food simply appeared from out of nowhere, mostly at times when the fugitives paused for a brief interlude of sleep. Even woollen blankets, admittedly much worn and unravelling at the edges, were found lying over fences at remote homesteads. The fugitives never saw a living soul, not even the Dene children who were always curious around strangers. Fed and nurtured by their countrymen, the fugitives could run on and on, regardless of bad weather or the roughness of the terrain. Arthur was amazed at how courageously the ordinary people could ignore the edicts of their king. The young prince said as much to Eamonn when they paused to sleep in the brief period between noon and late afternoon, for they had run during the night to hide from any pursuit on horseback.

Stormbringer had decided to flee through the coming night and the following day, now they were approaching their destination. Fortunately, the land here was flat.

'No one is openly disobeying Hrolf Kraki's edicts because the Dene set great store by individual and collective loyalty,' Stormbringer told Arthur during one of the short rest breaks. 'However, our king has used up much of the common folk's goodwill, especially since he's taken up with the White Witch, as the commoners call Aednetta.'

He paused.

'The Dene peasantry don't trust Aednetta because the king's latest decisions harm their interests. Their crops are heavily taxed, while their sons are taken to Heorot where they are required to carry out menial duties. Our people would willingly give these things to the king if he accorded them the thanks that their sacrifices warrant, but Hrolf Kraki has used his power arrogantly and has stretched their loyalty to the limit.'

Stormbringer's second-in-command, Sumarlioi, had listened to the conversation. With a sense of pride, he gave an additional reason for the Sae Dene's influence with the country folk.

'Stormbringer is a hero to these people, one who has always put the welfare of his people before his own comforts. Just like the local peasantry, Valdar Bjornsen is a farmer, even though the scale of his cultivations is much larger than their small acres. Wait till you see the size of The Holdings! In short, his people won't believe that Stormbringer has suddenly become a traitor, and certainly not on the word of a bitch like Aednetta Fridasdottar.'

Arthur smiled wryly and nodded in understanding.

Then Stormbringer set out once more and there was no breath left for talking.

'At least, this explanation is favoured by Stormbringer's lieutenant, who insists that the people already hate Aednetta like poison,' Eamonn added later in the day during another short rest break. 'According to one of the farm workers he spoke with when we were passing through the last village, Maeve's speech about impending sickness and the diminution of Dene power has been repeated constantly, and several women purported to have the Sight have cast the runes and they agree with her.'

By the fourth day, all the fugitives were weary and desperate for rest. Maeve's blisters had become infected, but she bit her lips and continued to run, although Arthur could see a spoor of blood left on the earth when she moved. Stormbringer noted this proof of her fortitude as well, and treated the girl with the same respect he usually gave to men. The Sae Dene ensured that her wounds were cleansed and well wrapped, although the treatment cost valuable time.

But she still refused to be carried.

The day was well advanced when the path suddenly turned towards the sea. From cliffs that beetled over stony beaches too wild to allow ships to beach, the fugitives could see the grey-blue sea and a steady line of breakers far below them. Arthur could also spot charcoal smudges on the far horizon that suggested islands in the far distance.

Arthur could tell that Maeve was at the point of collapse. But, before he could lift his sister up and carry her, Stormbringer appeared from behind and hoisted the girl bodily onto one of his shoulders. As he hefted the girl like thistledown, he barely broke his stride.

'We're only one hour from my uncle's village now,' he told Arthur. *Sea Wife* awaits us, although I doubt that she's seaworthy. It's just a little further, my friends, so we'll sleep under a roof tonight. If God is willing, we'll have a fire and good food to keep us warm.'

The Dene warriors managed to raise a ragged cheer, but most were so exhausted they could scarcely manage any enthusiasm. The men were no longer running – they were stumbling. While all the able-bodied men had been encumbered with shields, swords and armour, the girls had been the truly heroic members of the party and every man present knew how they had struggled to keep up with the main party. Obstinately, they had called upon their youth and willpower to keep going. And now, although she was slung over Stormbringer's shoulders in a most undignified position, Maeve had only ceased running when her feet had finally betrayed her. The warriors even approved of Maeve's predictions and her assertions that had brought them to this pass; she had simply voiced the words that so many of them had thought, but feared to say aloud.

Night was fully advanced by the time that Stormbringer saw lights on the foreshore below a particularly high and precipitous bluff. After sending several warriors to search for the point where the path plunged down to the village, he set Maeve down on the coarse sea grass and rested on his heels to regain his breath.

'We've found the path, my lord,' a large warrior called from the lip of the cliff, while Arthur's heart sank to see a group of figures appear as indistinct shapes against the slightly lighter skyline. He dreaded the thought of negotiating such dizzying depths in the darkness.

The Briton limped slowly to the cliff edge where one of the warriors was hefting a torch that would make the narrow track visible. Maeve hobbled to his side to examine what was visible of the steep drop. Decisively, she started the painful descent before Arthur could stop her. Every step must have been excruciating, but her retreating back gave no indication of it. Wherever the path became particularly treacherous, Maeve had the presence of mind to turn around carefully so she could find handholds and footholds more easily.

'I won't allow anyone else to fall because they feel compelled to carry me down this cliff,' she announced between clenched teeth. 'Agility is all that matters on a path such as this, so I can manage if I have light to show the way.'

Other torches were lit from whatever materials came to hand along the cliff-top, revealing a path more suited to the passage of mountain goats than humans. The climbers picked their way gingerly as they searched for assistance from handholds of long, coarse grass or stunted bushes that survived precariously along this strip of earth between the land and the sea. Occasionally, a foothold or the roots of a windswept bramble would give way and men would stumble, but other hands always seemed to snake out of the darkness to steady the windmilling arms of their companions.

Eventually, the whole party made their way successfully to the foot of the cliff.

The village of World's End was set back into the cliff face along a section of rising shale shelves that kept it above the level of the highest tidal flows. The small houses were constructed of grey rock taken from the foreshore and the cliffs that protected the dozen houses that clung, limpet-like, to their flanks.

Unlike the houses of Heorot, these small one-room structures were round or oval and made entirely of un-mortared stone. They reminded Arthur of the most primitive and ancient villages that clung to the cliffs along the wild coasts adjacent to Tintagel in Britain.

Moisture glistened on the stone as if the sea had washed over this hamlet and scrubbed it clean. Smoke leaked from holes in roofs made from sod, while the tiny slit windows sent narrow shafts of flickering light to expose the rough face of the cliff. A barricade of rough stone topped with dry, thorny briars encircled the whole community. Arthur felt a spasm of nostalgia for his homeland that was far more acute than he thought possible.

When Stormbringer pushed open the rough gate of young tree logs that led into the maze of cottages, he motioned for the rest of his men to wait outside the compound. Lit by stray shafts of moonlight, Stormbringer was a huge and menacing shape of slick furs and an armoured head, a sight that any timid villager would have mistaken for a monster. He stayed beside the gate where any watchers could see him clearly before raising his makeshift torch so his face was visible.

'Don't be alarmed over our late arrival at your village, people of World's End! You know me! I am the nephew of your dead master, Erikk Sea-Searcher, and as you know, I am his heir. As a child, I visited your village with my uncle. I recall that I sat at the forge and watched Poul Snaggle-tooth turn iron cherry-red as he made fish hooks and spearheads. And I marvelled then at the skill of old Rhun as he made nets in the sunshine.'

A harsh and untrusting voice rang out. 'I remember Valdar Bjornsen well, but any man can call himself anything he chooses if he's surrounded by armed men in the darkness. How are we to know that you are the Stormbringer? You can say whatever you want, with impunity.'

Arthur could tell from Stormbringer's lowered head that he was thinking quickly. Then, putting down his torch, Stormbringer ripped off his mailed shirt and his jerkin to expose a section of his broad, muscular side, almost under his arm. A massive scar, puckered and thick like rope, was exposed where Stormbringer had obviously been badly burned many years earlier.

'Do you remember the fire, Poul? I was ten and a coal fell from the forge unnoticed. The straw caught alight and I foolishly tried to put it out. But I was a clumsy boy who dreamed of heroism and great battles, not old enough to be wary of dangers that lay in my path. I had grown too tall and too fast, so I slipped when I threw a bucket of water over the blaze. I fell onto a bucket of coals which burned through my shirt. One of the embers became caught inside my leather jerkin and continued to burn like a finger of fire. I remember that you pulled off my tunic and smeared my burns with pig fat. I can still recall the pain of those wounds.'

'Aye,' another older voice answered. 'I also remember that burn. It tracked across the boy's side as if the trail of a fiery snail had burned into the boy's flesh. I welcome you, Valdar Bjornsen, for no one could counterfeit that scar.'

The doors to the nearest houses were swiftly unbarred and half a dozen men stepped out, still holding hoes, harpoons and the knives that were normally used to skin and gut fish. Arthur saw another man exit the narrow alley between his house and the protective wall, clutching a short bow with an arrow nocked into position. This village would be far from helpless in the event of an attack by a marauding force.

A short, elderly man with distinguished features came forward from the press of onlookers. He was wrapped in sleeping furs, but he carried an air of authority.

'What brings you to World's End, Stormbringer? A man of your influence and reputation has no need to visit a small community of no particular value such as ours. And why do you come with a whole troop of warriors at your back? Did you fear attack from this village?'

'I'm declared outlaw by our king! Hrolf Kraki calls me traitor because I argued that his dependence on his witch-woman is dangerous to our people. He has decreed that anyone who helps me is also declared outlaw, so you may turn me away and no one will blame you. I'd be shamed forever if harm were to come to this village because of me and mine.'

Stormbringer's honesty was written clearly on his shining face, although more than one person in the village wondered at the true story that lay behind his banishment. However, these villagers were bound to Stormbringer's family forever. His uncle had protected the small hamlet all his life because it possessed a useful cove for the repair of his ships. Likewise, Stormbringer felt he owed a debt to every person who dwelled within its stony walls. Even if they had denied him shelter, his allegiance to them would never change because, as his vassals, the villagers were his responsibility.

'Come into our house, Valdar, master of this village. We don't fear Hrolf Kraki, or the power of mere mortals. They cannot stop the waves or still the storms. We have our own wise woman, and the Serpent protects us. I, Sigurd, as headman of this village, will give you a roof over your heads. What we have is yours, as little as it is.'

Sigurd's dignity raised a lump in Arthur's throat, for so had Bedwyr offered succour to those dispossessed refugees who came to his home in Arden.

Hoisting Maeve up into his arms, he limped forward into the light.

'You bring strangers to our door, Stormbringer. Who are these outlanders?'

The elder spoke so reasonably that Arthur was comforted by his even questioning, even though the elder was wary of the young man's alien appearance.

To enhance the captives' prestige, Stormbringer introduced the four Britons by giving them their full titles and explaining how they came to be in the lands of the Dene. Once the captain had finished, Arthur inclined his head to all the villagers with a courtesy that had been ingrained in him at his mother's knee.

'Master Stormbringer failed to tell you that we four were responsible for bringing the wrath of the king down on your master's head. Eamonn pen Bors and I, with the strength of our bodies, proved that we had the right to stand in Heorot as free men, regardless of the spite of Hrolf Kraki and Aednetta Fridasdottar. One of the king's warriors, Rufus Olaffsen, was selected by Hrolf Kraki to uphold the honour of the king's court in a battle to the death with Eamonn. Rufus was fairly beaten by my friend and, despite the loyalty and courage he had shown during the contest, the king's champion was foully cast out by the king.'

Arthur gazed around at the absorbed faces of the listeners. 'My sister, Maeve, bravely informed the king that his dependence on his witchwoman would bring disease and disaster to the Dene people. The accuracy of her prophecy became ominous when a wounded courier arrived with advice that the king had been betrayed by traitors in Skania who had overrun his villages in the province. Before he died, the courier revealed that his subjects who inhabit Skania are in grave peril from the king of Gothland. They begged for help from the Crow King, but Hrolf Kraki wouldn't be moved.

'No blame can be attached to Stormbringer for the events that have brought him to this pass, for the ultimate responsibility for his banishment is mine. We are strangers to him, but I now owe Stormbringer for four lives. This is a blood debt which I, Arthur ap Artor, have sworn to repay. Should you take us in, I vow that the people of World's End will also become my responsibility and I will do everything in my power to keep you safe.'

'That's fairly said, young master! So you'll be the one they call the Last Dragon? You have the size and the bearing for it, but only time can tell if the goddess intends to favour you. You and yours may come into our village now and be welcome.'

Willing hands took Maeve from Arthur's arms and she was borne away by a cluster of women. Feeling lost and without purpose, Arthur stood loosely, but he was comforted by the Dragon Knife and the sword that hung heavily from his belt. After months of uncertainty, there was a degree of comfort in their weight, as if a part of his self that had been amputated by force had been magically returned. He was a man again.

Friendly hands guided him through the maze of narrow alleyways that wound between the outer walls and the village huts. Arthur's brain registered that this village was perfect for defence with its protective outer walls encircling all the huts and the curving alleyways that linked them and made ambush easy. Any attacking force could be easily cut off in those dark, claustrophobic spaces where there was scarcely room to swing an axe or a sword.

A doorway seemed to materialise before him and a grizzled man with a long grey head of hair plaited into two forks ushered Arthur into his home. The small, circular room was only four sword lengths in diameter and was dominated by a central stone fire pit. Arthur's head struck a rolled, hanging net and other unseen items that were hooked to the raftered ceiling. The bearded man pointed to a pile of straw in one corner that was covered with a length of coarse wool smelling strongly of fish. Silvery scales from a cleaned catch of fish gleamed on the undyed wool.

But for all its poverty and bleakness, the room was warm, the straw was soft and the bowl of fish stew that was thrust into his hands was still hot and very tasty. Simple pleasures, Arthur decided, would be enough to meet his needs for the foreseeable future. He ate, thanked his host and then slept like a child, thoroughly warmed from exhaustion and his new-found peace.

World's End had no name other than what the villagers called it.

Perched on the very edge of the land mass, the village must have seemed to its inhabitants to be the last place on earth, for no farms clustered on the cliffs above it and there were no towns within easy reach. Only the return of young men who had left the village in search of work or a wife could provide new blood to sweeten and strengthen families that had existed, unchanged, for hundreds of years.

Awake before sunrise, the village menfolk slid their small hide-and-wood craft into the sea and rowed out beyond the breakers to cast their nets into deeper waters as soon as the sun crept over the horizon. Their womenfolk cured the cleaned fish in small smokehouses while the children scoured the shoreline for miles in search of shellfish, crabs and the seaweed that bulked out their diet. More young boys and youths were busy tending livestock in the hills above the village where cows and sheep were allowed to graze. Fattened pigs were kept in pens at the edge of the cliffs outside the palisades, cared for by the women. On the bleak pastures that lay above the cliffs, shepherds' huts that were little more than ramshackle kennels provided shelter for the older youths who cared for the village's livestock. When winter came, the animals were penned in deep caverns in the cliffs similar to other caves where surplus food, hay and the valuables of the community were stored behind the stockade. If attacking marauders should pierce the defences of the village and reached the deep caves, the breach hardly mattered, for all the villagers would be dead.

World's End was as self-sufficient as the populace could possibly make it. The small, dark people were quite unlike their Dene cousins, and surely harked back to earlier settlers who had tamed this inhospitable coastline long before the Jutes, Angles or the Goths appeared in these lands.

The villagers had lived in much the same way for a thousand years and were sustained by their isolation, their worship of Mother Sea and a respect for all things that lived in the whorl of their narrow world. To face the capriciousness of the ocean, day in and day out, required a courage so fundamental that it shrivelled the contest of man against man, or army against army, into mere exercises of avoidable self-preservation.

Beyond all logic, and with the full knowledge that their frail boats could capsize in high seas and tidal flows could sweep them far out into the ocean where their oars could never hope to bring them home, these fishermen went out to sea, again and again, with smiling faces and laughing eyes.

Arthur was learning to see into the inner hearts that people kept hidden behind cheerful facades. As Bedwyr had often explained to him, eyes rarely lied. The disproportionately large number of single women of all ages in this community, coupled with a deep sadness that rested behind their eyes, reflected the losses of their menfolk to a power stronger than any god – the power of the sea.

When Arthur was woken by his host, Ivar Rhunsen the Netmaker, he was informed that Stormbringer awaited him with the elders, and that many of the decisions to be made would affect him and the other captives. With alacrity, Arthur dressed, paying particular attention to his tangled hair and trying to slick his curly locks down into some semblance of neatness. He regretted that he had no time to wash his filthy feet, but his boots would cover the worst of the grime. Chewing on a twig and with his face glowing from the cold water that he'd used to sluice his hands and face, Arthur hurried in the wake of his elderly host who was amazingly nimble for a man in his fifties.

A council had been called in one of the largest of the village huts which housed strange stones marked with odd symbols that Stormbringer called runes. Woodcarvers had created the likenesses of boars, bears, wolves, great whales, fish, serpents and birds out of bleached driftwood and painted them naturalistically. Stormbringer told him these figures were totems of the ancient clans who had once lived in this village. Around the familiar fire pit, three elderly men and one old woman sat quietly as they waited for Arthur to be seated. In the shadows of the windowless hut, Arthur caught a glimpse of Maeve's white face, but she slipped back out of the light to join two other shrouded female figures.

'Please apologise to Eamonn pen Bors, for he hasn't been invited to attend this meeting,' Stormbringer began. 'Sigmund, the village headman, deems that you should speak for your fellow Britons. I speak for the Dene but, as you've probably divined, the people of World's End are an older tribe than my own people. We need their help if *Sea Wife* is to be made ready for the voyage we must undertake because we have no other way to leave these shores.'

Nodding his head in greeting, Arthur bowed respectfully to the three elderly men, one of whom was his host with the forked beard. Then he seated himself cross-legged on the sod floor.

As the three old men spoke together in a language that Arthur couldn't hope to decipher, the young man spent his time examining his hosts through careful eyes. These folk were even shorter than Eamonn, and were quite dark in hair and skin colouring, despite having paler eyes.

The old woman was a withered crone. Her empty breasts sagged within a cowl of sealskin while a necklace of bear claws, obviously very old, adorned her scrawny neck. But her eyes were youthful, snapping and bright brown like berries that had just come to ripeness. Under her cool gaze, Arthur felt exposed and vulnerable.

The meeting continued in the same tongue, while Stormbringer translated for Arthur's benefit whenever such a service was needed. Stormbringer was told that *Sea Wife* had been beached in a nearby cove. Out of respect for Erikk, their erstwhile master, the villagers had dragged his vessel onto wooden rollers and positioned it above the level of the highest tide. Then the enclosure used for repairs had been made watertight to stop the winter storms from dragging the hull back into the deep waters.

These precautions had meant that *Sea Wife* was in far better condition than Stormbringer would have expected. The villagers had known that such a valuable craft would be needed one day, so basic maintenance was carried out assiduously. They still cared for Erikk's craft as if she had been one of their own fishing boats, by keeping her timbers supple and checking her hull for sprung boards.

Arthur was forced to marvel at the combined efforts of the villagers as they strove to complete these non-essential tasks when the strain of their daily battle for survival was so critical.

Stormbringer was pleased to hear that little maintenance would be required to make the ship seaworthy for its new owner. Her sails would need repairs and she needed all her joints waterproofed with pitch and resin. Other smaller repairs would take very little time for skilled sailors, and these could be carried out at sea.

With luck, *Sea Wife* would be ready for a sea voyage within a week.

The council decided that Stormbringer's warriors would be put to work on *Sea Wife*. The villagers would assist where they could, and would provide food and shelter for the thirty-three men and two women who had arrived on their doorstep unannounced, despite this decision straining their resources to the very limit.

'We can provide some assistance to the village,' Arthur announced determinedly when he was given details of the village headmen's discussion with Stormbringer. 'I can't help with the ship's repairs, but I can hunt for whatever game exists along the foreshore. Eamonn knows small boats and fishing far better than I, and Blaise is expert at making traps to catch wild game. Meanwhile, Maeve can help me when she is able to walk freely.' He shook his head with regret. 'The only skill I have in abundance is the world of killing, war and death, but I will offer my services to Stormbringer and to the village in any way that they can use me.'

Stormbringer translated Arthur's words while the three older men listened with bland, unreadable faces. Then, after conversing quietly with the other two men, the headman nodded towards Arthur and spoke rapidly in his own tongue.

'Sigurd insists that there is no debt to repay, for the Mother requires that all travellers who are in need should be given food and shelter,' Stormbringer translated. 'But they will accept our offer of a gift in the Mother's name, although there is no debt as such.'

Arthur pondered the similarities between the simple people of all lands. The worship of gods such as the Celtic Mother of all things, Don, or *She who must not be named*, seemed a common one the world over; he sometimes wondered if Mary, the Holy Virgin, simply presented another face of the Mother to the world. Nervously, Arthur crossed himself, for blasphemy still remained a sin, even if thought on rather than uttered.

During the silence of the morning, the fire pit glowed with a small explosion as a collapsing log flamed into sudden life. The old wise woman rose and moved around to stand at Arthur's side. Without any words, another woman picked up the old woman's stool and placed it beside Arthur so the old woman could rest her old bones comfortably while she was speaking to him.

Her power was tangible, and her status was so high in the eyes of the villagers that she had no need to flaunt it

'Give me your hand, young man,' the old woman demanded in the Dene language.

Then she smiled for a brief moment, and Arthur could imagine the beauty she had once been under her drawn bones and wrinkled skin.

'I am Freya. I am the wise woman of this village, and I'm sorry if I appeared to be rude. The people in the village treat me far too well, perhaps because I have a little knowledge of herbs and I am able to read the signs of weather that are given to us by Mother Ocean. May I be permitted to read your hand?'

The force of her nature almost overrode the warning voice in his head, but Arthur complied without a second's thought. The old woman began to massage his open palm and his long callused fingers with her own still-strong fingers and thumbs.

'Aiee! Your life is written in the scars on your hands, and you have worked overlong at your craft.

'Both of your hands are so marked,' she said quietly as she examined his other hand, paying attention to all the old breaks from battle injuries and the years of weapons practice.

'Will you cast my stones for me?' she asked. 'I know you don't believe in them and have sworn your life to the Crucified One, but please permit me my curiosity. As you can see, they are only black pebbles that have been washed up by the sea. They have been marked with ancient runes and handed down to me by my mother and her mother before her. I swear they cannot hurt you.'

Arthur took the smooth, black stones in his right hand. The faces of the pebbles were deeply inscribed with linear patterns that had been scratched deeply into the stone. Even after the touch of hundreds of fingers, the lines had scarcely been blurred. Arthur closed his eyes, and then rolled the stones onto the sod floor.

He heard the indrawn hiss of breath from between the woman's missing teeth, but he refused to open his eyes. Once again the stones were returned to him – this time in his left hand.

'Cast again, young man,' the old woman murmured. 'What is, and what will be, are only shadows of possibilities, so you should have no fear.'

Arthur threw the pebbles onto the sod floor again, this time from his left hand. He could feel the silence that followed the gentle thuds when the stones hit the foot-hardened earth.

He opened his eyes and stared directly at the old woman seated next to him.

The headman and his two companions looked questioningly at Freya. And so, slowly at first, but becoming faster and more assured as she warmed to her task, Freya began to speak. Stormbringer refused to meet his eyes and the three old men were looking at him with unreadable expressions.

When she was finished, Arthur tried to capture the Sae Dene's attention, but the tall captain kept his eyes steadfastly on the members of the council. Then, when they were dismissed, and Stormbringer and Arthur rose to their feet, they bowed to the elderly headman and backed out of the central hut. By the time they had moved away from listening ears, Arthur's curiosity was unbearable.

'What was that all about, Stormbringer? What was the purpose of the stones?'

Stormbringer's golden eyebrows furrowed with a blend of irritation and consideration.

'Freya is a soothsayer who has won fame as one who has been touched by the gods. In the past, she regularly travelled throughout these islands but, twenty years ago, when her daughter was murdered during a Jute raid, she retreated from the world. Only a select few know that she came here to World's End, so I ask that you remain silent about her presence – to everyone!'

It was Arthur's turn to be confused and distracted.

'But why? Why must we be silent about her, even if she's genuine and can read the future like an opened scroll? And why does everyone bow and scrape around her?'

'Why can't you take me at my word? Must everything with you be explained and kicked to death until you're satisfied with the answers you've been given?' Stormbringer was cross but, given Arthur's stiff mouth and impatient walk, he wasn't surprised.

Then, as they reached the seafront where the Dene warriors waited with their borrowed tools, Stormbringer came to a decision.

'The wise woman spoke mostly of Maeve, who she called the Woman of Blood. She is certain that your sister will be the mother of a line of kings that will, in time, rival the Scylding line. She ordered me to protect the Woman of Blood, or death would come to us all. She told me that Maeve would save us from the Great Horror – whatever that is!'

Arthur absorbed this information. If he was honest, he was a little disappointed at not being at the centre of the wise woman's advice. However, he nodded and felt a frisson of pride in his sister.

'I'm pleased that my sister has been placed under your protection, my friend. I can't think of a safer place for her to be if I can't take her home to Mother Elayne and Father Bedwyr.'

He paused because he knew that his eyes were beginning to tear up from homesickness. 'They must be desolated after losing both their eldest son and their youngest daughter on the one day. I hope they are well, and I pray for it nightly.'

'I should also tell you, my friend, that Freya swears that you will eventually return to your own lands and you will become the King of Winter, whatever that means! To set your mind at ease, Freya is a daughter of Hrolf Kraki's grandfather. She is of noble birth and is much beloved, but she was forced to leave the court while Snaer ruled, if only to ensure her own survival. Later, after Snaer was dead, the runes told her that she must remain in World's End, for it is a place where she can perform a great service for her people.'

'Hmmmff! That would be a wise decision to make, given the murderous ways of those persons who rule in Heorot at the moment. Can you imagine that bitch, Aednetta, allowing a noblewoman with the Sight to remain in her ambit? Freya would have died of poison before the first month was out.'

Stormbringer clapped Arthur on the back. 'Freya asked if you might stay in the village with a detachment of my men under your command. The rest of us will be working on *Sea Wife* by day and by night, so I can only spare six men. We won't be far away if any trouble should arise, but *Sea Wife* must be our first priority.'

'Of course!' Arthur agreed with pleasure, for he would have promised anything to repay these villagers. 'We haven't seen the last of Hrolf Kraki or Aednetta Fridasdottar. I don't need to be a sorcerer to know that he's not about to let us go free.'

Stormbringer nodded. Long years of serving the Dene kings had taught him that men of power will never forgive someone who has offended them.

Within half an hour, the Dene warriors had been formed into two lines. Then, burdened with tools and packs of supplies, they trotted along the beach while Arthur, Eamonn, their two sisters and the six men who had been detailed to stay behind watched their departure with the full gamut of emotions written on their faces.

The warriors who remained were eager to be part of the renovation and seaworthiness of Erikk's old vessel, so to be ordered to guard the village, to fish, to hunt and to work like farmers was almost an insult. Arthur understood the waves of resentment that hummed out of them.

Bedwyr had been more than a father throughout Arthur's childhood and young manhood, providing a living example of how a man should live and act. In recent times, Stormbringer had also filled parts of that role in a totally alien world where Arthur had no rights and no power. The young Briton was even forced to accept his captor's charity in the provision of food and shelter. The man in Arthur resented his loss of autonomy, but under a thin veneer of resentment, he both liked and respected Stormbringer as his lifeline for a return to Britain and the felicity of his family.

Arthur's booted foot scraped at the pebbles, mud and sand of the beach in a circular motion. The pebbles were like Freya's rune-marked stones, so Arthur was sure that she, or an ancestor, had picked them up on a similar shore in days gone by before they had been turned into a conduit to whatever power guided the universe. Lost in thought, Arthur barely noticed that the last of the departing warriors were clambering over the rocks on the headland, while the main body of the troop had disappeared beyond the breakers. When he looked up again, the black beach with its tide-line of seaweed, the grey sky and the heaving, slate-coloured sea were all bare. A single gull swept over the waves, screaming raucously at a sighted prey that was too large for its claws.

'Well, Eamonn, it's time to do what we promised,' Arthur said to his friend as bracingly as he could before turning to Blaise. 'I'll need your clever fingers to make me some particularly vicious and effective rabbit traps. Meanwhile, we continue to eat the supplies provided by our benefactors, so it's time to work and repay some of the debt we owe to them. I won't be happy until we find stores for these kind people that will replace the food we've eaten.'

Without needing to speak further, the Britons climbed up the shelving beach towards the village and the path behind it that led up the cliff. The first day of Arthur's stewardship of World's End had begun.

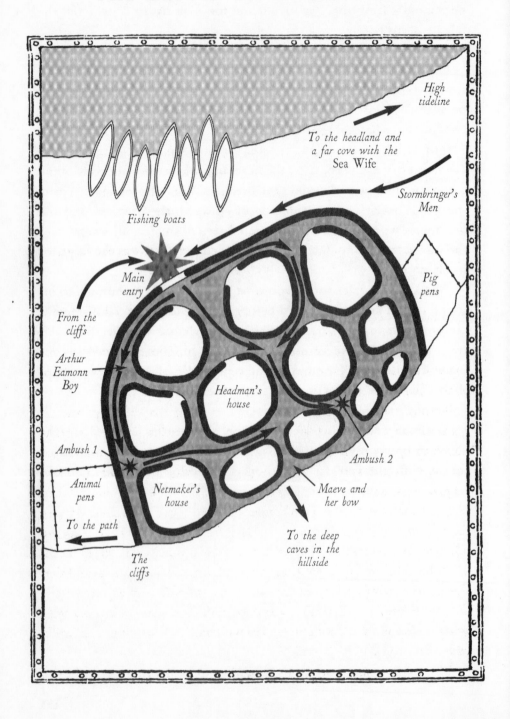

High
tideline

To the headland and
a far cove with the
Sea Wife

Stormbringer's
Men

Fishing boats

Main
entry

Pig
pens

From the
cliffs

Arthur
Eamonn
Boy

Headman's
house

Ambush 1

Ambush 2

Animal
pens

Netmaker's
house

Maeve and
her bow

To the path

To the deep
caves in the
hillside

The
cliffs

CHAPTER XV

BLOOD AND COURAGE

It is perfectly certain that the soul is immortal and imperishable, and our souls will actually exist in another world.

Socrates, recorded by Plato in *Phaedo*

Arthur spent several idyllic days out on the cliffs snaring rabbits with Blaise's traps, while Eamonn filled his days with the men of the village as they fished in the bay.

Arthur saw his skin begin to brown in the spring sunshine and he gained a boy's enjoyment from pitting his muscles against the cliffs, climbing up faster and faster as his confidence grew. He achieved some measure of success with the women of the village by presenting them with rabbits, wild fowl and a too-curious fox in its spring coat. He also became adept at catching and tethering wild goats in a makeshift pen for the boys to tame and milk. These young lads spent most of spring and summer away from the village as they tended their sheep and a small herd of prized cows. In his daily explorations, Arthur found that there were caves aplenty further up the coast where the paths to the sea were kinder and fresh water was plentiful. The additional wild goats he found in this area were very welcome as a new source of milk, hides and wool.

The young man found that killing the wild creatures he caught was far harder than destroying an enemy in battle. Naturally soft-hearted, Arthur experienced a bone-deep sadness when he was forced to inflict suffering on an animal, but accepted that such animal husbandry was necessary. Only Maeve could fully understand this squeamishness in her brother, reckoning that men were able to comprehend why death came to claim their lives, while beasts could only suffer in dumb silence.

Sometimes, his hunts were especially profitable for the villagers, and these occasions became a cause célèbre for the whole village.

While clearing his trap line, Arthur stumbled across a deer in a small expanse of woodland and managed to bring it down with a bow and arrow. Because the carcass was too large to carry, the young man was forced to butcher the deer where it fell and carry the meat and hide back down to the village in well-planned stages.

The women exclaimed over the meat and the internal organs, while the hide was carried off to be stretched and aired on a frame. Even the hooves provided a sticky substance that had a variety of uses when they were boiled, and the bones could be carved for utensils, hooks and other weapons. The small horns were especially prized.

Maeve also applied the skills learned from her mother, augmented by some of the herbal remedies contained in Myrddion's scrolls. Arthur grinned ruefully when he remembered how he had pored over those same scrolls to learn the secrets of his father's warcraft and Myrddion's strategic genius, while his mother memorised every casual reference she'd heard from her son of Myrddion's healing lore. Here, Maeve could put the knowledge learned so long ago to some practical use.

Still limping badly, Maeve began to hunt for mandrake root, radishes and comfrey. Herbs and plants were hung to dry in the hut she shared with Freya, while the young girl shared what knowledge she had with that old soul who, in turn, shared her knowledge of various seaweeds and remedies from the sea. Once her feet began to heal, Maeve climbed to almost inaccessible places along the cliffs which Arthur's weight would bar him from reaching. While there, she pillaged the gulls' nests for eggs while apologising to the angry birds for stealing their embryonic young.

Both girls spent time using simple spindles to spin the coarse wool from the small herd of black-faced sheep that the village possessed. These objectionable animals were very bad-tempered and the old ram resisted being shorn so violently that Arthur was badly bruised by its powerful head when he and the boys removed its heavy winter wool.

Like many British women, the two girls had been well trained at the loom and were able to create a yarn that could be woven into a coarse cloth, regardless of whether the wool came from sheep or goats. While the village women were adept at spinning and weaving, the British girls were more familiar with the sophisticated tools that had come to Britain with the Romans. They did everything they knew to share their knowledge with their new friends.

And so the days passed in pleasure and usefulness, so that Arthur almost forgot that they were fugitives and that Hrolf Kraki's dogs were still hunting for them. Ultimately, such idylls must end, but Arthur was unprepared for the suddenness and viciousness of that ending.

The villagers settled down for the night after eating their frugal evening meals of flat bread and stew. Then, just on dark, a boy ran into the compound with his shaggy hound trotting behind him. As the herders normally stayed away from home for several weeks at a stretch, the boy's arrival sounded an alarm, so tousled heads appeared at every door in the compound. This boy was like most of his kind. He was a little over ten years of age, but not yet a man, and was dressed for the summer in crude hide breeches, a coarsely woven shirt and rough sandals. His eyes wide and terrified, he spoke out manfully as soon as he had been ushered into the headman's hut, gabbling out what he had seen.

'There are men coming! Some are on horses and the others are on foot. Near to twenty of them! I saw them chasing Leaper here. He'd have fought them, but I thought it was more important to raise the alarm. We didn't want to leave the cows, so we drove them into a copse where they'll be safe. I'll kill the bastards myself if they hurt my cows – I swear I will!'

In spite of his fear, the boy was proud of his efforts and luxuriated in the praise of his elders for his foresight and bravery. Before he had completed his tale, Arthur had heard enough and instructed Blaise to run as fast as she could to raise the alarm with Stormbringer and the other warriors. Eight men, as well as a dozen able-bodied villagers, almost set the conflict on an equal footing, except for the obvious fact that their enemies were trained warriors, hard-bitten and brutal killers who would stop at nothing to succeed with their mission.

Then, with the aid of Eamonn and the six warriors loaned by Stormbringer, Arthur dragged the village gate into position at the entrance to the compound. Inside the barrier, a large, trimmed log was kept specifically to act as a blockade. The wall on either side of the gate had holes chopped into the raw stone where the massive log could fit firm and snug once it had been manoeuvred into position. Arthur admired the creativity shown by the builders of the wall and their foresight in constructing such easily erected defences.

'That wooden barrier won't hold them for long if they have their axes with them, but at least there's no way they can spirit their horses down the cliffs. They'll be forced to leave at least one of their warriors to guard the hobbled beasts once they find the path leading down to the beach. At a guess, we'll be fighting nineteen men, and I'll warrant they'll be heavily armed.'

'Can we hold them, Arthur?' Eamonn asked. His face was drawn with worry, but his eyes gleamed with the battle joy that ran through his whole tribe. As a direct descendant of Gorlois, the Boar of Cornwall, Eamonn was a true son of those wild coasts and savage seas. Blaise had already departed on her dangerous run through the darkness with the same expression glistening in her eyes, for she shared her bloodline with Morgan and Morgause, extraordinary women who refused to be tamed.

Arthur considered Eamonn's question. It didn't really matter whether they could win or not, because Arthur was oath-bound to protect the villagers with his life-blood anyway. Still, he started from the premise that he had to succeed at any task assigned to him.

'Yes, we can hold them! But we must win the battle, Eamonn,

or at least keep the king's men penned inside the compound until Stormbringer can come to our rescue. But we can only defeat our enemies if the headman agrees to give me command of the able-bodied men in his village. I must be permitted to place them in strategic locations where we can trap the warriors in narrow spaces, and then pick them off – one or two at a time. We are asking the headman to place his trust in strangers, so no one should be surprised if he refuses my request. But I have thought hard about our predicament because the Dene warriors provided by Stormbringer are unused to command, which leaves you and me to take control, Eamonn, and I've a lot more experience than you. The responsibilities will lie heavily on our shoulders. Many of the villagers will die, but it's the only way we can hold them – and survive the battle.'

Sigurd, the headman, was already translating the words of the two Britons to the gathering crowd of villagers. Arthur was visibly shocked that this elderly, uneducated man knew the Celtic tongue as well as the Dene language. His surprise must have shown on his face, because the headman answered his guest's unasked question in a reasonable facsimile of good Celt.

'The Old Ones say your people once came from lands near here in the days before the Romans laid waste to Gaul and the approaches leading into the north. They moved south into Gaul during the years beyond imagining. It was said that they built a kingdom in the new lands and became rich on trade. I cannot know how they came to arrive in your homeland, but I can still speak and understand a little of their ancient tongue.'

He paused and his eyes were sad. 'I have no particular learning, but I remember the old stories and some tribes near the borders of Saxony speak a version of your language that is even more pure than yours. I married a girl from one of those tribes when I went wandering in my youth, so I can still understand something of what you say. I only learned basic words and pillow talk, mainly because my girl was a dutiful wife who felt the need to learn my tongue. But when you love someone, it's a pleasure to do little things that will make them smile, such as learning the language of their childhood.' Sigurd smiled sadly. 'She died forty years ago, but I never forgot her stories or her language.'

The world is far smaller than I ever imagined it to be, Arthur thought as he began to formulate his plans for defence and attack in his head. When he finally spoke, he used the Dene language out of a perverse desire for privacy.

'All the women, children and elderly men must go into the deep cave. If Kraki's men should enter your refuge, you must defend yourselves as best you can until Stormbringer arrives. You must understand that the rest of us will have already been killed by the king's warriors if the enemy has penetrated this far into our defences. If that occurs, you'll have to fight to the death.'

The lack of understanding on Sigurd's face spoke more loudly than words that the old man had lost the thread of Arthur's rapidly issued orders. Briskly, and without any sign of panic on her face, Freya appeared and quickly and efficiently began to translate Arthur's instructions.

'Thank you, Mother. But it's time for you to go to the caves with the others, including my sister. I can't be distracted from my task because I'm worrying about your safety.'

'Of course, Arthur. I'll just wait for a short time until you have placed your men exactly where you want them. I'm concerned that they mightn't understand you. I promise you I'll go to the deep caves with Maeve as soon as you require it.' Freya spoke with such autocratic authority that Arthur decided he would be wasting his breath if he argued with her.

Off in the distance, a muffled cry of terror came faintly from the direction of the path that led down the cliff.

'With luck, that's one less man to worry about.' Arthur grinned with wolfish relish.

'I'm quite capable of using a bow, Arthur, if there's one I can borrow,' Maeve interrupted. 'I can help to guard the entrance leading into the deeper caves.' He nodded briskly as his sister's mulish expression convinced him that she had already made up her mind.

Then he turned to Stormbringer's warriors, who were armed to the teeth and eager to do something other than the domestic tasks that had occupied them for most of the past week. Now there were enemies to kill. As Fortuna would have it, they would probably see battle and become heroes. Their fellow warriors working on the ship would most likely arrive too late to take any part in the impending combat.

'Once the king's men have broken through the log barrier, we'll allow them to enter the alleyways. Their numbers are such that they'll have to divide to the right and to the left as the smaller paths are very difficult for a fully armed man to negotiate. There simply isn't enough room along the pathways for them to manoeuvre themselves, so it's a good strategy for us to divide their number and eliminate them individually. We'll let them come to us, and then we'll ambush them.'

Arthur turned to examine Stormbringer's warriors. Unfamiliar with their abilities, he selected them at random.

'You three will take the right fork. But I need a bowman to accompany you.'

With Freya's help, one of the villagers stepped forward. He was clutching an old bow and quiver filled to bursting with arrows, most of which were flint-tipped.

They must be very old, but they'll kill just as well as good iron, Arthur thought with grim satisfaction. In fact, they'll probably make nastier wounds.

'According to the village legends, they go back to the time of the ice,' said the headman, noticing Arthur's surprise. 'Although we no longer have a need for bowmen in our lives, these men still honour the totem of their ancestors and the sea-eagles, by keeping bows for . . .'

'Religious ceremonies?' Arthur asked.

'Aye, that's it!' the headman replied. 'But men of that totem could never explain their rituals to a stranger.'

Arthur nodded his understanding and thanked God that these old pagans possessed archery skills that were relics of some distant past. Whether the villagers were accurate with these weapons was of little importance. In such close quarters, a bowman could hardly miss their target.

'The rest of you will go to the left with another bowman. I need to divide the village men into three groups now, and these men will make up the second line of defence. When the pressure is greatest on Stormbringer's warriors, they will fall back once we have inflicted some initial damage. This retreat will draw the attackers in for the kill. The men from World's End must wield a mixture of weapons in each group. One man with a harpoon or a spear, and others with axes and hoes would be ideal, as the man with the harpoon or spear can kill from a distance while the others can come in closer. An archer would be even better, but I understand how unlikely it is to expect a number of men capable of drawing a bow in a small village, especially one that depends on fishing and grazing animals rather than hunting. And so we will do the best we can with what we have, such as the blacksmith's hammers. Be wary of every move of the enemy, for these warriors are savage killers who are blood-bound to their king. They will cheat and use every low blow they know. They won't give you any choice other than to kill them, so you can't be squeamish. They know they can't fail, for their oaths bind them to Hrolf Kraki – even beyond death!'

Arthur's sobering advice was more settling than any rousing speech. Then, as Freya departed for the caves with Maeve, the headman and the other non-combatants, Arthur spoke once more to his motley group of defenders and explained quickly, with the use of diagrams in the mud of the pathway, how these simple fishermen must tempt their enemies into advancing deeply into the labyrinth. When he was satisfied that they understood his instructions, he sent the men to their positions in the defensive lines.

As the defenders were about to depart, serious and determined, Arthur remembered one last issue that must be faced, by himself as much as by them.

'Before you go, you must understand what we are doing this night. We commit treason, so no enemy must be allowed to escape, or they will take a warning to Hrolf Kraki of our presence here. Every man who is part of the attack on the village must die! Do you understand me? I doubt they'll beg for quarter, but we can give none. Even the wounded must perish, although it seems cowardly. If we let even one man live, the king will return with a huge force and obliterate this village and kill everyone and everything in this place – men, women, children and livestock! By giving us shelter, the lives of every villager is forfeit, even the infants in their cradles.'

Such wanton revenge by Hrolf Kraki had never crossed the minds of these simple fishermen, because they were incapable of such gross disrespect for human life themselves.

Perhaps men who live in close proximity with nature, and are therefore prey to her whims, don't understand the wickedness that motivates some kings or jarls whose power has turned into hubris, Arthur thought sadly. Then he smiled savagely. 'Hrolf Kraki is due for a great fall and his own crows will feed on his eyes, if he's not careful.' Arthur spoke in his own language, so Eamonn was the only person who understood, which was just as well, given that Arthur's words were treasonous. His friend nodded in tacit agreement.

As the Dene warriors and the villagers disappeared into the maze of huts, Arthur gave Eamonn one final instruction.

'You're my second-in-command and we understand each other's capabilities, Eamonn, so you must remain directly behind me. We each know what has to be done. You must fight with your head rather than with your passion, my friend, because I can't afford to lose you.' When the point is reached where we're finally securing the village from the attackers, I have one final task for you, and this responsibility is yours alone. You must climb the cliffs and locate the place where the Dene's horses have been tethered. Once there, you must kill every sentry who has been left behind and ensure that no one escapes to raise the alarm with Hrolf Kraki. I repeat, Eamonn, no quarter must be given to any of the Dene warriors. Every one of them must die! Ride after any man who chooses to run, and then ensure he is killed.'

'I swear it, Arthur. None of them will escape, not as long as I can hold a sword.'

Eamonn's grin seemed wide and white below the bleached skull of the moon. Only a few torches were left alight to illuminate those parts of the village that could provide aid to its defence rather than give even a modicum of assistance to the attacking force. If the king's hunters required illumination, they must bring their own torches with them. After all, a warrior only had two hands, and Arthur's strategy depended on the enemy being out of their depth at every step.

Every enemy handicap was useful to the defenders, so the fire-pits in the village had been doused with water to ensure that the attackers had only minimal access to fire. Thatch could burn and fire might work against them, as well as leaving the villagers homeless after the skirmish was over.

As Arthur carried out one final inspection of his defences, he noted that most of the smaller stone buildings had roofs of sod, but the central hut where the headman lived was thatched for it was largely ceremonial. As the focal point of the village, Arthur expected it would become an important target, and a place where he could consolidate his reserves.

'One further matter remains for discussion, Eamonn. Distasteful as it might seem, you must use the boy – the one who brought us warning of the attack. Take him with you as your guide when the time comes. He'll move faster than you, because he can guide you up the cliffs even in darkness. He'll be around here somewhere, because he'll refuse to go to the deep caves.'

Predictably, a shadow moved across from him, for Arthur had spoken in the Dene tongue. The boy had been watching Arthur with narrowed and angry eyes; he was determined to play his part in the coming battle and had hidden himself away until the women and children were ushered towards the caves.

'Where's your dog, boy? He'll be of no use here, no matter how brave he is, because he won't have the space to fight or to protect himself. If you love your dog, you'll send him to the caves with someone you trust.'

The lad flushed at the tone of Arthur's voice, but he had spirit and raised himself to his full height of barely five feet.

'I've already sent Leaper to my mother. He'll protect her, so she'll be safe with him.'

'Can you use a knife, lad?' Arthur asked in the kindest voice he could muster. 'Are you capable of cutting a man's throat? You must tell me now! If you doubt your ability to do this, I will send another young man who is able to carry out this essential task. No shame will attach itself to you if you don't think you can kill a man at your tender age.'

'I've cut the throats of my ewes if they've broken legs or are dying during the lambing. And I've had to kill one of the calves after a fox savaged it. I love my beasts more than my own life, so I'll surely kill anyone who comes to hurt my family or any of our villagers.'

'Good lad! Do you have a serviceable knife? I know you have your stick, but it would be useless in close-quarter fighting.'

The boy extended a worn blade by the point and allowed Arthur to grip the plain wooden handle. The precious iron glowed with cleanliness, although the blade had been sharpened so often that it had become quite narrowed. When Arthur tested the edge along his thumb, he viewed the resultant thin streak of blood with satisfaction.

The boy must have spent many nights sitting on his bed-roll, while cleaning and sharpening this old knife until the blade had become razor-sharp. The thought of the lad's solitary life with only his dog for company filled Arthur with melancholy and respect, and a sympathetic lump formed in his throat. When he finally spoke, his voice was soft and friendly as he handed the knife back, handle first. 'Fair enough, boy! I'll personally give you a new knife to replace this worn one once this little skirmish is over and done with. If we survive this night, your old blade will become an honoured memento of our victory. What is your name?'

As he spoke, blows from a number of axes began to strike the wooden gate with a savage, disciplined intent.

'They're coming for us, Arthur,' Eamonn interrupted from deep within the shadow of the hut where he was invisible to any intruder. Arthur ignored the noise, although the boy's eyes widened and darted towards the sounds of destruction coming from the barricade.

'I am called Seagull in your tongue,' the boy replied proudly, as if daring Arthur to make any mention of the scavenger reputation of that particular bird.

'Ah, that is after the sailor's friend. Gulls tell seamen that land is close by, so you're well named, boy!'

Arthur smiled at him in encouragement. 'But it's time now for you to save all the families who live in your village. After the battle is over, I need you to guide Eamonn up the cliff to the place where the Dene warriors will have secreted their horses. I'd like you to choose a fast and safe route that will outflank them. When you get there, everyone must die at Eamonn's hand. Until then, you will stay with Eamonn at all times and take no part in the coming battle. You are crucial to the attack on the cliff-top, Gull, so don't fail me by getting yourself killed down here. Finally, if Eamonn should die in his attempt to kill the sentries, you must try to kill the sentries yourself and complete his mission in any way that you can. Do you hear me, boy? I know it's wrong for a grown man to ask you to kill another person – but I have no choice!'

'Aye! I hear what you say!' Gull answered solemnly.

The boy melted into the darkness like a wraith as the gate began to shudder under the pounding of the Dene axes. Even now, the timber could be heard to shake and splinter as Arthur freed the Dragon Knife from its scabbard.

'And now they are here!'

The gate collapsed inwards, further blocking the entry into the village proper. Dark shapes began to drag away smashed slabs of timber, while a dark figure leaped through the breach with braids flying wildly in his haste. Behind him another figure followed carrying a torch aloft, followed by another . . . and another . . . and another.

Gods! That boy has no idea how to count, Arthur realised as the press of men began to fill the small space at the open end of the yard. Of course, any number over twenty would be an impossibly large number for an illiterate shepherd boy to imagine. Arthur berated himself for his failure to question the boy more carefully.

Meanwhile, the attackers divided into two distinct packs that moved like wolves to encircle their prey.

'Just as I hoped.' Arthur attempted to comfort himself. In the past, he'd never had so many lives depending on his leadership abilities.

Within seconds, the first man through the gate had charged past the doorway where Arthur stood with his back against the wall. Somehow, it seemed dishonourable to kill him from behind, despite the defenders being comprehensively outnumbered. The young man yelled out a Celtic war cry, completely alien in this land. The hairs rose on Gull's neck as the undulating challenge rose over the sound of splintering wood. The Dene warrior turned and raised his axe, but before Arthur could run him through, Eamonn slid into position behind the man and sliced through the back of his knees with a scything sweep of his sword. He collapsed with a scream and Eamonn vaulted over his writhing body, his sword in one hand and a Dene shield in the other.

Before he turned back to face the oncoming Dene warriors, Arthur saw the shepherd boy dart out of the shadows and bury his knife to the hilt in the wounded man's eye socket. The Dene threshed his legs and arched his body in a final fit, but Gull dragged his knife free as the dying man's heels stopped drumming on the sod floor. Then, as the lad stripped away the dead man's sword and axe, Arthur turned away, his knife and sword slicing through the air in deadly parabolas of shining metal.

'Come on then! Come and meet the Dragon Knife,' Arthur snarled in Dene as one man broke away from the press of warriors in an attempt to corner him in the confined alleyway.

'Get back, Eamonn! Check on the others – and quickly! I can hold long enough to kill this fool,' Arthur ordered as blade met blade. This Dene was more intelligent than his predecessor and was able to swing his shield like a weapon, while keeping the metal boss aimed directly at Arthur's breast. He was also very fast, so the boss skidded across the plates sewn into Arthur's tunic.

But Arthur was faster still.

To attempt such a risky manoeuvre, the Dene warrior had been forced to expose the trunk of his body. Feinting with his sword, Arthur seduced his enemy's weapon further away from the man's torso in a move that allowed him to close to within a foot of the warrior's chest. The man's shield and sword were useless now, so Arthur had the edge. The Dragon Knife slid upwards between the second and third ribs like a hot blade slicing through cheese. The Dene's eyes gaped widely and a great gout of blood gushed out of his mouth when Arthur dragged his knife upwards and outwards in one smooth motion.

As this Dene fell, another took his place.

After several months of inactivity, Arthur found himself on comfortable ground at last, a feeling he welcomed. His blood sang, and he understood why the Dene seamen on *Loki's Eye* had gone into battle with the forces of nature with songs of defiance on their lips. Although the voice in his brain calmed his excitement, he felt truly alive.

Two men came at him. They rushed him, side by side, but they could scarcely raise their swords because they were encumbered by their huge, circular shields. Within the blinking of an eye, one man reeled away with his arm pumping out arterial blood when his right arm was severed at the wrist.

Arthur scarcely bothered to watch the warrior as he fell to the ground. Gull leaped onto him like an angry cat, with his reddened knife flashing in the indistinct light. Under the feet of struggling men, the boy was at an advantage. Even as he slithered away into the shadows, the worn knife flashed again and impaled a very dirty foot. Arthur grinned fiercely.

'Young Gull will go far. He has all the instincts of a born killer.'

The other warrior quickly learned that a British sword will cut just as deeply into the abdomen as a Dene blade, and he fell to the ground with his entrails spilling out like unravelling, reddened wool.

The boy screamed out a shrill warning that caused Arthur to take evasive action just as a sword blow slid harmlessly past his shoulder and caused sparks to fly as it skidded along the stone wall. One of the attackers had used a narrow space between two of the huts to outflank Arthur. With a desperate curse, the Briton stepped sideways and then forward until the man's extended arm was exposed to Arthur's sword as it sheared down through bone and muscle at that point where the shoulder met the neck. Grotesquely, the warrior's head rolled sideways. It was almost severed, but Arthur had no time to watch his enemy as the man's body fell to the ground.

A torch spat out a shower of sparks with a small explosion, and Arthur swore with the shock. If one enemy could outflank him, so could others. Cursing this oversight, Arthur swept the boy under his arm and swung him off his feet as he ran, with both weapons still at the ready.

The Dene warriors pursued him, as Arthur expected they would.

'Down, Arthur!' Eamonn's voice roared out in Celt from the darkness. Arthur dropped to his knees immediately and released Gull, who rolled away into shadows that immediately swallowed his slight form.

As he dropped, two arrows immediately whined past him. Arthur felt one shaft whistle past his ear as it impaled itself in the chest of the massive shape behind him. Only the black fletch was visible inside the ruff of black bear fur that was worn around the huge man's neck and shoulders. The arrow quivered obscenely as its victim tried to breathe.

Although the action seemed to take place in slow motion, only scant seconds had elapsed. Arthur's detached brain noted that two Dene lay dead in the narrowest part of the labyrinth and several of Stormbringer's warriors had taken Arthur's place in the defences. The sound of mortal combat could be heard only a few feet away on the left-hand path that had led half the invading force away from the caverns. Frustratingly, Arthur was unable to follow the true course of that battle, because several huts lay between him and the other village defences.

'We've killed at least five of the bastards,' he grunted to Eamonn as his friend led him at a trot down the passageways between two houses. These alleys were so narrow that the two men were obliged to turn sideways and slide along the sweating, wet-stone walls.

'Seven,' Eamonn responded. 'You're forgetting that we've been guarding the smaller paths, so we can't expect to retain all the glory for ourselves.' A ragged knife slice had twisted Eamonn's mouth out of shape and his smile would never be as wide or as innocent again, but the young Dumnonii prince seemed twice as alive as anyone else.

Behind them, Arthur could hear the soft susurration of Gull's sandals on the packed sod, but the darkness was absolute.

One section of the space between two of the houses almost defeated Arthur because of his wide shoulders. He could barely slide through this narrow section of curved tunnel, until he contrived to burst into a wider passage beyond. There, in the hellish light, Arthur was thrust into a conflict that was more suited to the Greek Hades than to a small fishing village.

In a bottleneck caused by heaped bodies, five village defenders were holding nearly a dozen Dene warriors at bay. Two archers were peppering away at any portions of exposed enemy flesh with their barbed, black-fletched arrows, while the Dene warriors were unable to use their own bows in the narrow maze. Because the archers were fighting on their own soil, they had the knowledge to seek out perches where they could unloose their arrows and then disappear like smoke.

'Eamonn, a fire arrow! Guard my back!'

Arthur realised that one of the Dene warriors at the back of the press of struggling men had raised a short bow which he was pointing towards a thatched hut in the densest part of the village near the headman's house. Attached to the barb was a length of cloth already well alight.

Without pausing to check on Eamonn's response, Arthur stepped away from the narrow passageway behind the bulk of the Dene warriors. Before him, the melee and its resultant chaos was loud, confusing and deceptive.

Arthur looked more like a Dene than many of Hrolf Kraki's ruffians, for many of the honourable warriors found various nefarious ways to avoid the pursuit of Stormbringer, who was a famed Sae Dene and a noted patriot. But others of Hrolf Kraki's men were warriors who served out of a desire for preference or payment, while some came from other northern lands where they had plied their skills for hire.

These venal creatures were more criminal than loyal, for they were bought and paid for with the king's coin. Hrolf Kraki, who knew the worth of such men, called them his *dogs*.

One of his *dogs* had managed to free his bow by stepping back from the press of his fellow warriors. Arthur's position outflanked the larger group of attackers so, as the archer raised his bow to shoulder height, Arthur appeared behind the man like a pale ghost. The archer had no time to scream before Arthur clapped his arm over the unfortunate man's mouth and chin.

Then, using both hands, Arthur snapped the man's neck like a carrot.

The cracking sound shuddered through Arthur's hands and the noise seemed to reverberate off the enclosing walls. But the battle was so fierce that none of the attacking Dene noticed an enemy was behind them.

Eamonn pushed his friend through a closed doorway behind him. It swung open under his weight and Arthur found himself in a small, smoke-filled space.

'We can be trapped in here,' Arthur warned in a whisper.

'No,' Eamonn whispered back.

'Can we resume the attack from here? From what I saw, there are six men still alive out there, but only three of our men are still standing.'

'And they're near to dying, master,' a child's voice said from the doorway. Gull had materialised silently from out of nowhere. 'We'll have to do something!'

'We're behind them, so we'll try an all-out attack from the rear, just the two of us. But we're on the knife's-edge now.'

Arthur gripped Gull by the shoulder.

'Whatever happens, boy, I congratulate you for the wicked knife thrust you used on the eye of that Dene warrior. But now I must ask you to stay in this room once Eamonn and I venture outside for someone has to let Stormbringer know what has happened if we should be killed. Remind him that none of Hrolf Kraki's warriors must be allowed to escape. This is the task that is entrusted to *you*, Gull.'

'I won't fail you, master, but why can't I help? You've seen that I can fight like a man.'

Arthur was halfway out of the door as he answered. 'This is red work, Gull. I'd rather you didn't see what that means until you're older. You must obey me in this!'

Impaled by Arthur's implacable eyes, the boy swore to obey. Then, using the darkness to full advantage, the Britons were gone.

The defenders of this section of the maze had been pushed into a slow retreat. They were fast exhausting themselves, for the limited fighting space acted against them as well as in their favour. Entering the fray from behind, Arthur screamed like the fabled Banshee of Hibernia and attacked the first Dene in his path as his sword and knife flashed in the half-light. His charge was so suicidal and unexpected that the six remaining servants of the Crow King were forced back against the defenders from the village, all of whom were now too weak to capitalise on the mad attack by their British allies.

Arthur felt a sudden hot wire of pain across his biceps, but he ignored the leak of blood where his armour had been sliced through. As he killed his next opponent, he thanked God for Germanus, who had taught him how to use a knife at close quarters, and for Father Lorcan, who had taught him to think rationally under pressure. As fast as a man wavered or stumbled before him, Arthur advanced to the next, leaving Eamonn to mop up the wounded. Arthur's longer reach and Eamonn's ferocity worked effectively in tandem to destroy the warriors who stood against them.

Two men could fight more effectively than six in these narrow spaces, no matter how large and how strong they might be.

Finally, none but his allies were left standing in the narrow labyrinth, while Arthur felt the warm stickiness of blood as it dripped all down him into the leather of his boots. He was a man dipped in gore as if he had waded through a tide of clotted blood. Sickened a little by the carnage of tangled bodies and severed limbs, Arthur hawked and spat, trying to clear his mouth of the stench of physical destruction in this confined space. He weaved a little on his feet before managing to stagger along the narrow cross-passage and return to the right fork in the pathway.

Another pile of heaped bodies was thrust against the external wall. With a pang, Arthur recognised the faces of three men with whom he had rowed, run and shared food. If there was a Valhalla, then Arthur was certain that their souls were already winging their way to the Abode of Heroes, aided by Valkyrie, the warrior women of the air.

Eamonn and Arthur broke into a run, while both men heard the patter of Gull's feet as he followed them, but all their haste was in vain. The last of the Crow King's *dogs* were all dead now, hacked to pieces by the villagers and their wicked hoes, and Arthur was proud to see a large number of arrows that were deeply embedded in the corpses. Maeve was retrieving her arrowheads, oblivious to the more gruesome aspects of this task as she tugged or cut the barbed fletches out of dead flesh. Now that these strong men were only so much useless flesh, the arrowheads were worth more than the corpses.

'We'll move this carrion outside the walls to places where their remains can be burned and their ashes scattered on the winds. Our own dead must be washed and cleansed, and then we'll prepare them for the final funeral pyre.'

Arthur's voice was filled with regret for so much loss of life, but the village had been securely held, and remained unburned.

'Eamonn, you and Gull know what you have to do. Start your climb!'

The man and the boy nodded and padded away, while the headman and Freya moved forward. 'You mustn't worry about those who have died during this conflict, young master,' Freya explained with great seriousness. 'Everything will be done for them as if they were our own honoured kinfolk.'

'We're in your debt, Lord Arthur,' Sigurd added. 'You are truly the Last Dragon of the Britons! Now that we have seen the mettle of you and your friends, we believe you are who you say you are. We live in times when there are still wonders to be seen, and while we are simple folk, we can still recognise greatness when it appears in our midst.'

'But I had the honour of leading Stormbringer's warriors and your own heroes – and that is all! I simply acted as I was taught to do since I was just a very young boy.'

Freya and the headman smiled and nodded, and gave their own praise to those who had taken part in the battle, including lauding Arthur as the hero of the Battle of World's End. While the skirmish was a small conflict in the larger scheme of things, it was now the stuff of legend in the annals of this small and undistinguished village.

Arthur was forced to endure the gratitude of the village until Stormbringer and his warriors eventually came running into the compound under the light of torches that were borne high to light their way. Their faces were bone-white with anxiety.

Stormbringer was told how World's End had been secured, and how twenty-seven of Hrolf Kraki's warriors were lying on a rocky outcrop high above the tidemark with their bodies stripped of all valuables. The shades of these warriors would enter the next world without wealth or arms, for they had failed their master and their possessions were now forfeit to the victors as spoils of war.

If the Green Dragon existed in her ossuary beneath the surge and violence of the waves, then her smile was an irritated sneer of chartreuse lips over wicked white teeth. As she entwined her scaled tail around her pyramid of skulls, she crooned to herself so that Arthur, in his dreams on that night of blood, could hear her sibilant whisper.

'You aren't free of me yet, King of Winter, for I can wait until you come to me. I am always prepared to wait for the greatest of prizes.'

Then Arthur awoke to a new day with the weight of forty corpses on his shoulders.

PLAN OF THE HOLDING

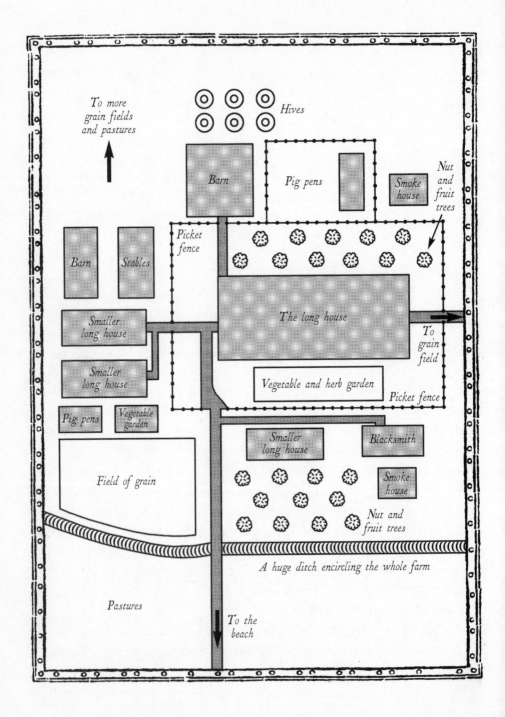

To more grain fields and pastures

Hives

Barn

Pig pens

Smoke house

Nut and fruit trees

Barn

Stables

Picket fence

The long house

To grain field

Smaller long house

Vegetable and herb garden

Picket fence

Smaller long house

Pig pens

Vegetable garden

Smaller long house

Blacksmith

Field of grain

Nut and fruit trees

Smoke house

A huge ditch encircling the whole farm

Pastures

To the beach

CHAPTER XVI

THE *SEA WIFE*

Fortis fortuna adiuvat.
(Fortune favours the brave.)

Publius Terentius Afer, *Phormio* 1

The ship scudded under its great sail which had been patched in places where the wool was torn and unravelling with age. Yet the plain sheets still bellied gracefully in the offshore breeze. Now that night had settled over the longship, the last of the crew moved effortlessly about their duties before settling on the sun-warmed decks to sleep dreamlessly under a huge yellow moon.

They had travelled far and fast since they had relaunched *Sea Wife* into the slapping waves of the tiny cove that lay to the south of World's End. Once the crew had pitted their strength against the drag of the waves with much cursing at her unresponsive bulk, *Sea Wife* had become a graceful and living thing that swam through the water with grace and power. Despondent and morose, Arthur had still been reliving the battle in his mind, so he welcomed the chance to leave that scene of carnage behind him.

Sea Wife was wider in the beam than *Loki's Eye*, so she wallowed in the troughs of the waves whereas Stormbringer's longer and narrower craft would have cut through the swells with ease. This ship, so ungainly and stubborn on the shore, would never have survived the devastating and sudden storm at sea that had so nearly sunk *Loki's Eye*. An earlier design, one constructed to transport goods as well as men, meant that *Sea Wife* would always lack grace.

For two weeks, time had seemed to unwind slowly on a huge spool after Stormbringer's small force had set sail. No longer afraid of the sea, although still wary of her caprices, Arthur leaned against the rail and stared out at the slowly moving waves. He watched as phosphorescence edged the swells with strange and eerie lights, while the moon left a long avenue of silver from the horizon to the ship – and beyond.

In days gone by, Arthur had loved the forests with their changing nature during the various seasons. He could see now how the great deep was loved by the Dene with the same devotion that he reserved for his oaks, elms and other giant trees. He had spent the last few days watching the small transformations of the seas as wind, rain and light altered the living face of the deep.

On this particular evening, Arthur was in a philosophical mood. Infinity stretched out into the vast reaches of space as the moonlight spread over the black skyline. The faint light of the stars was also argent against the thick black wool of space, like lights breaking through holes in a great invisible sail.

This could be the face of God! Arthur thought pensively. Whenever the young man tried to imagine the existence of his God, all he could see in his mind's eye was the countenance of Bedwyr, old but not frail, and still vibrant with strength and wisdom.

Thoughts of Bedwyr led to memories of his mother's face that swam into view and was imprinted over the soft gleam of the stars. Her loveliness was part of her bone structure rather than the flesh that had begun to sag with the inexorable passage of the years. Elayne was no saint, but in her son's estimation she was everything that a woman and mother should be. He was afraid he would never see her face or touch her hand again.

Off to his right, a light suddenly leaped into life on a distant, almost-invisible shore. *Sea Wife* was sailing parallel to the coastline for safety. A new breeze began to fill the sail and the sheets soughed gently as if a woman sighed with melancholy. But the wind brought the scents of land to Arthur: the sharp smell of pine resin; the wet and salty reek of seaweed and, somewhere below all the others, the aroma of freshly cut grass. Time slipped and he was a boy again, cutting grass for the horses with Bedwyr. The sun skidded over his foster-father's bush of curls and glinted on the small sickles they used for the cutting. The boyish Arthur was laughing because Bedwyr had shoved a daisy behind one ear and was making a comical clown's face at his foster-son. In the shadow of the mast, he hid his face from his companions and wept like a child.

Sea Wife was headed for Ostoanmark or Zealand, the largest of the islands that rose out of the wild sea between Skandia and the Cimbric Peninsula like jade beads strung across a lapis lazuli cloth. Stormbringer's family lived at Ostoanmark on broad lush acres. Although Ostoanmark was an island, nothing was beyond Hrolf Kraki's reach, so the Sae Dene's family must be warned.

Arthur understood. Stormbringer and his warriors had demonstrated the strong family and clan links that lay at the heart of Dene society. The Sae Dene went to sea during the spring and the summer when they sailed to foreign coastlines in search of trade opportunities and, if necessary, pillage, while the women of the Dene clans remained in the countryside to supervise the farms, the slaves and all aspects of agriculture. Stormbringer was genuinely afraid for his womenfolk and knew that he could be attacked and punished through them.

As well as protecting his family and his clan, Stormbringer was determined to raise a small force of warriors to sail to Skania. 'If the Crow King isn't prepared to honour his debt to his loyal subjects, then I'll have to meet these commitments myself,' Stormbringer had told Arthur and his crew before they commenced their voyage into the south. Stormbringer had crudely sketched their route into the hard-packed sand with a tide-soaked stick. Although they had not yet left the sandy cove where *Sea Wife* had been beached for so many years, the Sae Dene captain always kept them informed of their ultimate destination.

He described a number of small villages near the old Anglii borders in the south, trouble spots themselves, where he planned to raise a force of warriors and ships for the relief of the Skania Dene. His crew were eager listeners, for they understood that their captain was an honourable man who would never deliberately lead them into evil. Danger they would find, and sudden death, but their reasons for fighting would be just.

And there would always be spoils to share!

Sea Wife had already landed at one such settlement where Stormbringer had been met cautiously by the local jarl. That the ageing lord was friendly was proof of how far Hrolf Kraki's reputation had deteriorated in recent months.

'I have two ships at hand and enough warriors to man them, but you must see my problem, Valdar Bjornsen,' Ivar Hnaefssen explained as they sat at ease at a hastily prepared feast in the great hall. Ivar pushed one grizzled hound away as the animal rested his chin pensively on the table top.

'Down, Bear!' Ivar ordered briskly. The dog raised liquid-brown eyes in his master's direction, before turning his attention back to a haunch of mutton that was steaming on Ivar's wooden platter. 'I can spare these men at the moment, but who knows when the Hundings will return and burn everything we possess? They've been very active along the borders in recent times and my halls are less than half a day's journey on foot from the Saxon lands.'

Bear's fixed and melancholy stare at the food stated clearly that he was a poor, malnourished creature who was utterly devoted to his master and would never steal from his table. Arthur was amused by Bear's manipulation, because he was wise to the ways of great hounds. Bedwyr had always been surrounded by them, so Arthur was quite comfortable in their company. Eventually, Ivar took a small, meaty bone from the central platter and offered it to Bear, who took it daintily in his wicked jaws. Trotting slowly away, he began to gnaw on it in a discreet corner.

The jarl wiped his hands on his greasy robe and Arthur tried to repress a grimace as a new layer of grime was added to the stains that covered the coarse wool. Ivar had been a good host and was obviously a decent man, Arthur reminded himself.

'Well, Valdar, I've thought on your proposition and I'll be sensible. I'll give you my two ships because no one is likely to attack me from the sea, more's the pity! But I can only give you the equivalent of one crew. I need to protect my own back, you understand?'

Stormbringer nodded. He was a little glum, but he remained fulsome in his thanks to Ivar for the generous assistance he'd given so unselfishly.

Without doubt Ivar was a man of distinction, whereby his stained tunic and his softness for his hounds were irrelevant eccentricities in a man of dauntless courage and admirable diplomatic skills.

Now, with access to three ships and sixty men, Stormbringer pushed southwards towards the tip of Funen Island, the navigation point where *Sea Wife* should turn to port and follow the coastline towards the east. Then, island-hopping, the ship would make her way to the eastern side of Ostoanmark where Stormbringer's holdings were situated. Skania lay only a short distance across the straits from Stormbringer's home, a distance that was easily covered by the small, two-man fishing boats of poor fishermen, so Stormbringer had a strong motivation to save his beleaguered kinfolk who lived on the edge of Gothland.

Those few miles of water would easily be breached if Skania became part of the Geat kingdom and their king should cast his covetous eyes over the island of the Dene.

Much had happened to the Britons in a short period of time. Eamonn and the girls were sleeping deeply beside the rudder, covered with their cloaks to protect themselves from the bite of cold. But Arthur was finding that sleep was elusive.

Around him, members of the crew were taking their rest after a day of exertion and only the helmsman and the sentry on the prow were sharing wakefulness with him in this velvet night.

Now was the time for reflection, for recrimination and for guilt, so Arthur recalled recent history and blamed himself for much of the death and destruction that had taken place.

Arthur recalled how Eamonn and Gull had acquitted themselves so well in the aftermath of the battle at World's End. Although Arthur could hardly bear to think about the men who had died as a result of his orders, he accepted that the responsibility for the death of one wounded man along the path and the two sentries at the top of the cliff was his. These deaths had been necessary to avoid greater murders. As planned, Gull had led Eamonn along a circuitous route to a path where they could secrete themselves behind the Dene picket line. There, two sleepy sentries were guarding the hobbled horses, and Eamonn killed them both without any qualms.

Meanwhile, Gull had made a reconnaissance along the main path leading down to the village. Gull's feet made no sound on the rough tussocks of grass on the path. Nor did he dislodge stones or cause the bushes of gorse to betray his presence until he was safely ensconced behind an unkempt warrior with a wounded arm who had positioned himself as a sentry near the bottom the incline.

Gull showed no mercy to the wounded man as he crept up behind him and slit his throat.

Later, Arthur discovered the wounded man's remains while searching for Gull to present the boy with his newly earned knife. He was grateful that Gull had been too squeamish to look his victim directly in the eye. Arthur also noted that the warrior's arterial blood had sprayed out in a wide red arc in front of him, but Gull was scarcely marked with the flood, except along his right hand when he hadn't been able to remove his weapon from the man's neck wound as quickly as he would have wished.

Arthur wished Gull and Eamonn well and thanked them for fulfilling their dreadful orders. Given the circumstances of the attack on the village, Eamonn thought that Arthur's scruples were a little quaint for someone born to rule, while Gull kept silent for fear of giving offence.

Eamonn and Gull accepted the deaths of the Dene sentries as inevitable casualties of war. But Arthur was surprised when Eamonn told him that one of the warriors guarding the picket line was a woman, a camp follower who had obviously possessed some skills with weaponry. The young Briton had realised her sex at the last moment after seeing her long and distinctive braids from behind.

He killed her anyway!

In the long reaches of the night, Arthur considered his unmanly weaknesses, and doubted his ability to lead men in battle. He understood the need to silence all the warriors sent by the Crow King to kill them, but when he was faced with the actuality of his orders, something in his nature baulked at the task.

'I'm too soft,' he whispered to himself. 'I have no place in this company of men if I can't do what must be done.'

That night, the green she-dragon left his dreams in peace, but he was sure he heard her laughter just before he fell asleep.

The journey was wondrous during the northern spring. For the first time in his life, Arthur saw dolphins scudding along beside the hull of the ship. He watched in awe as the sleek, grey fish danced in the waters and frolicked in the swells whenever the breeze dropped and the great sail was barely stirring.

'Oh, Arthur! They really are playing.' Maeve had one hand on his shoulder and her body close to his as she shared the rail of the vessel with him. 'One of Stormbringer's sailors told me that they'll drive fish into the nets for the fishermen if they are familiar with the villagers. Isn't that remarkable?'

Arthur was acutely conscious of his sister's blossoming body so he moved a little way away.

'I'm afraid that you and I are creatures of the land, Maeve. Blaise and Eamonn aren't particularly impressed by the presence of the dolphins, because these giant fish are familiar to those folk who spend their lives along the coastline. Eamonn assured me that they often saw dolphins herding large shoals of fish in the seas near his home.'

As they sailed across the straits leading to Ostoanmark, several larger shapes suddenly broke the surface of the water near the ship and began to frolic in their vicinity. The great black and white shapes were finned and tailed, and each was the size of *Sea Wife*.

A cheerful warrior who was securing a long length of rope began to laugh at Arthur's look of amazement and answered 'Orca' to Arthur's unspoken question.

'Orca!' Arthur breathed in amazement, and watched as the leviathans of the deep breached the water with slaps of their tails that sent shock waves reverberating through the Dene vessel. The huge mouths seemed to smile, while water poured off their slick hides in torrents that left their skins shining in the morning sun. One great black eye was so close to *Sea Wife* that Arthur could have sworn it was gazing directly at him. More importantly, it seemed to understand him and sympathise with his inner fears and doubts. Then the great eye seemed to wink conspiratorially at him as it descended and disappeared into the depths. Arthur thought his heart would burst with wonder.

Shortly thereafter, the small flotilla arrived at Stormbringer's home island. *Sea Wife* skirted around a long headland of stone to approach a neat, shelving beach. The sails were lowered and the disciplined oarsmen rowed with a will into the shallow water until the boat embedded its bow in the smooth sand. At the last second, the oarsmen raised their blades on an order from Stormbringer, and the ship came to a safe halt with its keel secure in the beach.

Once more, Stormbringer blew on his ram's horn to warn the local population that theirs was a friendly visit, while his warriors began to unload the stores and valuable items of cargo that would be presented to the villagers. Even an urgent journey such as this one was an opportunity to carry trade goods and gifts for the country folk who were the inhabitants of this settlement.

With nowhere to run or hide, the Britons were permitted to leave the confines of the ship and regain their land legs after the weeks spent on board. Trying to straighten their hair and clothing, Arthur and his friends trudged up the beach and began to follow a sandy track that led into the flat landscape of thick green grasses growing along the sand dunes.

The children came running first, with the eldest in the lead. Several of the boys who were just short of puberty led the way, armed with knives and small bows that flapped over their shoulders as they ran. The girls followed, their long, flaxen hair crowned with loose daisy chains that leaked flowers at every stride. The little ones brought up the rear, stumbling in an effort to keep up with their siblings.

They greeted Stormbringer with crows of delight and quickly jumped up to cling to him. Grinning widely, Stormbringer staggered along the path in the direction from which the children had come. A trail of children dropped away from him, all of them laughing, singing and shouting joyously in his wake.

So infectious was the children's innocent welcome that Maeve and Arthur both started to laugh. Arthur picked up one toddler who had arrived late and was sucking his thumb in distress. Perched on Arthur's shoulders, the small boy was kicking Arthur's sides as if he was a horse, while a wide grin split his tear-stained and grimy face.

Other children were lifted high by crew members. Some of the crew seemed to be the fathers of the laughing little mites who crowed and capered all the way over the last of the grass-covered dunes until they all stood above The Holding, Stormbringer's ancestral home. The captives were immediately impressed by the buildings that lay below them on a long rolling plain rich with long grass, cattle, sheep and fields of new grain that was waving in the sea breeze, protected by the dunes from the worst of its storms.

The long stone houses that they had seen at Heorot were here too, wedded to the chocolate-brown earth with fieldstone walls and tall, pointed roofs that would resist the heaviest snowstorm. The buildings were clustered together in order to protect each other from the onset of inclement weather, and the barns, stables and piggeries were as carefully built as those houses constructed for human habitation.

This close to the coast, every tree that managed to survive and grow was cruelly bent into a tortuous shape by the ever-present winds. One pine tree twisted grotesquely to grow parallel with the ground, just below the top of the dunes, so that it looked like an ancient man bent almost double.

By comparison, the farm was situated below sea level so its trees were protected from the worst of winter's gales. In the glossy spring day with the sun dusting the landscape with golden pollen, Arthur could understand Stormbringer's deep passion for his land and the well-being of his kin.

Arthur could see that both men and women worked the fields, and he accepted that some of these people were likely to be slaves. But he also noted that when the farm workers heard the hubbub created by the children, they looked up, smiled, waved and completed whatever task they were doing before coming to welcome the visitors.

The Holding was surrounded by a huge ditch, not particularly deep, but perfect for a defence designed to slow attackers down rather than deter them completely.

Arthur shook his head in admiration. The heart of The Holding was surrounded by a picket fence that was heavily gated for protection in times of danger. Within this compound could be found the longhouse of the jarl with the farmsteads of his kin and servants clustered around his hall like chicks around a plump hen.

As they reached the ditch, a wooden pathway provided a dry, safe surface in times of snow or heavy rain. The path ran through to the inner compound, where it joined smaller paths that linked the various farmsteads and barns together. People were crowding onto these paths now, straightening clothing and surreptitiously wiping dirty hands behind their backs. As Stormbringer and his party reached the gate in the wooden fence, most of the adult population was already gathered to bid them welcome.

A beautiful woman walked out from the front of the crowd. Her long blond hair was bound with clasps of bronze and she had eyes so blue that Arthur was transfixed by their vividness. She threw her arms wide to allow Stormbringer to walk into them and embrace her.

'You've come unheralded, brother Valdar. What's amiss? Don't lie to me! I'm older than you and I know all the expressions your face makes when you're stretching the truth.'

A small boy tugged at her skirts until she bent and listened closely as he whispered in her ear. She grinned at her brother.

'My youngest son, Leif, has reminded me that our cooks are preparing a noon meal for you and your men. He says I'm being rude, because you might not wish to speak casually in front of the house servants. I am suitably chastised, Valdar.'

'It's true that I do have matters of great importance to discuss and I will share these with you and Raudi, your husband. But my men and our guests would welcome food first, and then I'll explain why you must be more careful of visitors in future.'

Stormbringer took his sister's arm while two little girls perched on his shoulders. Arthur wondered if these rosy little flaxen-haired girls were Stormbringer's children.

'It's time to introduce our guests,' Stormbringer added, and started with Arthur and Eamonn, while giving a full account of their titles and antecedents. 'And the two girls are their sisters, Maeve and Blaise. Blaise was promised in marriage to a tribal king in the north of Britain who was assassinated before her party reached the Vellum Hadriani where the groom's family were domiciled. I captured them during one of my forays and paid good rings of silver for them as hostages, but they have proved to be very troublesome for the price paid.' Stormbringer grinned with good humour, so his sister, Alfridda, frowned and smiled uncertainly by turn.

The British girls coloured slightly, insulted by Stormbringer's apparent rudeness, but the Sae Dene had saved their lives, and the Britons were mindful of their debts.

'Maeve, who is Arthur's sister, went so far as to attack Aednetta, Hrolf Kraki's white witch. Her effrontery caused us to be banished but, before you judge her harshly, consider that the Crow King was determined to find fault with me, regardless of the fortune in iron, gold and silver that I brought to his hall in Heorot. But explanations can wait until after we've eaten.'

By this time, the warriors had broken away to join wives or parents, or to gather with the other unmarried warriors in one of the long halls. The largest building, at least four times the size of the smaller farmsteads, belonged to Stormbringer's family and was a wondrous sight to the British captives.

On a stone foundation, Stormbringer's house was built of trimmed and dressed timber and any cracks between the logs were caulked with a mud mortar that repelled the cold of winter. As they neared the longhouse, the Britons could see that this large building was pegged together and whitewashed on the outside. Like the buildings of Heorot, the outer walls were low but, in this case, the great rafters that formed the bones of the roof continued downwards past the base of the walls and into the ground to buttress the heavy roof of reeds. From above, the longhouse seemed to have spokes on two sides that radiated outwards at the longer ends.

At each end of Stormbringer's house, the huge external rafters were far longer than their counterparts that ran along the remainder of the roof. These rafters crossed over at each end, to the east and to the west, with elaborate carving that was exposed along the crossed arms where the rafters entered the ground. Stormbringer pointed out that the decorative wooden rafters told stories about the heroic deeds of his ancestors.

The carving on the eastern doors was equally complex, with a large opening above them which allowed morning light to enter. Pig's bladders had been sewn together carefully to a wooden framework to ensure that the elements weren't permitted to enter the hall.

Stormbringer explained that there was another window on the western end, so that light and warmth gradually flooded into the hall as the sun set in the west.

Inside, The Holding was less smoky and close than the much smaller structures of World's End, or even those of Heorot. To keep heat inside the hall during the desperate winters, most halls had no windows. Once again, like Heorot, a wooden floor was sawn and erected to rest on a series of stone sills, guarding against rot.

Like the Crow King, Stormbringer refused to use straw on the floors, either for sleeping nests or to hide the accumulated dirt after a long and cold winter. Even now, servants were busy with birch and straw brooms, removing any detritus from previous meals.

As the Britons stood blinking in the semi-darkness after the bright glitter of spring sunshine, their eyes gradually saw the partitions of storerooms off to each side of the doorway. The Holding was a smaller and more compact version of Heorot, but a woman controlled the interior spaces of this hall, so the emphasis was on comfort rather than panoply and self-aggrandisement.

The familiar stone-lined and mortared fire pit was placed in the centre of the hall. Wooden cradles and a flat iron griddle showed where bread and meat were fried, while small ovens could be placed into hot coals. Wooden divisions in the hall created other half-rooms for sleeping.

Alfridda and her women obviously worked hard to make inroads on the accumulated soot stains from a long winter. A wooden bucket sealed with pitch to make it waterproof sat on the floor in one corner, along with a short brush of stiff pig bristles covered with a fatty substance used for scouring. The smell of beeswax was a pleasant addition to the usual stink of woodsmoke, animal grease and the sourness of soiled clothes.

Long tables were raised to run parallel to the long sides of the master's hall. A table across the top at the western end was obviously the head table used by the family for their day-to-day meals. For now, the head table and one longer table were set up with wooden trays; bowls of soapstone of such thinness that Arthur was amazed; spoons made of horn and wood and, in Stormbringer's case, silver. Hot pots of copper and bowls of fine pottery and horn supplemented the utensils usually presented for the use of the Sae Dene's family and guests.

'We're eating a little early, aren't we, Alfridda?' Stormbringer asked. 'Nadver isn't due for several hours yet.'

Arthur's eyebrows rose, so Stormbringer explained that the Dene people ate two meals a day, Davre in the morning and Nadver at dusk.

'But men can eat at any time, my brother, especially large lads like young Lord Arthur here.' Alfridda's tongue stumbled over the un-familiar name, but her smile was clean, natural and white. So far, Alfridda had kept most of her own teeth so her smile was unblemished.

'I'm sure you'll find much here that will tempt you, so eat your fill and more, sirs and mistresses.'

She kissed her brother heartily and settled the children at the same table where they perched on the bench stools with anticipation.

The table was laden with food. Heavy black bread was sliced carefully on a wooden platter. Large bowls of butter, cheese, boiled eggs and hazelnuts tempted the appetite. Using a metal hook, Alfridda deftly removed the lids from several hot-pots, releasing a wonderful heady aroma of herbs and meat in the process.

'The first stew is made of mutton, with carrots, cabbage and onions, while the other is made from salmon, limpets, oysters, eels and other seafood. We use coriander and garlic, so I hope you like them. There's a bowl of mustard near your hand, Master Eamonn, if you like your meat with bite like my brother here. We have supplies of apples, berries and other nuts, and there is beer or mead if you wish to drink them.'

Arthur savoured the fresh scents of mint, dill and horseradish, as his mouth began to water.

'Not even Stormbringer's warriors could have dragged me away if I were so well fed at home.' With a silent apology to his mother's cooking, Arthur bowed his head to Stormbringer's sister, a compliment that caused her to blush becomingly from the high neck of her dress up to her hairline.

Meanwhile, Maeve's eyes had become fixed on a ceramic pot filled with honey. 'I apologise for speaking out of turn, mistress, but is there honey in that jar? Do you keep hives for the little people?'

Maeve's quaint choice of words had simply popped into the young girl's head unbidden, and Alfridda had not heard the old term for many years. She smiled at her with real warmth for the very first time.

'Yes, we keep bees in wicker hives. You can see them just beyond the western gate in the sunshine and within a short flight to the vegetable patch and the fruit trees. If you choose to stay for an extended visit, you'll have many opportunities to observe them, if you so wish.'

Stormbringer glanced at the Britons, his sister and the two flaxen-haired girls whom Arthur took to be his daughters. The Sae Dene coughed awkwardly and began to explain the parlous situation that existed between himself and the Crow King. Alfridda became increasingly upset, and when Stormbringer described Maeve's unusual attack on the witch-woman, she clutched an amulet around her neck and visibly paled.

She's beginning to think that Maeve is also a witch, Arthur thought, appalled. She'll make Maeve's days here an agony!

'How could you have been so stupid, Valdar?'

The Sae Dene blushed under his sister's regard as she gradually released her amulet and smiled knowingly at her brother.

What's going on now? Arthur thought wonderingly.

'You must understand, Alfridda, that Maeve had no idea what she was saying to the king's court, how accurate her instincts were or how we would be punished for her attack on the king's woman. She was brave and dauntless, so I don't blame her for the predicament in which we found ourselves.'

Alfridda continued to smile enigmatically as Stormbringer told the tale of their long run, the village of World's End and the battle fought between his warriors and the attacking forces from Hrolf Kraki's dogs. The Sae Dene's natural storytelling skills came to the fore and Alfridda and her young sons stared gape-mouthed as he described the fierce battle. He was especially proud of Maeve's courage at the entrance to the deep caves and the courage the Britons had shown when defending this insignificant little village.

'But why? I cannot understand why our king would reward your years of service by outlawing our whole clan and banishing loyal tribesmen?'

Alfridda was puzzled as much as alarmed, and her arms went out to clutch her youngest son to her breasts. The boy squirmed away, for he was mad to hear the remainder of his uncle's story and was careless of any personal dangers.

'The Crow King is smitten with lust for the witch-woman. She poisons his ears so he sees enemies where there are none. Maeve is sure that she is treasonous, and is determined to bring our king and the

Dene kingdom to ruin. If Maeve is correct, then the bitch will need to separate Hrolf Kraki from his most loyal and powerful allies.'

'Such as us!' Alfridda exclaimed. Suddenly, Arthur realised how strange this whole conversation had become. Over the past few weeks, he had begun to feel that the Britons were far more civilised and urbane than the Dene, at least in standards of cleanliness, the sophistication of their food and dress, their use of metal and industry and their complex social structures.

So why was Stormbringer discussing matters of politics with a woman? Arthur was confused, as was Eamonn, for both young men had been brought up to believe that women had no place in the council chamber. Even Bedwyr, who discussed *everything* with his wife in private, would never consider asking Elayne's opinion on manly matters *in public*. Arthur decided to ask Stormbringer about this obviously unusual relationship between the sexes when the opportunity arose.

'And then there's the situation in Skania!' Stormbringer proceeded to explain the parlous situation that was playing out to a dreadful conclusion only a few miles away across the narrow neck of water, albeit far to the north.

Alfridda's hands twisted and she toyed with the bodice of her tunic.

'By the sainted hands of Mother Mary, brother! If Skania should fall to the Goths, then so too will Ostoanmark. We could never hope to withstand a prolonged attack by the ships of Gothland. That small strip of water and Skania itself are all that protects us from the Gothland king. In the past, he has sometimes shown himself to be friendly and a good ally but, at other times, he remembers old wrongs from the years when the first Scyldings took the coastal rim by force of arms and desperation. If Hrolf Kraki refuses to help the jarls of Skania, then he's turned into a stark, staring madman, or he's become ensorcelled by the witch-woman. Either way, these troubles could become the beginning of the end of all of us. I'm certain that if this island falls, then the others will also, and the Crow King will really be the Jarl of Nothing. May the gods protect us!

'You must call up all those men who are sworn to your standard and convince them to sail to Skania with you,' Alfridda decided firmly. 'You mustn't delay, brother! If the white witch plans treason, then the Hundings will attack the Crow King from the south and he'll continue to ignore Skania. Before Hrolf Kraki can blink, he'll be attacked through his safe underbelly, and they will march across our bones and blood.'

'Aye, sister, I believe there's a treacherous plan in that wicked head of Aednetta Fridasdottar, and it has already been put into motion. The game has begun, whether we like it or not. We live, or we die, by what happens in Skania so we must set sail as soon as I can raise a force that will put a stop to the machinations of the Gothlander.'

'I'll send out runners immediately, Valdar. Meanwhile you can take whatever you need from The Holding. Be about your work, Valdar, and I'll see to your guests.'

Valdar Bjornsen kissed his sister's rosy cheek and swung his daughters back onto his shoulders. 'Stay with my sister, Arthur, and she'll see to your lodgings. This struggle has naught to do with you, and I apologise for dragging you into the domestic troubles of the Dene people. For now, you can rest and enjoy the hospitality of my sister and her friends.'

'I'm coming with you, Stormbringer,' Arthur insisted. 'We brought trouble to you and yours, so we are obliged to repay our debt to you. We'd be lying dead in a cesspit in Heorot if it were not for the assistance you gave us. All that Eamonn and I will require is that our sisters be allowed to remain here in safety.'

Stormbringer glanced quickly in Alfridda's direction and she smiled secretively.

Is that the way the wind blows? My sister is only a child and Stormbringer is a grown man, Arthur thought. Does the Sae Dene captain hold more than admiration for her?

But Arthur decided not to voice his suspicions. Time was short; their enemy controlled territory that was visible across a narrow strip of water from Stormbringer's spacious lands. He could understand Alfridda's nervousness!

'If you are fated to perish in any future battle, Valdar Bjornsen, I'd prefer that it's not through any fault of mine.' Arthur's chin jutted forward with determination. 'Until our debt to you is repaid, I am obligated to shield your back from all harm or treason, and I'll not shirk my duty. In fact, I will enjoy the prospect of conflict. Come rack or ruin, I and mine will always keep our word.'

'Very well then, Arthur, but don't say I didn't warn you of what could lie ahead of us,' Stormbringer snapped, before setting off at a trot towards the warriors' hall.

Cursing under his breath, Arthur followed.

The afternoon had barely begun and their safe harbour had become a perilous place of shoals in the blinking of an eye. Fortuna had once again turned her wheel.

THE JOURNEY OF THE TRINE
THROUGH AUSTRASIA

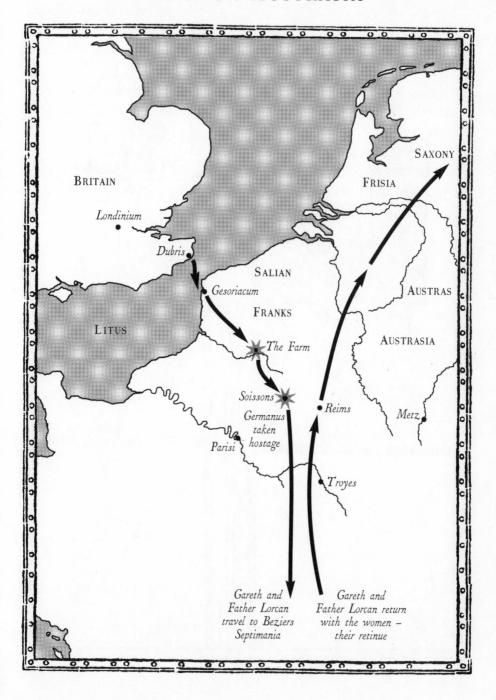

PLAN OF THE FARM IN AUSTRASIA

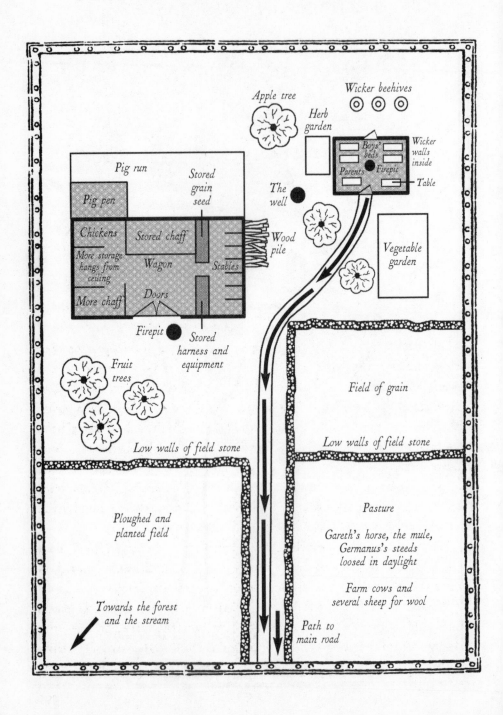

Apple tree

Wicker beehives

Herb garden

Boys' beds

Wicker walls inside

Parents

Firepit

Table

The well

Pig run

Stored grain seed

Pig pen

Chickens

Stored chaff

Wood pile

Vegetable garden

More storage hangs from ceiling

Wagon

Stables

More chaff

Doors

Firepit

Stored harness and equipment

Fruit trees

Field of grain

Low walls of field stone

Low walls of field stone

Ploughed and planted field

Pasture

Gareth's horse, the mule, Germanus's steeds loosed in daylight

Farm cows and several sheep for wool

Towards the forest and the stream

Path to main road

CHAPTER XVII

PLAGUE

Be happy, drink, think each day your own as you live it, and leave the rest to fortune.

Euripides, as recorded by Plato in *Phaedo*

The barn was warm but, most importantly, it was watertight. As they rode through the storm, the three travellers were subjected to the worst extremes of nature before they reached its dim protection. Germanus was sagging in the saddle when they reached their haven and was only partly conscious. It required the combined efforts of both Lorcan and Gareth to lift him from his horse and lay him down on a nest of straw as far from the open doorway as was possible. Germanus almost woke for a moment, because any pressure under his arms appeared to cause unbearable pain, although Lorcan checked under the Frank's clothes and found no indication of wounds.

Several indignant chickens looked down on the interlopers from their roosts in the rafters, while an old plough horse munched incuriously on newly cut grass in one of the primitive stalls.

Gareth left Lorcan to fuss over Germanus in order to strip the packs and saddles from their five horses. The beasts shivered in the cold draught from the doorway, so Gareth led them into the rear of the barn to pens that were obviously used in winter to protect the farm animals from deep snowfalls. Once the horses were penned, Gareth used hobbles to restrict their movements so he could fill their drinking troughs with fresh water from a well near the farmhouse, drenching himself once more in the process. Finding an open bag of stored grain, he made a mental promise to pay the elderly couple for anything he took, and then filled a number of pails of food for their precious horseflesh. The beasts snuffled companionably and their hobbles tinkled musically from the small bells that Lorcan had tied to them.

Gareth smiled at the bucolic scene and its familiar sounds and smells. A sense of peace flooded him with half-memories of early childhood. Then he returned to where he had left Lorcan and Germanus, and his pleasant mood cracked open like a smashed egg.

Lorcan had stripped his friend down to his shirt and Germanus now looked frail and elderly with his long white legs exposed. For the first time, Gareth noticed that Germanus's skin was creped and loose at the eyelids, the belly and under his chin. Carefully, Lorcan was engaged in inspecting the entire length of his friend's body as he sought for signs that would explain the fever causing Germanus to shiver with something other than cold.

'It doesn't make any sense,' Lorcan complained. 'Shite, his lungs are clear so it's not the coughing disease. There are no spots – except for a couple of bites, courtesy of the bed bugs provided by Priscus's establishment. And it's not the scarlet fever or one of the other illnesses involving a rash. The only symptoms are an over-warm body, a crippling headache and some swelling in the neck and under the arms.'

Gareth was surprised at Lorcan's anxious face. Up until this moment, he had known that Germanus was sick, but had failed to recognise any specific symptoms that could harm the large Frank warrior. He'd always seemed invincible during their short acquaintance.

Suddenly, their journey into the land of the Dene had come under threat. Gareth prepared himself for what could become a long sojourn in the barn until such time as the illness had run its course.

Surprisingly, given how ill the Frank was, Gareth wasn't terribly perturbed, partially because Lorcan claimed some skills in healing, but mostly because Germanus was like the mountains. He was indestructible. During the night, Gareth awoke to the quiet of the countryside, a silence that made him nervous after the earlier noise of thunder and lightning. The fierce storm had passed and left the landscape battered, wind-torn and glistening in the moonlight. The wildly scudding clouds had blown westward towards the sea to leave behind the familiar stars that had comforted Gareth for most of his life. Curled in the fresh straw close to his stallion's stall, Gareth listened to Lorcan's exhausted snores and the companionable whicker of his horse standing behind him.

The young man's reverie was broken by a moan from the indistinct shape of Germanus as he lay under a pile of cloaks used to warm his shivering flesh. Lorcan had fought against his own weariness for many hours, while urging his comatose friend to take in water and a little of the hot soup provided by the farmer's wife. Germanus had struggled to eat, but he was sliding in and out of consciousness.

As he gazed out at the stars through the open door of the barn, Gareth considered their plight if Germanus should die. The prospect was so fraught with potential disaster that he refused to dwell on the possibility. Grunting impatiently with himself, Gareth rolled over and fell into a deep sleep.

In the morning, the sky had that fresh blueness that comes after spring rains. Lorcan was still dozing in the straw, while Germanus had thrown off the restrictive cloaks. Gareth could see that the Frank's flesh remained hot and feverish, so he carefully pulled the disturbed cloaks back to cover Germanus's partial nakedness.

At the door of the small stone farmhouse, Gareth spoke to the elderly couple in his halting Frank, although he was unsure if his words were fully understood. The farmer was called Tominoe, an odd name that the grey-haired man told them was Breton in origin. His wife, Eleana, was a plump little creature with raisin-brown eyes and ruddy cheeks. The elderly couple happily accepted two silver coins for the use of the stables and the grain while Eleana brewed a tisane that she swore was an excellent medication for fevers. She also added a generous helping of a medicinal concoction that her mother used to draw out poisons. Gareth thanked her effusively and made the old woman blush when he gave her a courteous bow.

These farmers were excellent hosts. But Gareth could see that the farm was too large and too time-consuming for the elderly Tominoe to manage alone. The fields lay fallow while ploughing and planting were long overdue. Similarly, the stone walls along several fields were in urgent need of repair so Gareth offered to take their old horse out to plough the nearest fields if the elderly couple were prepared to carry out the planting. They agreed readily, and Mistress Eleana gave him a battered jug of fresh milk for the invalid. When they discovered that their other guest was a priest, their plain and honest faces shone with pleasure.

'Would the priest hear our confessions? We've not been shrived for near a whole season since our old priest died.' Gareth wondered aloud why no one had been sent to take the dead priest's place.

'Times are hard, young master. The king has no liking for the Roman Church, preferring to use the Aryan priests. Rumour says there's been trouble in the church hierarchy, but we poor worshippers are the sufferers from any disagreements between the great ones. Our sons went off with the army near to three years ago and we've heard naught of them in all that time. My wife feels it deep, can you understand? A few prayers from your priest would ease her heart, and we'd be grateful for any time he can give us.'

Gareth promised that he would ask Lorcan to minister to the spiritual needs of the old couple, once Germanus's condition had improved. Taking his leave, he returned to the barn to give the herbal simples to the priest, along with the fresh milk that might nourish Germanus if he could be induced to drink it.

In his absence, Lorcan had woken, checked on the health of his friend and then collected the eggs laid in the straw during the previous night. Lorcan accepted the milk with a little crow of pleasure.

'Fresh eggs beaten into milk will help Germanus to fight any infections, even those I can't see on my friend's body. I tell you truly, boy, that I've no idea what illness is devouring my friend, and I'm deathly afraid of it! Germanus would have caught the lung disease for sure if you hadn't found this pleasant little farm when you did – and then nothing would have saved him. Tell the mistress I thank her for the simples and I'll visit with them at nightfall.'

Lorcan immediately went to work, mixing the drawing potion and spreading it onto two pads of cloth that looked suspiciously like the old priest's spare shirt. Then he made two more pads, placed them into Germanus's armpits and lashed them into place with more strips of rag.

'He complains of pain there when he's partly conscious, so I'll see if this drawing ointment brings out any of the infection,' Lorcan explained. 'And the raw eggs and milk will help to ease his gut and provide him with some sustenance.'

Lorcan's mood had been lifted by the simple fact that he now had tools to use in his battle against this mysterious disease. Whether they worked or not was less important than the fact that Father Lorcan was able to make a real attempt to heal his friend.

Meanwhile, Gareth prepared himself for some heavy farm work. He had done his fair share of farm labour during his youth, so he was comfortable with the prospect of physical exertion.

'I'll take their horse and start ploughing their fields while you take care of Germanus,' Gareth explained to the priest. 'I'll feel less beholden if I'm doing something useful. If we can't continue our journey, I see no fault in keeping myself occupied here. Incidentally, I don't think much of a ruler who takes all the sons of such an elderly couple who can't care for themselves. Surely their king must realise that there'll be a famine if the land and crops aren't tended.'

'Some rulers don't care about their lands or their tenants,' Lorcan replied briskly. 'They only bother with their prestige and the gold that can be squeezed out of the peasants who rely on them for protection.' Gareth nodded and turned to go, but Lorcan called him back and presented him with a number of large, speckled eggs which were transferred into a pouch made from the front of Gareth's shirt. 'Please thank the mistress in advance, boy, for the few eggs I have already taken,' he added.

The grey-muzzled farm horse was huge when compared with Gareth's stallion or the pack animals. She was broad in the beam and her fetlocks were hidden under long hair that was light in colour, much like her uncombed mane and tail. Gareth untangled her mane and promised her a good brushing at the end of her working day, if she was compliant. The animal snickered gently through soft black lips. Her eyes were large, brown and long-lashed like a girl's and her reddish coat made the young man think of strawberries. Gareth decided to call her Berry.

Gareth could read the old man's mind as soon as Tominoe saw the quality and beauty of Gareth's stallion. The old farmer could visualise the foals that Berry would throw if she was covered by such an animal. He could only live in hope.

Well, if that's what our host wants, I see no harm in it, Gareth thought with a wry grin. And you'll not complain, will you, my lad? Gareth thumped the stallion's side and raised dust from his strong black coat. The horse whickered encouragingly.

Throughout the morning, and in the heat of the noonday sun, man and mare laboured under the spring sunshine. The ploughshare carved its way through the turf with more ease than Gareth had expected, given that the plough's blade needed sharpening. Gareth promised himself that he'd find out if Tominoe possessed a whetstone.

As Gareth guided the horse and plough through the turf and into the chocolate-brown soil, pushing with all his strength to assist the mare in her efforts, Tominoe and Eleana followed in Gareth's wake to clean out the furrows with hoes. Once the furrows were clean, they began to plant their precious seed before covering it lightly with soil to defeat the depredations of the blackbirds. For these poor farmers, it was vital that everyone worked hard to ensure a good harvest.

A row of the untidy birds sat on the paddock wall and watched the three humans with bright, cruel eyes. When Gareth pelted them with stones, they flapped away briefly before returning to preen their feathers on the un-mortared stones like ragged scraps of black cloth.

Gareth picked up a particularly large rock and tossed it hard into the row of birds. They squawked indignantly and flapped away, but this time they waited for their chance in an apple tree beyond the reach of Gareth's stones.

At noon, the provident housewife brought more milk, fried bacon, slabs of coarse bread and a soft white cheese. For all that the cheese was unfamiliar, Gareth ate with gusto. He felt alive and at peace for the first time in months, despite being mud-blackened from head to toe.

Eleana fetched a tin platter with more food and another jug of milk for Lorcan and Germanus, so Gareth left the traces with Tominoe and trotted to the barn to deliver their noontime meal. Lorcan, distracted, absently nodded his thanks and turned to heating the tisane over a small fire pit he had constructed outside the open barn doorway.

Gareth took the hint and returned to the ploughing.

As the sun began to sink through the heavens, Tominoe showed Gareth the way to a small stream that cut through the farm. There, Gareth frolicked in the shallows as he scrubbed his skin and hair free of clinging dirt before washing his clothes, then sunned himself in a small clearing beside the waterway.

The young man watched while butterflies of various colours danced about in the afternoon light. Weeds had flowered in great, white heads that would soon seed and all too soon become pests, but on that particular afternoon, Gareth's heart was touched by their loveliness.

But Gareth's pleasure quickly evaporated when he returned to the barn, for Germanus was worse. The Frank moaned and mumbled in his unnatural sleep, while Lorcan pointed to small swellings growing under his arms where the drawing ointment had been placed. The priest told Gareth that these lumps felt hard and hot, as if burning pebbles had been inserted under the skin, causing Germanus to suffer from a degree of pain much greater than the size of the swelling seemed to warrant.

Lorcan began to prepare another pair of pads containing the drawing ointment.

'It's all I can think of to do, boy. At least I'm forcing the infection to come to the surface. Could it be that the other nodes in the neck, groin and belly are also at risk of infection?'

Helplessly, Lorcan and Gareth could only watch in amazement at the agonies suffered by their friend. At dusk, Lorcan went up to the farmhouse to minister to the spiritual welfare of the farmer and his wife, while Gareth watched Germanus in his stead and used damp cloths to bathe the Frank from head to foot. The water seemed to ease Germanus's pain, so Gareth collected more cold water from the stream and continued to gently lave Germanus's sweating form.

And so the next two days passed, as Germanus sank deeper into a torpor from which his companions believed he would never awaken.

Germanus's temperature remained dangerously high. Pain racked his inert body and all movement of his joints seemed to cause him pain.

In the darkest hour in the early morning, when the soul's hold on life is at its weakest, Gareth became deathly frightened. Without Germanus, they would lose a fluent Frankish-speaker and the local knowledge so important to their journey. Whether Germanus lived or died, Gareth fully intended to go on into the north in search of Arthur and his companions, but his heart quailed at the idea of setting off into a hostile landscape without Germanus's comforting counsel to protect his back.

Now that the huge Frank was in such peril, Gareth could finally admit that he needed Germanus and, of even more importance, he actually liked and admired the sword-master. 'Don't die, Germanus,' Gareth whispered into the darkness. But the night wind continued to moan, while the young man felt tears begin to well at the corners of his eyes.

'The people I care about always seem to die.' He dropped his head into his folded arms to rest, sure that he would never be able to sleep. But soon the night washed over him in a thick black tide.

In the morning, Germanus appeared to be coming to some kind of physical crisis. The blue of his lips, his glazed and sightless eyes and the heat in his body that seemed to sear his flesh were killing him. The mystery illness had defied Lorcan's best efforts to save his friend.

His extremities appeared white or bluish, so Lorcan massaged the

Frank's fingers and toes, pinched his nose at the tip to stimulate the blood flow and massaged his friend's thinning lips. Lorcan understood that if the blood flow slowed or was cut off from the extremities, then the fingers, toes, nose or lips would die and the skin would begin to putrefy while the patient still breathed.

When Gareth asked Lorcan what he was doing, the priest dropped his head into his hands while his whole body seemed to shrink in defeat.

'I've no idea what I'm about, Gareth. The odd colour of our friend's extremities seems to indicate that his circulation is compromised and his flesh is dying. Would Germanus want to live without fingers and toes? No, I think not! If he should suffer that fate, he would kill himself before too long, and this would bar his soul from Heaven. That's something I couldn't bear to contemplate, so I massage his extremities and try to force the blood to stir through his body. I do it every hour without fail, but I have now reached the point where I must ask for your help because I have to sleep.'

He smiled wearily and sat down to rest.

'So heat me some water, Gareth, and I'll try to give him some more massage. Afterwards, there are some matters that I would like to discuss with you. I'd send you on without us if I could, but I need your help now and I don't like to risk the health of our hosts by asking them to assist me with the nursing.'

'We've been at cross-purposes in the past, Lorcan. Please forgive my impatience if I've been uncharitable or unkind. I'd never sacrifice Germanus just to achieve my quest. Besides, I don't think I can be successful without you both to guide me along the paths we will be forced to travel.'

Lorcan saw real sincerity in Gareth's moist eyes and wondered if Germanus had touched the boy's wounded heart.

When Gareth returned with the hot water, Lorcan was kneeling beside his friend with the Frank's right arm extended above his head.

'Look at his inner arm, Gareth. Then tell me what you can see there?'

'Dear Lord,' Gareth whispered. 'What is that thing?'

'I don't know,' Lorcan replied slowly. 'But he has the same massive boil, or whatever it is, under the other arm. I've checked his groin and neck but so far, beyond a little swelling, there are only two of these things that actually look like *that*.'

Just below the greying hair that grew sparsely into the deepest hollows, a massive red and shiny swelling distended the skin so it seemed that the flesh could tear open at any moment. Even more grotesquely, there seemed to be no head on this infection, just an egg of raw, red and burning agony that throbbed under Lorcan's fingers. The slightest touch caused Germanus such pain that Lorcan could only drizzle more and more cooling water over the terrible outward manifestation of this foul illness.

'Do you realise that this disease, whatever it is, could be contagious? Have you been feeling ill at all?' The twin swellings were so painful that Gareth had already started to check his whole body with exquisite care.

'No, nothing, I'm feeling perfectly healthy,' Gareth said. 'I'd be very sorry if we were to bring disease to this farm.'

'I feel as you do, Gareth, but I don't think we have to worry. Neither Tominoe nor his wife has been near Germanus, so we'll keep it that way. Now, help me to dip his hands in the hot water.'

Germanus screamed weakly when his fingers were placed in the hot water, almost as if every nerve ending had been abused. Gradually, because the swellings under his armpits weren't compressed, their patient quietened and Lorcan asked Gareth to prepare more milk with two raw eggs broken and stirred into the liquid.

'It seems to give Germanus strength, although he finds it increasingly difficult to swallow. I've been chewing his food for several days now, but it still pains him to swallow it. I've been depending on Eleana's milk. Those two old ones are decent, kindly people. They deserve more from their king than stolen children and a penurious old age.'

Gareth was touched by Lorcan's devotion. Although the comparison seemed ludicrous, Gareth was reminded of a mother bird regurgitating food for its chick.

The next morning, the swellings under Germanus's arms were even more inflamed and terrible, so Lorcan was forced to face the possibility that his friend might be close to death. Throughout that night, the Hibernian had prayed, reverting to the idealistic blacksmith's son who had gone into the priesthood with so much joy, before the cardinal in Rome had poisoned his heart.

Then, in the morning, Lorcan discovered that Germanus's pulse was thready and had weakened during the night. The priest gazed down at his friend and decided to face up to what he'd known for some time would become an irrevocable and inevitable course of action.

During a long life, the priest had contrived to survive brutality and sodomy, lost children and a murdered wife. He had also been forced to plumb the depths of human depravity and to wade through blood in numerous battles, but he had somehow found the courage to return to the priesthood and to the life-giving strength of his humanity. Lorcan prepared himself mentally to take a terrible risk.

What he proposed to do was dangerous and could mean death for Germanus within hours, but Germanus's plight was extreme now, and he'd die anyway if Lorcan did nothing.

The priest had made his decision during many melancholy hours of prayer, so he prepared to commence his battle with fate, while his heart was lighter for having arrived at this commitment.

'Please, Gareth, can you tell the farmer and his wife that your work in the fields will be delayed today? I know you were weeding the cabbages yesterday, but I need your strength here today. I'll wait till you return.'

The priest refused to explain any further until Gareth had completed his duty to the farmer and his wife, so Gareth hurried to the large vegetable patch where the farmer was already hard at work with his hoe. As quickly as he could, he explained Germanus's parlous condition and informed Tominoe that Lorcan needed his assistance. The elderly farmer crossed himself and muttered a short prayer before sending Gareth back to the barn with his good wishes for Germanus's health.

When he entered the barn, Gareth could see that Lorcan had moved the Frank's pallet closer to the door where the light was stronger. The strength that Lorcan must have expended to drag Germanus over the sod floor on his straw bed would have taxed even Gareth's young muscles.

'What are you proposing to do, Lorcan? And how can I help you?'

'I've sharpened the blade of my eating knife by using the whetstone Germanus uses to sharpen his sword. Could you please hold the blade into an open fire if you can build one? I need hot water as well, as hot as I can bear, and I wish to cleanse my blade the way the Jews and Arabs of Rome did when they healed hideous wounds. I've read Master Myrddion's scrolls, remember? His use of boiling water always seemed so odd, but I've tried everything else. I don't know why fire cleans metal, or why boiling cleans water so it doesn't contaminate a wound, but many of the patients of ancient times survived, as did Myrddion's, so I must be guided by their wisdom.'

'This is nonsense, Lorcan! How can water cleanse anything? To drink polluted water is to die. And no healer I ever knew cleansed his knives with fire.'

Every instinct told the young man that this course of action was wrong, although he granted that Myrddion Merlinus was said to be a sorcerer in his trade of healing. Perhaps magic was needed to save Germanus.

'I don't have time to argue with you, Gareth. Merlinus always used boiling water and fire to chase away the evil humours, so I intend to do the same for my friend. What can be the harm in that, boy?' Lorcan's voice broke with the force of his passion. 'He's dying before our eyes!'

'But what are you proposing to do?'

'Please, boy, just do what I ask, and I will take the responsibility for all that happens.'

More confused than ever, Gareth used his tinderbox to raise a flame in the outside fire pit that Lorcan had built on the day of their arrival. When he fed that small tongue of orange some shavings from the wood heap, followed by several substantial logs, he set a pannikin upon the heat and filled the vessel with water. He then bathed the elegant little eating knife in the flickering, cherry-red flame.

The delicate little knife and its wicked point began to glow red . . . and then white, so Gareth removed it and, using gloves to protect his hands, carried both the blade and the pannikin back to the barn. Lorcan thanked him distantly and dipped a cloth into the steaming water in order to cleanse his hands with the hot fabric.

'Now, my friend, hold Germanus down and put all the pressure you can on his torso and his right elbow. You can even sit on him, if you must! Cracked ribs are the least of his problems, and I must ensure that he remains perfectly still. I plan to lance both the swellings because the humours are eating him alive.'

'But there's no head on those lumps, just a gross tumorous swelling. You might be doing more harm than good!'

'Do what I ask, Gareth, for Germanus is dead if I don't act right now. If he dies from what I do, I have only hastened his end. At any rate, the sin and the responsibility are mine. I'll castigate myself far worse than you ever could.'

Then, as Gareth watched in dismay, Lorcan's bravado cracked and the older man almost wept. 'For God's sake, boy, obey me before I lose the nerve to do what has to be done.'

So Gareth threw the whole weight of his body on Germanus's chest and used both arms to hold the right arm above the Frank's head. He was forced to lie across Germanus's body, using his legs to hold down the left arm, while also providing space for Lorcan to reach the right armpit. The position was awkward for all three men, and Germanus began to thrash. A sharp blow struck Gareth across the nose and blinded him with pain for a moment, but he raised his right knee to hold down Germanus's left arm, leaving Lorcan free to act.

'May God guide my hand,' Lorcan prayed, and then sliced deeply into the hideous swelling in Germanus's armpit.

A rush of blood and serum came first, and then vile-smelling pus began to pour out. Quick as lightning, Lorcan thrust a hot piece of cloth into the open wound while Germanus howled and bucked like a wild animal. Gareth gritted his teeth and hung on to the wailing man with all his strength.

As Lorcan bound the cloth into a pad and secured it across Germanus's arm and chest, the Frank gradually quietened. Gareth heaved a huge sigh of relief, but his ordeal was far from over.

'And now we must lance the other armpit, Gareth. Please, wash the knife, and then reheat it over the fire. We must replace the water first, however, so I can wash again.'

Gareth hurried to obey, sickened by the terrible, rotting stench.

Soon enough, Gareth was back in the barn, and the whole prelude to the operation was repeated, only in reverse.

Gareth changed position and manoeuvred his body until his muscles began to crack with the strain. Under his weight, Germanus stirred as if, even in his torpor, he guessed that some new atrocity was coming at any moment.

'Are you ready, Gareth?' Lorcan asked. He used the knife with more confidence on this occasion. Once again, the Frank fought like a wild thing, but his great strength had been diminished by illness. Lorcan was obliged to cut a second time, much deeper, until the vile-smelling rot began to pour out. Gareth averted his head, because the stink was a reminder of the charnel house and of long-dead corpses. He feared he would vomit and contaminate the wound.

Once again, Lorcan packed and wrapped the wound and then asked Gareth to cleanse the blade with fire again, in case it required further use. This time, Gareth was quick to obey. He'd seen the corruption flow from within Germanus's body and he doubted that Lorcan would ever again be able to cut his meat with this dainty Roman toy. Beyond all doubt, the fire had cleansed the iron of that terrible pus, but what could cure the heart after the horrific wounds he had been forced to inflict on his friend?

Once Gareth had placed the knife into a fresh pannikin of boiling water, he looked to Lorcan for reassurance. 'What do we do now, Lorcan? Does Germanus have any hope of survival?'

'We can only wait, Gareth. My treatment might prove to be fatal. But he must be watched constantly now, so we can concentrate on keeping his temperature down. He must be washed regularly, and the dressings have to be changed at regular intervals as well. I'll still need your help, I'm afraid.'

'So we sit and wait. Is that all we can do?'

'You could try praying, boy. At this stage, even Germanus won't mind a prayer or two.'

Far away, a ship was found off the coast of the kingdom of the Visigoths near the town of Lisbon on the Tagus River. The vessel seemed to be wallowing rudderless in the waves, so several enterprising fishermen rowed out beyond the shallower waters and clambered over its stern.

Other than the absence of crew members aboard the ship, a disgusting odour was the first indication of something very wrong aboard the *Golden Nymph*. The grandiose name was etched into a plaque in Latin on the ship's side.

The vile stench came from the hatches leading down to the hold. One of the fishermen crossed himself and muttered a comment about the works of the devil before heading back to his rowing boat, but his companion was made of sterner stuff. Carefully, and with his fish-gutting knife drawn to protect himself, he crept stealthily towards the prow of the vessel.

Something about the dark and gaping hatch made the hairs rise on the back of his neck, so he gave it a wide berth.

In a narrow gap between the mast and an adjacent storage locker, the fisherman found a dying man. His lips and nose were black with rot, as were the stumps of his fingers; his eyes were glazed with pain and fever; while his stripped torso revealed hideous boils under his arms and in the folds of his groin. As the fisherman watched, appalled, the sailor went into his death throes with a great convulsion of straining and cracking muscles.

Any man of sense would have fled in terror and forgotten the ship of dead men with its grisly cargo. But this fisherman was far too poor to leave the gold cross around the dead man's neck or the silver rings that decorated his blackened fingers. Shuddering with revulsion, he went down below decks and stripped the dead and the barely alive of all the valuables that he could find in the foetid darkness, in spite of jumping in terror at the slightest movement or sound. The bright eyes of black rats watched him from the shadows, perched on the cargo and lashing the air with their scaly tails. Eventually, despite his strong constitution, the thought of these vermin feeding on the ship's crew sent him running up into the clean air and back to his boat. Safely ensconced, he vomited until only bile was left in his stomach. Even the promise of more gold wasn't sufficient incentive to tempt him back to the death ship.

In the morning, the *Golden Nymph* had disappeared from sight and was never seen again.

'I want you, woman! And I want you now! I don't feel well – so fetch me some hot milk.' Priscus was tired, headachy and nauseous, but refused to reveal just how ill he felt to his woman. He was sure she would take liberties.

Over the following days, she took more than liberties: she took everything. As the innkeeper fell into a deep coma that baffled the physicians she hired, Delia ordered the servants to move Priscus to a smaller room over the stables, citing the need for the master to sleep peacefully, without being disturbed. In private, the servants wondered at the illness until other people away from the Green Man began to contract the illness.

In a fit of spite that she found impossible to explain, Delia decided to burn his bedding and every loathsome piece of the furniture in his room.

'With luck, he'll have no use for it in Hades,' she said to herself as she watched the whole pile of bedding flame up. With some satisfaction, she watched Priscus's bed bugs and lice pop and die in the blaze. The servants thought she'd gone just a little mad with grief.

In his new room above the stables, she cared for Priscus desultorily, taking pains not to touch him. Within days, he fell into the sleep of the deathly ill, and died unattended. By good fortune, none of the servants from the Green Man became ill, so they began to view Delia in a whole new fashion.

During the terrible days that followed, people were told that Delia had used fire to kill her man's illness and her methods were copied by other prudent citizens throughout Gesoriacum and the surrounding district. The air was filled with the smell of burning and whole streets in the slums were turned into hell pits with the bodies of the dead still lying inside their burning beds. It would never be known how many sufferers died of the flames, rather than the disease.

Even priests and physicians died in the weeks that followed, for no one was spared – no matter how pious or learned they were.

The Green Man inn was taking no guests by this time and had barred its doors. Priscus was quickly forgotten, once Mistress Delia had removed all the innkeeper's possessions and burned them to cinders with his remains carefully stacked inside the makeshift funeral pyre. The hostelry was soon seen as a haven of safety in a sea of disaster, so Delia was left to wonder at the luck that Fortuna had placed upon her attractive shoulders.

She left the ashes of Priscus's bones to be scattered in the winds, which occurred quickly enough. For the moment, however, the inn had sufficient food and drink to last until autumn and the first traces of cold when nature would ensure that the most stubborn plague would die.

Meanwhile the ungodly took the opportunity to turn Gesoriacum into a living hell. There was no escape and no amount of wealth brought safety to the populace. Drunkards died just as quickly as the abstemious, so men drank and whored, and dared Death to take them.

And it came for them – again and again! It grew sated, and then became bloated with more bodies than even Death could stomach.

CHAPTER XVIII

THE END OF INNOCENCE

He who desires but acts not, breeds pestilence.

William Blake, *The Marriage of Heaven and Hell*

In the year before Arthur set forth from Tintagel and embarked on his disastrous journey into the North, a pestilence had begun to stir in lands around the Middle Sea. How such a strange and alien disease came to the blue waters and gem-like islands at the world's centre was a problem too complex for either philosophers or kings to understand. Did the illness travel with the camel trains in the caravanserai, led by dark-faced men dressed in robes of glistening white and wearing head-cloths that were bound in place with cords of silver, gold and crimson? Did camel bells welcome the fatal illness from the lands of saffron and spices where it coiled in the curled black hair of doe-eyed women with dots of gold and scarlet on their foreheads? Or did it originate first in the lands of the East where small yellow men immersed themselves in rice paddies that divided the landscape into bright green squares under a dusty, heathen sun?

Did the origin of the pestilence really matter? It simply came – in the folds of silk, in a woman's hair behind her ear, in a ship's cargo of spices, or in the thick white flesh of eunuchs who guarded young girls sent as tribute to the City of God.

Then, having trebled and quadrupled in strength and potency, the pestilence attacked the City of God like a great storm until, finally, strong men died in humiliating delirium, soiled and filthy, and women and children perished in their homes. The authorities soon realised that God had turned His face away from His people, for physicians also perished while trying to stem the tide of death. As Germanus was suffering in the Frank Lands, five thousand men, women and children were dying every week in Constantine's great city. And so, one death in the north was a bagatelle in the enormity of so much carnage in the area around the Middle Sea.

Shipping fanned out from the centre of the world that was the Golden Horn. In this place where large cities met across narrow straits of water, traders set out in heavily guarded convoys bound for exotic destinations in the north such as Dacia, Carpathia and Illyricum. Other enterprising ships' captains set sail for exotic ports such as Crete, Egypt, Italia, Burgandy, Numidia and Aquitaine, while other intrepid sailors braved the Pillars of Hercules to seek out the kingdoms of the Visigoths, the Franks and the Britons. Like a great web, the entrepreneurs of Constantinople traded with the whole world and, where their ships' keels cut through the invisible thoroughfares of the sea, pestilence went with them as an unwelcome and invisible passenger. The web was wide, well-travelled and complex, and pestilence followed its path like a black spider scurrying along the silver strands, as insubstantial as thistledown, but deadlier than all the poisons in the Middle Sea.

But such vast charnel houses of death become too huge for human-kind to comprehend. The Pope prayed that Satan's Curse would be lifted and the Cardinals flinched to discover that death came knocking on the doors of Mother Church. Innocent nuns and young priests turned the golden rings on their fingers as they prayed on cold stone floors both night and day, weeping for the deaths of so many citizens who had been cut down before the hour decreed by God. The Pope ordered the faithful to pray in their homes rather than come to the great basilicas to prove their piety. For if the Palace of the Pope in Holy Rome wasn't safe, where in the world could a man sleep free from care?

Once Death had silenced the cross-road fountains of Rome, or turned marketplaces in Lisbon into arid, empty and desolate expanses where farmers lay dead in their barns, even the guardians of Heaven were forced to notice.

Father Lorcan prayed throughout the long night over the waxen body of his friend, repeating every prayer he had ever heard in Hibernia or Rome. The weary, dangerous hours of early morning were broken periodically, when Lorcan was required to remove the packing from Germanus's wounds and insert fresh cloths. Lorcan threw the used cloths onto the dying fire and then thoroughly washed his hands. And so, in mournful labour, prayer and suffering, Lorcan and Germanus managed to survive the night in Tominoe's barn.

Gareth awoke with a rush. He had dragged a promise out of the priest to wake him after a few hours of rest; Lorcan had stretched his considerable strength to its limits during the previous day, so he was on the point of collapse. As soon as the young man opened his eyes, he realised that Lorcan had tried to spare him from any duties during the night. He cursed mildly in irritation.

But Gareth admitted to himself that he was glad to have been spared. The thought of touching those gross holes in Germanus's flesh made his gorge rise and he saluted the silent, sleeping mound that was Father Lorcan with genuine respect and awe.

Lorcan, exhausted, was sound asleep. Gareth left him curled up in his cloak within a couple of steps of Germanus's body and turned his attention to the dying Frank. Germanus was so still and his limbs seemed so flaccid and unresponsive that he appeared to be dead. With his heart in his mouth, Gareth placed his forefinger on the large vein in Germanus's throat and whispered a soft prayer.

There! A heartbeat! And another! Germanus's heart was still thudding away in his chest, impossible as that seemed after the trauma of the previous day's surgery. Gingerly, Gareth touched the patient's forehead and found it was beaded with sweat. In fact, the cloak that covered Germanus was soaked through, but his flesh was no longer burning to the touch.

Miraculously, the tall Frank's condition had improved and, with luck, he might yet survive. When Gareth washed the cooling sweat from his face, Germanus opened his eyes and, for a moment, Gareth thought the Frank recognised him. Then he mumbled something inarticulate and fell asleep.

Lorcan stirred, dragged out of a deep sleep by the noise around him, so Gareth helped the older man to sit up. The wind from the sea in the west was chill, and only a faint line of golden light touched the eastern skyline, giving the promise of a clear dawn.

'Is . . . is Germanus . . . ?' Gareth realised that the priest thought his friend had died during the night.

'Heavens, no!' Gareth said softly. 'His fever seems to have broken and I'm certain that he's asleep now.'

'I don't believe it! He was as hot as the fires of hell when I checked his dressing this morning. You've mistaken the coma that comes before death for a natural sleep.' Lorcan seemed afraid to check for himself. He was fearful that his friend would be snatched away if he even dared to hope that his prayers had been answered.

'Look at him, Father,' Gareth begged.

Lorcan placed a small mirror of polished metal against Germanus's mouth and watched the surface mist over from the Frank's warm breath. He felt Germanus's forehead with his palm and even the evidence of his own eyes and hands sent him searching for other indicators of the Frank's condition. He found a marked improvement, so Lorcan permitted himself a deep sigh of heartfelt relief.

'You see! Whatever these things under his arms were, cutting them open must have saved him,' Gareth said. 'You did it, Lorcan! You saved him!'

'But what of the disease? Can it come back and strike him down again? There are too many questions to feel any joy – just relief! God must have heard my prayers and I now owe him my service for as long as I live.'

'If that makes you feel better, my friend, then so it must be! But I'm going up to the farmhouse now to see if I can beg some milk from Eleana. Do you want to come?'

Lorcan shook his head regretfully. 'No, boy! I'll stay away from our hosts, just in case.'

Gareth was met at the door by Tominoe, who was obviously unwell. Cursing inwardly, Gareth assisted the old man to sit on a bench seat close to the open doorway.

A few quick questions told Gareth what he least wanted to hear. Both Tominoe and his wife were ill with the same disease that had struck Germanus down.

'Has anyone else come to the farm recently, Tominoe, either just before we arrived or just after? If there's an illness come to the countryside, I'd rather know if we brought it with us, or whether someone else has passed it on to you.'

Tominoe tried to think the problem through, but it was obvious that the elderly farmer was finding it difficult to concentrate over his sick headache. Gareth remembered the early symptoms experienced by Germanus and sighed.

'No one visited before the big storm – not for months, as I recall. But the same day that you arrived, my brother called in on the way back from Soissons. He was full of information that I didn't consider important at the time.'

'Where's Soissons?' Gareth asked. His conscience would be assuaged if it wasn't close to Gesoriacum.

'It's to the west of Reims, young master. The markets of Soissons are the biggest in these parts and my brother took his spring vegetables, thinking to make a good profit from his foresight in planting so early. I told him he was taking a gamble by turning the sod in midwinter. Who's to say that winter wouldn't be hard and long this year? But Bernard never listens to anyone. He's always been the same – a bag of wind on any occasion.'

Gareth was forced to interrupt Tominoe quite rudely, because the elderly gentleman was embarked on a pleasurable diatribe concerning his brother, a pastime he obviously enjoyed.

'What did Bernard have to say about the markets of Soissons?'

Tominoe chuckled crudely.

'He told me the markets had been cancelled because of some illness, perhaps the one that your friend has caught. The king's man sent out orders that public gatherings were forbidden. My brother ignored the warnings, because Bernard knows everything! He told me he was angry that the lords had been worried over nothing.'

Tominoe coughed with a rasping bark that was sodden with congestion from the evil humours settling into his lungs. Although Germanus had experienced no difficulty in breathing, who could tell what other unseen symptoms might come to the fore with this strange new disease?

'And Mistress Eleana is also ill? I pray that she will recover quickly.'

Tominoe's eyes leaked rheum and slow tears, as if the interior of his body was too dry to produce the normal signs of grief.

'Aye, lad. She's not been the same since the boys were taken, you understand? I think she's glad she's ill.' Tominoe paused. 'Oh, no, young sir, don't be thinking she'd ever harm herself in any way. It would be a mortal sin and my girl's faith is too strong for her to take her own life. But she told me that I'm the only reason she's clung to life. I think she'll die soon, Gareth me lad, for I think she's wishing herself to join them . . . and I don't know what to do about it.'

The slow tears began to fall more freely, so Gareth felt his own eyes dampen with traitorous sympathy. 'I'll fetch Father Lorcan at any road! He'll bring her comfort and he knows something of healing. Our friend is on the way to a full recovery after Lorcan's ministrations, and so it will be for you and your wife, if we assist you to become well again.'

'We don't want to trouble the priest, young man. He must be very busy with your sick friend to take care of.' Tominoe was sincere, although Gareth initially thought the old farmer was being sarcastic, since Lorcan might have been the carrier who had infected them with their illness. But the old man's worried and lined face convinced the Briton otherwise.

'Please, Master Tominoe, you and Mistress Eleana have been so generous to us that we'd be churlish indeed to leave you to suffer. We are in your debt, so we'll work to repay your kindness. I can care for Germanus now, while Lorcan will minister to you and your good wife.'

Then, because the old man slumped into his seat, Gareth placed his arms around Tominoe's shoulders. The bones seemed ready to pierce the old man's skin, for only a thin pad of flesh covered Tominoe's skeleton.

'I swear I will take care of you, Master Tominoe, regardless of the outcome.'

So Tominoe surrendered to the force of Gareth's will and another day began in sadness, confession and recriminations.

The wagon wheels turned slowly. The huge discs were rotating at considerably less than walking speed as the teams of oxen struggled to drag the heavily laden carts along the rough terrain. Bedwyr had been forced to choose the worst possible route leading to the Forest of Dean, for Saxons from Mercia had become aware of the evacuation and were searching for their quarry along the Roman roads.

So far, although the Saxons knew that Arden Forest was deserted, they had yet to determine the ultimate destination of the refugees. Bedwyr had arranged for the sixty-strong members of the rearguard to remove all traces of the cavalcade's movement and to prepare ambush positions if the Saxons should pick up the trail of the departing Britons. Such a huge baggage train could hardly be hidden forever, so Bedwyr had rejected the broad Roman road, forced to stay away from the flat, lush river valleys where his movement were easily traced. The cavalcade had been delayed for some hours while the forward scouts found a ford that permitted them to cross the fast-flowing Severn River, and even Elayne's calm demeanour had become ragged with impatience and anxiety.

Eventually, the river had been crossed without loss of life, except for two sheep that had bolted from their herdsmen in a vain attempt to lead the rest of their flock astray. Once over the river, Bedwyr had ordered the baggage train to turn in a southerly direction, insisting that they must strike into the lowlands along one little-travelled section of the river valley. This route provided ample pasture and water for their livestock, but was rarely frequented by Saxons with a curious disposition. Try as they might, the mass movement of four hundred people in the main party, with all their possessions and their flocks, left a trail of smashed vegetation and discarded objects. The dung of the various beasts also indicated that whole families were travelling with everything they owned; even the most cloth-witted enemy could be expected to deduce that the entire population of Arden was on the move.

So far, Elayne's God had been with them and the people of Arden had been left in peace.

Any journey is hard on old bones and Elayne suffered greatly, especially in her knees and ankles. But she scorned to complain, especially since her elderly husband could barely sleep at night as he suffered from his own aches and pains. Yet he mounted his horse at the start of every day, regardless of the agony that would soon come. And each afternoon, he dismounted racked with cramps and muscular spasms.

'If he can keep going then so can I,' Elayne told her daughter, a young woman nursing her mother's first grandchild at her breasts. 'I'd cry for my poor old man, if those tears didn't shame him. To leave Arden, where his ancestors have lived for hundreds of years, is painful for everyone, but Bedwyr feels it right here!'

Elayne patted her chest with one hand and smiled at Nuala, her youngest living daughter.

'You think Father will die soon, don't you?' Nuala asked, blinking tearfully. 'He has a bad cough now and his joints are very swollen, but Father is the oldest man in the tribe. I've heard some people say that King Artor gave him dragon's blood which is why he lives on and on, but I don't believe them. Father is a Christian and there's no such thing as a dragon.'

'It's a convenient fiction, because your father is sometimes too soft with his subjects. The threat of dragon's blood has always stopped the worst of them from taking advantage of him.' Elayne laughed. 'My darling old man has outlived his king by a decade. I cannot believe that our lord would have been eighty-one if he had lived, Nuala, but such is the way of the world. Men of importance never seem to die peacefully in their beds.'

Elayne and Nuala looked out at a land that should have been rich with agriculture and grazing animals. A few black-faced sheep still wandered on the hillsides with matted wool and the look of animals unshorn or cared for in several seasons. One old ewe in a thicket could barely walk or feed for the weight of the wool she carried. Briefly, Elayne considered ordering their driver to stop, collect the ewe and shear it before setting it free.

'We go on, because we must go on! Bedwyr assures me that we have at least a week to travel until we reach the outer margins of the Forest of Dean. We have to pray that the weather stays good, and the Saxons don't realise we've safely arrived at our new refuge.'

There had been little time for piety once the journey to Dean had commenced. When the wagons rested for the night and Bedwyr deemed the situation safe enough for fires, the women were kept busy preparing the evening meal but also cooking sufficient food to last for several days, in case a Saxon presence required them to survive for some time without fires. Bedwyr might be old, but he exhibited none of the forgetfulness that afflicted many elderly persons. He understood the Saxons and could accurately predict how they would react in most situations. So far, their journey had been uneventful, but as he sat on his horse on a low ridge above the long train of wagons, Bedwyr was worried.

His back was aching with a mind-numbing and endless pain that never seemed to leave him. Within his gloves, his fingers flexed and he winced at the persistence of a raw new pain. Weapons exercise was agonising, but to cease to practise weakened his muscles until he could scarcely use his hands or legs at all. Bedwyr must continue to ignore pain if he wished to oversee the safe transfer of his people to the Forest of Dean. So, under his wolf collar, the grizzled old man huddled in his armour and suffered.

Each night, while the sentries walked their horses through the wooded landscape, their eyes searched among the people of Arden to ensure that no enemy had infiltrated their numbers while the long, creaking line of wagons was on the march. As they patrolled, they ate cold viands under strange trees and mourned for their departed homes and lost peace. There was no easy way to transplant a vine so that it had a chance to live in new soil. Bedwyr knew he had made the right decision, but he saw himself as the uprooted vine, unable to feed on the new soil and prosper under a new sun. He sensed that his time on earth was almost done, so his grave awaited, along with the shades of everyone he had killed – or had ever loved.

Elayne watched her husband's tired eyes look inward to some place she had never known, so she too was afraid.

'Off to bed with you now, Tominoe. I've seen to Eleana and she's comfortable. It's your turn now, my friend. Come, lean on me.'

Lorcan took the strain of Tominoe's slender body, while Gareth cleared a stool and bench table away from the fire pit where a sleeping pallet was prepared and waiting. With a groan, Tominoe allowed himself to be lowered onto the bed. On the other side of the fire, his wife was lying on a similar pallet. Her eyes were closed, while her face was florid with fever.

Father Lorcan had opened the two doors, front and back, which provided cross-ventilation for the one-roomed farmhouse. Wicker partitions had provided privacy for parents and children in the past, and the half-walls, although flimsy in appearance, were strong enough to hold pegs on which the elderly couple kept the common items used in their day-to-day lives. Within two small, partitioned areas, Gareth found four beds and four chests in which lay the good tunics and breeches of four young men. Their small sleeping spaces had been left exactly as if the boys had been taken that morning.

'It isn't fair!' Gareth paused in the homely task of tucking the old farmer into his bed.

'Few things in life are fair,' Lorcan responded grimly. 'From my experience, the good seem to suffer while the wicked die peacefully of old age in their beds. God made this earth a perfect place, but He also gave us free will, so God has nothing to do with our misery. In fact, fair and unfair don't enter the equation either—'

'Please!' Gareth raised one hand to halt the flow of Lorcan's theology. 'All I want to know is whether the farmer and his wife will become well in time, like Germanus? I might add that he's still sound asleep in his bed.'

'Keep your voice down, lad. I don't want these good folk to hear your prattle.'

Gareth nodded, already suspecting the priest's answer.

'These two are very old, as is Germanus, but our friend is strong after a lifetime of hard exercise, warfare and constant sword practice. I'm afraid for Eleana and her husband. They're two good people who have done their best to help us.'

Although he longed to leave the farm and continue their journey to Reims, Gareth could never suggest that they should leave the two elderly sufferers to their fate. As Germanus slowly recovered, the young Briton split his time between caring for the arms master and completing the essential farm chores. Cows must be milked daily, while eggs must be collected to ensure they didn't begin to hatch. Similarly, the animals all needed to be fed. Gareth was grateful for his time in the open air, for he was spared the distress of having to care for the two old people who had been so kind to him.

Life on the farm continued for two days as the disease ran its course. Eleana died on the morning of the third day and Gareth took the woman's role of washing the desiccated body, dressing it in fresh clothing, combing and plaiting the long iron-grey locks and then stitching Eleana into a shroud of oiled cloth. He was not tempted to remove the silver rings in her ears and a much-worn ring on her finger. They had been worn every day of her married life and they were precious to her.

That same day, after Eleana's wrapped corpse had been placed in the woodhouse, a man was seen riding towards the farmhouse.

'Quickly, Gareth! Stop him! He mustn't be allowed to come too close, even to you, because we know this disease is contagious.'

Lorcan's last patient was struggling to breathe and Lorcan had decided not to use his knife on the swellings under his patient's arms because of Tominoe's age and weakness. The shock would kill the old man faster than the disease.

Gareth set off towards the main road at a brisk run. The stranger had reached the first pasture by the time that Gareth shouted out a warning to him.

'Come no closer, sir! There is illness at this farmhouse and I don't believe you'll be safe if you come any closer to me or any other person on this farm.'

'And who might you be?' the stranger asked rudely. He was a middle-aged man with a coarse, untrained black beard and a rather dirty yellow robe of fine fabric. His leather belt sported a long knife in a scabbard once gilded, but now very worn. Above his unprepossessing appearance of past wealth, the stranger's face was fat from good living and was topped with thick eyebrows like hairy caterpillars. Gareth wished he had paused to pick up a weapon.

I wouldn't trust this man on a dark night with my back turned, he thought. 'More importantly, who are you?'

'I am Bernard, brother of Tominoe and master of many broad acres to the north of Gesoriacum. How is my brother? Is he ill? And what of Eleana, his wife? Tell me, man, for I've a mind to call out the troops of the city of Reims to arrest you for theft. No doubt you're in the process of picking my brother's farm clean of everything of value.'

Affronted, Gareth drew himself up to his full height. 'I am Gareth, son of Gareth, sword-bearer and personal body servant who protected Artor, the High King of the Britons. I have no need to steal from farmers, especially those who have been kind to us.'

Gareth's scorn cut no ice with Bernard who sneered unpleasantly from his vantage point atop his horse.

'Hoity-toity aren't we, you foreign shithead. I'll repeat my question! How is my brother? Is that question simple enough for someone with your grasp of the Frank language?'

Gareth ground his teeth. 'Father Lorcan, a priest, is treating your brother, the good Tominoe, inside the farmhouse. The priest believes that your brother will die. Your sister-in-law, Mistress Eleana, has perished earlier today and I have conducted the rites to ready her for burning and have sewed her into her shroud. She lies in the woodshed yonder if you wish to pay your last respects. I've been milking the cows and feeding the farm animals, so I'll be more than happy for you to take over these duties if you wish to do so.'

Bernard coughed harshly, and then seemed to recall something important. His eyes narrowed craftily and Gareth longed to kick the avaricious pig of a man in the balls.

'Eleana always wore rings in her ears and another on her finger,' Bernard snapped. 'Tominoe's sons are all dead by now and that makes me the heir to all they have. So hand over the jewellery!' He held out one hand impatiently. Gareth fantasised about cutting off the offending digits, but his manner remained courteous.

'I had the greatest respect for Mistress Eleana, who was a fine woman and a good Christian, so I left her jewellery on her body where she always wore it – even in sickness.'

It was time now for Gareth to grin craftily.

'As the heir to their farm you can feel free to cut open the shroud and remove her baubles, if you so wish. I'll just sew the shroud closed again once you've completed your appropriation.'

'You're an impertinent young man! How do I know you are telling the truth? You could be lying and I couldn't possibly know.'

'I'm not stopping you from looking inside the shroud,' Gareth said equably. 'I suggest you go up to the woodshed and check her body or, if you're of a mind to take over the nursing of your brother from Father Lorcan, we'd be happy to oblige with that as well. We would gladly be on our way rather than risk death from this particular pestilence.'

Bernard was torn between greed and self-preservation. It was obvious to Gareth that he had no intention of nursing his brother, or of risking his own health and welfare by crossing the threshold.

But nor did he wish to leave his brother's valuable property in strange hands.

Finally, Tominoe's brother made up his mind. 'I'll send some of my herdsmen to move the livestock up to my farm. These are terrible times, young man, whoever you might be, and if Tominoe survives, he'll want his beasts to be safe and cared for. You'll have to leave eventually and then where will Tominoe be? The roads are thick with folk who are fleeing to God knows where, and I know that people are dying from Gesoriacum to Parisi in the south and Reims in the north. From what I hear, some sufferers manage to survive, but the largest numbers perish in agony. There's no explaining it!'

'None at all,' Gareth answered curtly. 'If Tominoe doesn't survive, I'll wait for your herdsmen and hand over all the livestock that can be moved. Or I'll pen them inside the lower pasture. I assume you want Berry, the plough horse, and the chickens, although I'm not sure how you intend to move the birds. Some portable cages, perhaps?'

Bernard overlooked the obvious cynicism in Gareth's voice and continued to rattle on about the many deaths from the plague which seemed to have started in Gesoriacum and then spread out into the rural areas as travellers moved around the Frankish lands.

'Like passengers on a ship?' Gareth asked, while Bernard nodded slowly in agreement.

'Yes, I suppose that's possible. Or even people who are staying at an inn.'

'Wouldn't travellers stay at many different establishments?' Gareth asked slowly, his mind going back to the *Golden Nymph* and her regular travel from city to city. Had the ship left something else behind her, as well as passengers and trade goods?'

'Yes, I suppose they would,' Bernard answered brusquely and pulled on his horse's reins. 'Anyway, what does it matter? My lads will be back within the week. I'll take your advice and send cages with the boys for the chickens. Good layers are hard to come by. They'll not want to come near the house, mind, for they'll be frightened of catching that vile disease, so I'd be obliged if you'd help by penning the animals down on this bottom pasture as you have just suggested. I'll pay for your trouble.'

Gareth bridled with indignation.

'Keep your coin, Bernard! I'd rather have Berry! She's an old mare, and she's grey-muzzled, but she's a fine creature. 'I'll pay you for her, but I have no coin other than one silver piece.'

Greed and amusement slid through Bernard's piggish eyes. The old horse wasn't fit for the saddle. And the Briton was prepared to pay a silver coin for it? The lad was off his head!

As Bernard rode away, Gareth was touched by sadness for Tominoe and Eleana. Inevitably, their loathsome kinsman would survive the pestilence and would ultimately profit from it. Lorcan and I will remember you, Gareth thought to himself. Germanus would have died for certain without a roof over his head and without their eggs and milk to keep up his strength.

Tominoe died after another twenty hours of suffering. To give the old farmer some comfort in his dying hours, Lorcan held the old man's hand and pretended to be Eleana while Gareth stood in for the four sons at various times as Tominoe experienced his last deliriums.

Gareth spoke of riding with the king into battle and how he would be home by the end of summer. Tominoe smiled weakly and seemed much eased by Gareth's promise. For the next hour, he rambled on to Lorcan in his guise of Eleana and spoke of fishing in the local streams in the old days, and of how they'd once again fish for trout and roaches. Tominoe muttered about killing chickens and feasting long into the night once the boys returned, while he smiled peacefully in his semi-conscious state.

When Tominoe breathed his last, Lorcan and Gareth washed his body and prepared him for the fire. Limping a little and still very weak, Germanus gradually moved all the burnable timber from the woodshed into the cottage which would be burned to the ground. The two bodies were laid out on the table where the couple had eaten so many meals, and Lorcan conducted a brief and touching service for the souls of the dead. Then, when there was nothing left to be said, Gareth lit the pyre where the old couple had been laid out, united in death as they had been throughout their lives.

The thatch went up with a rush, lighting the dusk with sparks that swirled in the small firestorm. Inside, the wicker walls blazed fiercely, especially when the rafters of the roof collapsed to windward, which further fanned the flames. When the fire died after midnight, the stone walls were still too hot to the touch.

Lorcan had collected all the eggs he could and then boiled them over a fire. These staple items would flesh out their diet once they resumed their trek into the north. Lorcan also wrung the necks of several chickens, before setting Germanus to work by plunging the birds into hot water and then plucking out them in preparation for cooking.

'Why should Bernard take everything of value?' Lorcan had asked once the farmhouse animals were penned in the lower pasture and the three men had filled every container they could find with fresh milk. With varying degrees of regret, they bade their farewells.

'How long were we at the farm?' Germanus asked. 'My mind is still hazy with confused memories, so I don't know what's real and what must have been a bad dream.' Germanus was very thin inside his armour, but his eyes held their customary blue calmness and his smile was as genuine and as wide as ever.

'It was near enough to two weeks, you big lug! Two long, sad weeks, during which we looked after you – and then the farmers who took us in. At least you remembered that part.' Lorcan's affection softened any hurt in his words.

'Their deaths were my fault.' Germanus seemed to shrink in the saddle.

'It was I who took you to the farm, Germanus,' Lorcan pointed out. 'You had no choice in the matter. Did you catch this pestilence deliberately?'

'For God's sake, can't you both give it a rest? We're all alive and we have a hundred miles to cover. And who knows what troubles we'll

331

find on the roads? This pestilence is killing whole communities. Brigands are abroad and madness is supposed to have taken over the living, if Bernard is to be believed. How are we planning to survive any tests that are thrown in our path before we reach Reims?'

'A lot faster now that I'm riding Berry! I must say that I like my mule, but he's better as a packhorse,' Lorcan replied cheerfully. 'We'll surmount any other difficulties as and when we come to them.'

Gareth ground his teeth in frustration as he watched the two older men jest and jostle in their usual fashion. A minor detail like the presence of a deadly plague was hardly likely to change the attitudes of these remarkable old men as they rode down the long, dusty road towards Reims.

At least we now seem to be immune to the disease, Gareth thought.

The day had that special soft shine that comes in springtime, the grass was vividly green and the trees were budding with new, lime-green leaves that blurred their nakedness.

Birds sang in the hedgerows which were heavy with daffodils and wild iris. Even Gareth smiled at the beauty of the morning.

In the distance, a single kite circled over a hill as if something had died there, or was in the process of perishing. Gareth was forced to look away.

Somehow, the morning was no longer quite so fair. There would be no loveliness without pain, for nature had her rules that humankind would never control.

The three men rode on towards Reims and an uncertain future.

CHAPTER XIX

IN THE DARK OF THE SUN

In friendship false, implacable in hate: Resolved to ruin or to rule the state.

John Dryden, *Absalom and Achitophel*

Before the sun had set and risen twice, the three travellers saw at first hand the results of plague on the land and the devastating reach of this cruel epidemic. They also saw the human animal at its most avaricious, brutal and superstitious. Gareth's youth would be washed away forever by their experiences at Soissons and Reims.

The full indication of the seismic upheaval caused by the plague was the movement of desperate people heading in all directions. Most of these desperate refugees were pushing carts piled high with their meagre possessions, the vehicles topped with ragged children and toothless, elderly grandparents, as whole families struggled to escape from the nameless horror. Some lucky few had a destination in mind when Lorcan asked them courteously where they were heading. Many of the other families fleeing from their homes were seeking the hospitality of kinsmen, but most were running mindlessly, afraid to stay in places where the plague held sway – but ignorant of its range or its exact location.

Evidence of the mindless violence and capriciousness that came with the plague was gruesome and ugly. Scavenger birds warned travellers of farms where the dead lay in their cottages. Their bloated, abused corpses affronted the eyes of the beholders nearly as much as the pathetic condition of the farm animals. Many of these poor beasts had been locked in barns by the farmer when he first became sick, in order to protect his livelihood and prevent theft. Later, these dumb beasts were set free by kindly people such as Gareth whenever they found horses, cattle and even chickens suffering in their confinement. Cows were always milked prior to being released into their pastures. With luck, given that the three travellers tried to ensure that the animals had fresh water and food, those farmers who survived the pestilence would take these animals into their own farms. In many cases, the first true warning that a farm was dead at the heart came with the lowing of the cows as they called out for relief from painfully distended udders.

Lorcan was horrified at the condition of starving dogs that had reverted to the wild and were hunting farm animals for food, often in packs. But domestic pets were the worst. If no other form of sustenance was available, farm cats and dogs weren't averse to feeding on the corpses of their dead masters.

In every case where human deaths were involved, Lorcan felt obliged to give the dead the last rites so that their souls would be freed from Limbo. Gareth and Germanus collected firewood and once Lorcan had finished the prayers, they set fire to each cottage to ensure that the plague would find no further unwary victims who visited the farm.

Nor were they the only persons carrying out these sad and necessary duties. As the miles to Reims passed by like a steadily unrolling scroll, the three travellers saw great plumes of smoke rising in the distance on both sides of the road, evidence of the steady march of Death as it strode inexorably forward. Carrion birds grew fat and sluggish on dead beasts and other unclean meat.

There weren't enough arrows in Gesoriacum to kill all the predatory birds or stop the farm and wild animals taking whatever food they could. Death and his followers grew fat on the road to Reims, while all other living things went sadly malnourished.

One day, a shy pale young man approached the trine carefully, while all three noted that his body was noticeably thin from a recent illness. His eyes never left the three travellers, as if he was waiting for an inevitable attack. He ensured that he was beyond the reach of their long swords as he carefully approached them. The priest drew Berry to a halt and looked down at the anxious stranger.

'You're a survivor of the pestilence, aren't you? What's your name, young man, and where are you going?'

The thin young man was obviously frightened of the three warriors. His eyes darted from their scabbards to their armour, their packhorses and even Germanus's pallor that was so like his own. Finally, still wary, he made his way to the verge of the road, sat on his heels and haltingly told his story.

'My name is Louis and I was a baker's apprentice in Reims. My father's name no longer matters because my whole family is dead. It all seems to have happened so long ago that I can't imagine life before waking under a tree and finding I was surrounded by my dead family. When the illness first came to our village on the outskirts of Reims, my mother insisted that we should run. I would have preferred to stay because the illness travels faster than human feet can move, but we packed up everything we could carry and fled into the west.'

'How far did you get before the illness struck, Louis?' Lorcan asked.

'We were only two days from home, so it was a nothing in distance. We were already infected when we left, I suppose. When my mother and my sister became ill, we settled into a copse of trees close to a streamlet and strung blankets between the trees to keep us under cover. Then we cared for each other as, one by one, we all began to sicken.'

'And when it was all over, you found you had survived,' Germanus said dourly. 'Like me, you endured when better and stronger people perished.'

'Exactly so, friend! I thought you were a survivor as soon as I saw you. We all wear the same look – and the same guilt!'

The young man examined his hands closely, as if trying to make up his mind.

'Do you have anything to drink? I have some food, but fresh water frightens me at the moment. The streams are fouled near their sources, and most of the wells are contaminated. Sufferers of the pestilence burn up with inner heat and they will do almost anything to obtain cold water to ease their symptoms.'

'We have milk and you're welcome to share it with us,' Gareth replied and smiled at Louis. With exaggerated care, he dismounted and placed a leather bottle on the ground a few feet from the stranger's hand. 'There are cows enough that need milking on abandoned farms, so there's no need to suffer from thirst during your journey.'

Louis moved swiftly, snatched up the bottle and emptied it in three gulps.

'Excuse my bad manners, but those persons who survive the disease are considered to be in league with the powers of darkness. I've been attacked several times by folk who don't understand the illness.' One hand indicated a nasty contusion on the side of his head. 'They nearly got me with that attack.'

'What of those few persons who are immune to the plague?' Gareth asked.

'Is anyone truly immune?' Louis asked. His eyes were wide and amazed.

'Aye! Father Lorcan and I have been exposed to the disease on many occasions. We have nursed sufferers of the plague, but we haven't become ill at all, not even a sniffle.'

Under his black humour, the young warrior was grim and angry, and Louis recognised his rage.

'I'd heard that some people don't sicken, but I thought the tale was a fable,' the young man replied. 'Such persons are said to be demons and are killed on sight, along with Jews, Huns and old women who are skilled in herb lore.'

Louis examined the three warriors carefully from under his lowered eyelids. They were obviously experienced fighting men, possibly mercenaries, and Louis smiled as he wondered how the bullies who had tried to kill him for the sin of survival would tackle men such as these.

I hope these warriors kill every one of the bastards who tried to kill me, he thought with grim relish.

'Where are you going then, now that all your family members are dead?' Lorcan's voice remained calm, although inwardly he shuddered at the tale of innocents being killed out of hand in the name of superstition.

'I'm heading for Orleans. I have an older brother who lives near there, so I'm hoping I'll outstrip the disease if it hasn't reached there yet. How can I know? I could be heading into even worse conditions than exist in this hell-hole.'

Lorcan moved forward on his huge horse and the young man finally had proof that the old man was a priest when he saw his vestments, his tonsure and the beads that hung from the cord round his coarse robe. Bowing his head respectfully, the baker's apprentice rose to his feet, handed the bottle back to Gareth and prepared to set off on the road once again, when a sudden thought caused him to stop and turn back.

'Please forgive me, but my illness has caused me to forget my manners. Should you come to Orleans, look for Louis or Bernais at the bakery on the Street of the Metal Workers. You'll always be welcome there. After all, we survivors should stick together.'

Germanus touched his forelock in salute, as did both Lorcan and Gareth. In the weeks to come, Lorcan would comment that Louis had been the only person who had even pretended to be civilised during their experiences on the road to Reims.

A day later, they reached a small village where thin dogs lurked just beyond the reach of cast stones, while gangs of feral children ran from their approach like wild creatures, shaggy with dirt and sly with unhealthy wisdom.

No adults appeared to be alive, although half the houses in the village were blackened and burned like the hollow, broken shells of diseased teeth. The stink of rot hung in the air and seemed to seep into hair, clothing and the folds in the travellers' skins.

Several other groups who were ahead of them had run, spurred their horses, or rushed their carts through the main street of the village. All that the strangers desired was to brush the dust of this hellish place off their bodies as soon as possible. Nevertheless, Germanus raised his fingers to his lips and then drew his sword from its scabbard with a nasty little hiss. Gareth and Lorcan followed suit.

A thin, high-pitched scream ululated through the air, grating along stretched nerve endings and raising the hair on the arms and backs of the three travellers.

Gareth dismounted and handed the reins of his horse and pack animals to Lorcan, while gesturing to the priest that he should wait with his sword at the ready until he returned. Almost as quickly, Germanus did the same and trotted after Gareth as nimbly as he could.

As Lorcan waited, a lone figure on a huge draught horse on an empty road with deserted and ruined houses on each side, he began to feel his anxiety increase as the moments dragged by.

He could hear shrill, childish laughter teetering on the edge of hysteria. It reverberated across the fields from a row of cottages along the edges of a road leading north. 'Sounds like wild children!' he muttered softly to himself. 'Dear God, who could conceive of such a thing? But then if their parents and siblings are dead, what can children do? They must eat and they must drink, so it's logical that they'll band together to steal, or do anything that will help to fill the emptiness in their bellies.'

Lorcan's voice sounded old and thin, even to his ears.

Time stretched out painfully and his friends still hadn't returned. Lorcan's nervous eyes scanned the street and the ruins for any signs of life. His warrior instinct was screaming at him that something was terribly wrong in this godforsaken place.

Then, another scream made the priest jump. This time, the voice was clearly masculine and the naturally baritone voice rose up and up in an extremity of agony too terrible to be imagined. In quick succession,

Lorcan heard the laughter and giggles of children, followed by another ghastly scream that, this time, was suddenly cut off. Almost immediately, he heard the clatter of running feet.

'Father Lorcan! Dear God, you're needed! Bring the horses and hurry,' a high-pitched adult voice was yelling from across the field. 'Just come, Father!'

Lorcan recognised Gareth calling for him.

When Gareth realised that Lorcan had heard his call and was responding, he ducked down a laneway between two cottages. In a fecund garden bed, spring cabbages had been allowed to rot and the stink caught at the back of his throat. The young man picked up the pace to run across a neglected field towards the cluster of stone houses on the north road.

Kicking Berry in the ribs, Father Lorcan dragged the packhorses behind him as he caught up with Gareth. Cursing as the reins became tangled, Lorcan slowed to speak to his companion, but Gareth simply waved him on. The younger man's face was as white as new bone.

'Ride ahead, Lorcan! You're needed! I'll see to the horses. For God's sake, hurry, Father.'

The sense of urgency in Gareth's voice drove Lorcan onward to where the tall figure of Germanus had stepped out from behind a fieldstone wall.

Germanus's face was as white as bleached linen and Lorcan could smell the stench of vomit as he approached his friend. Something had shaken Germanus to the core, so badly that Lorcan could see the shock written in his stiff expression and the rigidity of his shoulders as if the Frank had tensed every muscle against something truly frightful.

'What's wrong, Germanus? You look as if you've seen a whole host of demons.'

Germanus shook his leonine head and pointed to the back of a cottage. 'See for yourself! There's a man out there who needs extreme unction, if he's still alive! I think he's a Jew! But all dying men need the comfort of Heaven – Jew or not – don't they?'

Lorcan dismounted and picked up the small bag which held his holy oil and the precious tools of his trade. He moved behind the cottage and found the obscenity that had been enacted in this nameless village.

An entire family had been crucified on the timber frames used to hold their vegetable vines in place during the summer. Where beans, peas and gourds would normally have been entwined and flowering, five bodies were hanging from nails that had been driven through their wrists.

'Dear God!'

In a daze, Lorcan began with a tow-headed boy of about five whose contorted corpse was an abomination against nature. As he struggled to breathe, the real suffering of crucifixion, the young boy had torn his wrists from the cruel nails that bound him into position and had actually managed to free one hand. The torn and broken wrists continued to leak slow drops of blood to join the huge, drying puddle that had formed at the foot of the frame.

With his trembling fingers on the boy's throat, Lorcan confirmed that the boy-child was dead. His sister had obviously been raped before she had been nailed into place, as her swollen genitals and a snail trail of blood and semen on her thighs revealed. Her wide-open brown eyes stared out at eternity with a sick horror. Fortunately for her, Lorcan was certain she had died quickly from the shock and pain of the indignities she had been forced to endure.

The last and eldest child, a boy of twelve or so, had obviously fought back because his body was covered with bruises, scrapes, cuts and deep stab wounds. Even in such a weakened state, the boy had survived on the agonising frame for longer than could have been expected, because his body was still warm. Perhaps he had released those first terrifying screams as he gave up his spirit. Lorcan closed the boy's staring brown eyes and smoothed the spiky matted black hair on the lad's forehead.

'Sleep now, my child,' Lorcan whispered with tears prickling at the backs of his eyes. 'Whatever your name was, you were a brave boy.'

The mother of the household had been raped repeatedly and half-strangled before she was nailed up. From the stiffly fixed state of her body, the clustering of flies that were already laying their eggs in her mouth and the clammy discoloration that had begun in her feet where the blood from her body had pooled, this poor woman had died quickly. Muttering a hasty prayer, Lorcan was glad that she had been dead before her children perished.

Then the funereal silence of the afternoon was shattered by an agonised howl. Belatedly, Lorcan realised that the hanging man who had been left to last for attention was still alive.

Lorcan shouted for Germanus and Gareth to join him.

'Help me to get him down from here. He's still alive, for Christ's sake, so we might still save him – if we hurry.'

Lorcan's companions came around the corner of the building and, although they were obviously aware of the man's condition, neither of them responded with any degree of urgency.

'He doesn't want to be moved, Father Lorcan,' Gareth told him. The ruined and battered head nodded vigorously, as if all the destroyed body's strength was focused on its neck muscles.

'Then he'll have to tell me so himself,' Lorcan retorted as he dragged a battered stool across the cobbles in the garden bed to stand on while he attempted to prise the nail from the dying man's wrist.

'He can't speak, Lorcan. They've cut out his tongue,' Germanus replied and then grabbed the stool away from his friend. 'Ask him to nod if he agrees with me. I'm sure he'll let his wishes be known.'

'Do you want us to cut you down, sir?' Lorcan asked. 'The position of your arms is causing you to choke slowly, so you'll die if we don't move you soon.'

The man's bruised, bleeding and lacerated head shook vociferously in denial.

'I think he wants to see someone,' Germanus explained softly, 'A religious man, I imagine. Perhaps he needs to be blessed by his Rabbi? I've tried to explain that there's no one of the Jewish faith alive in the village. And there's no one else living in the village that I can find.'

'I can shrive him, but I'm a Christian priest. Does he understand the difference?'

The man nodded emphatically, and two fat tears slid out of his eyes to roll down the slick of blood, sweat and dried tears that dirtied what was left of his face.

'There is no sin in what we do,' Lorcan stated. 'But if there is, I will accept any blame on my own soul. You can stand in front of your God and mine, washed clean of all the sins of a lifetime by the wounds inflicted on you. You have finally atoned for any transgressions you've committed during your time on this earth.'

Lorcan's voice grew in strength and authority as he decided how best to comply with the dying man's wishes, despite the tears that ran unchecked down his craggy, grey-whiskered face.

'Could you guard the horses, Gareth? There is something evil in this village and it wishes to inflict harm on us. I'd like to know we can escape from this shithole if the need arises.'

'I'll kill anything that moves if they threaten us,' Gareth snapped grimly. He turned and ran back to the road where the horses had been tethered.

Lorcan returned to the task at hand.

'Find me something that will support my weight, Germanus. This stool's too rickety to hold my extra poundage for too long. I want to be able to look our friend here in the eyes when I give him Extreme Unction.'

'Can you be burned in Hell for giving this ritual to a Jew, Lorcan?'

When Lorcan didn't reply, Germanus shrugged and found a bench table inside the cottage which he dragged into position.

'I can't believe that a loving God would deny comfort to any of His children, regardless of their beliefs. If our God objects, then He's not worth worshipping!'

Germanus's voice was rough with emotion, but Lorcan blotted out his friend's agony of spirit. Another soul was suffering hideously and needed urgent help.

Then the most holy of all Christian rituals began.

When Lorcan had completed his solemn task, the crucified man closed his eyes briefly and his smashed lips smiled beatifically through his pain. Lorcan could see from the delicate bones of his face that the victim of this atrocity had once been a handsome man. The breath was dragged into the dying man's lungs slowly and his chest heaved in response to the enormous effort, so Germanus tried to support the hanging body at the knees to minimise the pain. But he soon realised that this simple act of mercy was placing almost unendurable agony on the man's body where the nails were still holding the torn feet in place.

'Fetch the poppy juice from my saddle bag, Germanus. At least we can give him some release from his agony.'

Once a heavy and almost lethal dose had been dribbled through the man's mashed lips and his head started to nod, Germanus and Lorcan struggled to release the survivor from the cruel frame that had killed his family. When he was lying on his back on the spread cloaks of his benefactors, Lorcan was able to check his wounds more carefully. With a shudder, the priest discovered that the dying man had been castrated before he was crucified.

Normally, such a hideous wound would cause the sufferer to bleed to death, but someone had wanted this victim to die of suffocation, so hot pitch had been slapped around his hideous amputation to seal off the blood vessels.

'It's a miracle that he didn't die of shock. God would have been kinder to this man if he'd permitted him to die alongside his wife.' Disgusted, Lorcan spat on the ground. 'People sicken me most of the time, especially those fuckers who enjoy inflicting pain on their victims. They deserve a special place in Hell.'

A sudden indrawn gasp came from the crucified man. After the best part of a day hanging from the frame with his shoulder and chest muscles in spasm from the strain, his condition had weakened with pain and the exhaustion from blood loss, prolonged pain and the incalculable cost of despair. But the need for struggle was over now, and he was about to join his loved ones. As Lorcan held the farmer's broken and damaged hand, the man struggled for breath and died when his heart stopped under the strain.

'Why were they killed?' Gareth asked later as they placed the bodies of the small family in their beds, almost as if they were sleeping.

'Remember what Louis said on the road?' Lorcan reminded him. 'The Jews are becoming common victims of the superstitions that exist in plague-infested areas.'

'So these children were sacrificed because they had been lucky enough to escape illness and they happened to be of the Jewish faith.' Germanus's disgust was mirrored in the eyes of his two companions.

'So, we'll send these innocents to their God and shake the dust of this pest-hole off the soles of our boots. How we can hope to remove its stains from our souls, I don't know,' Lorcan decided quietly as he gathered up an unlit torch and led the way out of the cottage.

At the doorway, Germanus used his flints and tinder to light a small collection of twigs and dried moss, and coaxed it into the semblance of a fire. Once this starter fire had caught alight, Lorcan thrust the fat-soaked torch into it. Then, once the torch was blazing fiercely, Lorcan went back into the cottage and set fire to the woodpiles, the beds and any other flammable materials. Finally satisfied, he threw the torch back into the conflagration and stepped briskly out of the splintered door.

As they rode away, choosing to travel into the darkness rather than sleep in this ugly, contaminated village, Lorcan looked back over his shoulder.

'Germanus! Gareth! Turn and look! The children are dancing around the fire.'

Gareth saw the shapes of children and youths as they capered around the burning cottage. With a whoosh, the roof collapsed in a shower of hot sparks, and both Gareth and Germanus saw excited, young faces barred with stripes of drying blood, leaping and prancing like crazed animals.

'Children did this?' Germanus exclaimed, outraged by a thought that he struggled to grasp. 'I don't believe it! Children couldn't commit such hideous crimes.'

'Children are more likely to survive the plague than adults,' Lorcan explained. 'They would never survive alone in the aftermath, so it makes some sense that they'd band together for mutual protection. But children can be very cruel, my friend.'

'But a village of this size would never have so many young ones among them. I counted nearly twenty of them dancing around the funeral pyre,' Germanus protested.

'They're like a tribe that constantly moves from village to village, gaining in number and scavenging off the dead for some time before moving on again.' While Lorcan knew his assertions were correct, part of his mind continued to rebel at the thought of murderous children running amok among the population.

'And children can be cruel and curious by turn,' Gareth added. 'I can imagine how they'd respond to the plague by using pack violence against those people whom they think could have caused the deaths of their families.'

'Whatever they were once, they're hardly human now. I'd rather not think of the little animals, so the sooner we reach Reims, the better.'

The city of Reims had been a beautiful metropolis before the Hun had swept into the north a hundred years earlier. But these barbarous warriors had burned every city that lay in their path, including this one.

The town had been rebuilt, but much of its classical Roman character had gone and many buildings housing the poor had been replaced with structures that were tawdry and temporary in nature and appearance. The town's sewerage system had been irreparably broken, as had its water supply. At this troubled time in its history, the city fathers had little idea how to counteract the plague and even the stout walls that had been repaired and reinforced in the years since Attila's attacks could offer no protection for even the least significant citizen or slave.

At Soissons, a much smaller township to the west of Reims, King Theudebert had settled his army into bivouac just beyond the outskirts of the walled centre. Here, in the fallow fields that had been left unploughed and unplanted by farmers who would never tend their crops again, a small army of fifteen hundred men had set up two-man tents, dug latrines and spent all their free time whoring and drinking in the town's stews. Although Theudebert had instructed his officers to keep the men away from the town to minimise the risk of plague, those same officers received small sums of coin from innkeepers and the owners of brothels to recommend their establishments to the troops. For a further golden stipend, those same officers provided guaranteed protection from bar fights, damage to their girls and problems with the king or the city fathers. As always, corruption made the world go round.

The general consensus seemed to be that what the king didn't know wouldn't hurt him.

Theudebert had a strong and virile face, made even more masculine by bristling, luxurious moustaches and a neatly clipped beard. His dark golden hair fell in heavy waves to the neck where it was shorn off in a blunt, straight line. The king's nose was narrow at the bridge but his nostrils flared to a broader tip than would have been expected. Above heavy brows and permanent frown lines at the bridge of that jutting, arrogant nose, his forehead was wide, deeply lined and surprisingly low. Theudebert was a handsome man who was suited to armour and military dress, he also loved jewellery and elaborate, highly decorative ornamentation.

But, for all the richness of his dress and the many jewelled rings upon his fingers, the great chains of kingship around his neck and his heavily gilded armour, Theudebert had a serious and persistent problem: two problems, if he chose to be accurate.

Wisigard, the queen of the Franks, had died of the plague and her remains were lying in a glorious tomb in Cologne Cathedral. Encrusted with her favourite gems and richly attired in the dress of her Lombard birth, she had gone to rest with all the panoply of the Christian Church, while special candles had burned, night and day, to disguise the reek of a plague death.

Once the days of mourning had been completed, Theudebert had fled from Cologne with the army at his back. All thoughts of conquest in Thuringia vanished from the king's plans once the possible effects of the plague entered his considerations. Indeed, Wisigard had never been so much trouble in the seven years of their betrothal and the four years of their marriage as she had become in death. Subsequently, Theudebert had ridden as far south as he dared – only to find that Reims was already afflicted with this new illness that had been called the Wrath of Heaven.

'That stupid bitch! Trust her to catch Justinian's Disease. No one else at court even had a cough, but Wisigard would insist on distributing bread to the poor and other such nonsense! She put herself in harm's way and so she contracted her illness. But what if she had passed the plague on to *me*?'

Theudebert was in his cups and was belligerent and melancholy. He had lacked a confidante during his Roman wife Deuteria's absence, not to mention the pleasures of the bed that she had mastered, perhaps because of her first marriage. The Frankish lords had insisted that Deuteria be sent home to her family in Auvergne, partly because her arrogance had irritated them, but mostly because good alliances could be forged with a more suitable wedding to Wisigard. Theudebert needed a sounding board that was able to listen tactfully to whatever was irking the king, but in Deuteria's absence, he was forced to depend on his servant, Hubert, who only had one conversational advantage, his absolute discretion.

'The queen took her responsibilities seriously in the old ways of the Lombards,' Hubert answered in a conciliatory fashion while cleaning up a spill of red wine on Theudebert's folding map table.

'Meaning she wanted to be loved.' Theudebert snickered gently into his half-full wine cup. 'Is there anything to eat around here? I'm the king, so I shouldn't have to cook for myself, as well as everything else. Doesn't anyone fucking think around here, other than me?'

Hubert sighed gently and tried to keep the irritation out of his voice and off his face. The king had already sent two hot meals back to the kitchens in petulant exercises of petty contrariness. When he was drunk, the usually alert and decisive monarch became almost childish in his fits of sulkiness and high-handedness.

'What would you desire to eat, sire? I will send orders to your cook immediately.'

'Whatever's available! My cooks should know my appetite, or I'd hope they do.'

Hubert was unconvinced that Theudebert would accept the meal when it came. When he was in a contrary mood, Theudebert was unpredictable. The frustrated servant sighed again and sent orders to the kitchens for a haunch of mutton, a fish stew, several roasted chickens and some honeyed confectionery.

One of these meals will strike his fancy, Hubert decided. But I'll probably have the others thrown at my face. When my father sent me to court at Reims from our broad acres at Troyes, I doubt he envisaged me as a glorified butler.

Hubert was the son of a minor nobleman who grew up outside Troyes. His father had hoped for family preferment by sending his second son, at fifteen, to the court of Theuderic I, the father of Theudebert. The boy had possessed organisational gifts and Theudebert had grown to depend on Hubert's loyalty, discretion and his ability to anticipate his master's smallest desires. The relationship was mutually advantageous because Hubert had grown rich and powerful in the prince's service and, when Theudebert had taken up the crown after the death of his father, Hubert's star had risen even higher among the nobility of the land.

Hubert continued to straighten the palatial tent that was the king's home for most of the year, for Theudebert was only truly happy when he was on campaign. Their enforced bivouac at Soissons was driving the king demented with inactivity, so he drank to alleviate his boredom. Unfortunately, he missed the terrifying Deuteria when he was intoxicated.

'My father was a clever and ruthless man, Hubert. Did you know that?'

Hubert's spirits sank because the king's voice had that whine of self-pity that signified a period of maudlin confidences. Did the king ever remember what secrets he revealed when he was in his miseries? He hoped not, for such a possibility could herald a death warrant if he was the sole possessor of too much of the king's business.

'Yes, my lord! King Theodoric was a man of many talents,' Hubert agreed, while his mind was turning and twisting like a basket full of rats trying to escape.

'So – if he was so clever, why did he betroth me to Wisigard? I told him I'd never marry that blond milk cow, but did he listen? No, not him! The mighty Theodoric knew *everything*!'

Hubert could tell from his master's discontented face that no answer would satisfy him, so decided on presenting his king with a novel approach: the truth.

'Your noble and clever father sought to make an alliance with Wacho, the king of the Lombards, whose lands adjoined yours, so marriage to his daughter was the most simple and effective means of securing the eastern borders.'

'True, Hubert, but I never wanted to marry that silly woman, so her presence at court in Metz was embarrassing, to say the least.'

Theudebert's normally firm mouth was pursed unattractively as he pouted.

'Unfortunately, Princess Wisigard was forced to live in the palace at Metz for seven years, my lord, which must have lacerated her feelings. She was still unmarried at twenty-one! As well, your love for the lady Deuteria was no secret, was it? In the twelve months before your father died, the queen heard nothing but rumours of your passion for the daughter and kinswoman of Roman aristocrats and Emperor Avitus. And when your father died, she found herself still betrothed to you while she constantly heard gossip that you were married to the Roman woman. How would you feel in her shoes, my lord?'

Theudebert was angry, drunk and sullen now, a dangerous mix, so Hubert feared he might have gone too far. The servant held his breath as Theudebert staggered to his feet and weaved his way towards Hubert's side. But, instead of striking Hubert viciously or flying into a rage, Theudebert draped one arm conspiratorially over Hubert's shoulder and whispered in his ear.

'These women, Hubert! They'll find ways to castrate a man between them, one way or another. Wisigard was so frigid I thought she'd freeze my prick off. But Deuteria! Gods, Hubert! She killed her daughter because I expressed some ... affection for the girl. Much as Deuteria is an itch I can't quite scratch, she still scares the shit out of me. These women frighten me, Hubert! Even Wisigard – and she's dead!'

'I understand, my lord.' Hubert tried to look wise, but the revelations that Deuteria had killed her own daughter would take any man some time to accept.

'I still want the bitch in my bed, that's the trouble! Have you ever loved someone or something that was so bad for you that you were likely to die if you gave in to your desires? No? Well, Deuteria is my death wish. From the moment we met in Auvergne, I had to have her and she's one of those women that one can never tire of. I miss her!'

'Then send for her, master. The queen is dead, so there's no reason why you can't have Deuteria if you want her to be with you, is there?'

Hubert was trying to be reasonable, although his heart was racing at such dangerous confidences. If the Frankish lords should realise what he knew, he'd be dead within a week. Gods, some of them were monsters!

'I'd already married Deuteria privately when the Council of Franks decided that I should honour my father's word and marry Wisigard. They knew the situation, but they ordered Deuteria back to Auvergne. I was left in no doubt that they would withdraw their favour, *and their men* if I didn't act as they wished. So much for the rights of kingship!'

'Yes, master. Sometimes it isn't easy to be a ruler.'

Theudebert nodded owlishly. 'Then the silly cow caught the plague and now she's viewed as some kind of saint by the common people. There's no impediment to my taking Deuteria back into my bed, but the lords say the people wouldn't like it. Who the hell cares what the people think?'

Hubert coughed politely. It was perfectly obvious that the lords cared, so Theudebert was certainly caught in a trap of his own making.

'Perhaps you could visit her incognito, my lord? Maybe she could move to Reims and you could visit her when the need arises, without raising the suspicions of the lords?'

Theudebert's handsome face expressed a series of emotions that ran the full gamut of frustration, hope, fear, a dawning idea and, finally, conviction.

Oh, no! What has this drunken fool decided? And does it concern me?

'Whenever I become angry with you, Hubert, I forget just how brilliant you can be when situations are difficult. Metz would be far too dangerous for any liaisons, but Reims would be perfect, especially now when the plague is such a danger. You will organise Deuteria to come to me as soon as possible, Hubert, and you'll be well paid for your trouble. Just make sure that nothing can be traced back to either of us.'

'Lord . . . are you—'

'Yes! Yes! Use mercenaries to collect her, and then settle her into a suitable house on the outskirts of Reims. This plan will solve all of my problems, Hubert. It will work!'

The king's face was flushed with excitement – while Hubert knew that his own face was pale from horror.

'I feel so much better now, Hubert. I swear I could eat a horse!'

Then the king smiled and Hubert knew that he had been trapped by his own stupidity.

The sumptuous feast arrived while Hubert considered his options. With a sudden fit of appetite and good humour, Theudebert commenced to eat, while the night continued to darken and the overcast sky threatened rain.

In his heart of hearts, Hubert knew he could only be saved by a miracle.

The three travellers reached Soissons late in the evening. Because they had approached the city from the south, they were ignorant of the presence of Theudebert's bivouac to the north of the town until after they selected an inn for an overnight stay. As they arranged for their horses to be stabled they learned of Theudebert's presence, but they had already paid for the care of their horses and their feed in advance, so toted their valuables into their inn which carried the colourful name of the Leopard and the Unicorn. The inn's sign swung on a metal arm above the entrance and moved fitfully whenever there was the slightest wind. The noise of the creaking and grinding metal was both threatening and sinister.

Germanus led the way into a large room that took up the whole length of the building and offered a large bar where drinkers could sit and eat with friends. The din of shouts, snatches of song and arguments hit the three men like a physical blow as they fought their way through the crowded, smoky and dimly lit room towards the bar where a large man and several equally buxom women served beer in huge pottery, tin or horn containers.

Germanus used his height and weight to negotiate his way through the crowd while Farther Lorcan used his religious habit as his *entré*. Gareth's nimble flexibility allowed him to slide through gaps in the press of drinkers as he followed a zigzag path to keep Germanus's blond-grey head in sight. Eventually he found himself pressed against Arthur's tutors at the bar where Germanus was questioning the barkeeper as he paid for three huge, foaming mugs of local beer.

'Our beer hasn't the quality of the brew that comes from Cologne, of course, but I'd say that quietly around the locals who live here,' the bartender was telling Germanus with the loquaciousness of his breed. 'They're too fond of wine in these parts, although I don't care much for it myself. Give me a good amber beer and I'm happy!'

'Are rooms available here?' Germanus asked, and then took a large swig of his beer. 'Very good indeed! Better than British beer, I can tell you. Theirs is cat's piss, and it isn't even worthy of that name.'

With the exception of Gareth, all the listeners laughed cheerfully. Even though he knew that Germanus was playing up to the locals, Gareth still felt thoroughly annoyed.

'Yes, sir! We have rooms, but we're almost empty since the Wrath of Heaven came to these parts. King Theudebert has forbidden citizens to gather together in large groups, not even to attend church, but as you can see, we're not prepared to give up *everything* to save our necks. If the plague should come for us – well that's as it may be!'

He smiled across the bench top at his new acquaintances.

'May I ask your names, good sirs? It's not often that three armed men come to Soissons, or at least men who aren't signed up to the army or acting as a bodyguard to some useless nob. You've the look of a local man, sir, but I'll be a horse's arse if your friends aren't Outlanders.'

'True, good barkeeper! I'm called Germanus – a working name, you understand – and I'm seeking a runaway prince of the Burgundians.'

Germanus pressed the side of his nose and winked broadly. 'You know what young people are like! He doesn't want to marry his betrothed. Heaven knows she's no beauty, but what can you expect with the huge dowry she brings to the boy's family.'

The barkeeper nodded with a sly grin. 'I can't say I blame the nipper. The rich nobs have more money than us, but they have to marry as they're told whether they like it or not.'

'Aye, the princess from Dacia is no painting, it's true. At any road, this priest is called Lorcan. He's a Hibernian and he's really a heathen who also serves my master as the tutor of his children. And the dangerous-looking young cock here is a servant of the son of our master. We've been told our boy is heading towards Saxony or old Jutland. He's been known to speak well of the Dene, and we think he intends to join with them. Do you know of the Dene people?'

The bartender rubbed his whiskered chin with a harsh, rasping noise.

'Well, I've heard that the Dene are those bastards who've banded with the Geats to pillage our coasts. Trade ships are often captured by these devils and they've got no respect for anyone. Our king, Theudebert, is said to have killed the Geat king when he was little more than a boy, decades ago, God bless him. Until then, they'd invade our coasts every year, but things have been quiet since then. But if you're planning to take your prince back from them, I should warn you that the Dene warriors don't give back what they consider to be their property.'

'So we've heard,' Germanus replied drily. 'Still, we're not novices with the sword, as you can tell by our grey hairs. In fact, our Gareth is considered something of a genius with a blade.'

'I've heard rumours of three men who were seeking a lost Briton, only I believed there were four young outcasts who took off from their homeland. But I could have heard about different runaways, of course.'

Gareth's heart almost stopped. Who could have known so much of them? Who could have known that Arthur had been taken with three other Britons? Was the tale a part of common gossip? And how did such a state of affairs come to be?

'Who told you about the Britons?' Lorcan asked silkily, with a wide, gap-toothed smile.

The barman felt a frisson of anxiety as he glanced at Gareth's intense face, but Lorcan soothed everyone's nerves with his usual pragmatic charm.

'Priscus of Gesoriacum, an innkeeper there, sent word to all the inns in Soissons and Reims that you might be coming in our direction. The barkeeper smiled with a veneer of sorrow. 'It was a pity about Priscus, wasn't it?'

All three visitors looked blankly at their host, but to keep the barkeeper's attention away from several noisy patrons who were demanding to be served, they drained their beakers and Lorcan ordered another round of drinks. As he poured out fresh beer, the barkeeper continued to gossip, his large gut moving like jelly as he picked up a filthy cloth to wipe down the bar.

'Priscus caught the disease...' The barkeeper crossed himself piously. 'He was a terrible gossip, that man, but he was a mighty source of information. He went to the fires several weeks ago. Where have you been that you haven't heard of what happened down there? The word has spread that one out of every two men, women and children in Gesoriacum was taken by the disease. May God preserve their souls.'

'So! I wonder what was so intriguing in our movements that caught Priscus's interest,' Germanus said as he gulped his beer with practised ease.

'I've no idea, friend, but if you wish to take the three rooms, I'll have one of the girls take you upstairs. However, given the times in which we live, I insist on payment in advance.'

'So you're the owner of this establishment! Can we know your name, sir? We'll be needing food before we sleep and hot water as well, for my young friend likes to wash. He's a little peculiar, you know, like many of his type.'

Conspiratorial looks were exchanged at Gareth's expense, but he pushed down the desire to kick the innkeeper hard in the balls.

'The name's Egbert of Wurms! I've lived in Soissons since I was twenty, raised children and had three good wives – and I'm still an outsider! You know how it is in these small towns!'

'I know! Narrow-minded peasants, for the most part,' Germanus agreed and Gareth decided that the Frank would have told any convenient lie to win Egbert's confidence or to keep him talking, at least. 'Here are three silver coins. Let me know when you need more payment and . . .' Germanus's voice trailed away, but he winked broadly. 'Let me know if anyone comes looking for us, Egbert. Although he's dead, I trusted Priscus as far as I could throw him. He probably sold us out to someone – although I can't imagine what use we are to anyone in Soissons. Still, I'll happily pay you good coin if you pass information to me as soon as you get it. Do you understand?'

'Absolutely, master.' Egbert chuckled until his belly and his jowls jounced and bounced with his mirth. 'You can depend on me!'

After following the maid up a narrow, creaking staircase, the three men were offered either one large room that would be shared with two strangers or three small rooms, little larger than alcoves. For security's sake, and to ensure the safety of their valuables, Germanus decided they would take the one large room.

'We'll be sleeping in shifts so there's always one of us awake at all times. Egbert of Wurms is even less trustworthy than Priscus – and that bastard's dead! Sleep lightly, friends, with one eye open. And keep your weapons close at hand.'

The maid brought more beer in large jugs and bowls of mutton stew, very tasty after the fare they had been forced to eat on the road.

Even Gareth, who cared little what he ate, remembered his last good meal back in Gesoriacum and wondered if that wasn't an omen of the troubles to come.

Once they were lying down to sleep against the walls closest to the door, and as far as possible from the two snoring drunks who had taken the pallets near the only window, none of the three travellers found sleep easy to catch and master. Too many dangers were emerging around them for comfort. Priscus had announced their approach to the local authorities, the king's army was in bivouac outside the town and plague had already struck in some of the outlying parts of Soissons. As Lorcan remarked before he wrapped himself in his cloak, the prospects of a profitable visit to Soissons couldn't be further away.

'Yes, they could,' Germanus mumbled sleepily. 'Egbert could sell us out to someone who needs seasoned warriors in their service. At least we can be reasonably certain that none of us is likely to catch the plague. I know that I'd have to be very unlucky to catch it twice.'

Gareth cursed and pulled his cloak over his head. 'Thanks to you, I won't sleep at all now. Thank you very much, Germanus!'

Then, within ten minutes or so, the Frank and the Hibernian were amused to hear the young warrior begin to snore.

In the small tent where Hubert slept, and where he kept his clothes' chest and the small casket that contained his secret cache of coins and jewels, the king's body-servant accepted a message from a tall man-at-arms that a courier had come from one of Hubert's informers. Like all good servants, Hubert paid well for information and gossip that might be of use to his king. For the cost of a few coins, Hubert assembled important sources of information that ensured he had his finger on the pulse of whatever was happening in his king's world, especially information that couldn't be garnered by informers within the army. In essence, Hubert was a most useful spy-master and Theudebert paid him well for the intelligence he collected.

Perhaps the coin that had brought the loyalty of Egbert of Wurms might be about to pay a rich dividend. After he had heard the memorised message from an ostler from Egbert's inn, Hubert smiled quietly to himself. He tossed a small coin to the man to ensure his silence before sending him on his way.

'Sometimes a man doesn't need to be anything other than lucky,' he muttered. Then he hugged himself with secret glee and executed a little dance around his tent.

Outside, the guards looked at Hubert's dancing shadow on the tent walls and made the universal gestures that described madness. Then they sighed. Who was really the mad one? Hubert, the king's body-servant, would soon be sleeping on a soft, cushioned camp bed while they were required to guard the king's quarters throughout the hours of darkness.

And as he slept Hubert wove large and financially successful dreams that would swell the contents of his secret casket two-fold. If either his sleep or his grandiose plans were disturbed, it was only through the melodic sound of harness bells as mounted warriors patrolled the perimeter of Theudebert's camp site, protecting the king and his servants from harm throughout the long and lonely night.

THE JOURNEY TO VAGUS RIVER

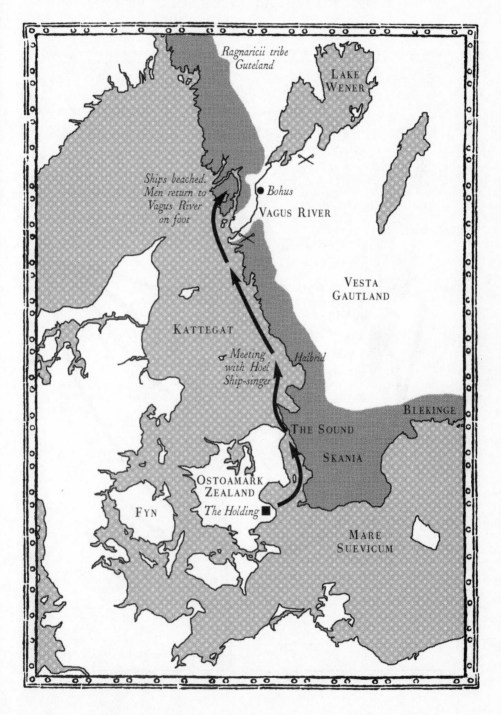

THE SIEGE AT VAGUS RIVER

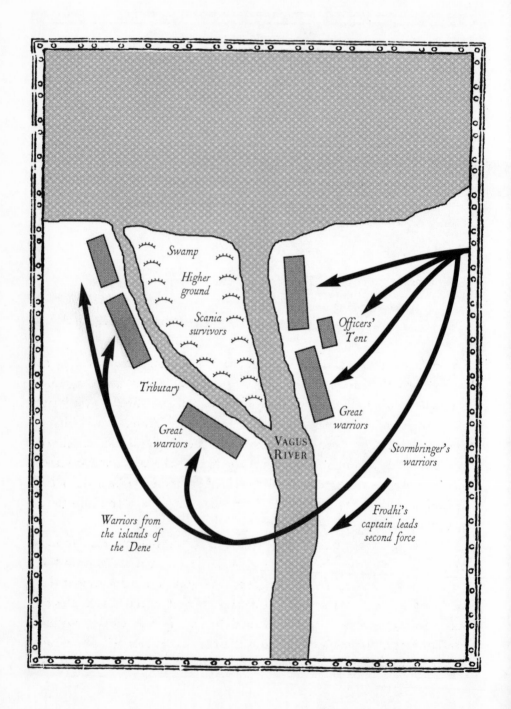

Swamp

Higher ground

Scania survivors

Tributary

Great warriors

Officers' Tent

Great warriors

Stormbringer's warriors

VAGUS RIVER

Frodhi's captain leads second force

Warriors from the islands of the Dene

CHAPTER XX

THE SIEGE OF
THE HEALFDENE

Veni, vidi, vici. (I came, I saw, I conquered.)

Julius Caesar according to Suetonius and Plutarch

Sea Wife tugged hard at the rudder, much as a restive horse struggles with the bit to free itself of constraint. With her sail straining against the rigging, she ploughed across the narrow sea in company with forty other ships and a force of over a thousand men. Under a black night sky, with summer warming the sea and the ship's planks, the fleet headed slowly towards Skania. The warriors of the traitorous outlaw, Stormbringer, were going to war against their ancient allies, the Geats of Gothland, so the brief hours of darkness hid the size of the large fleet under the Sae Dene's command.

Men sang as they honed their weapons to razor-sharpness. Around him, rising like white birds, Arthur could hear stirring tales from the eager crews spiralling upward to greet the night breeze. He caught the sense in fragments of the songs, especially those that told heroic tales of great warriors who fought and died in cataclysmic battles against foreign kings, monsters or the gods themselves. Arthur felt hot blood rise to his head in response; this day could, indeed, be a good day to die.

Such singing was worthy of Taliesin himself, yet these sturdy men were simple warriors who were unused to the poetry of bards. Their voices were coarse and lacking in any training or musicality, yet their songs almost stopped his heart with their beauty. Without the assistance of musical instruments, their voices wove the tune: some voices were high and almost womanish, while others were strong baritones that intimated a sense of power.

When Arthur thought back, he realised that the Dene sang often – when they were happy or sad, for weddings and funerals, before a battle and after a disaster. To these barbarians, song was an essential part of every aspect of daily life, as vital as breath, water or food for the belly.

Long ago, when he was still a boy, Arthur had been educated in the battles of the past, so Father Lorcan had related tales of long-distant campaigns such as the doomed Battle of Thermopylae in the city-states of ancient Greece. Arthur had never forgotten the tears of sympathy that prickled at the back of his eyes when he heard the tale of that memorable day for the very first time.

According to Lorcan, the last of the Spartan soldiers had oiled and braided each other's hair during those final hours as they readied themselves for the battle that would take place on the morrow. Even after many days of death and mayhem, each man had decided that he would go to Hades looking his best. In some cases, the Spartans had nothing left to fight with other than their teeth, their fingernails or the shards of their broken swords. But, in the morning when the Persians massed to kill them off, the defenders fought and killed their enemies and dragged out the inevitable until the last Spartan fell, singing joyfully. All that the Persians received were songs of defiance as their enemies died, contemptuous to the end.

Arthur had mourned for the ancient days of reckless courage, matched with disciplined sacrifice, that were now long gone.

But as the convoy ploughed onward, the young Briton could see how wrong his assumptions might have been. These Dene warriors would welcome death if their honour could be left intact and their heart's-blood was needed for a noble cause.

Over the previous months, the fleet had assembled gradually as Stormbringer and his guests rested at The Holding and enjoyed the sweet, hot days of early summer.

Maeve developed a sprinkling of attractive freckles across her nose as she helped Stormbringer's sister with the mundane details of domestic life on a farm. Blaise wove wool and amazed the other women as she displayed her remarkable skills, while Eamonn exercised his very able tongue to charm and bed any number of willing girls. Arthur smiled indulgently as he practised his swordsmanship in the warm sunshine.

Eamonn had laughed at Arthur's single-mindedness. 'When will you fall in love, Arthur? Or at least enjoy a mild flirtation? I've seen you with several beauties and you've bedded them too, if Maeve is correct. But your heart hasn't been touched at all. You aren't natural!'

'I'm unnatural? You're always dying of love for some girl or another, while I never seem to meet one who would be worth living with for twenty days – least of all twenty years. But the girls fill the hours, I suppose.'

'You're a devil, Arthur!' Eamonn was a little shocked by his friend's bluntness. 'They say that when men like you fall, they can really tumble into love.'

Arthur laughed with light-hearted humour. Silken thighs existed to be kissed, stroked or used as a conduit to the softness of every woman's greatest weakness, her sex. He was a practised lover, after a somewhat slow start to his education. After he discovered the erogenous zones that governed the gates to every woman's pleasure, he came to understand that men were hot, quick to arouse and, just as quickly, forget the experience, while women were slow to feel the heat rise in their bellies and genitals but, once the fires were lit, their pleasure grew stronger and stronger, and forced the patient man to be set alight until he drowned in female eroticism. Once a man tasted such fruit, he realised that a casual, quick slaking of lust was never acceptable again. Arthur was a master of this latter form of lovemaking and his respect for women was limitless, but . . .

363

'Admit it, Arthur. There are too many wonderful women in the world to settle on just one.' As usual, Eamonn was right.

While they waited, the ships began to arrive at the sheltered cove where *Sea Wife* lay on the beach at the high-tide line. Men came as well, tall and grim warriors shamed by their king's failure to protect their Dene kinfolk. In haste and desperation, Valdar Bjornsen had sent out a call to arms, and all right-spirited men heard his message, although the Sae Dene's name was never mentioned openly among Hrolf Kraki's loyalists in Heorot. At the slightest mention of Stormbringer, Hrolf Kraki lost his temper. One unfortunate jarl who invoked the memory of the great Bjorn, Valdar's father, had been slapped and kicked by the king's guard until he fell to the ground. He was left to lie in a shivering and shocked huddle of armour and blood until the Crow King's attention was diverted by other imagined ills.

Those warriors who remained loyal to their memories of the Crow King of long ago still tried to find excuses for his failure to honour his treaties, but more and more of the disaffected Dene came to join Stormbringer's fledgling army.

Some volunteers were rascals and cheats, and were more suited to signing on as mercenaries than as warriors of honour, but when Stormbringer explained that there would be no payment other than an equal division of the spoils, the worst of the ruffians departed. Most of the volunteers came because they had suffered as victims of Hrolf Kraki's intemperate rage.

Rufus Olaffsen and Thorketil came, both out of a desire to fulfil their oaths and because they had nowhere else to go where they could wield their swords with honour. The Troll King, as Thorketil had taken to calling himself, had healed as well as he ever would. His right leg was encased in a sleeve of iron and leather so it could bear his weight. With a full staff to redistribute the weight of his massive body, he could walk, although very slowly. But he could row, and easily took the place of two men while, in any fray, he was able to stand upright and surround himself in a ring of swinging metal. Rufus guarded his back, for the two men had become almost friendly as they convalesced and, finally, they had agreed to place the blame for their injuries and their individual humiliations squarely on the head of Hrolf Kraki.

Ivar Hnaefssen remembered his vows, even though scouts warned him that Anglii warriors were massing on the frontiers of his own lands. His youngest son, Vermund, led a force of thirty men who had been split between the two promised ships. Stormbringer met the young jarl personally on the shelving beach, embraced him warmly and welcomed him to The Holding.

'I know how important your thirty good men are to your father at such a perilous time as now. The frontiers are boiling with tension and our king is far away in his thoughts, if not in actuality, so he won't move to warn off any aggressors. Your assistance is a matter of great importance to the Dene people – and we thank you and your father, who is a true man of honour.'

'I was angry at first when my father ordered me to come here. I believed he was trying to protect me from the Anglii warriors that are certain to cross our borders.' Vermund examined his toes with a shamefaced expression. 'But my father took pains to show me that the debt was owed. How can we expect aid from other jarls if we show no loyalties ourselves? I am here as his representative and as proof of his personal regard for you. We are hoping that you and yours will respond in turn if, as is almost certain, the Anglii enter our lands and we require assistance.'

'There's no need for oaths or high-flown language between men of honour, Vermund. It only requires a handshake between you and me. If you need my help, I'll come, as will my kin, in answer to any call for assistance from your clan. Although I'm a Sae Dene, we are both jarls and our oaths are iron-clad.'

Vermund saw the sincerity in Stormbringer's eyes and was comforted. He had feared to leave his father's lands, for Ivar had grown old and his two other sons were not the warriors that their father had been. However, his brothers were more than able to obey the orders of their sire and would fight to the death to protect their broad acres. Stormbringer's oath convinced him that this man would always keep his word. They would be assisted by the Sae Dene if the Anglii, or the Jutes, attacked their lands in force.

The men embraced and walked up the long, shelving beach. For Vermund and Valdar Bjornsen, the point of no return had passed.

Frodhi kept his word and ten ships arrived, fully armed with crews and fighting men loyal to their master, although Stormbringer's cousin remained at Heorot.

Stormbringer understood his cousin very well and the duties that kept him there. As a member of the ruling family, he was bound to the Crow King by the sacred oaths and responsibilities of kinship, so Frodhi was caught in a moral dilemma. To send ships and men to another kinsman was a betrayal of sorts, but Frodhi had chosen to do so, while refusing to give the public support that his own presence would have excited.

Stormbringer had called to his other kinsmen and they responded to his summons. As well, neighbouring jarls from the islands between Heorot and Skania measured their safety by the distance across the small body of water called the Sound. When their loyalty to Hrolf Kraki was measured, they found that the peril from Geat aggression was more pressing than abstract issues of loyalty. Any fool could see that if Skania fell, then so would all the Dene Islands along the Sound's narrows. The Crow King could afford to be high-handed from the safety of Heorot, but the island jarls looked towards Gothland with jaundiced eyes.

And so, once forty ships had been assembled and every spare patch of land at The Holding was groaning with armed warriors, Stormbringer decided that the time for action had come. Calling Arthur and Eamonn to him before commencing his council of war, Stormbringer asked the Britons to declare their intentions.

Arthur looked at Stormbringer blankly. 'I'll fight alongside *you*, Stormbringer. You've treated us like guests, rather than captives, and you've saved our lives on a number of occasions. We're not fair-weather friends! As much as Hrolf Kraki owes you a debt for your bravery, so do we owe debts of honour to you for your generosity towards us.'

Arthur grinned. 'I must sound very formal, but you bring this stuffiness out in me, my friend.' He began to laugh at the surprised expression on the face of the Sae Dene. 'Personally, I'd follow you anywhere out of loyalty and friendship, but I have practical motives as well. You hold the keys to our return to Britain, so I'd be a fool to spurn any endeavour to which you have committed your men and your word. Besides, Hrolf Kraki is no friend of mine. But for your intercession, he would have killed my sister out of hand. He refused to accept our victories in single combat and he refused to accept us as equals. I have no loyalty towards the Crow King and would willingly do him harm, if I had such an opportunity.'

'Well said, Arthur,' Eamonn agreed. 'I agree with you and I will also be travelling with you to Skania. We don't know where we're going, but I'm sure you'll eventually tell us.'

'And we'd be grateful if our sisters could be kept safely at The Holding,' Arthur added.

'Of course, Arthur! Both your sisters are welcome to stay for as long as they wish.' Stormbringer was very serious, as if he was embarrassed.

Wisely, Arthur said nothing.

The day of departure came with many tears. Because they had wailed at the sight of their father cleaning his weapons, Stormbringer's daughters were chided gently by their aunt, so the little girls tried to control their sobbing. Some of the older women also wept to see their sons depart, but theirs was a restrained grief.

As the warriors moved towards the beach, Maeve came running, her arms filled with daisy chains. Gently, she crowned Eamonn, then her brother and, finally, she asked Stormbringer to bend his head. Quickly, before he could change his mind, she placed the last daisy crown upon his amber curls.

'Hail to our Three Warriors of God! You do His good work – and so you will come safely home to us. We love you!'

Her words were lost in the wind as Stormbringer and the Britons trotted to *Sea Wife* and joined with the rest of the crew as they pushed her keel back into deeper water. Once they had clambered aboard and hurried onto their rowing benches, the warriors put their shoulders to the oars and the ship turned and shot away as it gained some assistance from the light breeze. As they left the cove and entered the waters of the Sound, the sun was sinking slowly into the sea.

Somehow, Arthur and Eamonn both lost their daisy chains while they were rowing vigorously away from the shore, but Stormbringer stood beside the rudder and removed his crown himself. As Arthur watched surreptitiously, Stormbringer lifted the string of daisies from his tangled hair, held them briefly to his nose and his lips, then placed them inside his clothing so that the bruised blossoms rested over his heart.

Ahead of the fleet, the land had fast become a darkened spool before them, except for the glow of moonlight on the white beaches. On Stormbringer's order, the fleet turned to port and the forty ships began their long, slow prowl up the coast of Skania.

When Arthur had asked Stormbringer for their destination, the captain had explained that while the centres of both the Fervir and Hallin clans were close to the Sound, these tribes had already been betrayed and their populations had been overrun by the Geats. To the north, the Vagus River cut deeply into the landmass, and this fast-flowing flood emanated from a great inland lake called Wener. Years earlier, the Dene had fought a decisive battle against the Geats on the margins of this lake and their success had won them a large stretch of land that extended from the confluence of rivers in the north controlled by the Ragnaricii clan to the southern tip where the Bergio clan held sway.

'Is there a great town at the entrance to this lake?' Arthur asked.

'*Town* is too large a description! It's a village that comes to life in the spring and summer when the king and favourites among the court and his army arrive for a time of feasting when war is no impediment to their pleasure. We describe the place as Vaster Gotland, the name of a province taken from the Geats who inhabit this rich area. It's populated by farmers and a few rich traders who live near the confluence of the

Vagus and Lake Wener. In spring and summer there are markets and trading houses that enrich the township.'

Eamonn cocked his head sideways and grinned disarmingly at Stormbringer. 'So the Geats finally became sick of the Dene controlling the west coast of their country, not to mention being so close to their richest and most favoured army bivouac! The Geat king must flinch whenever he swims in his lake for fear of Dene arrows being trained on him.'

His observations were only marginally short of rudeness, so Arthur's cheeks flushed at his companion's tone and effrontery.

Fortunately, Stormbringer chose to overlook Eamonn's slip in manners. 'Of course! But we have always feared attack from our backs, so we have ensured we have a strong and self-sufficient colony behind our flanks. We don't want to control all of Gothland – just a coastal strip that will always be a strong buffer between two warring races. As yet, we've kept to our part of the bargain for more than four hundred years.'

'He's caught you fairly, Eamonn,' Arthur retorted. 'Why would the Dene attack the Vastergotland? It's upriver, and we'd be surrounded by hostile warriors.'

'We have traded with Vastergotland for generations, and we've lived side by side with them. Up to now, the Geats have ruled the game on this campaign, but we must take back the initiative that we previously held. Unfortunately, the Geats are caught between the Swedes on the east coast who are hostile and aggressive and the kinsmen of the Dene who inhabit the lands along the west coast. I understand their anxiety about any aggression from either side, but we were their allies in the past. And now they have broken their solemn oaths.'

Stormbringer's upper lip twitched with the contempt he felt for all oath breakers.

'Our only hope for success is to attack their precious lake settlement, the one we let them keep so long ago until they decided to use guile to turn on our people and destroy them. A victory by our forces at Vastergotland would bring hope to the Dene towns in the south and turn the Geat conquest into a retreat towards their own lands.'

'People who fight for their lands are never easy to defeat,' murmured Eamonn. He was still pushing his luck, but Stormbringer seemed undeterred.

'We Dene have nowhere else to go, Eamonn. We have always been prepared to remain inside our old borders. But we are willing to fight for this strip of land, so let's see who is the most desperate. Will it be the Geats with their thousands of acres, or the Dene whose total kingdom would fit into Gothland many times over? Don't misjudge these people. They look like us, and they sound like us. But, in fact, they are not Dene!'

'So?' Eamonn was genuinely confused now.

'We took their land as a springboard for further expansion of our kingdom, but we never sought more land than we needed. We are little different, but the Geats love battle and power even more than we do, for we are reminded of the ancient days in Opland when our people suffered in the snowy wastes.'

'I acquit you of any hubris or self-delusion, Stormbringer, but don't ask me to believe that Hrolf Kraki and his poisonous woman wouldn't steal the whole wide world if they thought they could get away with their treachery.' Eamonn's voice had a nasty edge to which Stormbringer finally responded.

'Thank you, Prince Eamonn, I'm forever in your debt for stating the obvious.' Stormbringer managed a serviceable, if sardonic, bow. 'Your personal approval is very important to the Dene people.'

'Do shut up, Eamonn! You're making a fucking ass of yourself,' Arthur warned his friend, while cuffing him lightly across the right ear for good measure.

'Ow!' Eamonn yelped. 'That hurt, Arthur!'

'It was supposed to,' Arthur retorted.

'Enough, Arthur, for I can understand Eamonn's doubts,' Stormbringer added. 'After all, neither of you would be here if the Dene weren't under constant pressure to expand their lands. Still, Eamonn, I'd prefer that you thought well of my people and were prepared to fight for our cause with a whole heart.'

'You'd have that oath anyway, Stormbringer, even if I believed your cause to be wrong,' Eamonn replied quickly. He looked puzzled at the idea that his opinion could matter at all to the tall Sae Dene.

The longboats cut through the water at an amazingly fast pace, but the warrior atop the sail called out an alarm when he spotted a warning beacon on a distant headland. While the other longboats moved through the early, still-darkling morning, *Sea Wife* lagged a little behind so that Stormbringer could monitor other beacon fires being lit along the coast as the passage of the fleet was plotted.

A small craft crossed the bows of *Sea Wife* at speed almost before Stormbringer's crew noticed its presence. Leaf-shaped and narrow from stem to stern, there was only room within her elongated shape for four rowers, while a simple sail had been provided to extend her range. On this Eamonn could see that a white swan with a roughly sketched crown around its crest had been daubed.

'Who goes there?' Stormbringer roared. 'Identify yourself or we'll run you down.'

A voice drifted up from the craft. The warriors sat at their rowing benches, poised to act immediately that the ramming order was given, while Stormbringer walked slowly to the prow and showed himself.

'Who enters the waters of Ingeld Sea Sweeper, master of the coasts of the Hallin?' The voice was arrogant, so Stormbringer raised one hand to give the attack order.

'Wait, Captain! Wait! We are the servants of Ingeld, but he's in hiding with what's left of our people in the caverns in the southernmost reaches of our lands. We've been overrun by the Geats and I thought you might have been a part of their fleet passing northwards to wipe out our last defenders along the Vagus River. I apologise if I've misjudged you.'

'What is your name?' Stormbringer shouted back. His temper was stretched tight by the seaman's prevarications and the danger of their discovery. The whole invasion could be at risk!

'I'm called Hoel, the Ship-Singer, so I beg your pardon for any rudeness. But, sir, I should remind you that your ships are the strangers in our waters.'

'Aye! And your beacons have announced our presence to the enemy more effectively than a personal announcement at their main camp. I'm Valdar Bjornsen, the Stormbringer, and I have come in answer to the call of Leif, the Sword of Skandia. I was at Heorot when his emissary arrived in search of aid from Hrolf Kraki, King of the Dene. So I have come with forty manned ships to make the contest against the Geats more even.'

'Thanks be to Loki then! And to Thor! His companions cheered with gusto, and Hoel's face was split in a grin so wide that his face seemed to be divided into two parts.

'The warriors of our master, Leif, are confined within a narrow triangle of land that is bounded by the Vagus River, the sea and a smaller tributary of the river. They can't advance or retreat, so the Geat leader, Olaus Healfdene, has left a small force to starve them into submission. Olaus has camped at Vastergotland where he and his army are growing fat on the wealth that has been stolen from our people.'

Hoel spat over the side of his vessel into the oily sea.

'You're late in coming, Stormbringer. Our women have been raped and our children are dead. Our acres are blackened, our boats have been burned and our horses have been stolen. But you have come, nonetheless, and you give heart to an old man. I had readied myself to flee to the west, but now I'll gather together what men and vessels I can and I'll meet you at the Vagus River. I'll send couriers to the north and explain that relief is at hand.'

'And you will be welcome!' Stormbringer pointed to the line of warning fires that marched into the north. 'But take care that your couriers aren't captured or we'll be defeated at the Vagus before we arrive. Can I depend on you, Hoel?'

'Aye, master. You're well named, for you bring the storm with you and, if the gods are kind, those raging winds will blow Olaus Healfdene away like straw in the tide. Fare thee well, Valdar Bjornsen.'

Without waiting for an answer, Hoel released a rope, the sail filled and the small boat sprang away like a hunting hound released from the chain. Within moments, the elegant little craft was a dark sliver in the gold-tinged world of waves as the sun began to rise on the first day of war. The sail, with its crowned swan, rode above the waves as if it flew on the breast of the morning wind while, on the prow, a small figure raised one hand in triumph and salutation.

'That ship is a beautiful thing, Stormbringer. I would consider myself a fortunate man if I possessed a larger version of her. Hoel Ship-Singer must be a master craftsman.' Arthur followed the track of the vessel until it was hidden behind the headland with its blazing beacon.

'He's a master builder, so perhaps he'll sing you a ship one day, if we should prevail in the coming battle. All things are possible under Heaven.'

'I doubt I'll ever be able to afford such a beautiful ship – and certainly not here in Skania. I could have her if I were at home in Britain, although I don't know what I would do with a lovely vessel like *Sea Wife* or *Loki's Eye* in Arden Forest. The nearest water to Arden is a five-day trek on horseback.'

The Sae Dene captain smiled politely and Arthur remembered that he had seen the east coast of Britain at first hand and that sighting hadn't always been in the most generous of lights.

Stormbringer issued a series of rapid-fire orders to his crew. Then he returned, his face calm but grave, and Arthur felt a frisson of concern.

'You're young, and barely a man, Arthur, but it's time we had a serious discussion about your future because it's time for you to put off all your more childish habits. Don't stiffen up on me, lad, for I'd like to speak to you as if I were an older brother . . .'

Stormbringer coughed awkwardly in embarrassment.

'You're the best hand-to-hand warrior I've ever seen, Arthur. I'm not just flattering you. 'You're a master with those twin blades of yours, and you have all the natural skills of a born leader. I can assure you that my men would already follow you if I were to pass on – except for the fact that you don't trust yourself.'

Arthur opened his mouth to protest, but Stormbringer brushed his complaints aside. 'I understand that your father's death left large boots to fill. I know better than you imagine, for my father was a legendary swordsman, a genius on a ship and universally loved by all who served with him. Yet he saw nothing in colour, so he existed in a half-blind state that ranged from black through to white. As a child, I was sure I could never hope to earn a name for myself. Not like him!'

What was there for Arthur to say in response to his friend's truth?

'You see every mistake you make as proof that you're a failure. You paralyse yourself by thinking and talking endlessly about your perceived weaknesses. I've watched you analyse every simple flaw, real or imagined, since we first met. I've told myself that you would grow out of these mannerisms, but you need guidance in how you must plan your life, if you ever hope to see Britain again.'

'That's my problem, Stormbringer! I've been living with the certainty that I'll never see it again, and my father and my mother will die without me. I know that Arden Forest will be lost to the Saxons and burned for charcoal, all the people I have loved will grow old and forget me, while I will dwindle, become old and ultimately die. I can easily remain a landless beggar once my strong arms and legs begin to fail me, if I survive at all.'

Stormbringer laughed, riotously and hurtfully.

'I can see I appear amusing to you, my lord, so I'll leave you if I'm such a figure of fun.'

Suddenly, Stormbringer slapped Arthur with his open hand across the face. The young man gasped with the shock of the unexpected blow and his furious eyes blazed like burning ice.

'Such masterly self-pity! If you were a priest, you'd need a whip that would allow you to flagellate yourself. You Britons amaze me sometimes! If you don't like the situation, do something about it.'

Arthur gnashed his teeth with fury, but Stormbringer was far from done with him.

'Has it occurred to you that talent, rather than birth, is everything to the Dene people? You too can become a man of wealth with ships and wide acres, and good men will follow you wherever you lead. You can build your own ships and sail back to Britain like a king. If you wish, you can carve out your own kingdom from the British lands that are now ruled by the Saxons. Why not?'

This time, Arthur was unable to find the words of protest needed. His mind was filled with the prospects that Stormbringer had described, so he was dizzy with a sudden rush of blood to his brain.

'What are you thinking, Arthur?' Stormbringer's voice was surprisingly gentle.

'My dreams, my friend! I'm wishing that all you describe might come to be.'

'If you wish it, so it will. Did you doubt the words of the wise woman, Freya, who said you'd become the King of Winter? I don't, and I believe fervently that you will become a great king in Britain because that is what your heart desires. Now, sleep for what remains of the darkness because you might not get another chance.'

Some two days later, the Vagus River made its presence obvious by a brown stain on the blue waters. Although the Vagus wasn't a large river, it was strong and deep, and swept from the inland lake through fertile lands until it reached the waters of the western sea. Arthur plucked a small pine branch from the floodwaters and, although the sharp, spiny foliage was waterlogged, the bough brought the scent of sap with it, as familiar as the smell of his mother's hair.

If Stormbringer is right, I can return to Britain like a king, Arthur thought. I need to determine that I will win a name for myself, collect a following of good warriors and then purchase a ship with the rewards of the victories that will surely come to us. If all goes well, I will smell the pines of Arden, hold my mother in my arms and once again become a complete man.

As one, the fleet turned and the ships veered to the north, just beyond sight of land.

'Do we disembark to the south of the river, or do we beach the ships and make a direct attack?' Eamonn asked with an eager smile on his face. His eyes flashed with the excitement of the coming conflict.

'No! We'll beach our ships north of the river in a place that will ensure our vessels can be guarded and kept safe. Then, on foot, we'll attack Olaus Healfdene's troops who are keeping Leif and his warriors confined in their encampment on the Vagus. Next, in company with Leif and the remnants of his force, we will take to our ships to attack the main body of Olaus's army at Vastergotland. He won't be expecting an attack at this early stage in his campaign, especially from the river. We'll sail upstream as far as we dare, and then beach our ships. Again, we'll need to select a well-protected landing spot, because we'll need our longboats to sail south to those places where we can teach Olaus's allies in Southern Skania that they must keep to their own borders. Our ships must remain safe and undamaged, so their protection is paramount to any tactical decisions we make during the course of the battles.'

'Where will this second battle be fought then?' Eamonn persisted, with little lights dancing in his eyes like small red fires.

'You're very eager, my friend, and you'll become a berserker if you're not careful.' The Sae Dene captain smiled. 'It's my intention to take the fleet upstream until we reach Myrkvidr, which is deep in Vaster Gortland, the land of the Geats. We'll make our attack at a place where the Dene infiltration and settlement is negligible. Do you understand why, Arthur?'

'No one ever asks me,' Eamonn interrupted, grinning; Stormbringer was left confused by the odd sense of humour of these Britons.

'Hush, Eamonn,' Arthur responded. 'I think I see your reasoning, Stormbringer, but correct me if I'm wrong.'

'Go on then, Arthur! We still have some time before we'll need to muffle our oars and maintain complete silence.'

'To attack the Geats in an area where they consider themselves to be completely secure will give us an unexpected tactical advantage. Considering the fact that the Dene, the Geats and the men of Noroway are all closely related by blood, there's a strategic gain in defeating the

Geat forces at a time when the Dene position in Skania in the south is so parlous.'

'That's all true,' Stormbringer agreed equably.

'The Dene forces in Skania are demoralised and more than half defeated already. Normally, they would fight to the last man for every foot of land, but not only has Hrolf Kraki deserted them and left them to the mercy of their enemies, but his name was used to betray them. Only a stunning victory will rouse them from the torpor of defeat. With luck and good planning, our counteroffensive will be successful before the Geats have even commenced the second wave of their aggression. Is that assessment true?'

'Absolutely!'

Arthur felt pleased with himself.

'Of course, we must defeat them comprehensively if we're to gain the ascendancy that we need. There must be few survivors, if any, from the forces of our enemy.'

'This Myrkvidr, Captain! What an ugly name! It must mean something particularly unpleasant,' Eamonn put in.

'You would call it *Mirk Wood* in your tongue; it means a murky, dark or black forest, and it's not a place where you'd really like to be unless you had good reason. In the summer, Lake Wener is very beautiful and the Geat jarls enjoy the pleasures of sin, women and feasting once their enemies have been crushed. We will attack their encampment from the forest south of the shores of the lake. It's said to have a dangerous reputation. Unclean things dwell there in a half-darkness too thick to be breached, even during the height of summer.'

'A pleasant spot then!' Arthur's sardonic expression was everything that Stormbringer had hoped for. 'Because of its reputation, Olaus Healfdene would never expect an army to arrive out of its depths. A successful commander and strategist will always choose the ground for his battles and will bring his forces as close to his enemy as he possibly can *before* he is discovered and loses the initiative. That's what I'd like to do if I were in command!'

'And so do we all – but we must rest now! We sail north to a spot only twenty miles from the Vagus, but we'll move at speed once we leave the fleet, for who knows if we've been seen already? We must be fast, disciplined and silent. That means no berserker rage from you, young Eamonn!'

Stormbringer's navigators found a pebbled beach that was just large enough for the beaching of their vessels, so the Sae Dene approached the shore with the caution of men deep inside enemy territory. With a practised economy, Stormbringer used hand gestures to order a dozen men to create a perimeter before *Sea Wife* was finally dragged above the high tide line.

Beyond the pebbled foreshore that was thick with black, bleaching seaweed tossed down by the last high tide, an area of coarse grasses and flowering vines formed a transitional area between the sea and the thick forest. Arthur imagined that this wood of midnight-blue shadows, brooding silence and deep drifts of pine needles hid enemies behind every tree. Stormbringer hissed out the information that these woods were green and pleasant places in summer, although when winter came and the snow fell in thick drifts, many peasants became frightened of the growling of the frozen branches.

Once the perimeter was established, Stormbringer instructed his jarls to select one hundred men who could be trusted to fight to the death to protect the ships. None of the warriors relished such a task because it promised no spoils, no glory and scant excitement. With an apologetic grin, Stormbringer asked Vermund to volunteer to lead the hundred.

'I can see from your face, my young fire-eater, that my request doesn't please you. But I must leave my ships in the hands of a man I can trust. I promise you that you will be part of the fighting when we arrive at Myrkvidr, if you successfully guard my fleet for me. You will not be required to stay behind twice. Remember, we have to rescue Leif, the Sword of Skandia, and his men. If so, we may have to escape at speed and will be relying on these ships. We may be expected when we arrive at the Vagus! If that disaster happens, this duty will be critical for, without the fleet, we'll be trapped on this beach – and here we'll rot.'

The silence was deep and ominous while Arthur watched Vermund's eyes closely. At first, he thought the young man would refuse out of hand, but then Vermund stiffened his back, squared his shoulders and bowed his head in obedience to his commander.

'I will do as you ask, my Lord Stormbringer. These ships will suffer no harm unless we are all dead. Your ships are safe!'

'I believe you, Master Vermund, and you have my hand on my promise.'

Then Stormbringer and Vermund clasped each other's wrists in the way of warriors the world over: toe to toe, and eye to eye.

Without delay, the Dene warriors were strung out through the forest with scouts moving ahead and on each side of the main body of warriors to disguise their number and warn of problems before they arose. The main force was organised into independent platoons comprised of ships' crews under the command of the ship's captain and officers. Each commander was directly answerable to Stormbringer, who was in overall command of the attack force.

Before they left the dunes above the beach, Stormbringer had stolen the time to hold a conference with the thirty or so officers who would control their crews once the assault began. The strategy chosen for the attack was simple, but its success depended on perfect timing and teamwork.

When the prevailing geographical conditions became fully apparent, Stormbringer decided to divide the force into two groups. Leif was trapped between three distinct bodies of water. The sea approaches couldn't be traversed and running at attack speed through dry sand or pebbles was treacherous, exhausting and foolish, so Stormbringer excluded any attack or escape from the sea and its beaches with no regrets.

The two rivers, the Vagus and its small brackish tributary, were another matter entirely. As the command group observed the lie of the land from the top of a low dune overlooking the Vagus, Stormbringer, his captains and Arthur stared down at the trap that Olaus had sprung on the Dene imprisoned in their enclave.

The Vagus was broad at its confluence with the sea, but it was spread over a wide area. A smashed path through the dried grass and the low, stunted bushes that could tolerate these salty conditions showed where the Dene warriors had been driven, so Stormbringer was sure that the river, in this section at least, would allow armed men to ford the waters with reasonable safety. Of course, the Geats had set up an encampment that prevented any escape into the north by Leif's warriors, who had been trapped in the marshes between the two confluences for nearly two months. That any of the Dene defenders were still alive was a miracle in itself.

Across the swamp with its higher ground covered with tents, Stormbringer could see the shallower tributary. All the trees that had grown in this marshy, malodorous and muddy stretch of waterfront had been cut down for cooking fires. The camp was deceptively quiet, almost deathly still, and Arthur tried to imagine what life would be like, trapped and defeated in a world of dirty water, slimy mud and minimal supplies of food. The plagues of midges and insects would make life unendurable. With a jolt of horror, Arthur recognised dried meat hanging in the Dene camp. The Dene had been forced to butcher their horses and dry the meat, because they had no use for their beloved beasts, coupled with insufficient food or fresh water to sustain them.

'We must attack from both sides simultaneously,' Stormbringer decided. 'The river is deep enough to permit the passage of low-draught vessels but we may have to swim for it, if we fail in our attack. On the other hand, that tributary is shallow and more mud than sand, because the water is very slow-moving. We'll have to cross the Vagus from upstream where the Geats won't be expecting us, but it'll still be a long run to the battle with the besiegers.'

He singled out Frodhi's captains. 'Can you swim the Vagus, run to the enemy positions and then carry out a successful attack?'

One hard-bitten commander, Halgar, bridled at the question. 'My men's resolve will not be weakened and no ground will defeat them. My master, Frodhi, sent his best men and his fairest ships in answer to your call, and no man present will outclass Frodhi's warriors.'

'I'm pleased to hear you say those words,' Stormbringer answered calmly. No trace of irritation at Halgar's curt response was permitted to show. 'At dusk, just before the sun sets and at a time when no one would normally expect an attack, I will light a beacon right here, which will be the signal for the attack to begin on both sides of the rivers. If the fire is on the reverse slope of the dune, you'll be able to see it from your starting points, while it will be mostly hidden from the Geat positions. With luck, we won't have to swim unless we are defeated – and I refuse to consider defeat! After all, there are only two hundred of them and near to a thousand of us. If we fail, the clans will sing songs forever of the foolish tactics and stupidity of Valdar Bjornsen. So, my friends, we won't lose, will we? We will relieve our brothers and then we will strike the Geats where we can really hurt them.'

'Do we take prisoners?' Halgar asked, his mouth pursed in a thin line of determination. Stormbringer thought quickly, as did Arthur, and they both came to the same chill conclusion.

'There will be no prisoners! We can't afford the warriors to guard them. Besides, I don't expect that there'll be many of Leif's men left alive and sound. We'll have problems enough caring for them.'

'You can't allow any of them to escape and warn Olaus Healfdene that we're here and hunting,' Arthur added. 'Surprise must be everything in this campaign!'

'You've heard the Briton,' Stormbringer told Halgar, and was rewarded with a jaundiced smile. 'Give no quarter and permit no one to survive.'

'Does that include the women?' Halgar asked.

'If there are women in Healfdene's group, they'll be camp followers and shield maidens.' Arthur's reply was adamant. 'They'll understand the ways of war.'

Stormbringer answered reluctantly. 'Kill the women, but there will be no rapine, do you hear me? We're not barbarians, and I want our people to praise you and your men when they sing of our victory, not compare you to the animals of the wilds. Finally, before you ask, any children who may be present will be spared and given to Leif as slaves. I don't make war on children!'

So, with the sun on its downward slide into the afternoon, Stormbringer's forces divided and Halgar led his men into the inky shadows of the trees. When Arthur looked, his sun-dazzled eyes could find no trace of the three hundred men under the dour Halgar's leadership. All sound from Frodhi's warriors was lost in the forest and the entire force had vanished like smoke.

'You and you,' Stormbringer pointed to two of his captains, 'secrete yourselves and your men in ambush along the beaches. I can see Olaus's men attempting to escape in that direction if they have no other choice. But remember – no quarter!'

'Depend on us, Valdar Bjornsen,' the tallest man responded. 'No one will escape.'

Stormbringer turned his attention to Arthur. 'And you, my friend, take my crew and build me a beacon fire sufficient to be seen by our men, once they have taken up their positions and are awaiting the order to attack.'

'I live to serve,' Arthur answered and immediately leaped to his feet to obey. Because his nerves were stretched taut, the young man was grateful to be occupied during the interminable hours that stretched out before him until the battle commenced. Every warrior feared these hours, because each man was tortured by his own imagination.

And so the afternoon dragged on, in impatience and taut anxiety, while the sun continued its descent towards the horizon and the coming battle.

CHAPTER XXI

THE CROWS OF HUNGER

We have made a covenant with death, and with hell are we at agreement.

The Bible, Isaiah 28:15

The sun had crept slowly towards the western horizon and the red-flecked sea as Stormbringer stirred, rose to his feet and moved to the summit of the vine-strewn sandy dune. Below him, the enemy camp was a careless jumble of tents and cooking fires.

'Is the beacon ready, Arthur?'

'Yes, Stormbringer, ready to light as soon as you give the signal.'

'There's no reason for delay then. Halgar will be in position and the Geats will be engrossed in eating their supper, so let's light the beacon and introduce these fools to Hell.'

Arthur had prepared a small mound of kindling, wood shavings and dried leaves in a small hollow in the ground and this tinder was quickly ignited with his flint. He had also prepared a torch, wound round with cloth soaked in the pitch which Stormbringer carried on his boats to repair sprung planks and timbers. Once the flame roared into life, Arthur thrust the torch into the beacon and waited until the dry wood caught alight.

'Lord!' Arthur acknowledged the command softly as the blaze leaped up with a sudden flare of scarlet and gold flames that were almost too beautiful to announce the start of a battle.

'Attack!' Stormbringer ordered, his call to arms clearly heard over the squabbling of feeding seabirds and the soughing of the freshening wind. As Stormbringer charged down the dunes with Arthur and the Dene warriors in pursuit, the young Briton could hear distant roars of challenge across the river from the besieged Dene encampment near the banks of the tributary. Desperate not to trip over the trailing creepers that rendered this area between the sea and the tree line an obstacle course of considerable danger, Arthur shouted to Stormbringer that Frodhi's warriors had commenced their attack.

At full pelt, a line of Dene warriors forty foot long struck the Geat force like a tidal wave. It was inevitable that the Geats would hear Stormbringer's call to arms, but they had been engrossed by one of the few high points of any soldier's day, the evening meal. So it took the besiegers a moment or two to realise that they were under attack from an unexpected quarter.

Shouts, curses and bellowed commands filled the air and added to the confusion among the Geat warriors. When Arthur reached the first cooking fire, he kicked over a triangle of iron supporting a heavy cooking pot filled with bubbling mutton stew. The hot slop of food hit the glowing coals with a deadly hiss, but Arthur now knew that he wouldn't trip over the cauldron during the fighting.

A huge, dishevelled Geat with a plaited blond beard and long, uncombed locks vaulted over the mess around the fire pit with the determination of a man who was crazed or confused. In one hand, he wielded a wicked axe on the end of a long handle which he swung with such force that Arthur felt the breeze of the blade as it sliced past his chest. Too experienced to look downwards, the Briton responded with an underhand slice of his sword. He knew the Geat would evade the blow, but the warrior must be prevented from swinging that unusually long axe again.

Arthur stepped inside the arc of the axe, even as he swung his sword. Now less than four feet from his enemy, most Dene warriors would be too far away for knife work and too close to wield their swords effectively, but Arthur already had the hilt of the Dragon Knife in his left hand. He drew the blade out of its scabbard and the pommel embraced his hand like a lover. He scarcely took the time to think as the wondrously crafted knife sliced open the Geat's throat with the practised neatness of a fisherman filleting a fish. Quickly, as the arterial blood sprayed over the space where Arthur had just been standing, the Briton sped towards the next warrior.

And the next!

And the next!

The Geats had been caught completely off guard. Two men had even been in the malodorous latrines when the attack began and had lost valuable time dragging up their unlaced trews. As the shadows deepened, it was only the presence of firelight that gave any sense to the chaotic struggles of men as they fought and died.

Now, Arthur could appreciate why the success of the Dene attack depended on men who had fought the sea together and knew each other's faces and the timbre of their voices. One huge man appeared before him, eyes wild with battle-lust and his braids swinging like snakes around his head. Arthur almost castrated the warrior before he recognised Rolf Sea-Shaper, the helmsman from *Loki's Eye*. At the last moment, the young Briton managed to control the deadly momentum of the knife-thrust.

'Rolf! You fucking idiot! I'm the Briton – you know me!'

Rolf shook his head and the redness left his eyes.

'Arthur, the Last Dragon! Shite! I could have gutted you!'

'Look down, Rolf Sea-Shaper.' Rolf saw the Dragon Knife almost touching his genitals. He winced appreciatively.

'Congratulations, young Arthur! You'd have trimmed me in ways my wife wouldn't have liked. Stay careful, friend!' Then the warrior turned and pursued a running Geat who seemed crazed and disoriented, for he was heading pell-mell towards the Vagus and the besieged enemy. Without identification to mark the chains of office, the Geat and Dene warriors were interchangeable, so only familiarity saved

Stormbringer's men from killing each other rather than their enemies. Sensibly, the Sae Dene commander had ordered that warriors from his ten ships should provide the nucleus of troops for the first wave of attack, so the second wave would only be used if, for some inexplicable reason, Stormbringer's crews failed to achieve their objectives.

Later, Arthur would realise that the battle had been quick and vicious, although time seemed to stretch out as the Dene hunted down those Geats who were trying to retreat. They had realised their position was hopeless within ten minutes of the commencement of hostilities, but were far too proud to beg for mercy. Once trapped, most of them died bravely and attempted to take their attackers into the shades with them.

Arthur was faced with one ugly choice as the camp was being mopped up and the corpses piled onto a section of the river bank once they had been stripped of all their valuables. Stormbringer had determined that the families of the dead would receive the first cut of the spoils, while the remainder would be kept and equally distributed among the entire force at the end of the campaign. Once the Sae Dene had explained his intentions, the warriors in the various crews worked together with cheerful enthusiasm.

In the corner of one large tent, Arthur stripped away a bundle of clothing that had been thrown into the corner near a sleeping pallet. Then he felt a sting in his hand and a hellcat came after his eyes, her long claws bared and her teeth searching for the soft skin of his throat. Without a further thought, Arthur struck out with his clenched fist on the side of the head. The figure yelped, then slid unconscious to the floor.

'Mercy, my lord! Mercy! My daughter was trying to protect me,' a shrill female voice called from the back of the tent. 'The girl's only thirteen and she's still a virgin. Please, lord, don't kill her! She's already seen her father slaughtered in front of her! Please . . .'

'Hell's fucking bells!' Arthur swore in the Celtic tongue, and then began to ask questions of the woman, a striking strawberry blonde of some thirty years. In her arms, she nursed an infant who couldn't be any older than one or two days.

What do I do now? The girl's a child and she falls into the category of a slave. I should kill the mother immediately, but her baby will die if we can't feed and care for the infant.

Arthur thought quickly. 'Get on your feet and all three of you might survive.' Arthur shoved the reluctant woman forward as she tried to rouse her daughter. A narrow snake of blood slid from the girl's nose. Then, half-dragging the semi-conscious girl-child and with the nursing mother bringing up the rear, Arthur picked his way through the dead to where Stormbringer was overseeing the clearing of the Geat camp.

'Hoi, Stormbringer!' Arthur shouted in warning in case any of the Sae Dene's companions killed his captives before he had time to explain his plan to the captain. 'I've a favour to ask and a problem to solve.'

Stormbringer looked up and felt that odd shiver of premonition that raises the hair on the arms and sends shudders through the soul.

Arthur was walking out of a thick drift of charcoal-grey smoke and, behind him, a wall of fire and showers of wind-born sparks created a halo of light around the tall Briton's figure. The nimbus of fire caught Arthur's curls and seemed to crown him with a diadem of yellow, orange and scarlet flame shot through with gold. The woman, who was nursing the infant at her breast to silence it, was a black blur against the brilliant backdrop, as was the figure that sagged over Arthur's shoulder.

Then the Briton dumped the small figure unceremoniously on the ground.

The child, for she was little more, sprang to her feet and spun to face her captor with the speed of a striking serpent. She had been dissembling, feigning unconsciousness to attack Arthur as soon as he put her down. As Stormbringer watched this largely silent tableau, the girl's headscarf tore away and her white-blond hair came loose, seemingly yards of it, for the child's locks had never been cut. Stormbringer couldn't recall the last time he had seen such thick, lustrous hair on an adult, least of all on the head of a child.

She launched herself at Arthur with the intention of scooping out his eyes with her nails, but Arthur gripped a handful of that wonderful hair, turned her so that she faced Stormbringer and then used his boot on her boyish backside to shove her down onto the muddy, blood-soaked earth. The child's right hand landed in a puddle of clotting gore and she wailed thinly before bursting into tears.

'What have you brought me, Arthur? We agreed that there were to be no prisoners except for children!'

'Aye, Stormbringer! That was our agreement!' The light played across Arthur's face and, momentarily, the features appeared to be moulded out of gilded bronze, except for his eyes which caught the light like two prismed crystals – colourless, yet striking.

He's a god! the superstitious pagan in the Sae Dene whispered from inside his brain. No! He isn't a god, he's just Arthur! But God seems to be giving me a glance into some future glory. So what under heaven does He intend for this troubled young man?

'I've decided to claim these three souls as part of my spoils from our campaign. I know! I'm a landless and untried man and I should be more sensible, but this girl is younger than my sister – for all that she's a hellcat. Her mother says she's been rendered half-crazy because her father was killed in front her, so it appears that she is maddened with grief.'

Stormbringer welcomed the opportunity to break the moment and gaze down at the child.

He saw immediately that the girl's eyes were an unusual shade of grey, with navy rims around irises which were almost colourless within. Those flat eyes, fringed with long, pale eyelashes, were threatening and angry. The child's milk-white skin and pale flesh was so delicate and transparent that Stormbringer could have sworn he could see the veins just under the skin.

She's a frightening child! An intense child! But is she dangerous?

'I can't, and won't, kill a child who's younger than my sister, Master Stormbringer. But my scruples don't extend to her mother.'

At this threat, the young girl wailed like a wild beast and she struggled to rise. Arthur's boot pushed her back onto her knees, although he felt a momentary stab of pity.

'Unfortunately, the mother has recently given birth and her infant son will die if I kill her. Such an action is at odds with the upbringing that governs my manhood so, for good or ill, I ask that these captives be given to me as slaves. I'm prepared to vouch for their silence until our campaign against their kinfolk comes to an end.'

Stormbringer bit on his thumbnail and his magnificent brows furrowed in concentration. 'Step forward, woman, so I can see your face!'

The woman complied so that the Sae Dene commander could see her expression and come to a conclusion concerning her fate. She could have been no older than thirty and the girl had inherited her mother's fine white skin and delicate features.

'Bare your head, woman, and tell me your name,' Stormbringer demanded.

The woman complied and the assembled warriors could see that she possessed a beauty that was unearthly, almost fabulous, lit as it was by the fires from the burning tents and the detritus of a savage conflict. So would Helen of Troy have seemed when she watched her husband take his revenge on her adopted city for his humiliation at the hands of Prince Paris, her lover. Her thick, sword-straight hair had been plaited into long braids which she had wound into a coronet around her head. No diadem could have been more beautiful. The tendrils of curling hair that had escaped from the plaits softened the harshness of the constraining locks and made the mother appear more vulnerable, especially to impressionable male eyes. Whether she had intelligence, Arthur couldn't tell.

'My name is Ingrid and my husband was the commander of this encampment. My daughter is Sigrid. Any harm that comes to my children is my fault, so I should bear the punishment. I was pregnant and refused to stay behind in safety in the lands that lie beyond Lake Wener. In my loneliness, I wept and refused to eat. Eventually, my husband weakened and permitted me to join him here, since his duty to his master, Olaus Healfdene, was considered to be a relatively simple and safe task of guarding harmless prisoners.'

'Why didn't your husband send you to safety once your son was born? There was no reason for you to remain any longer. You should have been packed off home immediately.'

The woman bit her lip, as if only a flow of blood could ease her feelings of shame. 'I should have gone, but my son was only born a few days ago and I never recover quickly from childbed. I was supposed to leave in the next few days . . . oh, Inge! Would you still be alive if I had acted reasonably? Would you have travelled with me to Vaster Gotland and survived this massacre? Is your death my fault?'

She opened her mouth and would have wailed aloud. Instead, she began to tear her robe in distress and scour her perfect cheeks with her nails until Stormbringer ordered her to be restrained. Arthur released Sigrid, who ran to her mother and held her protectively. The girl stroked her mother's forehead to comfort her, while she glared at Arthur with a fierce rage. The child was more adult than the parent.

'Yes, Arthur. Like you, I lack the callousness to damn an infant to die of starvation. Take all three of these Geats as slaves if you wish, but you are responsible for their behaviour.'

'Aye, Stormbringer! I accept that all blame and shame will be mine!'

Stormbringer, Arthur and his captains made their way across the river to the Dene encampment. They were forced to take the longest route, which involved wading through waist-deep water and then swimming across one of the deep channels at the widest point of the river where it entered the sea. Arthur knew from the captain's expression that Stormbringer was worried, because Leif and his warriors had made no attempt to take part in the twin battles along the banks of the rivers. Such behaviour, or lack of it, was a warning that the prolonged siege of over two months might have been successful in killing off most of the Dene survivors through starvation and illness.

As they swam they held torches high above the water so they could see their way in the black waters and on the insect-ridden swamps.

In the predominantly Stygian darkness, Arthur could see several lights flickering in the swamps ahead of them. 'Look, Stormbringer, the signs aren't entirely gloomy. Some fires have been lit, so some of your kinsmen are still alive.'

When he reached shallower water, Stormbringer quickly found his feet, for his torch was one of the few still sending out a bright light. His spare hand immediately started to slap at invisible insects which were biting any inch of his skin that wasn't below the waterline.

'They need as much fire as they can get to kill off these fucking insects,' Stormbringer shouted, with his voice rising angrily on the last word. Arthur realised he'd never heard the Sae Dene curse before.

The river was fast-running in the main channel, but the stones on the uneven bottom had grown beards of weed, moss and slime near the river edge. The smell of rotting weed was stronger here, even though the Vagus had a powerful flow. Arthur almost dropped his own torch when a stone slid out from under his leather soles and brought him down to his knees with a sharp and painful jolt. Waterweed and reeds were choking the margins of the river.

'Fuck! It should be too damned cold for this shite to grow on the rocks.'

Several of the warriors had already slipped and fallen while trying to keep their footing. They snickered in understanding.

'Shut up, Arthur! Did you hear that?'

Stormbringer's body was stretched and taut like a hunting hound that has taken the scent of prey and was now readying itself for a deadly attack. His every sense was straining now towards the shore only a hundred feet or so away.

'There! I thought I heard someone weeping, and I'll swear I heard a cry for help.' Stormbringer picked up the pace, trying to maintain his balance in the river current.

'I heard it too,' Halgar added, so every man struggled to remove themselves from the treacherous waters.

The current slowed significantly once they reached the reeds, but the hard, dry vegetation resisted them at every step. Cursing, the warriors heaved themselves onto solid ground.

Solid ground?

Mud! Clinging, reeking mud further slowed their rush towards any survivors of the siege. Stormbringer called out to his men to be still and maintain their silence.

'Rescue is here – and we have food and clean beer aplenty. Just call out so we can find you.'

The answer, when it came, was almost under Stormbringer's feet.

A man clad in full battle gear, but dreadfully gaunt and frail, had forced his emaciated body to crawl towards the river bank.

'You're skin and bone, man! Who are you, and where's the main body of Leif's defenders?' Stormbringer's voice was rough with emotion. In response to a gesture from the Sae Dene, Arthur raised his torch over the starving man who flinched away from the cruelty of the light.

'We're all ill, master. All who are alive, that is! I've not kept count, but Leif assigned his young cousin to that task after the first month. Leif swore that the Crow King would come, but you've been overlong in arriving. I am Hrolfr, and my grandsire insisted that we were kin to Hnaef Healfdene, king of the Dene, near to a hundred years ago. Anyway, my name is much like that of the king so perhaps there is a family link there in the distant past.'

The young man was babbling and he knew it. Prolonged hunger had taken away any appetite, but he was so weak that his brain had slowed alarmingly. Fruitlessly, he tried to stand.

'I'm sorry, master.' The young man's eyes filled with tears of shame at his weakness. 'I don't have the strength to take you to Leif, who is our commander. But if someone were to lend me a shoulder to lean on, I'll be able to show you the way.'

Stormbringer swallowed a lump in his throat and pushed the man down gently so he could lie in the long grass of the verge in relative comfort, despite the insects that were attacking his flesh in tormenting clouds.

'Smear your bodies with mud,' the young man suggested helpfully as he caught the direction of Stormbringer's thoughts. 'It helps a little bit.'

The Denes hurried to smear their skins liberally with stinking, slimy sludge from the river bank.

'Halgar! Swim back to the encampment. Once there, bring Arthur's women to Leif's encampment. They can make themselves useful by nursing those living who are the victims of their kinsmen. We'll need makeshift litters to transport the injured and dying back to the ships as soon as we bring them to the river bank. Horses would help if you can get them! The Geat warriors are supposed to love their steeds, so I imagine you'll find a picket line somewhere. It'll be near clean water beyond their camp.'

Halgar started to move, but Stormbringer stopped him with one hand.

'Put the warriors to work who aren't clearing out the corpses of the Geat scum. We need hot food – nothing too solid or difficult to chew. And we need beer! Send some men back to the longboats to fetch whatever is needed. If Hrolfr is anything to go by, his companions will be in dire straits. Hurry, Halgar! He must be one of the strongest of our patients, because he managed to crawl this far.'

Halgar ran and dived in. In a matter of minutes, he became a black dot in the water, and then he was gone.

'Horik! You'll remain here with Hrolfr,' Stormbringer instructed one of his warriors. 'Ensure he remains as comfortable as possible until such time as we take him back to the longboats.'

'Aye! I'll care for him, Stormbringer. I'm afraid of what we're going to find in there, my lord. The smell is disgusting whenever the wind freshens.'

Horik had no need to say more. As the captain of one of Stormbringer's ships and a distant kinsman, he understood the Sae Dene better than most. He also knew the sweet reek of old death and he had seen Stormbringer's efforts to control his rage. The Sae Dene had berserker fury in his heart, so wanton waste of life could unchain the beast that lived within him. Stormbringer could foretell what waited for them when they entered the encampment.

'Be careful, Valdar! Danger and peril lie in the darkness within these swamps.'

Confused by the interplay of information between the two kinsmen, Arthur started to move towards the flickering light and whatever horrors awaited them there. As Stormbringer joined him, Arthur could sense the heavy foreboding in his captain.

'Why do you want the females brought here? To nurse the sick? Or do you want to teach them a lesson? It's possible that Hrolfr is the only one who remains alive. He's young and he would have been strong before the siege.'

'You're very calm, Arthur, but I suppose these men aren't your people,' Stormbringer hissed. 'Yes! I want these women to see what their man did.'

Arthur tripped over a tussock of coarse grass that managed to survive above the salty marsh that surrounded it. His right foot sank to the ankle in foul-smelling, clinging mud, so he cursed creatively.

'I'm not afraid of what's tangible, Stormbringer. I was under ten when I saw my best friend's corpse, and nothing's changed since then. I couldn't survive if I allowed myself to be squeamish. I've seen burned churches and nuns who were hacked to pieces after they were raped to death. It was all so unnecessary! I firmly believe that torturing these women, especially the girl, would be pointless.'

Stormbringer nodded, raised his torch and then ploughed on into the swamps.

'I know, Arthur, but I'm not always a good man.'

Suddenly, a wind shift caused both men, and the warriors who were moving carefully behind them, to hear the slow, soft sound of moaning. They realised the thin, reedy sound had come from human lungs.

Arthur tripped again.

'Oh, shite!' Silence, appalled and chill, followed the curse.

'Stormbringer! You need to see this.'

The shock in Arthur's voice filled Stormbringer's throat with bile. The Briton was rarely upset by violence.

Arthur raised his torch and scrubbed his left hand on his shirt in an attempt to remove the stain of something he had touched with his fingers. The man whose moans had warned them of his presence breathed his last just as the light exposed his body. The breath rattled one last time in his throat and chest – and then he was gone.

Some ten yards away, three bodies lay on the margins of the swamp. They had been dead for some days. One corpse had the green tinge of old death and insects rose from its open mouth and nose in clouds when Arthur pushed his torch close to the ghastly, contorted face. Maggots crawled on the purple, engorged tongue, so Arthur had to force himself to control his disgust.

But the evidence of death, ugly as it was, hadn't caused Arthur's cry of distress. The first corpse had been stripped below the waist and the fatty flesh of the buttocks cut away with a butcher's efficiency. The meat from the thighs had also been harvested: someone had flensed portions of edible meat from the body of this dead warrior.

'This body has been cannibalised,' Arthur said with finality and disgust. 'And these two men, I believe, must have been the butchers.'

Stormbringer allowed his torch to play over the corpses of the perpetrators of the crime and the rotting meat near the bodies. Unlike their victim, these two corpses bore marks of violent death. Their bodies had been hacked about with sharp knives and each corpse had been almost beheaded by blows that had cut their throats. The hands of these corpses were black with old blood, while their stained knives were lying in the mud where they had been dropped. Nearby, separated from the bodies by a small space, several lumps of blackened flesh crawled with maggots.

For the first time in his life, Stormbringer completely lost control of his stomach.

When only bile was left to be scoured out of his gut, Stormbringer ordered his warriors to stay back.

'Else you'll have this hellish view of our own ugliness burned into your brain, like me. Go on into the encampment! Whatever we find there can't possibly be as bad as this.'

'I'll burn the bodies later, Stormbringer,' Arthur promised. 'At least, there must have been someone with scruples here who has executed those sods. Forgive them, Stormbringer, for weak men can become crazed if they're dying of starvation and consider the means of salvation is close at hand.'

An angry, frustrated and shocked Stormbringer finally reached Leif's camp which was on the only significant piece of dry land on this island. This camp was drenched with the same misery and despair that Arthur imagined would rule in the realms of Satan.

Every portion of dry land was in use.

Coarse, primitive pallets had been constructed out of reeds and water-grass and simple coverings made of cloaks covered this makeshift bedding. Some tents were also in use but spear shafts had been used to suspend them over several rows of beds. Their fires burned in crude fire pits where pots of vile-smelling herbs and grasses burned, ostensibly to ward off the hordes of insects. Other large iron pots, filled with water, were boiling on the untended fires.

On the pallets, men lay in various stages of illness. Some still had enough strength to grip the hands of their saviours in gratitude and mutter their thanks through tears of joy. Others lay in a waxen silence, lost in the sleep that comes before death, so Arthur wondered if any of these men could be saved. Some raved in their delirium, their bodies burning from within in a fever that was melting the flesh from their bones. A few of the shaky, but less seriously ill, warriors were trying to nurse over a hundred of their comrades and, try as he might, Arthur saw no one who could be considered well and able-bodied.

'The Geat could have walked into this camp at any time they liked.' Arthur's voice was thick with contempt. 'Instead, they chose to let these poor bastards starve in their own shit. I've glad now that we killed them all without mercy. No commander who could issue orders that caused such an affront to nature should be permitted to lead men.'

Stormbringer was beyond the release of words. One trembling young man, trying to spoon some boiled water into a dying man's mouth, pointed towards the centre of the pallets where Leif, the Sword of Skandia, could be found.

Leif had been a tall, robust man in the prime of life before starvation and dysentery had melted the flesh off his bones. Now he sat, supported by his saddle, and attempted to eat a watery stew made from horsemeat and grass, but his stomach kept rejecting the better parts of the food.

Stormbringer introduced himself to Leif while, around them, the camp gradually came to some semblance of life. The women had arrived and, white-faced, began to clean and wash down the patients with the assistance of the Dene captains. One of the characteristics that Arthur admired about the Dene was their ability to take on the caring and often demeaning tasks of females, if there was no one else to give succour to the dying.

'How did you come to this pass, Leif? I apologise for our tardiness in answering your call, but I had difficulty in assembling our fleet, so many of your casualties can be sheeted home to me. But I don't understand what has caused . . . all this.'

'Where is the king?' Leif interrupted. His green eyes were hot with fever. 'I must give him my thanks for his assistance in our time of need.'

'He's not here right now, but I'm standing in his stead,' Stormbringer replied tactfully as he pushed the jarl back onto his dishevelled bedding. The warrior lord continued to try to rise with ineffectual hands until Arthur stopped Stormbringer's distortion of the truth by interrupting his commander.

'This noble jarl who has saved you and your warriors is Valdar Bjornsen, the Stormbringer, who has been declared an outlaw by Hrolf Kraki, partly because he spoke out that it was necessary to come to your assistance. If it had been left to Hrolf Kraki, then you would never have been relieved. Stormbringer called on all Dene jarls of honour and pride to assemble in a fleet that would come to your aid.'

Leif's face was a study in rapidly altering emotions. At first, his confusion was clearly written on his face, but then rage engorged his green eyes with blood. This emotion was followed by regret and, finally, despair. The sick man's fists clenched and Arthur stared at the large bones of the wrists which were virtually bare of muscle. Suddenly, the charcoal and purple shadows around his deep-sunk eyes seemed deeper, as if Leif had accepted that his death was inevitable.

'I should have surrendered to the Geat and brokered a truce whereby my people could survive. I was foolish to put my trust in the honour of others, so these good men became ill, hungered and perished because I held to old treaties and allies.' Leif's arm gestured to all the pallets and patients who lay around him. 'This is my fault.'

'What shite!' Arthur muttered under his breath, but Leif's sharp ears had heard his insult.

'What did you say?' he demanded.

'You're being a fool! We're here, aren't we? I'm a Briton, so I've got no axe to grind, but I can see clearly that, while your king might have been disloyal to you and your tribe, the Dene warriors haven't failed you. Look at them! Those men cleaning up the piss and shit of your men are jarls, not slaves. Forget the self-pity and show some gratitude.'

'Arthur!' Stormbringer was outraged at Arthur's bluntness, but Arthur ignored him.

'Leif must be forced to understand the chances you've taken to save him and his command. And the plans that you've made to turn back the tide of the Geat invasion. I know he's ill, almost to death, but I won't have any criticisms laid at your door.'

'Your lad is a fire-eater, Stormbringer. This Briton, whatever that is, is right,' Leif said softly with a slow grin. 'I was wallowing in self-pity and I failed to value your efforts to save my people. My apologies, Stormbringer! I have heard of you in the past and I know you to be the Sae Dene king. I'm glad to have finally met you, and my heart is lighter to be part of your plans.'

Arthur was shocked, for this was the first he had heard of Stormbringer's formal title.

'Right now, you're a hindrance rather than a help,' Arthur added crudely. 'I'm sorry, Stormbringer, but this warrior is entitled to the truth. He's a man, and he'll react just like you. See!'

Leif clenched his fists and dashed tears of weakness and frustration out of his eyes. 'Yes, Stormbringer, your Briton is right! What do you need? Tell me, and I'll do what I can to help.'

Stormbringer patted Leif encouragingly on the back and began to brief him on the plans he'd devised to transport the sick to a site upriver where the air was clean and local villagers could be paid to help with the nursing and the recuperation of the invalid warriors. The Sae Dene captain was loath to divert too many of his fighting men to the task of caring for a hundred survivors suffering from dysentery and breathing problems.

Even though he was sick, Leif was a clever man and knew the landscape intimately. And so, within an hour, a temporary plan had been put in place for the evacuation, while Arthur's females and other volunteers went from row to row to keep the survivors supplied with fresh water and tiny serves of well-mashed fish and vegetables, in an effort to rebuild some of their strength and prepare them for transport upriver by longboat.

Sigrid looked at Arthur with eyes darkened by resentment and dislike, while her mother clicked her tongue at her daughter and apologised for the girl's resistance.

'She's not used to manual work, Lord Arthur, so please take her inexperience into account.' The woman's beautiful face had no power to tempt him because he only needed to look at the starved faces, hollowed eyes and protruding bones of the sick Dene to be reminded that her husband had been the architect of this suffering.

'She's a spoiled brat, Mistress Ingrid. I grew up in a privileged household, but I would have been beaten for such unattractive fits of sulking.'

Sigrid dropped the cup of water she was giving to a delirious young man all over the patient and then thrust her face into Arthur's, although she was too short to reach higher than his chin. Arthur noticed, irrelevantly, the she was tall for a girl who hadn't yet reached womanhood.

'It's obvious that you weren't the object of your parents' love then, else they'd have tried to protect you from sick and smelly men who could make my mother and my brother very ill. My father would never have risked my life.'

'Your father caused all this! It was a cowardly way to fight and win a battle, don't you think? And he took no risks with his own skin!'

Arthur was far from finished although Sigrid's eyes filled with tears.

'My foster-father thought too much of his children to allow such ignorant, crude and bad-mannered behaviour to take place in his household. Had we so disappointed him by acting like peasants, he would have been very ashamed of us. As for my mother? We would never shame her by any of our actions – never!'

The child flushed hotly. As the colour rose up her striking face, Arthur decided that she would become a beautiful woman one day, if she survived to adulthood.

'I knew it! Your real father left you, so you must be a bastard! Hhhhm! That explains how you could set me to work like a field slave.'

'My father was the High King of all the Britons, you silly little bitch. One day, you might learn not to criticise any man's family or acquaintances at times when you don't know what you're talking about. As of today, I own you – body and soul! I also own your mother and your brother. Your mother will explain to you what that means, because the time for any pride on your part is over. You can consider yourself fortunate that I'm not Dene, or you would already be dead.'

Sigrid's face was ashen now, but Arthur showed her no mercy.

'I'll be forced to protect you from the wives and mothers of these men who may, or may not, return to their homes. Do you now have the common sense to understand what I'm saying?'

The girl nodded and pressed her face into her mother's breast.

The wind howled and the rain lashed the Forest of Dean in an unseasonal storm of particular savagery. The newly sawn pine timbers in the house were still bleeding sap, like the slow leak of pink-stained tears. But the forest smells survived in the timber and Bedwyr woke to the perfume of pine needles, the scent of Elayne's hair and the aroma of dog that emanated from his old hound. For one short moment, his memory failed him, and then one last recollection of sharp pain surfaced in his head and he heard himself groan.

'Beloved? Bedwyr? Oh, bless the Lord, Bedwyr has woken!'

Somehow, Bedwyr managed to pry his gummed eyelids apart and

saw the face of his beloved Elayne floating above him. He tried to speak, but the words were guttural nonsense.

'Don't try to talk, my darling. The children are here, so all you need to do is hold their hands and feel how much we love you.'

Bedwyr looked at the circle of faces round his familiar old bed. He tried to raise his right hand to stroke its honey-coloured carving, but his muscles refused to obey. He pushed his feelings of panic away, for a warrior must know when his time has come.

'God has finally taken pity on me,' Bedwyr murmured, but what came out was a series of grunts and distorted sounds. 'Arthur and Maeve are still not at home, but yet I must go. What will become of you all?'

With the wisdom of a loving wife, Elayne interpreted her old man's attempts to communicate, took him in her arms and set about putting his mind at rest.

'Lasair, your eldest son, has become a man now, and he'll rule in your place, my precious darling. You brought us to our new home and settled us into our new surroundings, but it's time for you to rest. And Barr is here as well! He's taken over the defence of our new forest home and he's been busy training the young men to use their bows effectively along the margins of the trees. All is well within your family.'

Bedwyr wanted to weep for the loss of his children, but after a life full of losses, he had learned the value of keeping up a façade of strength. He smiled and nodded, to show the boys that he was proud of what miracles they had wrought in moving the entire tribe from Arden to Dean, although his thoughts remained fixed on the two children who had always been closest to his heart.

Elayne's eyes were glistening with unshed tears. 'We will be safe and well without you, Bedwyr, so if God calls for you to come to him, everything here has been done and you are permitted to rest.'

Her hand pressed his, while his daughter wiped his mouth of its spittle. How undignified old age is, Bedwyr thought, and how shameful! And now I find myself dribbling like a child. Like me, Myrddion must have hated growing really old, so I won't regret being called to meet my maker.

Bedwyr's mind ranged back to a stony hilltop. Ranges of mountains marched across the horizon in rows like the helmed and armoured legions from Rome. Although he had never seen the Romans in action, his father had told him stories of a time long, long ago, before a Saxon knife had terminated his father's ability to speak.

The room in the half-built fortress behind sturdy walls in the Forest of Dean melted away and Bedwyr's memories returned to a distant time and place. He felt the weight of Caliburn in his hands – so heavy and so weighed down with the invisible chains of duty, self-sacrifice and patriotism – and a beautiful woman who was telling him to throw it into the tarn that lay behind her. The face of Nimue, the Maid of Wind and Water, who became the Lady of the Lake after Myrddion Merlinus died, swam into his fading vision.

And what would become of Elayne? Bedwyr had loved her for so long that he had forgotten what existence had been like when he was on his own. He recalled that he had lived a solitary life fuelled by the need to revenge himself against all Saxons, but he no longer recalled the *sense* of it all. Their shared communion of souls had been more important to Bedwyr than sex, friendship or united desires for their country, and they had been one person from the moment of their first meeting.

Except for one short period of time! It was a brief and painful hour of betrayal, as fleeting as a breath. Even then, Bedwyr had lacked the heart to chastise his lady for loving the High King of the Britons, a man whom everyone adored. She had given the king her mind and her companionship in Cadbury at a time when the man Bedwyr had served and loved best in the world had been assailed by traitors, murderers and the horror of personal doubts. Artor had valued the same things in his auburn-haired wife that Bedwyr had loved so, when disaster threatened to kill them during a snowstorm that froze their bodies, they had betrayed him. So long ago! Bedwyr had been angry for a time when he was faced by the proof of that small time of disloyalty that was made flesh in the warm, rosy body of Arthur, their son. But Bedwyr could never reject his lord for more than a week or two, so the Arden

Knife had been present at the final battle when Artor had taken his mortal wound. Ever faithful, Bedwyr had closed Artor's eyelids over his grey eyes for the last time and he had folded the huge, scarred hands onto the breast of his king. Bedwyr had removed the pearl thumb ring to comply with his master's instructions, but Artor went to the grave with an amulet containing a part of a scroll around his neck. Even then, with Artor dead and beyond caring, Bedwyr had refused to read that scrap of super-fine vellum because his master had insisted on keeping it close to his heart.

So much had been lost, but more had been saved from those terrible days of failure and defeat. Somehow, Bedwyr had gathered together the courage to patch up the ragged edges of the king's life and maintain the old, civilised ways in the face of a world gone berserk and brutal. 'A rearguard action against fate,' Bedwyr had always called their way of life, but circumstances swept Arden away in any case, along with his children, and he couldn't grow in this alien forest where he had been transplanted.

Bedwyr closed his eyes.

Somehow, the old man had expected death to be more painful than this gradual slowing of mind and breath. He felt the love of his family enfold him, but the fierce ties to them that once would have forced him to remain alive had weakened. And he was glad!

There was so much for his sons to do to secure this new forest, but his shadow was too large for his sons to stand alone without asking for his advice. Yes, it was better that he go now, before he failed in his wits, allowing his boys to grow strong in the sunlight without his form blocking it out. But, by God's good graces, he sorely missed Arthur, now that he had come to the end of all things.

From a great distance, he heard his wife call out to him as she wiped the tears of a great loss from his eyes. But she was such a long way from him when he opened his eyes to see her once more. Elayne seemed dim, as did the whole breathing, changeable world below his hands. Bedwyr could see the light now and his soul longed to follow the beam of unbearable whiteness to its source.

'Go, my darling! We are safe and well, and we will endure the world without you.'

Elayne's whisper seemed to come from far away, but the message was so strong and true that Bedwyr rose and looked down on her as she folded her body over the chest of an ancient, twisted man who was lying on his deathbed. Still, the white light called him and he saw figures in the rays of light. A hound ran out of the whiteness, and Bedwyr knew the beast at once. Together, they had served in the fortress of Caer Fyrddin a lifetime ago. And there was Myrddion Merlinus, by God, grown young and lithe again. His parents embraced him and he felt complete.

Finally, Artor embraced him in the old way and Bedwyr found no shame in weeping into those still-young, still-vibrant arms.

In the Forest of Dean, an old legend died and was mourned overlong after the corpse went to the fires. He had known the gods when they walked upon the earth and he had served a righteous cause with other legends. The pyre burned for two days, while Elayne ordered tree after tree sacrificed to the spirit of the Arden Knife until, at the last, she handed that venerable weapon to her eldest son.

The time for miracles was now truly over.

CHAPTER XXII

A DIFFERENT BREED
OF WOMAN

Truth lies within a little and certain compass, but error is immense.

Henry St John, Lord Bolingbroke, *Reflections Upon Exile*

The three travellers had unwillingly succumbed to the power of Hubert's argument. Gareth was especially incensed at the idea of heading south when he was determined to travel to the north so they could continue their journey. His fury was so intense that Lorcan was surprised that the air in Egbert's barroom didn't catch alight. Germanus became their spokesman by dint of his experience with his own people, even though he had been a rover for several decades.

Along with Lorcan and Gareth, he had been woken before dawn and dragged down to the empty taproom at sword-point by four armed Frankish thugs who had been sufficiently proficient as to remove the trine's weapons before rousing the three men. They had been drugged, so the three travellers were easily captured, but they knew immediately who had betrayed them. Egbert of Wurms was absent, but a terrified girl of the house was serving mulled wine to the red-dressed lordling of no name, when the travellers were unceremoniously shoved into the room. She was still dressed in her underwear, with only a blanket tied over the top for modesty's sake.

The fair-haired, elegantly dressed man stared at them as if the three travellers were some new form of life, interesting, but hardly important to his well-being.

'He wants something very badly,' Lorcan hissed at his two friends in Celt, while Hubert frowned in frustration that he was ignorant of the language.

Germanus nodded blandly, while Gareth continued to scowl. Hubert commenced their discussion by spelling out their lack of choice in whatever matters he wished to raise.

'You are strangers in the Frank lands, so no one is going to miss you if you disappear from view. In fact, it would be child's play to prove that you're sources of the plague, or spies. The mob would happily tear you to pieces over whatever story I choose to tell, and Egbert, our good innkeeper, will happily swear to it as well.'

'So you're showing us that you have power over us,' Germanus commented. 'In these lands, almost everybody has greater influence than unknown travellers.'

'You're about to become my body-slave for a month or two, so I hope your friends are fond of you. Frankly, the old priest smells and I can't trust the young dog with my back turned, so I'll need to retain you as a hostage. At the very least, you speak my language and you're almost house-trained. Perhaps their task will be more difficult to complete without your presence, but I'm sure they'll find a way to meet my demands. The priest, in particular, appears to be resourceful and the young cub has the muscle to ensure your safety. As my creatures, they'll be very well paid for what I expect them to do for me.'

'And what do you want my friends to do that you can't?' Germanus's voice was unchanged and Hubert gave him credit for being able to keep his temper under control. The youngest of the three strangers was furious and would need to be restrained before too much longer, if Hubert read his mutinous face correctly. The courtier of the king raised one finger in Gareth's direction and two large Franks moved to flank the young warrior with impassive faces, while they tensed their muscles in anticipation of trouble.

'The task I expect you to carry out is simple. While Germanus purchases a town house in Reims suitable for the domicile of an aristocratic Roman woman, your friends will be delivering a personal letter to a high-born lady in Septimania. They are required to guard her when she journeys to Reims, and then assist her to settle into her new home. That's all I require!'

Father Lorcan spat crassly on the floor.

With obvious contempt, Hubert wiped his mouth with a wisp of silk.

'All? That's all? Do you know where Septimania is? And where in Septimania do we find this woman? It's a moderately large state on the western shores of the Middle Sea and it's near enough to five hundred miles away. That's three weeks' minimum travel on horseback, and probably longer if we have to escort a woman and her entourage in a wagon.'

'Of course I know where Septimania is! Your destination is the town of Beziers and you must go to the House of Sedonius whose family members are domiciled there. Your charge is the Mistress Deuteria, who is now the head of that excellent family. I don't believe there's anything else you need to know if you're to successfully carry out my instructions. Frankly, I don't like your face, your manners or your effrontery.'

'It seems my charm is working again,' Lorcan retorted as his Hibernian irony won out over his priestly common sense. 'You have the upper hand in this conversation, and we'll be forced to traipse across the countryside doing the actual work. Where are our rations to come from? What – and where – will we be paid? And how are you going to force me and my young friend to comply with your demands? You can't watch us every minute of the day!'

'I'll be holding your friend as my hostage, and I must tell you that I can be imaginative when it comes to punishment for perceived failures to comply with my wishes. On the contrary, you'll certainly enjoy a great deal of my patronage if you obey.'

'Can you guarantee us free movement through the lands of Theudebert, leading to the border of the Cimbric Peninsula once we have completed this task for you? We are on a mission to rescue kinfolk and your task slows us down. I'd imagine you'd want us to disappear anyway once we've carried out your little chore for you.'

Lorcan raised a hand in Gareth's direction to keep him quiet, while Germanus registered his understanding at this new turn in the conversation. Perhaps the priest could still salvage something useful out of this mess.

Hubert grinned like the shark he most resembled in character. How perfect! He had thought it might be necessary to assassinate these three pawns on their return, a task that would probably cost the lives of any number of good men if he judged the physiques, skills and cunning of the potential victims. However, if these men continued on towards the Dene lands, especially in light of the imminent invasion by the Saxons and the bastard Anglii, they'd be wearing extra grins before they passed through the northern border regions. It would be child's play to send couriers to his Anglii allies who'd happily remove these three annoying travellers for the few coins and the goodwill that Hubert was offering. Hubert was always happiest when someone else could be found to clean up his messes at minimal cost to himself.

'Of course! I'll issue you with documentation in Latin that will take you through all lands under the control of King Theudebert, and I'll have these papers ready for you as soon as our arrangements are completed. I'll pay the expenses for your travel into the south in gold, and each of you will receive three gold pieces for a little over two months' work. I'm fully aware that I needn't give you anything except the body of your friend, whole and well, but our bargain must be taken on trust if it is to arrive at a satisfactory conclusion.'

Hubert's smile was sincere and dazzling. 'Of course, I expect you to leave within a few hours, so it only remains for you to decide who between you will be carrying the coin to cover your expenses for the journey?'

Lorcan held out one hand and Hubert dropped a purse into it. The leather pouch made a satisfying series of clinking noises as Lorcan weighed it on his palm.

'We accept your offer, so we should be back within forty days if all goes well,' Lorcan said neutrally. 'Have the money and the papers in Germanus's hands and ensure he is ready to depart into the north with whatever documentation he considers necessary to get us up to our destination in the Dene lands. One word of warning, my lord! I will devise ways and means of ensuring our well-being while we are about your business. I will also make a special effort to ensure that we are safe from retribution from you should the arrangements not work as well as we would wish. You can be sure that my retaliation for treachery will be simple, but very effective. I would be especially displeased if anything unwise should happen to my large friend here. I don't think I need to elaborate on my views!'

Lorcan smiled toothily at Hubert, an effect slightly weakened by a missing canine. Hubert nodded and responded with the practised sincerity of a politician.

As the three men were ushered out of the inn's barroom, Gareth lagged beside the door as he bent to straighten his leggings. His young ears overheard Hubert's reaction when he realised that Egbert's barmaid had heard the entire conversation. Gareth could easily imagine how the poor drab had tried to become inconspicuous when she found herself trapped in the corner.

'Strangle that creature for me as quietly as possible,' Hubert ordered his bodyguard. 'I want no loose talk about this meeting. You do understand, Cully, don't you?'

Gareth was trying to decide what to do when the girl's neck snapped and his guard shoved him in the back with a naked blade. As he followed his friends back to their room, he thought furiously about their likely fate when they had finished this mission for Hubert. This man, whatever his motives and his source of power might be, could never be trusted. Forewarned was forearmed!

Meanwhile, as Cully removed the body of the dead girl, her blanket slid obscenely away from her pendulous breasts. With his lip curled in distaste, Hubert fished through a pouch on the table and removed a small square of vellum sealed with red wax. Idly, he smelled the faintest hint of perfume that still clung to the fine writing surface. It held the scent of money, prestige and untrammelled power.

A name had been carefully written on the front of the sealed vellum – *Deuteria*.

'Make sure the priest gets this letter before our friends leave,' the courtier told his bodyguard. Then he wiped his hands clean, before sniffing at a perfumed pomander made from cloves in an attempt to cleanse the stink of humanity from his nostrils.

Then he retreated to the peace and quiet of his tent.

The two travellers let their horses have their heads and set off with their legs crossed over their saddles for comfort. The two tall steeds plodded along patiently, much as they had done for the twenty-two days it took to reach the outskirts of Beziers.

Gareth opened his mouth to speak. But Lorcan interrupted, for the priest rarely let the young Briton finish a sentence these days.

'If you're going to rehash the mess we're in, who this Deuteria bitch is or how little you trust the puppet-master, then I'm sick and tired of talking about these subjects. For once, try to think about Germanus, who is being forced to pander to the needs of that soft-bellied, unscrupulous mongrel. That bastard of a man is capable of any humiliation.'

'I've been thinking about Germanus. There's no guarantee that he'll still be alive when we return with this Deuteria. That arrogant prick ordered the serving-wench to be killed as if she was a nothing. We don't know his name or what power he has at his command, so we don't even know how to find him when we return. Germanus is the only person among us who has the ability to obtain any information, so he may even decide to kill our friend to keep his mouth shut. Shite, I hate this country!'

'Stop trying to change the subject,' Lorcan snapped. 'He'll have to keep Germanus alive until such time as we deliver Deuteria to Reims. After that, I believe we'll be on our own! But I'm reasonably certain that he'll permit us to travel into the north, though he'll let the Saxons know that we're entering their lands. That's what I'd do if I were in his shoes.'

'That smells right! If anyone ever warranted death it's that bastard. Insects like him always do very well in this world and they feed off the dead. Egbert, the innkeeper, knew what he was about when he sent the girl to serve our friends in the barroom. He knew that anyone who overheard any conversations would probably be killed, but better her than him. Both of those beasts are evil!'

'After we've reunited with Germanus and we've headed north again, perhaps you could make a detour and give our compliments to our associates in Soissons,' Lorcan suggested. 'If you were to watch the king's quarters, you'll be certain to discover the identity of our mystery man. We can be sure that he's a parasite who hunts for wealth on the fringes of the court.'

Gareth grinned in a way that promised an unpleasant outcome for someone at the end of this particular mission.

'Meanwhile, we have to consider our immediate task. By my reckoning, Beziers is over that line of hills and we'll be there by this evening. We've been on the road for more than three weeks, and summer is almost here. So, the question for tonight is do we sleep rough, or should we enjoy the hospitality of an inn? I confess that I'd like a bath, and if this family is as important as we've been told, we will need to look safe and clean when we arrive on their doorstep. Otherwise we'll be tied up for days convincing them that we're harmless or have the authority to act on behalf of our mystery man. Either way, I'd just as soon be out of this place quickly. Our biggest problem is that I've never known a woman who could pack speedily or lightly. From my experience, she'll want to take enough with her to furnish several homes, including her robes, jewels and sandals.'

'Let's stay at an inn then! Our benefactor is paying for it, so why not?'

Lorcan and Gareth had been more companionable than ever before during their journey into the south. Without his friend as the subject and the source of his banter, Lorcan talked sensibly and descriptively, as if Gareth was a young pupil. As Gareth had been taught nothing other than the art of warfare or armaments, the young Briton was ignorant on many subjects and responded in a childish manner to tales of the Merovingian kings and their ancestors, Clovis and Merovech. The challenge of keeping Gareth interested gave Lorcan pleasure on even the most tedious of days on the road. Gareth asked constant questions, much like a toddler who wants to know the name of every unfamiliar flower or tree.

And the Briton was forced to admit, if only to himself, that he thoroughly enjoyed the journey to Beziers. Lorcan possessed a brilliant mind underneath the quixotic sense of humour, so Gareth discovered that he was quite fond of the devilish old priest.

Beziers was a pretty town on the River Orb, and it was sufficiently far from the main roads to have avoided Justinian's Disease, which was still cutting a swathe of despair and destruction from the port of Massilia to places deep inside the Frankish kingdoms. The travellers found that the citizens who frequented the inn in Beziers were eager to talk about the world beyond Septimania and showed no fears of the two strangers, once Lorcan had scrubbed himself from head to toe, including his habit, which immediately changed colour from a pale shade of brown to a heavy cream. The dampened material had shrunk so much that Lorcan's bony ankles were exposed, as were his angular wrists. Somehow, the overall effect suggested the wearer was trust-worthy, harmless and vulnerable.

A brief conversation over a glass of indifferent red wine seemed to oil the tongues of the regular drinkers who were eager to talk about Deuteria and her family history. In fact, as Gareth said later that night as he led a tipsy Lorcan to bed, it was impossible to shut them up. One red-nosed wine merchant was particularly chatty. 'The Sedonius family shove our noses in their noble background, so we are all aware that they're descended from St Avitus and his namesake, the Emperor Avitus. The family rules Auvergne as if they hold the divine rights of kingship, although what they have to boast of now is a wonder to me.'

'You don't like them overmuch, I take it,' Lorcan hinted, and called for another flask of the good red that the wine merchant had been guzzling.

'Like them? They think their shit doesn't stink like the rest of us in this world of tears. As for that Deuteria bitch, I don't begrudge you having to escort her on a journey where you are forced to spend time with her. Rather you than me, priest! Did you know that she drowned her daughter because of a man they were fighting over?'

'Charming!' Lorcan replied drily.

The wine merchant sniggered and then continued.

'Deuteria used to be the wife of that Frank king, Theudebert, who rules up in the north. He's the one who's causing such a fuss with the emperor of Constantinople over Italia. Still, the man's got an uncertain temper and a reputation for executing anyone who doesn't bow fast enough for his liking. He's a hard man, I suppose, so he's busy with his wars most of the time. Strangely, business does well in his kingdom, so his people have little to complain about. Anyway, where was I?'

Gareth was sardonic in his reply. 'Explaining why Deuteria killed her daughter.'

The wine merchant looked at Lorcan for sympathy. 'Is that boy always so impatient?'

'Yes, he is! Gareth has always been lacking in the godly virtues, I'm afraid.'

'Young people are a trial these days. My son ... Well, priest, I won't get into that, or we'll be here all night. Theudebert was looking rather closely at Deuteria's daughter, who was about twelve at the time. She was just about ready for plucking, so he liked what he saw!'

The wine merchant winked.

'Adia – that's what her name was! She was a pretty little thing when she lived here. But she was only about five or six then, so who knew what such a daughter would turn into? Anyway, the Frank lords weren't impressed with what happened, although Deuteria wailed and wept that she'd been misunderstood. The lords took umbrage at such monstrous behaviour in their queen and kicked her out, regardless of what Theudebert wanted. And so Deuteria has lived in Beziers ever since. By the gods, the bitch owes money to everyone, including me.'

'Why do you let her buy your wine if you know she's not going to pay for it?' Gareth asked bluntly. 'Isn't it bad business on your part?'

'You'll know why when you meet her,' the wine merchant replied and swallowed deeply while spilling some of the ruby coloured liquid down his food-spotted tunic. 'I wouldn't put anything past a woman who'd drown her own daughter.'

Lorcan continued to drink with the wine merchant in the hope that more information might be dredged out of him, but the man knew little else that would be of use to the travellers. However, even Gareth had to concede that they had gained valuable advance information for the cost of a few flasks of indifferent red wine.

Lorcan had a mild headache the next morning, but he was also familiar with some details of the people he would be dealing with at the Sedonius house, which was located on the outer fringe of the city. The residence had once been part of a large Roman complex, so Father Lorcan felt a little shiver of superstition as he remembered such buildings from his youth when he had been a wide-eyed boy in the City of the Seven Hills. A row of cypress pines pointed skyward like dark green fingers from behind a wall of fieldstone.

The two travellers entered the premises through a very small gate and rang the large brass bell at the heavily chained door at the front of the building.

Both men cooled their heels outside until a servant slouched to the gate and unlocked the huge padlock and chain, before ushering them into the villa's old-fashioned triclinium, all conducted in sullen silence.

'Obviously Rome wasn't the only thing destroyed at the end of the empire. Along with the bricks and mortar, they lost their manners as well,' Lorcan stated audibly. The servant ignored the insults, shrugged and wandered off.

'Did Romans lie down to eat?' Gareth asked with a curious, bemused expression on his face as he gazed at the antique couches covered with slightly soiled but very expensive cloth. The central table was low by modern standards, but the polished and inlaid woods were set at a perfect height for men and women who were reclining on couches.

'I don't think I fancy lying down to dine,' he added, using one hand to check how comfortable the upholstery might be.

'Oh, it has some advantages!' a drawled contralto voice purred with sexual promise, as both men turned rapidly to face the speaker. 'You must remember that the old Romans were hedonists. Do you know what a hedonist is, young man?'

'Uh!'

The woman who had entered the room was tall, even by Frank standards, but she was curvaceous and voluptuous in ways that were rare in northern women. Her hair was so black that it shone blue by the light that filtered in from the central garden and, instead of braiding her hair as was considered appropriate for older or married matrons, this woman had permitted her mane to hang to her knees unbound. She was somewhere in her thirties and was neither lined nor weather-beaten, but her face seemed to be frozen into a contracted and expressionless mask.

Will her face crack if she smiles? Gareth wondered. And why is she looking at me like I'm a tasty meal?

A man could get lost in that hair, Lorcan thought wistfully.

'I'm Deuteria. I've been told you have a message for me.'

Lorcan fished the square of vellum out of his pouch, while checking to ensure that the wax seal was still in place. Deuteria would be assured that her message hadn't been read by either of the couriers for the scarlet seal was quivering on the ivory-coloured vellum like a drop of fresh blood.

'Sit if you want while I'm reading.' Deuteria waved one hand absent-mindedly while perching herself on the edge of an ornamental marble bench in the atrium. The men sat awkwardly on the nearest couch.

Gareth now had the leisure to examine the face of this repellent woman without staring rudely. Her features were aquiline and beautiful in repose, although she could appear haughty by lifting her strong, pointed chin. Her eyes were an unusual shade of amber, almost yellow.

Later, Lorcan would speak of her similarity to a huge sand-coloured lioness that he had seen in Rome almost a lifetime earlier. The great cat had possessed those same blank, yellow eyes.

By contrast, Deuteria's mouth was small, full and richly red. She worried at her lower lip with unusually large white teeth as she read the message. She seemed to be fighting an internal battle with greed and gratification on one hand, and caution and annoyance on the other.

Lorcan and Gareth watched Deuteria think from totally opposed perspectives. Lorcan was immediately drawn to her Latin beauty, while Gareth found her hot eyes and the blatant exposure of her breasts in the flimsy robe to be grossly inappropriate. Deuteria had read the young man wrongly, a mistake she rarely made. On this occasion, vanity had clouded her usual masculine grasp of situations and persons.

Finally, having devoured the contents of the letter several times, Deuteria rose to her feet gracefully while her silken green gown parted suggestively over her long legs. Gareth tried not to watch the spectacle and concentrated on ignoring her heavy perfume. The fragrance of lilies, sandalwood and something strange, depraved and repulsively attractive nestled in her hair, her clothes and the folds of her skin.

'I believe you're aware of the contents of this letter, so I assume you've been instructed to accompany me to Reims.' She laughed sardonically. 'If I had any sense at all, I should cut this letter into tiny pieces, burn them and send the ashes back – but I won't.'

She sighed deeply. Her fabled understanding of men had saddened her.

'I'm growing old and I'm lonely. For that reason alone, I'll accompany you to Reims.'

'Good!' Gareth interrupted rudely. 'We'll be ready to ride tomorrow, so—'

'Goodness, young man. It will take me three days at best to pack, organise a wagon and what servants I need to accompany me for my journey into the north. At the very least, I'll need a cook, a maidservant and a bodyguard.'

Deuteria's flippant manner caused Gareth to clench his fists and wonder if he would be punished if he tied the confounded woman over a horse and dragged her to Reims. Lorcan intervened immediately.

'Then we'll return in four days at noon – hence to depart. And now, sweet mistress, I thank you for your patience and candour with us.'

The lady began to consider a mental list of what had to be taken when undertaking such a long journey. Even when the men left she was still standing in the same spot while biting her full lower lip in confusion.

Three days of boredom.

Three days of rest.

Three days of restive pacing for the two men as they sharpened their weapons and planned how quickly they could complete the journey.

As a Roman matron of over thirty years, Deuteria had driven her staff to agonies of packing, despite the criticism and threats from a younger brother and two sisters. As a widow of mixed reputation and considerable fortune, Deuteria could do as she chose and, after a lifetime of autocratic behaviour, she was unlikely to change.

Deuteria had read the brief message from Theudebert in which he swore undying love and devotion, but still proposed to maintain the same old secrecy regarding their relationship. His lords had insisted on her banishment over that silly little slut, Adia, and Theudebert had no intention of alienating the lords, even though he was the king. She had been unceremoniously dumped back into the backwaters of Septimania once, but she swore it would not happen a second time.

'Even kings can become ill and die unexpectedly,' she promised herself, as she gazed at a bewildering tangle of silken gowns of every possible colour that had travelled all the way from Constantinople before being stored away for future use.

Deuteria was a proud woman and no one dared to mention Theudebert's name for three years after she had returned from the north. As queen she'd been revered by her subjects but then, in a heartbeat, she had been transformed into a Roman widow. Finally, she became the cast-off of her king, so her cheeks were burning with the memory of her disgrace.

So why was she contemplating a life in Reims as the concubine of the Frankish king?

Even Deuteria, a Roman matron of the most arrogant and unbending type, longed for admiration and love as she was ageing. To be the secret love of a king is no small thing, nor is it to be so feared that strong lords would defer to her influence. Theudebert's proposal brought a rush of blood to Deuteria's head in a year that had been tedious in every possible way. Callous and cruel to the core, she was also a brave woman and to be transplanted over five hundred miles to a city of strangers was of little consequence when compared with the endless predictability of life in rural, bucolic Beziers.

When Gareth and Father Lorcan arrived with packhorses that were laden with supplies, the gates to the villa had been opened and a wagon was piled high with furniture, carpets, caskets and chests of clothing. A large marble bust of the Emperor Avitus was teetering atop a mountain of clothes' chests, while four large carthorses were set in the traces, readied for departure. Finally, a weeping girl, a plump man and a muscular bodyguard stood in the midst of their personal possessions while Deuteria paced around the forecourt issuing rapid-fire instructions. Confusion reigned, and any hope of leaving in the immediate future was clearly at risk because of Deuteria's high-handedness.

'May I assist, mistress?' Lorcan cooed in his oiliest, most fawning voice. 'A beautiful woman should never have to soil her hands with menial tasks like these.'

Deuteria knew she was being manipulated but her pride was left intact, so Lorcan was permitted to organise their departure.

The crying maid was cajoled into the back of the wagon and instructed to protect the marble bust, while the bodyguard agreed to take the reins of the wagon's horses. The cook preferred to ride his showy black horse, the proof of his success in his trade, while Deuteria, with an open sunshade to protect her complexion, consented to ride on the high wagon seat next to Crispus, her bodyguard. As Lorcan organised his human geese into a semblance of sensible order, Gareth checked the traces and fixed the odd pieces of harness that were too loose or too tightly buckled for safety. Finally, he checked that the teetering load was securely tied down. He came to the immediate conclusion that no one in Deuteria's retinue had the common sense or the practical application of a gnat.

Finally, they were ready. Long past noon, they were on their way while Deuteria kept up a wall of complaint that built higher and wider with each milestone that they passed. The carthorses were never going to be fast travellers, but they could plod along all day and half the night at a steady pace. Deuteria had suggested that they should sleep in the villa overnight since the hour was so advanced, but Lorcan had insisted that the journey must begin and, by the time they reached the first milestone, he had decided to punish Deuteria for her endless whining by continuing to travel long into the night. They would remain on the road for as long as the moon gave them sufficient light to see. By the time Lorcan called a halt for the evening, the Roman party had learned their lesson: complaint served no purpose other than to extend the day's journey.

Deuteria was furious! She sulked, she refused to eat and even refused to drink until she realised that Lorcan didn't really care, one way or the other.

'No one has stipulated what condition you should be in when you eventually arrive in Reims, my lady, just that you arrive alive and in one piece,' Lorcan informed her in a completely unpriestly manner. 'You may starve yourself by all means, but that leaves more food for the rest of us. I will be very sorry, of course, because you're a beautiful woman and I'd hate to see you become ill. But I'm in charge of this journey, and you will obey my instructions. If you wish to harm yourself, I cannot stop you, but I must say that your personal cook is certainly an excellent chef and I'll happily eat his stews and pies all day and all night.'

Lorcan saluted the chef, Coptus, who was seated in the back of the wagon, while peeling and dicing a pile of wilted carrots, turnips, swedes and other unidentifiable root vegetables. He had already expertly skinned the rabbit that Gareth had dropped with his bow an hour earlier, and the travellers knew that he'd produce a hot stew an hour or so after they stopped for the night. Coptus had discovered that riding a horse could become a painful task if a man was in the saddle for ten hours a day. Besides, the showy horse had a dreadful, uneven gait that almost jarred the teeth out of the chef's head. He had now decided to remain permanently on the wagon while his horse carried some of the luggage.

Deuteria rode occasionally during those times when she decided to flirt with Gareth as the most attractive male present. Unfortunately, Gareth had no idea how to flirt and even less inclination to spend time in the company of the Roman matron. Disconsolately, she was forced to practise her seduction skills on Father Lorcan, who might have been a priest, but possessed an appreciative eye for a pretty ankle and a generous expanse of thigh.

And so no one was totally happy during the four long weeks that their journey into the north was to take. The maid developed a tendre for the bodyguard who appeared to be repelled by females of any age. Ultimately, Lorcan was forced to intervene and explain the situation to the callow girl, which both shocked her and sent her into torrents of hot, embarrassed tears.

'The silly little slut has no idea!' Deuteria complained. 'What woman of any reputation would have a personal bodyguard who might compromise her? Crispus loves men, and he's far too pretty to be a real man. He plucks his body hair, for the sake of the Virgin! What did Adelia expect? Did she think he was naturally hairless?'

Crispus and Deuteria competed for Gareth's attention, but the young man was afraid to sleep close to the nightly fire for fear that he'd waken to find a warm body pressed against his. The very thought of plucking out his body hair repelled and fascinated the young Briton, who was wholly occupied with his belated lessons in sexual matters.

'Stay away from all of them and stick close to my side,' Lorcan suggested, trying hard not to laugh when Gareth came to him after being harried all day by one or the other of his admirers. 'Better still, you should spend your time with Adelia. Her heart is broken! She needs a friend now, because she's been in love with Crispus since she was a little girl. He used to tell her stories and he was kind to her after Deuteria sold her mother.'

'Deuteria sold her mother?' Gareth was round-eyed with shock and contempt. 'How old was Adelia when her mother left the villa?'

'According to what Adelia remembers, she thinks she was about nine or ten years old. She's belonged to the villa all her life and when Deuteria returned from the north, she trained the girl to dress her hair and keep her clothes mended, sweet and clean. Apparently Adelia is very adept at what she does, or Deuteria would have removed her long ago.'

'I hate this stinking country,' Gareth said. 'Slavery, plague, betrayal, mindless talk and violence! A man can't keep his head straight in this place.'

Lorcan grunted at the young man's prejudices. 'It's long past time you became less censorious, Gareth. This land is much the same as any other, including Britain, for that matter. Stop being such a prig, boy! I have to stomach the performances of everyone else ... but I'm not prepared to put up with too much nonsense from you.'

And so the journey went on, stumbling from one small crisis to another, so that when Reims was only one day away, Deuteria swore that she would never travel by wagon again. Gareth and Lorcan had other problems, especially the knowledge that they had no idea where they were going when they arrived.

'Our murderous friend seems to trust to luck, unfortunately,' Lorcan told Gareth when the younger man asked how they were supposed to conduct Deuteria to her destination. 'You'd best ride to the gates of Reims and see if you can get some information from the inns on the whereabouts of Germanus or his anonymous master.'

'You'd be far better at carrying out this task than me, Lorcan. You know I don't have the knack for talking to strangers.'

Lorcan snapped his fingers irritably. It was a sure sign that his temper was stretched.

'How can I trust you not to annoy Deuteria to the point of murder? She's already killed her own daughter, so I wouldn't trust your chances if you irritated her sufficiently. And, boy, you do irritate the lady a great deal. If you'd bedded her as she wanted, we wouldn't be having problems with her now.'

'She's loathsome! I couldn't! . . . I wouldn't.'

'And I suppose you never have,' Lorcan retorted, his temper breaking out like hot lava to burn anything in its path.

Gareth's face flushed hotly and the priest's bad temper was leached away with the realisation that the boy was either still a virgin or so inexperienced that he was completely ignorant of the ways of sex. In fact, Gareth had enjoyed the sexual favours of Kerryn, the servant-girl at the Forest of Arden, but she had approached him. As for homosexuality, the boy had known servants aplenty at the Villa who loved persons of the same sex, but he'd never considered himself in this light.

'Shite, boy! Your father was so busy creating the perfect warrior that he forgot that an idealised swordmaster would have to be a person as well, someone who'd have needs and desires.'

Lorcan sighed and cupped Gareth's cheek with his horny right hand. 'I understand, Gareth! You've had a difficult time of it, and I've not helped you by being insensitive. Why didn't you tell me?'

Gareth simply looked at the priest with a wide blue stare and Lorcan was forced to grin ruefully.

'Aye! It's not easy to have discussions about your sexual experiences if you haven't had many. No, Lorcan! I can't keep this bitch away from me by sleeping with her, because I've never had sex with anyone like her, and I wouldn't know how to perform what she wanted, even if I wanted to. In any case, I don't want to! I'm sorry!'

The priest thought for a moment.

'Very well then, Gareth, I'll go into Reims. I'll see if I can find Germanus near the city gates first, and then I'll just follow my nose. There must be a number of inns suitable for pilgrims who are eager to pray in the cathedral where all kings are crowned. Perhaps we can find our friend through them.'

Gareth sighed with relief, but Lorcan hadn't finished his instructions to his young novice. 'Stay outside the gates, Gareth. Lie if you have to!

Say anything to shut the Roman bitch up, but don't go into the city until I greet you again and let you know that all is well. I'll find Germanus, one way or another, and then we can shake the dust of this place off our clothes. Keep the whole party silent and safely outside the city walls – tell our charges how the death carts circulate daily through the city and how the dead are burned in communal graves outside the walls. Besides the fact that this tale is true, Deuteria knows nothing about Justinian's Disease, so just explain what the illness is like and don't be afraid to exaggerate.'

When Lorcan galloped away just before nightfall, Gareth knew how demanding Deuteria would be once she realised the priest had left for Reims without them; his prediction was all too correct.

'Why has the priest deserted us? What is the problem that he must go to Reims without us? Tell me, boy! I'm tired of being treated like a servant. I swear that I'll not move another step until you tell me what is amiss.'

As Deuteria's hysterical speech was shouted shrilly and was accompanied by a purple-red flush around the neck, cheeks and breasts of her usually luscious body, Gareth found himself recoiling in disgust. With considerable effort, he struggled to keep his voice even and reasonable.

'Reims was badly affected by Justinian's Disease at the time we left these parts to travel down to Beziers. The plague was the main reason that Theudebert's army was quartered at Soissons. Now that autumn has arrived, we believe the disease has halted its inevitable march towards the north, but we want to be absolutely sure of your safety. Lorcan and I have experienced this ghastly illness and we believe it's advisable to wait until the situation has been clarified. Lorcan is putting himself at risk by entering the city.'

'My ... friend wouldn't risk my life by allowing me to undertake a journey to any place where death is possible,' Deuteria snapped spitefully. 'Nor would that smelly priest risk his life for me.'

If you only knew, you stupid cow, Gareth thought in the full knowledge that the courtier they had met would have her throttled if it suited his purposes.

'The disease kills unpleasantly and your ... gentleman friend knows that the risk of contagion is in every town and every village throughout the land. My friend, Germanus, who survived the disease, was only in the Frankish kingdom for eight days before he succumbed to its horrors. Neither Lorcan nor I caught the illness, although many thousands of other poor souls did, and died. While coming to Reims, we have deliberately avoided all the major towns to bring you this far in safety, my lady. Did you not wonder why we never stopped at inns and other places where travellers are prone to catch the illness?'

Something in the young Briton's demeanour spoke of truth. When he went on to describe the huge boils that filled with pus and poison in the armpits and the groin areas, Deuteria looked sickened and Adelia wailed with fear. But when he continued his description to include the dead flesh that destroyed noses, lips, fingers and toes, all four of his charges paled and Crispus vomited discreetly into the bushes.

'Very well then, we'll travel to the outskirts of Reims and wait there until your priest returns. But if you're lying to me, Gareth, I'll personally arrange for your dishonest tongue to be removed from your mouth.'

Gareth had no doubt that she would try to fulfil her oath if she deemed it necessary.

'Crispus would happily obey me, especially if he thought you had risked his perfect, aquiline nose by keeping us out of Reims,' Deuteria averred. 'Isn't that right, Crispus?'

Crispus nodded impassively, but the large and over-muscular bodyguard touched his nose to assure himself that this perfectly formed feature had not suddenly been afflicted with the contagion.

The party of travellers waited within sight of the great walls of the city, yet they were still some distance away from the houses, shops and markets that existed beyond the outskirts of this venerable and ancient town built by the Goths and originally called Durocortorum by these long-dead artisans.

But the plague hadn't quite relinquished its hold.

While they waited, Deuteria saw the black carts filled with corpses leave the city for the burning pits where the bodies would be cremated and she quailed to think that these carts still came daily to collect plague sufferers.

Then, just before dark, the travellers saw a row of slum houses, all in the same district, burning fiercely. They were afraid that the city might have caught alight, but then Gareth pointed out the small, ant-like figures carrying buckets in long lines to and from the blazing street of derelict buildings. There was order in the chaos of this fire and the observers were soon aware that streets nearby were being drenched to ensure that storms of sparks wouldn't set light to the thatched roofs of other buildings.

'I've heard they burn the houses of the poor to kill the disease carriers. This usually means that a city is finally defeating the sickness and the townsfolk are taking action to isolate the infected areas and bring the contagion under control. Fire seems to destroy the evil humours that feed it during the warmer weather. Now that the cold has come, the citizens are removing the slums in the belief that the plague will have nowhere to live during the winter months.'

Deuteria was struck by a sudden thought.

'I do believe that's true! Any of my kinsmen or women who have died in contagions in the past seemed to perish during spring or summer. I always thought it was unfair that my parents died when the weather was so warm and lovely.'

Gareth nodded and prayed inwardly that Deuteria's fear of becoming ill would be stronger than her desire for the comforts of Reims, including a soft bed, her latest wish and the subject of much nagging.

The very next morning, after three days of waiting, Father Lorcan appeared on Berry. He was followed by a smiling Germanus who was looking hearty and healthy. The two men were accompanied by two other Frankish warriors, watchful and suspicious by nature. They were obviously keeping a close watch on their charges.

Gareth could barely contain his relief and joy.

'Well, my boyo, I can see you're still in one piece,' Lorcan said with a wink and a grin. 'Look who I found? He'd been checking every alehouse near the southern gate for a week or so, when we happened to walk into each other.'

'He'd been sampling the quality of the beer in a number of inns, I'm afraid,' Germanus quipped in his usual slow and reasonable manner. Joyfully, Gareth realised that nothing had changed and that the two old reprobates would probably needle each other until one or the other died.

'This is Mistress Deuteria and her servants.' Gareth made the necessary introductions while Germanus brought an attractive flush to Deuteria's cheeks by taking her hand and kissing her fingertips in a display of obvious admiration.

Gareth could almost read the Roman bitch's mind. A real man at last!

'Shall we go now, mistress? I have personally selected your villa, which is a charming little palace on top of a hill away from the press of the subura, as your people in Rome called the crowded streets where the commoners live.'

Deuteria simpered.

'Of course, I have ensured it is well furnished. It even has a small bathhouse which, as you know, is very difficult to find in these uncivilised days. A well provides fresh water, there is a fine orchard bearing every kind of fruit, a kitchen garden to please your cook and neighbours of the highest quality in all of Reims. I believe you'll be very pleased with your purchase.'

Deuteria almost skipped as she hurried to the wagon to depart for her new villa. All thought of the plague had been forgotten in Germanus's clever description of her luxurious new home.

'I didn't know you had become a merchant and taken to selling palaces to rich and foolish women,' Gareth jeered at the Frank, whose eyes swivelled towards the two tall Frankish guards who were examining Gareth and his weapons with particular care.

'Keep your voice down. These, er . . . nursemaids have been sent to ensure that Deuteria is well and happy in her new lodgings. They are carrying the payment for our services and a letter from the king that will grease our way through to the Dene borders.'

'If you believe in the effectiveness and integrity of those documents, I can assure you that I happen to possess a ship full of Falernian wine that I can sell to you at a very, very cheap price,' Lorcan added with his usual irreverence.

Two weeks had passed since the travellers left Reims.

The night was gelid with cold, while a slight wind stirred the icy tree branches. The first few raindrops from the coming storm fell on the solitary man who had settled himself into the shadows of ornamental trees in the grounds of a small villa on the outskirts of Soissons. Winter was almost here and the Frankish army would soon be snowed into its new barracks that Theudebert had ordered to be built on the fields where they had camped in tents during the spring and the summer. Although there had been no further incidents of plague in Reims during the past month, the king had decided to honour Soissons with his presence, so he had settled into the palace that he owned in the centre of that thriving city. His officers and aristocrats were forced to hire whatever rooms they could find and, of course, Hubert had found a small, congenial estate that was a little out of the way, but had the advantage of complete privacy.

Inside his scriptorium, Hubert lazed in a comfortable chair with a soft cushion behind his back. A glass of superior red wine winked beatifically in the ruby light from a torch which lit the room adequately, so he could read the notes of the accounts he had been assembling. Deuteria was very happy with her new home, which the barbarian had purchased at a much-reduced price after the death of the original owners from Justinian's Disease. Finally, the three bothersome strangers had been paid for their work and had departed into the north. Unknown to them, Hubert had sent couriers to the northern frontiers, ordering their immediate execution the moment they presented their travel documents that promised safe passage.

Hubert sighed with satisfaction.

The king had asked his devoted servant for an account of the coin spent to facilitate Theudebert's felicity. With a gentle smile that resembled the grin of a hyena, Hubert took up his stylus and added a stupendous and unearned extra charge for his trouble. The king was content in the arms of his woman, so Hubert would be satisfied by a profit commensurate with his expert planning and devoted silence.

The lords of these lands would never know who had brought Deuteria to Reims, even when they eventually became aware of her presence. Hubert had ensured that his master, as well as himself, was protected from gossip and unseemly rumour. Hubert had already planned for her poisoning in case Deuteria should weary of her tenuous position in Reims. One more death would scarcely be noticed and in any case his master rarely thought so far ahead.

Hubert toasted his intelligent use of the three travellers with his ruby wine. Life was very, very good.

The courtier felt a draught of cold air behind him and the icy blade of a very sharp knife against his throat at the same instant. His flesh tried to shrink away from both, and he gasped involuntarily.

'Are you cold, Hubert?' a young voice said from behind his back. 'I am so sorry, but I need the window open so I can leave just as quietly as I came. Your guards are pathetic! A child could find them and kill them without being seen, and I can assure you that I'm no child.'

'Who are you?' Hubert croaked, but he already knew the answer. He'd only heard the voice once, but he remembered the hot blue stare very well.

'You know me, my friend! I'm one of the travellers from Britain whom you sent on a wild goose chase to Septimania. For forty-four days of my summer and autumn, I have had to endure that woman's company. Really, Hubert, I'd happily force the same fate on you if I had more time, but I've another gentleman to see tonight and I needs must be in the land of the Dene before spring. Do you understand my dilemma, Hubert?'

'No!' Hubert found his teeth were chattering. He hated to show any weakness in front of a cur such as this man, but something about this young Briton filled Hubert with terror.

Something warm trickled down his legs and soaked into the

cushion of his seat. Hubert flushed with shame.

'You're a very dirty boy, Hubert! You've pissed yourself! But never mind, for I'm sure they'll clean you up before anyone sees what you've done to yourself.'

'Please don't!' Hubert whispered. 'I have gold, so there's no need to be hasty.'

'But you killed that poor little barmaid at Egbert's inn. Now, I didn't know her, but I can imagine that if you'll kill a harmless creature like her, then you'll have me slaughtered without a second's thought. Am I right, Hubert? I can't hear you.'

'Please?' Even to Hubert's ears, his voice sounded ineffectual, so he was hardly surprised when the Briton carefully and delicately cut his throat from ear to ear from behind.

'You can try to hold the wound together, I suppose. But I don't like your chances, Hubert. I'm sorry that I can't wait to see you bleed through to the end, but I've promised myself, and that harmless little girl, that I'd also visit Egbert of Wurms before this night is over. You do understand how it is when your life is so busy.'

Hubert struggled to hold his wound closed, but his blood jetted out in front of him. As his eyesight began to fail, he watched as the Briton moved in front of him, carefully avoiding the bloody puddle that was spreading far too quickly over the tiled floor.

'Goodbye, Hubert. I hope Hell is really hot for people like you, just as the priests promise. I'm sure there'll be a queue of sufferers who'll come from your past who are *dying* to meet you again. Forgive the pun, but I couldn't resist it.'

Then, as the Briton laughed at his little joke, Hubert drifted away. Staying alive was just too much trouble.

Uncharacteristically, Hubert's very last thought was about someone else.

'Jesus Christ, won't Egbert of Wurms be surprised!'

And so Hubert passed into the shades.

THE BATTLE OF MIRK WOOD

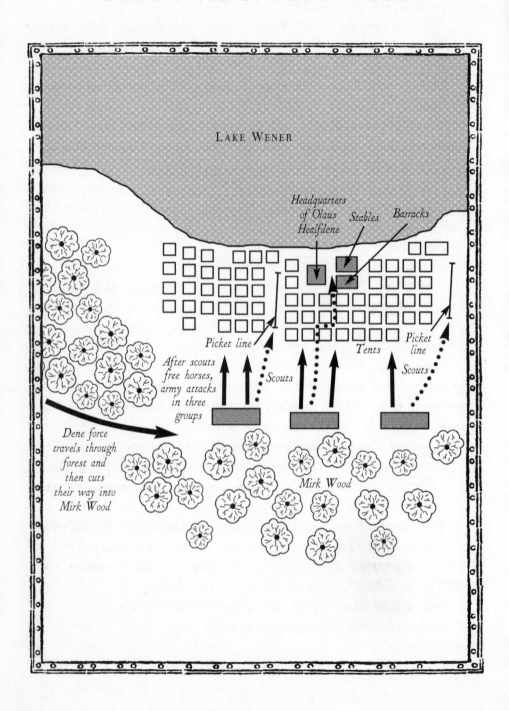

LAKE WENER

Headquarters
of Olaus
Healfdene

Stables

Barracks

Picket line

Scouts

Tents

Picket line

Scouts

After scouts
free horses,
army attacks
in three
groups

Dene force
travels through
forest and
then cuts
their way into
Mirk Wood

Mirk Wood

CHAPTER XXIII

THE BATTLE OF MIRK WOOD

Vain the ambition of kings
Who seek by trophies and dead things,
To leave a living name behind,
And weave but nets to catch the wind.

John Webster, *The Devil's Law-Case*, Act 5

Arthur awoke from a night horror of particular clarity. His skin was fast cooling in the crisp northern air, but the dream was so pervasive that he was unsure if he still slept. The fearful lassitude that comes after terror drained his limbs and made him feel ill and dislocated.

The forest of this dream was unfamiliar. At first, he had thought himself at home in Arden, but the trees and the terrain were so different that Arthur felt a little jolt of disappointment. Then, as if the earth had vomited him forth, a man in black appeared under a hazel tree, playing with a handful of nuts which he tossed carelessly from hand to hand.

'That tree is sacred, so you should beware,' Arthur warned the stranger, as if such a chance meeting was a normal matter.

The man in black recoiled back within the shadow of his cowl, ensuring that Arthur could see little of his face except for a curl of amber-coloured hair.

'Do you know the secret language of trees, boy? I think not! Your foster-father taught you very well, but Bedwyr was a man of oak trees. And so he had no need for any other green and growing things. His wife, the lovely Elayne, knew him very well, so she bundled him up with oaken logs when he died, and spared no expense. I never met Bedwyr in the flesh, or his compelling woman, but I have heard tell of him. But I belong to the hazel tree. And you? I will think on it . . .'

Arthur felt as if he was caught in a mire of cloying mud. His feet refused to move, although he willed them to run so he could escape the concealed eyes of this stranger who saw too much and said so little. The cords stood out on Arthur's neck as he twisted and tore at his feet, trying to will the deep drift of mouldering leaves that surrounded them to set him free from an inexplicable, fantastic bondage. The black-clad figure extended one arm, which was reassuringly solid, muscular and vigorous, and then patted Arthur on the side of his face with the casual affection that a man shows for his dog.

'You think I'm your father, come in a dream to tell you that Bedwyr is dead. Well, you're partly correct, but I'm not the shade of Artor . . .' The black-clad figure laughed, the sound grating unpleasantly.

'I, too, have a part of your blood and your bones, although whether I become lodged in your heart and your brain is up to you. Can you see? I came to you in my youth, because your aunt made me a caricature of myself at the time of my death. I, too, have a beauty, like the son I fathered. Do you know me now?'

Arthur recoiled in horror. Bedwyr had told him stories of Uther Pendragon; if this was a truth-dream and not some fantasy conjured by the horrors he had seen on the Vagus River, then how could Uther Pendragon be dragged back from the cold vastness of Tartarus to send a message to one of the last survivors of his bloodline? Uther had never embraced the ties of kinship.

'Why would the hazel tree be your symbol, Dragon King? The *Old Ones* worshipped this tree because of its cleanliness, its power of prophecy and its spirituality. But you only lived for death and the torture you could inflict on the human heart. The hazel would reject you!'

'Yet it doesn't!' the funereal figure laughed and one hand swept away the cowl to reveal a divided face. One side was as fair as any imagined angel could be. But the right-hand side of the face, although each detail was ostensibly the same, was repellent, grotesque and fascinating, like looking into the eyes of a great hunting cat that had no empathy or sympathy for its prey.

'I can see it now!' Uther giggled and the sound was a travesty of laughter. 'I know what tree is yours – and dark is its message! You are the yew, the tree of the graveyard. Try as you will, Death will follow you, because I am your sire and your blood comes from me as its fount.'

The dreamer felt sick to the bottom of his soul.

'I reject you – and everything about you,' Arthur gasped and recoiled until he felt the bark of an oak at his back.

'But you can't! Like your father, you'll discover that I'm impossible to remove. I'm the hazel in your bloodline, the voice in your head and the ability in your strong right arm. Ask your friends! You're just as monstrous as I am, if not more so because you drag the innocents along in your wake with little understanding of what you're doing to them. As I've said, you are the Yew of Death.'

Racked by tears and shame, Arthur began to waken and the oak tree became the vigorous young body of Bedwyr standing firmly behind his foster-son while generously pouring his own essence and strength into the child he had cared for as if the boy was his own flesh. Words of love sprang into Arthur's mouth and told the demon that Bedwyr's voice rang true.

'The yew binds past to present and beyond. It endures when the hazel dies. The yew stands alone and draws nourishment from the earth which it repays as a memorial to life itself. As a symbol of self, it is no bad thing to be – so the yew will be Arthur! But the boy isn't for you, old wight, so be gone and trouble him no more. Arthur belongs to a new way that will replace everything you fought for, even what his father struggled to achieve, and you have no part in what he will become. I say again, this boy is not for you – and never will be!'

Arthur's mouth framed the words, but they came from Bedwyr

behind him and the core of wood that was the soul of the oak tree. Warmth flowed through that conduit between tree and man so that Arthur stood in his dream, embraced by the ancient accord between tree-men and the miracle of God's genius that ranged itself against the demon of self-delusion that raged and gibbered as it tossed away the last hazelnuts and stamped at the earth with its cloven feet.

'Be gone now, demon of the dark. Don't bother to argue because he will know how to avoid you when he wakes. You came to poison his mind! He'll be on his guard against you now, even in his sleep, and I will remind him through his voices how you deal out petty games of sleight-of-hand. You are a fairground trick to cheat the unwary and a pale shadow of malevolence used to frighten children. Arthur has now become a man.'

The figure in black shrieked furiously and thrust its jaw towards Arthur's face, until the young man could smell the foetid breath of the wight's anger.

Then Uther Pendragon began to shrivel ... smaller ... smaller ... until he was the size of a hazelnut. Then, with a wisp of smoke, the small creature disappeared into a hole in the earth.

With the sound of a metal door clanging shut, the crack in the earth closed and the demon was gone.

'You're deep in thought, Arthur. We'll be on the move again tomorrow, so you'd be best placed if you're well rested.' Stormbringer sank down onto his haunches on the moist earth where Arthur had wrapped himself in his cloak and was now resting with his back against the trunk of a spreading oak. Stormbringer noticed how the Briton surreptitiously returned the Dragon Knife to its scabbard.

'I've been having a bad dream, Stormbringer. What of you? The commander of an army should be well rested rather than spending his time checking on sentries and doing menial work. You have to trust someone, my friend.'

Even as he spoke in the companionable darkness, Arthur wondered when Stormbringer had ceased to be his captor and slave-master and become his companion and friend. Eamonn kept his distance these days, preferring the fireside of Rolf Sea-Shaper and his young friends where good ale, mead and song were more important than strategy, the politics of the Dene throne and the complex heritage of the Sae Dene. Arthur understood that the exuberance in Eamonn's nature called out for entertainment and fun, but he required something more out of life. Arthur did his best to take his pleasure when he could, but he knew he'd always prefer the company of men like Valdar Bjornsen.

'I know, friend, you've told me often enough. But of all men, you understand the responsibility I feel for my warriors. Have I thought out our plan of attack with sufficient detail to achieve the task we've set for ourselves? Or have I misjudged the number of enemy warriors that we'll face when we arrive at Lake Wener? Thank heavens that Hoel Ship-Singer, arrived with his reinforcements when he did, because it allowed us the leeway to ferry the sick and wounded to the villages up the coast. Just as important, he brought intelligence with him that will be essential to my plan of attack.'

'You have Loki's luck, Stormbringer,' Arthur replied. He recalled how the shipwright had arrived with one hundred men in three ships. As a man who knew the local waters, Hoel cautioned Stormbringer against sailing up the Vagus River; there were too many enemy villages on the river banks to bypass them without such a large number of vessels being seen.

'It would be impossible to arrive unannounced, lad. It's far better that we run to the enemy on foot. We've no horses left to give you, certainly not in the numbers that you'll need, so we should do what Olaus Healfdene will least expect. I suggest that we should run to his summer quarters, across country and in the darkness of night, while resting during the day when sunlight prevails.'

And now, here they were, almost at their destination.

They had avoided the small village called Bohus, which provided many of the stores and servants used by the king and his favoured jarls as they camped on the margins of Lake Wener. As the entire army slid silently past the village in the early hours of the morning, Arthur's heart almost stopped when he thought he saw a horse dancing in the sky above the village, its hooves and mane turned to silver in the reflected light from the full moon.

'It's the village good-luck horse,' Stormbringer told him later when an incredulous Arthur asked his friend if he had imagined what he had seen. 'The skin of a dead horse is kept intact, including the skull and the bones in the legs. Its carcass is lightly stuffed and hung over large stakes so the legs dangle, giving an appearance of movement whenever a strong wind blows – especially at night.'

Now, as Stormbringer and Arthur talked quietly on a low hill above the cleared edges of the river, Stormbringer sighed with relief. 'We're only one day distant from Hoel's estimate of the place where Olaus went into bivouac with his army. I intend to travel inland now, pass through the edges of the Myrkvidr and attack the Geat force from the rear.'

Stormbringer shuddered.

'I react badly to the thought of entering the Myrkvidr in much the same way that you responded to the Flying Horse of Bohus. Myrkvidr is a dangerous place that is reputed to be the haunt of trolls and outlaws, all of whom are perversions of nature and unclean things. I feel the hair rise on my arms when I think of entering its black shadows – and I've never even been there! It has a foul reputation.'

'I grew up with trees and forests hold no fears for me. Forests are places of richness and life, even here in the north where the summers are short and the winter nights are very long. No trolls or dwarves can harm me.'

Stormbringer laughed at his friend's show of bravado. 'I had forgotten that you are the Last Dragon and can, no doubt, destroy trolls with your poisonous breath.'

Used to the way that his friend's mind worked, Arthur felt no insult in the jibe. 'I refuse to be frightened of trees, Stormbringer, but I'll not think the less of any man who's been raised to distrust the wild places.'

Stormbringer had obviously been manoeuvring his way to his real purpose for seeking Arthur out. All their talk had merely been a polite prelude.

'I expect you to assume command of my thirty men from *Sea Wife*, Arthur. As the overall commander of our forces, I'm responsible for over one thousand warriors, but the crew of my personal ship still need a strong and capable leader who isn't distracted by larger issues. Many of my warriors are capable of handling this duty, but I'd prefer that you assumed this role because you know them – and you've already fought with them as their leader. My men are used to being at the forefront of any battle so they would resent not being in the van of the attack. I'm reluctant to trust their lives with anyone else but you, because you'll worry about them as much as I do.'

Arthur was rendered speechless. Stormbringer's men were more important to him than The Holding, probably as close to his heart as his own daughters. He sailed with these men; he ate and drank with them; he fought with them; he knew their families and he was fully aware of their fears and hopes for the future. In the uncertainty of this war of honour, Stormbringer had accepted that his crew was his lifeline in a sea of trouble, banishment and loss of favour.

'I would be honoured to accept this command, Stormbringer. I promise too that I'll lead them into the forefront of the battle, but I'll not waste their lives like base coin that is useful for nothing but thoughtless spending.'

Arthur took Stormbringer's hand in gratitude and their bargain was sealed.

A force of over one thousand men is difficult to deploy across wooded countryside without attracting attention from the local population, so Stormbringer decided to continue with the tactical ploy of individual crews commanded by their own ships' captains that had been used during the attacks on the Geats at the mouth of the Vagus River. He issued orders that each group of men would make a concerted dash through the Myrkvidr as quickly and as unobtrusively as possible.

Congregation points had been determined for each night's trek through the woodlands until such time as the force reached their final jump-off point on the western edge of the Mirk Wood, the British name Arthur considered more fitting for an obstacle that seemed to engender such superstitious concern among his Dene compatriots.

Only five miles remained between their present position and the bivouac site, the place where Olaus Healfdene's warriors were comfortably ensconced in what they believed to be a safe and secure encampment. But the forest blocked the way of the Dene attackers. Stormbringer issued orders that, if the Dene scouts should encounter shepherds or hunters, these unfortunates were to be despatched immediately – without mercy.

The element of surprise would be crucial during this attack, for Healfdene's force was believed to be well in excess of one thousand warriors. And more were gathering, according to Hoel Ship-Singer. The Geats were preparing for a major campaign into the north of the Dene lands before the advent of winter.

'If Healfdene's force wins ground in the north-western coast, the Dene crops will go unharvested or be burned, so those of our people who survive the war will starve during the winter. Such a fate for our women and children cannot be contemplated by true men. We must stop the Geats, here and now!'

Stormbringer had obviously lost kin to starvation in the past, for Arthur recalled several occasions when the Sae Dene had become upset by references to famine. As before, Arthur wondered but refrained from asking questions. He knew the captain would tell him when he was ready.

On the second last evening before the battle, Stormbringer called a council of war for all the ships' captains. The entire Dene force had completed their trek through the open forest with few incidents and they were now settled into positions close to Mirk Wood. All the officers agreed that the woods had been very quiet, for their scouts had only encountered five skin-clad hunters, all of whom appeared to be antisocial individuals who preferred to live apart from the local villages.

One cause for alarm was the news that tracks had been found, indicating that isolated groups of men were heading towards Olaus Healfdene's encampment. Large bands of men from the south were on the move, obviously Geat war bands hurrying to join Olaus's force where they would win some of the spoils from the fertile lands of the north-west. Horses, gold, ships and women were there for the taking, so the enemy force was growing with every day.

'Our scouts have found the edge of Mirk Wood and can report on what is happening on the Vagus River and the approaches to Lake Wener. They've seen these places clearly, albeit from a distance,' Stormbringer stated and welcomed two disreputable men dressed in deerskins. Both were armed to the teeth. The eldest was introduced by the Sae Dene captain as Fridrik Haroldsen, a Dene from the south-western coast who had lost his family, his crews and his ships in the recent treacherous attacks by the Geats.

This man has an axe to grind, Arthur thought as he examined the harsh, weather-beaten face set in uncompromising and bitter lines. Stormbringer is too acute to trust this compromised man entirely, because Fridrik would lie or exaggerate information to bring us down on his enemies.

'The lake is huge, so its margins can't be seen from one side to the other. When the great ice sheets covered this land hundreds of years ago, the river was gouged out by the gods so there is flat river-valley land close to the lake, although the forests rise above it.'

The officers nodded, able to visualise the terrain.

'The lake itself is beautiful, a paradise with wide margins where small villages cluster to fish the bountiful waters. The land grows most grains, vegetables and fruits because there's rich soil and plentiful, year-round water.

'The army has settled near the confluence of the river, but the small insects that caused us so much trouble near the mouth of the Vagus are kept away by the breezes that regularly come in from over the lake. I can imagine that the lands around Lake Wener are cool and clean on even the hottest of days.'

'Our enemy is domiciled in Paradise then,' Stormbringer commented. 'How is their army disposed within their bivouac? Did you spot any weaknesses or mistakes in the disposition of Olaus's forces?'

'The entire force is widely spread out over a five-mile length along the lakefront which is at their backs. The area already has several luxurious houses built for the king's use when he and his favoured jarls are in residence, so there are barracks which house Olaus's horses and his personal troops. Roughly, these buildings house about two hundred men, or perhaps a few more. Olaus's house and the accompanying two buildings, which I believe are barracks, comprise the central command post at the heart of the bivouac.'

Fridrik's voice was grating from overuse, so he hawked and coughed to clear his throat. One of the nearby captains thrust a cup filled with ale into his hand. Fridrik drained the liquid in one long swallow.

'My apologies, Master Stormbringer, but I spend little time with other warriors now, so my voice becomes rusty from disuse. To continue ...'

Stormbringer's strong right hand gripped a stick and used it to carve a picture in the dust of what Fridrik was claiming to have seen. His eyes never left the scout's face, but his hand was busy plotting the site of the battle.

'To the right and the left, the force is strung out around central tents or small circular houses that are obviously summer residences. Each officer or jarl has his own banner flying over his section of earth, and his men are bivouacked in hide tents or in any building that can be used as a barracks, depending on their importance in the hierarchy. The force is thinly strung out on either side of Olaus's house, rather than massed in areas between him and the woods.'

Fridrik cleared his throat again and narrowed his feral eyes.

'In my opinion, this bivouac has major weaknesses. A well-organised enemy could drive through to Olaus's command centre with relative ease, although they'll be quickly swamped by his reinforcements if the Geats are allowed the time to regroup. Still, such a disposition of troops is a definite weakness, so I'm of the opinion that Olaus is complacent after his recent successes. He thinks that all Dene opposition has been eliminated, while the Crow King stays within his halls to brood on God's edict that he shall not make war if he wishes to remain alive. Olaus has not considered the existence of a warrior such as Valdar

Bjornsen who might have been offended by Olaus's hostility to allies of the Dene.'

Fridrik paused and considered his next words carefully, while the captains looked at Stormbringer and stamped their feet with approval. Arthur felt their excitement bubbling as every sinew and muscle geared itself for war.

'I believe that an attack on the centre of the main defensive line, encompassing Olaus's house and undertaken an hour or more before first light, would cause such confusion that his forces would be unable to recover the initiative and would be caught with their backs to the water. If the jarls were unable to join their commander and were forced to fight a dozen individual battles, they would be defeated. But the secret of this strategy would have to be total surprise.'

'How would you suggest we take advantage of this bivouac area?' Stormbringer asked.

The eyes of the Dene warriors swivelled to assess Fridrik's response.

'Your force must attack in three prongs. Because Olaus Healfdene is the commander and will be sleeping in his apartments, the Geat headquarters must be attacked first in a lightning-fast foray, followed immediately by coordinated attacks to the right and the left that will pin down the Geat jarls and add to the confusion.'

'Yes! I agree with your assessment,' Stormbringer replied and Arthur peered down to see a series of arrows drawn in the dust to pierce the three rectangles that represented the major features of the Geat encampment.

The Sae Dene smiled at his audience and they looked at him with the devotion of good hunting dogs, for the men who sailed with Stormbringer were utterly faithful.

'Are there any other suggestions, my friends? Any other strategies that could enhance our chances of victory? Remember that we'll be outnumbered – so any thoughts now could prove invaluable when the fighting commences.'

Arthur coughed. 'I'm an outlander, so I don't know the protocols here. Am I permitted to speak in this council?'

Stormbringer frowned with irritation. 'Of course, Arthur! You've fought with and against my men in recent times and you're familiar with our fighting techniques. I'd be an idiot not to listen to you, if you have useful suggestions to make.'

Some of the officers and jarls had reservations regarding the extent of Arthur's expertise and wondered at his usefulness to the Dene cause, so a few faces in the audience flushed hotly. But then, as Arthur began to speak, they gave him their full attention. The Dene warriors were prepared to use any honourable means to achieve their aim of winning this war.

Stormbringer admitted to himself that he was prepared to use dishonourable means as well, if nothing else worked. Here, on the eve of a major test of strength, Arthur was presenting strategies that the Sae Dene's grandfather would certainly have considered to be so.

'Fire!' Arthur intoned dramatically. 'I've fought in unequal conflicts where the use of fire doubled the effectiveness of the warriors available to a commander. Being burned alive is one of the most hideous ways to die for those men who must fight in metal armour. The victims eventually cook.'

To a man, Arthur's audience shuddered at the thought of such a death.

'Aye! I've heard tell of burning oil that was poured off city walls onto the troops below to catch the flaming liquid within breastplates or helmets.'

Arthur paused delicately to allow the full import of this image to sink in. The attention of the audience was focused on Arthur now, exactly as he intended.

'Fire is capricious, and it never acts as we expect. The smallest change in the wind direction or speed sends the flames racing away along a totally new and unexpected course. All it needs is fuel, anything that will burn. Yes! Fire will always bring confusion and chaos to the battlefield and, if used properly, it can make a difference to the outcome.'

Several jarls nodded in agreement. Arthur's suggestion had made good common sense, but he hadn't finished, not quite.

'I take it that Olaus Healfdene uses cavalry. If so, his horsemen will cut a swathe through our forces that will change the result of this battle, regardless of the courage shown by our warriors. His cavalry must be neutralised *before* the battle commences. In fact, it would be useful if the horses could be set free and panicked in such a manner that they trample their way through the Geat tents and the heaviest concentrations of men during the battle's initial stages.'

'I agree.' Stormbringer nodded decisively. 'Our forward scouts can eliminate the Geat sentries and gain access to the horses if they know where the animals are stabled or picketed.'

The older jarls, those who had seen the effectiveness of cavalry at first hand, growled in agreement.

'If we take up positions where we can see the encampment, our forward scouts should be able to discover where the horses are tethered, even in darkness. The horses must be fed and watered,' one eager young jarl from Stormbringer's own island suggested.

'I agree, Jormund.' Stormbringer's smile of appreciation caused the young man to flush with gratification. 'Each crew will assign at least one scout to ascertain the position of any picket lines, stables or other shelter used for the Geat horses. That's a force of anything between fifteen and twenty men who should be sent out in darkness an hour before the battle begins.'

He smiled once more at the young warrior.

'You, Jormund, will be in charge of the scouts. You'll select suitable men and divide them into three groups to make a reconnaissance of the right wing, the left and the centre.'

The youngster stammered out his thanks, while assuring Stormbringer that the horses would be found and set free to charge through the Geat encampment.

'This is a dangerous ploy because it might cost us the element of surprise. However, the chaos caused by five hundred crazed horses would be worth the risk,' Stormbringer explained slowly to ensure that his jarls were aware of the implications of this decision. 'In fact, I'd like to purloin some of Olaus's horses for myself as trophies once the battle is over. That would be a fitting punishment for that Geat bastard.' He smiled wolfishly. 'Right! Is there anything else, Arthur?'

'Aye,' Arthur responded. He now sounded slightly shame-faced because he was a little embarrassed at thrusting himself forward. 'Bowmen! Do you have any bowmen among your warriors?'

Stormbringer was surprised, but his jarls were openly contemptuous. He had rarely used bowmen in battle; most Dene believed there was little personal glory in long-distance killing. Like the Saxons and the Anglii, the use of longbows was mostly confined to the peasantry who used these weapons to kill deer during the animal migrations or wild boars that ravaged their fields and livestock. But Stormbringer was fully aware of the effectiveness of archers in certain situations, particularly close-quarter battles at sea and drawn-out sieges.

'Yes, I'd certainly like some bowmen to be available,' Arthur explained. 'The roof of a barracks building is a very large target, so any archers would be useful if they could set fire to the thatched roofs of the Geat buildings. Even hide tents will be vulnerable to burning if pitch is added to the cloth used on the arrows.'

With the clarity of a born strategist, Stormbringer saw the potential advantages of these tactics immediately, but many of his jarls found the concept of death dealt from a safe position to be cowardly.

'Do we *have* any warriors who possess bows?' Stormbringer asked. 'Check with our men! If I understand you correctly, Arthur, you're proposing that archers mark the beginning of the battle by using fire arrows on the thatched roofs of the buildings and the tents. Then those same archers would resume their normal role in the battlefield as foot soldiers. Am I correct?'

Arthur nodded in agreement, while the jarls looked much happier. 'If we are to win, we need to be prepared to use different strategies than would normally be required. Olaus won't be expecting an attack by fire arrows, will he? I estimate we'll need at least fifteen men with fire arrows if we're to set the enemy bivouac alight and achieve maximum disruption. What the bowmen do after the fires are alight and burning would be the business of their commanders,' Arthur added.

Then the young Briton added a final sentence that won him cautious approval. 'If someone has a bow, I'll set Olaus Healfdene's house alight myself.'

Several of the younger jarls crowed at Arthur's effrontery, while an equal number of the older men pursed their lips at the unseemly boasting of this outlander. However, most of the captains remained silent, content to wait and see if Arthur's actions were as strong as his words.

'There is one last detail that I feel is of vital importance, Stormbringer.'

Arthur gazed around at the audience.

'At the conflict on the Vagus River, the only way we recognised each other during the heat of battle was through our daily familiarity when we were at the oars or on long voyages. There, because of the scale of the battle, we were able to fight as individual crews. But such a method of recognition won't work on a large battlefield. Unless we're happy to kill each other – and we aren't – we need some method of identification.

'To add to the confusion, I can't tell the difference between a Geat and a Dene – even in daylight! I'd like to propose a simple solution. Mud!'

'Mud?' Several of the jarls scoffed aloud and even Stormbringer seemed confused.

'Do you recall the situation we encountered at the mouth of the Vagus? The only relief we could find against the insects was to smear ourselves with thick river mud. We'll be near to being devoured alive by insects in Mirk Wood too. Once the mud has dried, it leaves a pale crust on the skin that should clearly indicate to our fellow warriors that we are Dene, even if we don't know each other.'

He paused so that his audience could absorb his words.

'Perhaps we could attach a scrap of coloured cloth to the plaits in our hair as an additional means of identification. If we use different colours, we could indicate our particular formation as well.'

Arthur sat down again, beginning to feel distinctly embarrassed by the number and variety of his suggestions towards the battle strategy.

The Sae Dene captain seems to want me to develop a higher profile among his trusted officers, he thought. Why would this be so?

Once all the suggestions had been discussed, Stormbringer instructed his officers to find large pieces of different-coloured cloth. He tore out the finely woven red lining from his cloak and then arranged with one of his bodyguards to have the cloth cut into a number of strips that would mark his men as part of the phalanx which would attack Olaus Healfdene's headquarters.

One jarl provided a saddlecloth of heavy, coarse cloth in a yellow shade, while still another found that he and his brother had spare tunics in the more exotic pale green of the islands. With mud on their faces and these colours in their hair, the Dene would be able to recognise each other with only minimal difficulty.

And so the council of war was adjourned, to be reconvened on the next afternoon at the margins of Mirk Wood. Here, more questions would be raised and answered. Before the captains left to brief their warriors, Stormbringer divided them into the three attack groups, saving the central core of the red force for his own kinsmen.

Lest some of his allies should believe that he was taking most of the glory for his own men, Stormbringer gave a small heartfelt speech in gratitude to all those men in his command who would fight and die in the coming battle.

Stormbringer outlined his plan of attack with great passion, which won him cheers and foot-stamping from the jarls. Arthur could sense the purpose building in these officers as Stormbringer's calm and even voice hardened their resolve.

Lifting his horn cup of ale to his lips, Stormbringer paused to gauge the mood of his audience, who were absorbed in their commander's impassioned concepts of honour and their own oaths of loyalty to the Dene of Skania and the other lands of the west coast. The commander moistened his lips and spoke again.

'If I am to die in the combat that is to come, I pass on the leadership of our forces to my cousin, Jorn Oleson, and, failing him, to his son, Gorm. If any other heir is needed, then we are surely defeated. But, in such a disaster, I would advise you to follow the leadership of Arthur, the Last Dragon, who will be leading my personal crew. You can trust Arthur to save those who can be saved, just as I trust him with my own men.'

He nodded to Arthur to show his personal respect.

'If God deems that our cause is righteous, then we will prevail, although our master in Heaven seems to assist those men who are prepared to fight and die for justice. The siege on the Vagus River tells us that Olaus and his Geat forces are overconfident and ruthless. Such an affront will merely offend the gods, who hate hubris above all things. Pray tonight, for tomorrow we will teach Olaus Healfdene what it is to be a warrior and a man.

'Now, to sleep! We'll veer to the east to enter Mirk Wood before dawn arrives.'

The jarls were very quiet as they walked away to rejoin their crews. Stormbringer had given them clear warning that any victory would be hard won.

Arthur woke his crew before dawn and the men greeted him with the casual bonhomie of those who slept and toiled together. Several had fought with Arthur and Eamonn at World's End, so they were content with their leader's decision to appoint Arthur as their captain.

Quickly and efficiently, Arthur instructed his men to seek out water once they entered the wood and daub themselves liberally with mud to repel the clouds of insects that would send the calmest man demented within half an hour of entering the dim shadows of Mirk Wood. His men shuddered as they remembered the island created by the Vagus River, so Arthur was certain they would obey without argument.

The whole troop, and the other warriors clustered behind them, moved on silent feet and surveyed the first trees of Mirk Wood with jaundiced eyes. Because it was so swampy, the forest floor was actually lower than the areas of forest that had hidden them all the way up the Vagus from the sea. Small streams cut through it, contributing to puddles, pools and ponds that were full of threat. The steamy summer atmosphere was close, so the warriors quickly became soaking wet from sweat. At the first clearing, a place where shallow sheets of water glimmered under a distant sun masked by heavy foliage, they scooped up handfuls of mud and began to smear their bodies on every square inch of exposed flesh.

Water ran down from the woods behind them and flowed through shallow swampy areas before finding its way to the shelving, open ground that slowly drained into the lake. Mirk Wood was useless land for woodcutting or farming, even if the land could be cleared. Many of the swamp trees grew twisted through competition with the prolific seedlings and the thick growth of forest shrubs chasing the intermittent light. And so Mirk Wood had been left to thicken, to become more brooding, and to develop a reputation for danger.

Any outlaw seeking to prey on the villages of the lake or the aristocratic holidaymakers, made his home in its darkened thickets. For mutual protection, only large bands of villagers would normally enter the pathless wilderness.

When Arthur looked at Mirk Wood, he saw aged trees leaning together like old men; he noticed the occasional oak, with vivid, poisonous mushrooms nestling in its exposed roots; he ducked under trailing, twisted vines as thick as his wrist that were wound with flowering tails of white night blossoms that gave off a smell like rotting flesh; and he heard a thousand rustles and tiny noises in the thick underbrush that spoke of a hidden world of predators and prey under thick drifts of leaf mould. Mirk Wood always gave the impression that any intruder was being watched.

The day was hot under the heavy underbrush, so the Dene crew were sweltering in their thick covering of reeking mud. Adding to their discomfort was the presence of vines with wicked thorns that could tear through cloth and even pierce leather if a thorn should find its way under the sole of a boot. Seamen prefer the clean, open spaces of water and sky at the best of times; Stormbringer's force cursed as they struggled with the landscape.

'Anyone who chose to come this way would have to be a fucking idiot,' one of the seaman said to another. Arthur overheard the complaint and clapped the other man companionably on the back.

'As a man who prefers to ride rather than walk, I agree wholeheartedly with you. There's no way that people who know the terrain like Olaus, the villagers and the Geat warriors would ever expect an attack from this direction. It's no wonder their defences are so casual.'

'Do you ride horses in Britain?' the sailor asked, his curiosity overriding his natural reluctance to ask questions of an officer.

'We use horses as a natural part of our battle strategies. To be honest, we learned about cavalry from the Romans and their tactics were the means whereby we kept the invading Saxons at bay for so long. Until recent times, the Saxons never used horses, because they chose to go into battle with the same tactics and strategies as their grandfathers.'

'You speak as if that's a bad thing,' the sailor, Knut, retorted with an edge of resentment in his voice. 'I see no fault in preserving the tried and true methods if they continue to work.'

'Don't think me foolish, Knut, but if we can't change, then we don't learn. We really need to grasp at every good idea that comes our way and use it, if we can. What I admire most about the Dene people is their willingness to change for the better.'

Knut and his friend swatted away at a cloud of offending insects with frighteningly long, spindly legs. Then they grinned up at Arthur.

'You're right you know, Master Arthur. I just never thought in that way before. I can see how archers could be an advantage in a battle, especially if they pepper the enemy before the first line attacks. Fewer enemies to kill our boys so, aye, I'll grant you that new ideas aren't automatically bad.'

Gradually, as the sun slid down the horizon, light became stronger in front of them as the dense foliage began to thin. Arthur halted his men and sent Rolf and Eamonn ahead to scout the land before them, a task which was quickly completed as the two men returned with a new layer of mud plastered on their faces.

'Well, Rolf, what lies ahead of us?'

Rolf grinned irrepressibly. The singer's voice held a mellifluous and pleasant sound that seemed unnatural when it was used to speak of death, especially when Rolf smiled with such a broad flash of white teeth.

'We've reached the far side of Mirk Wood without incident, master. Because we know what to look for now, we could see signs of movement in the margins of the forest as our men took up their positions. Shite, Master Arthur, that lake is one huge hunk of water. You really cannot see the far shore and there were Olaus's men swimming in the water, taking the horses for a dip, preparing food and generally . . . well, enjoying themselves. They've got no idea that we are here, or that we're looking straight at them!'

'Very good, Rolf . . . Eamonn.' Arthur could see Stormbringer approaching, and the margins of the woods were suddenly alive with hundreds of men.

'It's time to settle the crew down, Rolf. As the helmsman, I'll filter my orders to them through you, so that they know my requests are genuine – and that they *are* orders! For the moment, the men must take up their positions and stop moving about, unless movement is absolutely necessary. Tell them to make themselves comfortable, because we'll be eating and sleeping here until Master Stormbringer decides to make his move. It will be dry rations for tonight, I'm afraid, but we'll be after Olaus's residence and barracks before dawn. Our job is to smash the headquarters. You can let the men know how much Stormbringer trusts us.'

'Tomorrow will be a very good day to die or, better still, to live and win huge spoils from those lazy swine enjoying themselves down on the lake.' Rolf sauntered over to the remaining thirty men of the crew, including Rufus and Thorketil, who had managed the long and tiring journey through Mirk Wood despite the difficulties they had experienced with their wounds. Enthusiastic whispered comments were passed from man to man among the crew, all of whom had been impressed with the heroic efforts of these two men to arrive at their destination without being a burden on the other warriors.

When he decided that a suitable time had arrived to approach his commander, the Troll King respectfully called Arthur over to the fallen log on which he was sitting. Arthur understood how difficult it must be for Thorketil to raise himself to his feet after his long journey through Mirk Wood, so he strolled over to Thorketil with good grace.

'May I ask a boon of you, Lord Arthur?' Thorketil asked. His eyes were earnest and passionate in their protuberant sockets.

'I'd rather you didn't give me titles I haven't earned, Thorketil. I'm not a lord. Not yet, anyway! But you can ask for your boon, although I can't swear that I can help you.'

'I can use a bow, Master Arthur. I heard what you said about archers and, coincidentally, I have my own weapon with me. I was taught to use it in my youth and spent much of my younger days hunting for game. Although some men would say it isn't an honourable pursuit for a warrior, archery is something that I can still excel at on the battlefield without being a drag on my fellows. May I join tomorrow's fight with the bow as my weapon of choice?'

'I thought you were going to ask for something difficult,' Arthur replied, grateful that the problem of Thorketil was so easily solved. 'You may become our archer with my thanks and blessing. Between us, we'll set fire to the headquarters building, if I ever find a bow to borrow. Go to the margins of Mirk Wood now and examine the ground closely for yourself. At the same time you can consider how best we can invent a supply of fire arrows.'

Stormbringer, Arthur and the other captains organised their lines of communication between commanders and the officers who would lead the green, the yellow and the red groups during the course of the battle. Then, while the last of the light remained, the three attacking phalanxes were arranged into battle lines and the men were given their strips of cloth or coloured leather to identify themselves. Finally the men of Stormbringer's army set to work plaiting their forelocks, shining their metal and honing the blades of their weapons. At Arthur's instigation, volunteer scouts were selected from men who were prepared to go into the sleeping camp before dawn to release the horses from their restraining tethers. Then, once the warriors had applied a goodly layer of mud on their faces, and each man had raided the last of their food pouches and drunk the remnants of the beer supply, the officers allowed them to settle down to sleep.

'Eat everything you can find, boys. We'll be breaking our fast in the morning when we'll be eating Olaus Healfdene's fine foods,' Arthur told his men before he rolled himself in his cloak and attempted to calm his overactive mind.

Within minutes the Last Dragon of Britain had fallen fast asleep.

Arthur woke a little after midnight when silence reigned over the woods and a thousand men curled into the landscape as if they were being birthed from the soil of Vastergotland itself. The moon had risen and the skies were clear, although Arthur scented rain in a line of clouds beginning to scud through the dark skies towards them.

'Yes, it will probably rain after dawn, but most of the bad weather will come later in the day. I'm confident your thatch will still catch fire, even in intermittent showers,' Stormbringer whispered. The Sae Dene was standing like a huge statue that brooded over the partially visible men who stirred, coughed, moaned and snored in their sleep. 'It always surprises me that men are restless before a battle, although I suppose it's natural to be unsettled.'

'Aye! So I've seen.'

'I'll be sending the scouts out in about two hours to find the horses and scatter them. Once that task is complete, we can start the battle at any time. I hadn't mentioned it to you, but your friend, Eamonn, has insisted on serving as one of our scouts.'

Arthur squinted at the position of the moon and the horizon, so he could chart its movement. 'That's typical of Eamonn. He loves danger and living on the edge. He'll enjoy this morning's entertainment.' He smiled at his little jest.

Arthur could see that the commander's face was drawn, almost as if he was already imagining the large piles of Dene warriors who would go to the gods on the morrow on his orders. Such a responsibility could crush a lesser man, Arthur decided, but Stormbringer was born to carry responsibility. This battle might be his first major conflict, but the young man was sure that it wouldn't be the last.

Then, when the waiting seemed to be dragging his nerves over iron spikes, inch by inch, Stormbringer nodded his head to the captains and the scouts were sent out, like unleashed hounds. Eamonn waved a negligent, muddy hand as he dropped onto hands and knees to crawl out from the tree line.

Arthur recognised the heavy presence of Thorketil behind him. 'You can move yourself into firing range of your targets and light your fires, my friend. If the enemy is awake, they'll see the lights, but we can't have fire arrows without flame.'

The silence was still complete.

Stormbringer was standing by himself some feet away, deliberately distancing himself from everything but the battle that was about to start. Arthur supposed that his friend needed a physical space to separate himself from those men who were soon to die for him.

'But not you!' the voice in his head chuckled grimly, as it woke and extricated its substance from the roots of his brain. 'You have your father's cold nature. Be grateful for it, for men who lead usually suffer.'

Arthur tried to close the door of communication between his thoughts and the voice that was also part of his true self. He knew that his dream had been born out of some primal fear that his extra sense was the spirit of Uther Pendragon. In response, the voice simply laughed at him.

'There's movement below, Arthur,' Thorketil called out to the commander. The time for silence was over now.

'To me, Rolf! To me!' Arthur called, without even the slightest tremor in his voice. Every time he had been forced to fight in his life, the action had felt right and natural, exactly as was happening now.

Rolf Sea-Shaper was at his shoulder immediately.

'The men must be ready to run as soon as I give the order. See that patch of ground? It slopes downwards, but it is about two hundred yards across at the closest point and it's all that separates us from the enemy.' Rolf was about to run to the crew who stood waiting with their comrades poised like hunting hounds to respond to the order to advance, but Arthur pulled him back.

'There will be no shouting, singing or insults until the enemy are engaged. We attack in silence, and this ploy will add to the confusion. Do you understand?'

'Aye!' Rolf replied with a swift smile. 'And I'd just learned a new song to sing.'

'You can sing it while we're killing the Geats,' Arthur said. Rolf was a little taken aback by Arthur's intensity, but he decided that it was no bad thing, considering what lay ahead.

The darkness stirred below them, then roiled with sudden movement. The moonlight glanced off the pale backs of several horses in a long, dark stream of running, panicked beasts, and Arthur realised that the barracks had been breached. He estimated that upward of a hundred horses were running at speed towards the small tent city clustered to the right of the larger dwelling, a torrent of sharp hooves and tons of muscle and sinew, to scream and pound the tents out of their way in their terror. The herd of stampeding horses joined other freed mounts that had been released from the picket lines. They would run until sweet grass tempted them to stop.

A lit torch seemed to wave from the closest barracks, then arced and tumbled through the air to land somewhere in the thatch.

'That has to be Eamonn! Thorketil! Set fire to those roofs for me. Burn the bastards!'

The Hammer of Thor had used his stick to brace his ruined leg into his firing stance and he pushed one of his arrows into the small fire. Arthur had been unable to find another bow or a cache of arrows within the whole company, so a great deal of responsibility was lying on Thorketil's broad shoulders.

The arrow flew high. When it plunged back to earth, it burned itself out in the area immediately before the doorway of the building, just as a dark shape heaved itself out of the shadows.

'Again, Thorketil! Again! Keep firing until you're successful.'

The next arrow also missed its mark, but the third flew high and true, and buried itself deeply into the thatched roof of the building. Within seconds, the fire began to spread as the dry roofing caught alight.

Thorketil continued to fire his arrows, even as the two buildings flamed scarlet along their roof lines. 'Well done, King of the Trolls. Ignore us now and fire at will. You can use every arrow you have to set the night ablaze.'

'It shall be so,' Thorketil grunted, even as he bent over to light another arrow in the fire pit. Arthur was watching Stormbringer's hand now, and was soon oblivious to the Troll King, who had served his purpose. The Sae Dene raised his arm, while the air seemed to quiver with taut muscles that were held in check by willpower alone. And then the arm dropped.

Along the margins of the forest, officers leaped out into the open, to be followed by their men, a ragtag army covered in drying clay and filthy mud. They were bedraggled and soiled after many miles of running – but they were an army that was fixed on destruction, and eerily silent.

Arthur's long legs cleared obstacles at a run and he had soon outstripped his equally long-legged warriors. His eyes were fixed on a group of half-clothed, lightly armed men assembling between the barracks buildings after abandoning their billets in confusion. They had poured out of the building with loud curses and the occasional scream when a man was set alight in his haste to flee. There, in the heart of the fray, was Olaus Healfdene, the architect of all the suffering on the island at the mouth of the Vagus. For his disregard for human life, Arthur had judged Olaus to be guilty, so his focus was fixed on the Geat commander alone. Arthur would kill whoever stood in his path until he was killed in turn.

A stray horse almost knocked Arthur over, but he avoided it by changing direction, thereby avoiding an axe that was swung to remove his head. A warrior sprang up before him, seemingly out of the raw earth. He must have been more acute than most of his fellows and expected an attack would have to come from the woods. For his intelligence, the Geat died quickly, his throat severed to the spine by a slash from the Dragon Knife while Arthur tried to regroup his attack towards Olaus Healfdene's headquarters once again.

Arthur was almost at the barracks before most of the Geat warriors realised the space between the lakefront and Mirk Wood was crawling with Dene enemy. Because the attack had been conducted in silence, aided by the use of fire and the loosened horses, the Geats had awoken to scenes of chaos. Nothing had prepared them for a surprise attack from out of nowhere. Arthur was upon them with his crew at his heels before the Geats even realised the danger they were in.

'For Stormbringer!' For Leif, the Sword of Skandia! For honour!'

Arthur continued to roar out his challenge as he engaged a huge, bear-like man wrapped in sleeping furs to cover his nakedness, despite wielding a huge sword that matched his impressive height. Behind him, Arthur heard the cry repeated again and again, as other crews took it up. The night that had been so silent was now reverberating with the constant sounds of mortal combat.

Somewhere nearby, a voice began to sing of death. Other voices joined it, so the sound added to the chaos of fire, blood and confusion. Arthur found that he was dancing and killing to the song's rhythm. All too soon, he was awash with blood so that he blessed the long-dead craftsman who had made the Dragon Knife so exactingly. A man struck out at Arthur and would have killed him, but his bloody fingers slipped on the sodden pommel of his sword and the blow glanced off Arthur's helmet.

Arthur shook his head to clear out any cobwebs, and then killed his foe with the Dragon Knife firmly gripped in his left hand. Bedwyr had ordered that shagreen and rope should cover the pommel of his son's sword and now, Arthur could see the wisdom of that choice in the charnel house of the lake's foreshore. The coarse sharkskin gave his sweating, blood-soaked fingers some purchase and the rope absorbed the blood.

The rope will never be white again, his inner voice chuckled.

'Shut up!' Arthur roared, and swung his weapons like scythes so that men avoided the crazed giant who was covered in blood from head to toe, except for his maniacal grey eyes.

The first light struck the horizon behind him and the rational part of Arthur's brain blessed the luck that Stormbringer possessed, whereby the rays of the early-morning dawn would dazzle the eyes of the Geat warriors. But there were more men to kill, so Arthur continued to scour the surrounds of the collapsing barracks, while killing all who stood in his path.

Suddenly, the sounds of singing were cut short, so Arthur turned to see that Rolf Sea-Shaper had fallen, his arm pouring blood. Above him, a giant Geat was poised to bury his axe into Rolf's skull.

Arthur shouted to deflect the Geat's attention, so when the axeman wavered in his stroke sufficiently for Rolf to roll away from the downwards blow, the axe-head was buried in the bloody mud of the barracks' forecourt.

'Never take your eyes off the enemy,' Arthur instructed the man kindly, just as he removed the warrior's head.

'He'll remember now,' Rolf chuckled weakly from the ground as he accepted Arthur's left arm, with the hand still holding the Dragon Knife, to haul him to his feet. 'Go, Arthur! Keep killing the bastards. I'll survive!'

'Be sure you do, helmsman,' Arthur growled. 'There'll be no songs without you and I've grown accustomed to them.'

Arthur continued to kill Geat warriors until his arms were almost too tired to lift his sword. As the yellow and green phalanxes demolished the wings to the right and the left of the Geat headquarters, the survivors had bolstered the forces around the collapsing barracks at the centre of the Geat camp. The red phalanx took terrible losses but Denes from the green and the yellow phalanxes joined them in a contracting circle of death. For most of the engagement, the Geat warriors could have escaped at any time, because the Dene lines were stretched so thin that they could not have stopped any organised breakout or retreat. But the Geat warriors refused to run and there was no organising brain to mitigate their appalling loss of life.

In the end, the battle of Lake Wener was an exercise in sheer butchery, as the element of surprise and a superior strategy gave the Dene an edge which they never lost. The sun rose on a scene from Hell, with piled bodies of dead Geat around a shrinking perimeter where the defenders were reverting to the use of the shield wall as their final line of defence. The Geat warriors were being mercilessly picked off by the sheer number of survivors in the Dene force.

Arthur felt a slap cross his face and raised his knife to gut the misty figure in front of him.

'I'm Stormbringer, you fool! Snap out of it, Arthur! I need you!'

'Lord . . .' Arthur gasped. The reek of fresh blood and entrails washed over him and, for the first time that morning, he became aware of the filth. The young man almost vomited at his master's feet.

'Better now? Good, because I need a man I can trust to persuade these Geat fools to stop fighting. There are fewer than a hundred of them left alive. I'll permit them to leave in peace, but they must take a message back to their king from me.'

The Sae Dene paused. 'I can parlay with the remnants of Olaus's army myself, but I'll lose prestige with those same survivors if I do. Besides, with your appearance, you'll scare the last Geat warriors into submission.'

Stormbringer was only half joking, which made his language and mien even more effective. The commander rapidly outlined what he wanted, although he was hard put not to twitch away from the stink surrounding his friend.

'Are you hurt, Arthur?' Stormbringer asked, his forehead furrowed with concern.

'My lord, I truly cannot tell! If these brave Geat are prepared to listen, I'll try to force them to lay down their arms, although I can understand why they would be prepared to die here on the spot where they were defeated, rather than accept an abject surrender.'

'Yes! I understand their need, my Dragon, but I must send a message to their king, so I want them to live.'

And so Arthur made a pact with the last officer of the Geats, a lad of

Arthur's age who was completely unsure of what he should do. Arthur convinced the young officer that the Geat warriors would be doing their last duty to Olaus by informing their king of the death of his general, and by granting mercy to the remaining warriors. After an hour of truce, the Geats capitulated.

Within another hour, the last survivors of Olaus's vast horde had left their encampment to undertake the journey back to their king on foot. They were unarmed except for knives and had been supplied with enough food and drink for two days' travel. If they needed more, their countrymen would have to supply it.

The young officer repeated Stormbringer's message regularly as he ran, determinedly placing one foot in front of the other while he learned the taste and smell of defeat. When he eventually stood at the foot of Heardred's throne, the message was imprinted in the young man's brain.

"'I, Arthur Dragonsen, tell you that the Stormbringer, Valdar Bjornsen, is come from the land of the Dene. He will take reparation for the cowardly murders of the Geat allies, his kinsmen who have been foully murdered, and he will kill all those Geat thieves who have taken Dene lands.

"'The Last Dragon swears to you in the Stormbringer's name that this will be, so ask for parlay or you will perish.'"

CHAPTER XXIV

THE DOLOROUS DAY

Be happy, drink, and think each day your own as you live it and leave the rest to fortune.

Euripides, *Alcestis*

The Battle of Mirk Wood would become the stuff of legends, while Arthur would become the red dragon who flew out of a burnished sky to destroy the enemies of the Dene. Arthur would laugh when he heard the sagas woven by Rolf Sea-Shaper, who would never again have a right arm strong enough to fight the rudder or carry a sword. He would become a singer, a chronicler of Stormbringer, the Last Dragon and those golden days of blood, death and triumph that made some sense of the horrors of life.

But that was all in the future. On that grim morning, Arthur faced up to what battle had made of him. He was a creature of death!

As he strode towards the water's edge at Lake Wener, the Dene warriors lowered their eyes respectfully and stepped aside for him so that even his shadow shouldn't touch them. Many of them had seen the Briton in action and they had been awestruck by his power, his coldness and his mastery of his weapons. 'He isn't human,' one warrior decided. 'You only have to look in his eyes to see that the dragon in him is alive.'

'Aye! When he's angry, the master's eyes change from golden to grey, but by all the gods of Asgaad, he's a wonder with those blades of his. I never knew a man who didn't need a shield until I met Arthur,' his companion added. 'But he's also a good leader – and he cares about his men.' In fact, Rolf had defended Arthur so successfully that the Dene warriors gradually ceased to treat him as if he was a man-monster.

As he scrubbed his body with coarse sand from the lake, Arthur believed that nothing could possibly peel or scour away the blood that tainted his skin. Fully clothed, he sat in the wavelets and ignored the water on his armour and his weapons. At this moment, all he wanted was to feel clean again.

Suddenly, Arthur remembered. His foster-father had once described how he had sat in the ocean and attempted to scrub away the blood of Saxons he had killed at Moridunum. Bedwyr had learned much about himself from the carnage of those war experiences, so the wise old man had counselled his son in preparation for the time when the boy would suffer from the same pangs of guilt. Arthur immediately felt a warm sense of camaraderie with Bedwyr, which mitigated his disgust at the number of men he had killed in this battle.

'Blessed Bedwyr, you always seem to be here when I need to think straight. I have been a man who was so crazed by killing that he doesn't even feel a blow that strikes him. Well, I can feel every blow now!'

Arthur made it to his feet with a deep sigh. Now that he was almost clean, he could feel the pains from a dozen small cuts, slashes and contusions caused by deflected swords or the hilts of weapons used to batter his face and body. None of the wounds were serious – but they hurt!

Once his muscles had cooled, Arthur allowed his unbraided hair to stream down his back while he carried his helmet by the cheek-strap. His fellow Dene seemed to meet his eyes more easily now that he wasn't covered in blood.

'Where's Stormbringer?' he asked Rufus, who was wrapping a superficial wound on his arm with a strip of cloth torn from his shirt. Laconic as ever, Rufus nodded in the direction of the partly burned headquarters which had already been co-opted as a makeshift hospital.

Arthur thanked Rufus, who remained dour and glum, then ambled off in the direction the warrior had indicated.

As he entered the building, he noticed that the doorway had been built for tall men, a relief after some of the structures he had been forced to use. He remembered the cramped quarters at World's End with an affection that was marred by the pain he had felt every time he hit his head on a doorway.

Inside, the once-spacious building was pungent with the smell of woodsmoke, fallen rafters and illness, but part of the roof had survived in the capricious ways of fires. Without any way to care for them, Stormbringer had decided that any Geat warrior who couldn't walk in the retreat should be put to death rather than die from starvation or be savaged by scavengers after the Dene army had departed.

The gloom was thick in the building, but Arthur could see that there were surprisingly few wounded men here. All told, there were fewer than a hundred.

'Yes! We fight – or we die!' Stormbringer exclaimed at Arthur's shoulder. 'The north is a testing place, as you have seen. We have no surgeons like the ones you have described to me. We even lack camp followers who can help us to care for the sick, as is the case today. Here, the wounded must fight until they die in the full knowledge that they will suffer that fate anyway. In death, my friend, there can still be glory.'

'My father would say that while there's life, there's hope, and a warrior must try to stay alive to strike further blows against his enemies.' Arthur grinned ruefully. 'My teacher, Father Lorcan, often told me that it was better to be a live mouse than a dead lion – or a dragon in my case! I'm still wondering if he's correct in that assertion.'

'I suppose it depends on the reasons for the battle,' Stormbringer said.

'Aye!' Arthur replied. He was too tired to make moral judgements on the ambivalent nature of warfare. 'Have you seen Eamonn?' he asked the Sae Dene, but then felt his stomach drop to his boots at the flicker of regret in Stormbringer's eyes. 'He's dead, isn't he?'

Arthur anticipated the answer before Stormbringer gave him the confirmation, but the young man needed to hear the words to actually believe it. He could still see Eamonn laughing with devilry when he looked back at Arthur before dropping to the ground to begin the long, dangerous crawl to the Geat lines. Even more poignant, Arthur remembered the short, plump boy who'd been so mercilessly bullied by Mareddyd, the British prince, who'd believed he was the strongest and most-royal of all the noble youth assembled by Taliesin to build a protective dyke in the marshland close to Glastonbury. In reality, the true purpose of the building project had been to bond together the next generation of the lords of Britain. Arthur had been thirteen at the time, so he had known Eamonn for nearly ten years, but adversity had caused them to become closer than brothers. Arthur had enough muscle for the two of them, but it was Eamonn who possessed the true joy of living.

'It's unfair that Eamonn is dead. He took so much pleasure from living when less worthy men have survived him.' Arthur was afraid that he would burst into tears. With some difficulty, he pursed his lips and squared his jaw.

'Eamonn and I were friends as boys,' he explained to Stormbringer, who was feeling helpless in the face of Arthur's naked grief.

The young man wanted to scream at God for killing Eamonn and for taking his parents, whom he still hungered for, just as every child will in those times when their world is shattered.

'They've laid his body out under the sky with the other dead officers. We'll burn the bodies of our warriors, but our jarls and Eamonn will go to the gods on a ship. There are some small rivercraft at the village where the Vagus meets Lake Wener. I've sent some of our scouts to bring back one of the largest boats which will be used as a gift to our noble dead. Unmanned, the vessel will sail out over the lake where it will be set alight, burned and allowed to sink in the deeper waters.'

Arthur sighed deeply. He must honour his friend in this rite so he could bear witness to King Bors and Queen Valda of Eamonn's fate. Then he snorted with laughter, for he was presupposing that there

463

would be a time when he actually returned to his native country. But in his heart of hearts, he knew that Eamonn's untimely death had helped to sever the bonds that tied him to his homeland.

Stormbringer called to a young warrior who was still proudly wearing a thread of the yellow phalanx tied into his hair. Then, with a serious expression on his face, the Sae Dene instructed the warrior to conduct Arthur to the site where the Dene dead had been laid out in readiness for the flames.

Outside, in the cleaner air where sickness had no place, Dene working parties were labouring to strip the enemy bodies of their valuables. Once naked, the corpses were dragged to a long, eroded fissure in the earth where their remains would be burned and their ashes left to dissipate in the elements. Everything of use, including a number of fine horses, had already been collected and stored. Surprisingly, as the Dene warriors continued to search the bivouac for wagons and harness to transport the captured spoils, they found further caches of supplies that Olaus Healfdene had stockpiled for a long campaign.

'Would the Geat have stayed here for the winter?' Arthur asked the young warrior, Ole Skuldesen, who was awed at being in such close contact with a man already spoken of as a living legend, a new Thor who had come to save the Dene.

'The lake is too big to freeze in the winter, so there's a constant source of food here. Also, my lord, the large body of water creates warmer air along the coast, so this place is a perfect spot in which to spend the winter. Olaus stored plenty of ale and he kept a goodly supply of dried meat, fish and game. He even had barrels of apples! By the gods, Olaus thought of everything when it came to his creature comforts.'

The young man grinned and looked at Arthur with the glow of hero-worship clearly visible in his eyes. 'Everything but the best warriors!'

'The credit for our victory belongs to Stormbringer's strategies, my friend. I merely tagged along in our commander's wake,' Arthur replied gruffly.

464

'But you killed Olaus Healfdene, Lord Arthur. Don't you remember?'

Arthur looked as thunderstruck as he felt. 'I killed a number of men, Ole, but they didn't pause to introduce themselves. Where is Olaus Healfdene?'

Arthur was led to a line of Geat dead who had, by their dress, been more important than the ordinary warriors. Ole pointed to the corpse of the large man wrapped in bear furs that Arthur had killed at the very beginning of the battle. The long and slightly portly body was thick with muscle and was still decked with heavy, golden arm-rings that were clamped around his biceps and wrists. Arthur realised the man's importance when he saw that a blood-spattered torc of three strands of plaited gold was still lying on his chest and his valuables hadn't, as yet, been pillaged. The head of the Geat commander had been cut through at the neck with amazing precision, and placed next to the body.

'Lord Stormbringer instructed me to present you with Olaus's sword, his torc of office and his arm-rings. You stripped the Geats of their leader and saved many lives by doing so.'

Ole was so proud of the task he had been given that Arthur lacked the heart to argue with him. The torc was made of orange gold, so Arthur shoved it inside his leather vest where it clunked painfully against his ribs. With the massive Geat sword and its scabbard slung over his shoulder, Arthur could no longer put off the awful moment.

'Where are our own casualties, Ole? I need to see my friend and pay my respects.'

Although he was very young, Ole seemed to understand Arthur's feelings. As they walked behind the barracks, the young man tried to explain his background in response to Arthur's questions.

'I am one of the southern Dene, and my kin live close to our borders with Saxony. We live in a state of constant battle readiness. We must, for the Anglii and Jutes have been waiting for an opportunity to obliterate us for many years.' The young man coughed and surreptitiously wiped moisture from his eyes. Arthur pretended not to notice.

'I've lost two brothers, a cousin and my betrothed to the enemy, so it seems my whole life has been lived between burials or periods of mourning. My father died when I was an infant and my stepfather will never see clearly again.' Ole touched the side of his head and shrugged. 'A sword blow to the head, you understand?'

'Aye, Ole, I do! I understand how it is, for I've had much the same kind of life with the same enemies.'

The two shared a glance of complete understanding. Our differences are born out of our natures, Arthur thought sadly. Fortunately for Ole, he still joys in life, much as Eamonn had done.

Ole came to a halt beside a long line of some twenty bodies lying swathed in their cloaks. We've lost half our captains in one engagement, Arthur thought. He was dumbstruck by the waste and the tragedy of it all. We may have crushed the Geats, but these fine young men will take generations to replace.

'Would you like me to wait for you back at the barracks?' Ole understood that Arthur might be embarrassed to show emotion in front of a stranger.

'You've lost friends too?' Arthur asked.

'Aye. We've lost many good men today, Master Arthur.'

As Ole walked away, his shoulders squared and his face turned away from the grim line of bodies, Arthur took in the scene, including the four guards, two per side, who'd been placed on duty to protect the dead from scavengers: human, avian and beast. Already, Mirk Wood was heavy with crows, ravens and shrikes, all waiting for a chance to feast on the dead. Fastidious as always, Stormbringer had set guards over the enemy dead as well, deep in their pits in a tangle of stiff arms and legs.

Grateful that Eamonn's physical remains were safe, Arthur walked down the line of corpses. Eamonn's short size meant that many of the shrouded faces needn't be bared because the taller bodies were far too large. Then he saw a familiar pair of boots that were more sophisticated than the Dene leggings.

As he folded back the corner of the enveloping cloak, he prayed to his Saviour that his friend might have gone into the shades with his face unmarked.

'Oh, Eamonn, you foolish bastard,' Arthur whispered. 'Why did you always have to be in the front line when you were called to battle?'

'Because I'm a short-arse, you fucking idiot. Why do you think I do it, you great beanpole?' Eamonn's voice was clear in Arthur's head, and he could almost believe that Eamonn had been wounded rather than killed.

He twitched the cloak away. Blood had run out of Eamonn's nose and mouth and left three sanguine trails. Arthur's sleeve was still damp, so he bent, kneeled at his friend's head and gently scrubbed away at the dried blood, leaving Eamonn's face familiar, but strange. Whatever was Eamonn was long gone now, and this husk had been discarded as no longer of any worth.

Blood had pooled and dried behind his head and his thick, black curls; Arthur's probing fingers soon found a long axe-wound. Another knife wound had struck him from behind, just below his shoulder blades.

'It took two men to kill you, my brother, and, even then, they had to take you from behind. I hope we killed the curs that sent you into the shades.'

Arthur forced himself to check Eamonn's whole body so he could give an honest report to the young man's kin when he returned to their home. Certainly, Blaise would want to know! Eamonn's ring still rested on his hand and Arthur eased it off his friend's thumb for Blaise, as well as a chunky chain that was still hanging around his neck. Arthur decided that this was his bulla, or birth gift, for King Bors had persisted with many of the old Roman ways. This trinket, more than anything else, held Eamonn's essence, so Arthur slid it off and cleaned away the dried blood with his shirt. He flipped open the clasp which resisted him for a moment, and then emptied the contents of the small casket onto his palm.

Arthur began to weep in great agonised sobs. He cried without shame, for so much of the sadness within him demanded to be set free.

There, on his open palm, lay a shell made of gold, probably the original birth gift from Eamonn's father. Alongside it was a small, grey pearl from the distant lands of the north, perhaps a gift from a lover, although Arthur was ignorant of any special woman in his friend's life.

But the third item was the reason for his tears, the final item that unlocked his misery and reminded Arthur that life is brief, like a butterfly that exists for a single day in beauty and joyfulness. Eamonn had kept a lock of Arthur's hair, stolen when he had been shorn at some time during his youth. His friend had bound it with a little twist of gold wire and retained it with his other precious objects. He had kept his love for his friend against his heart.

Three hours before dusk, a longship nosed into the shore and was pulled above the tide-line by its rowers, for this lake was so large that the body of water still felt the pull of the moon.

The Geat ship was broader in the beam than a Dene longboat and, in many ways, it resembled a Saxon ceol. As it approached the shore, it had seemed to walk on the waves, whereas *Sea Wife* snaked through them with such flexibility and grace that it was hard to see the boat as simply a number of overlapping boards nailed into the shape of a leaf. Later, when Arthur examined the Geat trading vessel, he discovered its keel was heavier, its planks were thicker and every line was more utilitarian than the poetry of a longboat. This ship was meant to carry cargo on the only western ocean access that Vastergotland possessed – down the Vagus River and out into the sea. Now the *Wind Eagle* would serve a different purpose.

'It's a pity this eagle looks more like a duck,' Arthur observed to no one in particular, but Stormbringer spluttered into a brief bout of laughter that was quite inappropriate on this occasion. The Sae Dene had seen the redness in Arthur's eyes and the blotchy skin across his cheekbones, so he knew that Arthur had visited his friend's body to pay his last respects.

'Our friends will go to their various heavens in this particular duck, so I hope she gains decent wings by this evening when she sails out into the centre of the lake,' the Sae Dene responded seriously. He was staring resolutely at the ship as it was stripped of all unnecessary fittings, to allow the shields of their Geat enemies to be piled onto the decks where they would make a bed of weapons on which the dead jarls would rest on their journey to Paradise.

Warriors were out scouring the fields and the margins of Mirk Wood for more fuel that could be added to the fire. Others collected flowers, the enemy's blankets and any cloth that held value. Sweet grass was laid as a pillow for each man's head, and jars of wine and beer from Olaus Healfdene's own stores were placed where the twenty-two men could find them when the time came for drinking contests with the gods. A haunch of venison, a wheel of fine cheese, apples and perfect fruit taken fresh from the vine or tree was placed alongside the wine.

As the sun sank lower, a long line of warriors bearing the dead bodies on quickly constructed stretchers came slowly to the *Wind Eagle*. Rolf Sea-Shaper led the procession, his voice rising in a song that shivered through the air, so that Arthur was reminded of keening women. One man stepped out of the crowd of warriors, carrying a strangely constructed brazen horn. As he raised the instrument to his lips, Arthur could see that the beautiful object was a long, sinuous and delicate tube that widened gradually and flared out into a partly enclosed horn shape, rather like the head of a flower. Arthur could scarcely believe his eyes, or his ears, when the older warrior raised the instrument to his lips, and blew.

The sound, which consisted of several high, thin notes, turned and twisted round Rolf Sea-Shaper's voice, wailing and mourning as if alerting Heaven to new heroes whose souls were poised to wing their way to its gates. That single horn brought Eamonn's loss sharply back into Arthur's imagination, as if that instrument could encompass all his deepest feelings. Perhaps it did, because Arthur and many of the warriors wept without shame.

Once the bodies were in place and flowers heaped around their feet, their swords were placed in their hands. Then, one by one, warriors came forward to extol the virtues of each of the jarls so that all the warriors still alive felt as if they knew the dead man and regretted his loss. One by one, singers praised the dead, until Arthur could no longer bear the thought that no one spoke for Eamonn. He moved to stand in front of Stormbringer as the ceremony began to draw to a close.

'Lord Stormbringer, one man lies unnamed and without kindred to shed tears to speed his way into the grey vastness of death. I speak of Eamonn, son of Bors, the king of the Dumnonii tribe of Britain. He is my oldest friend!'

Stormbringer nodded his head ceremoniously and Arthur turned to face the dead with a dry mouth, trembling hands and a pair of shaking knees.

I'd rather face a dozen huge warriors than speak on such an occasion as this, Arthur thought. But Eamonn must be honoured and I'm the only person who knew him well enough to do him justice.

He coughed, cleared his throat and tried to quell his nerves. 'Warriors of the Dene, hear what I, the Last Dragon, say to you. I speak for Eamonn pen Bors, a young man who was a prince of the Britons. Many times, he shared a joke with you and, on many occasions you've called him *little man* because of his short stature.'

Several of the Dene warriors from the crew of *Sea Wife* laughed affectionately, then realised that the insult they had laid upon Eamonn, albeit in fun, could never be recalled. They fell silent and looked down at the earth in regret.

'I, too, called him by that same insult and I can assure you that he felt no resentment for a simple statement of fact. Eamonn saved his anger for deeds of cruelty, depravity or dishonour. I recall that he once fought ferociously in a small, faraway village to save people who weren't his own, having no shame in his passionate defence of the weak and the helpless.

'But more than for his courage or for his decency, every man on *Sea Wife* and *Loki's Eye* will remember him for his joy in the whole wonder of being alive. Eamonn taught me about the beauties and pleasures of women, of the fun of being footloose, of fishing in a green bay, of dancing with pretty girls late into a warm summer's night and how there is no need for shame if we weep to see great loveliness. Everything I know about living, I learned from Eamonn.

'He was my friend, but he has gone to sing and drink with the gods. And he'll probably find a pretty wench to tumble.'

The warriors laughed at Arthur's accurate reading of Eamonn's irreverence.

'And so, my friends, I say my last Ave to Eamonn who will always be my friend.'

'Ave, Eamonn.'

Led by Rolf Sea-Shaper, the cry was repeated by the crew of *Sea Wife*.

Arthur stepped back, while refusing to wipe away his tears. If men thought him weak, then let them prove their claim with sharp iron.

With a sombre face, Stormbringer made a sign and a dozen men pushed the *Wind Eagle* into the current. As half a dozen torches were thrust into the ship, the waiting warriors launched her out of the shallows and then stood waist-deep in the wavelets to see if the ship had been accepted by the lake. A breeze suddenly sprang up from the land and filled the woollen sail, so that it rattled and soughed before bellying, causing the ship to turn till it faced out over the lake.

As if the ship itself had taken a great breath and leaped forwards, the hull cut cleanly into the waves. On board, the torches set the fine cloth and timber alight and the flames began to catch, licking at the decking and snaking towards the mast. The descending sun set the whole western horizon aflame as if the lake itself was burning, but the ship drove on and on, its rudder swinging uselessly as the sail captured the breeze.

As the light from the sun slowly began to fade, the ship burned from prow to stern. With an explosion of hot air that could be imagined from the shore, the sail caught alight, but the wool burned slowly with great gouts of white smoke. Arthur longed to turn away, yet the rites were so compelling and so final that he was afraid of being disrespectful.

The night seemed to thicken as, slowly, fire engulfed the *Wind Eagle*, and the ship began to slow. Hissing like a serpent, the fire died at the waterline, but the vessel was wallowing in the water now and the sail collapsed with a great shower of sparks as the ropes and spars burned through. Like a wounded bird, the prow dropped and the rudder rose into the air. Then, faster than Arthur thought possible, the ship and its precious cargo slid below the surface and vanished.

Eamonn was gone, and he would never return.

Three days later, the ships sailed upriver to the Lake Wener encampment and, regretfully, Arthur rose out of a stupor of indecision to slake his curiosity. The great sails flouted the Geat sky with their symbols of Dene power and, when the forty-three ships drove ashore, manned by skeleton crews under the command of Hoel Ship-Singer, Stormbringer and the jarls walked down to the sandy stretch of beach to greet them.

'Hail, Stormbringer, victor of the greatest battle in the history of Skania,' Hoel called loudly from the bow of the ship and raised his arm in salute to the Sae Dene captain. His eyes were shining with admiration. 'We have come to transport you out of this place and take you to Halland where the banners of the Geat king fly over my land. I beg you to bring relief to the south, and I swear that all able-bodied men who have survived in Guteland and Skania will flock to your standard.'

'We have taken serious losses here—' Stormbringer began, but Hoel cut him off.

'But not as many as your enemy has suffered and not as many as common sense indicated you could have lost. Your warriors have won a great victory and word of it is already travelling through the villages like fire. Once we have left this accursed place, able-bodied men will come willingly to join your warriors as you continue your campaign.'

'Very well, Hoel.' Stormbringer's voice was tired. 'I will be ready to leave in three days. Meanwhile, we must load the wounded, determine what spoils will be taken, decide what to do with the horses and store as many supplies as our ships can reasonably be expected to carry.'

Hoel was so pleased with the concessions he had wrung out of Stormbringer that he would have agreed to anything. Depressed, Arthur turned away and would have left the shore had Stormbringer not called him back.

'Hoel, I should point out to you that Arthur is the true hero of this battle, for it was he who killed Olaus in hand-to-hand combat. He denied the Geats the value of having a commander to lead them during the course of the battle.'

Once again, Arthur felt embarrassed at having to accept unnecessary praise.

Stormbringer turned back to Arthur. 'If we are leaving with Hoel in a few days, Arthur, I want you to select two of Healfdene's horses as my personal gift to you and Eamonn. These animals are in addition to your share of the spoils. I know that the Britons set even greater store by horses and cavalry than we do, so please take these gifts as a token of my gratitude and friendship.'

Hoel could see Arthur's discomfort clearly enough, so he watched as Stormbringer sent him off with Ole to make his choice of the horses on the picket line.

'Why do you worry about this Briton, Stormbringer? He's just another man from a far-off land. I expect that you have a dozen more who are as capable as he is, so why should you concern yourself over his fits and starts?'

'Arthur is one of the most exceptional men I've ever encountered.' Stormbringer smiled affectionately. 'And he feels everything so very deeply, as you can see. He is unsettled and miserable after the death of his friend and is at a loss to know what to do in a foreign land. But, if you saw him on the battlefield, you wouldn't ask me why I concern myself with him. He's cold, distant and impersonal in combat – the perfect weapon! For him, the goal becomes everything, and such focus actually saves the lives of his comrades and inspires those who fight beside him.'

At the picket line, Arthur's mood picked up considerably when he saw the fine display of horseflesh that was on offer. He had missed horses, although he hadn't realised it. These northern animals were heavier and longer in the leg than their British cousins, with large rounded rumps that were ridged with muscle and equally powerful, bowed necks. The faces of the long string of horses looked at him with eyes that reminded him of Eamonn: huge, dark and fringed with extraordinarily long lashes.

Arthur walked down the line of beasts, checking them carefully. One particularly large black horse had the same warmth in its brown eyes as his friend, so he knew that this stallion would give pleasure to Blaise once she had recovered from the loss of her brother.

For himself, he searched for something other than good looks, so he had almost despaired of finding that *something* that sparked his imagination and his emotions when he heard a pained scream from further down the picket line. One horse in particular was being fractious and refused to be fed with its fellows. It was reluctant to accept cut fodder when succulent, belly-deep grasses stood, green and growing, just nearby. The mare was very tall for a female, and Arthur could see that it was an indeterminate colour that was neither brown nor grey nor black, rather like watered silk. One white sock marked her changeable hide and, when Arthur ran his hand down her back, he was surprised to feel the vigour and crude strength of the hair in her mane. He had expected smoothness under his fingers. This beast was a chameleon.

'I'll take the black stallion and this mare,' Arthur told the warrior who had appointed himself to the role of horse-master.

'She's trouble,' he warned. 'She's a real bitch and I imagine her temper won't improve if you want to ride her. She argues with my lads over every little thing and now she's complaining about the grass.' He sighed with irritation. 'She's a real female!'

'But you can't ignore her, can you? In ten years, you'll still remember the fractious mare that caused such grief at Lake Wener. And that's no bad thing! I don't want a docile horse, I want a fighter.'

'Then you'll be a happy man,' the horse-master advised him. 'Just watch her teeth – she bites!'

The next morning, Arthur selected a saddle from the supply taken from the Geats and, as he placed the harness alongside his horse, she tried to bite him. He actually raised his fist and was about to strike her when he glimpsed a shadow of terror in her eyes. He quickly decided that fear was the last thing he wanted in this horse.

'Be aware, Horse, that I intend to make you love me.' Arthur's smile was competitive, wicked and, for the first time since they had left

World's End, boyish. 'I'll think of a suitable name for you soon. In the meantime – stand still!'

Given the mare's obvious intelligence, she should have known that this particular human was likely to be difficult. But she was determined to win their battle of wills. For the first half-hour, Arthur struggled as she tried to defy him at every step.

She had turned in continuous circles whenever he tried to mount her, then she had bucked ferociously as soon as he attempted to settle himself into the saddle. Finally, she steadfastly refused to obey any instructions conveyed through the knees and boots. Eventually, Arthur kicked her hard in the belly as he lost his temper.

'Horse! That's enough!'

Arthur dismounted with a thunderous face and decided to take the horse's training back to basics. He knew he had two options: he could use brutal methods that would force her to bow to his demands, or he could convince her that she could accede to his demands with dignity. He decided to take the easier option.

The young man placed a halter over the head and nose of the horse and allowed her a lead of about twenty feet. Then, with a piece of whippy cane about three feet in length, Arthur forced her to circle around him, while flicking the cane to let her know that it could be used as a method of punishment, if she refused to obey his instructions. Within half an hour, the horse had decided that she would be compliant and was happy to walk, trot or canter in a circle as her new master required.

Then, having demonstrated that he intended to become dominant, Arthur made a further attempt to mount.

For one short moment, the animal stood perfectly still and was contemplating her options. She was obviously undecided as to whether she should resume the contest.

But sanity eventually prevailed, and the mare showed her intelligence by making no further efforts to dislodge here master. Arthur had won the battle of wills so, from that point onwards, the beast would always be compliant when Arthur mouthed her newly acquired name, Horse.

Two hours later, they went on their first amicable ride, a journey along the shore of the lake with no particular destination in mind.

Riding along the margins of the lake, while permitting Horse to have her head and determine their destination, gave Arthur a sense of peace that had been missing from his life for months. He had been engrossed with his duties towards his sister and her friend, and to Eamonn, so he hadn't known a carefree moment since their capture. Now, with the wind in his hair and bound for nowhere in particular, Arthur felt his guilt and troubles begin to fall away.

Eventually, Arthur resumed control of his steed and they cantered up towards the margins of Mirk Wood. Then, about a mile or so outside the forest, he saw a bald, treeless tumulus off in the distance. Such a hill was a rare sight in these flat expanses, for it seemed to rise straight out of the dense vegetation and swamps. Piqued with curiosity, he turned his mount towards the hill.

Once he was under the shelter of the trees, he discovered that Mirk Wood was far wilder and denser here where he was away from the western edge. Even hunters didn't venture this far into the woods, so Arthur was surprised when his mare stumbled upon a footpath beaten flat by feet that had travelled in a single file towards the low hill. She turned to follow the enigmatic path, grateful to be separated from the worst of the thickly woven climbers, shrubs and stinging branches that created impenetrable barriers on either side of the track. Without any effort, Arthur imagined that the forest had packed itself around the track, leaving the earth untouched in a manner that made the Briton shudder.

'Well, Horse, has the Green Man built this path that leads up from the lake?' Arthur asked his steed. 'Never mind! We'll continue onwards and see where it leads.'

Horse seemed relieved and almost skipped as she walked along.

The heat generated beneath the glowering trees beat down on them and autumn seemed far away when Arthur arrived at the bottom of the hill. The rising ground was surprisingly smooth, perhaps because the track widened as the thick vegetation relinquished its hold on the smooth slopes. As with the path, there seemed to be no logical reason why vegetation didn't grow there. With his overactive imagination, Arthur saw himself mounting a smooth, stone skull leading upwards towards a broad forehead where he would discover what this strange place was meant to be.

Eventually, the flinty earth gave way to sheets of shale that had been laid down in ages long gone, even before the earth had cooled. Mirk Wood could not gain a purchase on this bare stone, for even the strongest, most deadly of invasive vines cannot force its way through a foot of solid rock.

Putting aside his superstition, Arthur kicked his mare into movement, even though she turned her head back to look at him and eyed his calf longingly. Then another light kick reminded her that he wasn't for eating and she moved forward in a relatively good temper.

A huge monolith was standing at the front edge of the shelf of rock which served as the crown of the hill. The stone was three times the height of a man, and it seemed to be wedged into a fissure in the stone. What craft had been used to move such a massive weight? And where had it come from? Arthur reached over Horse's back and stroked the monolith. He knew as soon as he felt the surface that it was made of sandstone and was roughly hacked into shape, probably with stone axes. He shook his head in wonder.

Beyond the monument, an odd structure seemed to have sprung out of the bare earth in one of the rare spots that wasn't entirely shale-covered. Arthur had seen such structures in the land around the Giant's Circle in Britain, when Eamonn had dragged him on an impromptu holiday around the south-west. The standing stones, with a large flat rock over the top, had once been covered with earth and sod, and Arthur had been told by an old woman that the *Little People* had built these structures as graves. Now, partly open to the elements, the structure offered a little shade from the baking sun, so Arthur decided to dismount and explore the area.

Leading Horse, he soon discovered a gaping black hole that plunged into darkness within the dolmen. Arthur resisted an overwhelming urge to throw himself in Horse's saddle and ride back the way he had come as quickly as she could carry him. He would have acted on his instincts had he not heard wood being dragged over stone.

Almost unbidden, the Dragon Knife leaped into his left hand while his right hand continued to hold on to Horse's reins. The animal's ears were pricked and she whickered quietly while scraping at the dirt with her left front hoof in obvious nervousness. As his eyes fixed on the black hole, he saw a figure that suddenly materialised out of an invisible passage like a conjuring trick. A knotted tree branch, long enough to use as a serviceable stick and polished by the hand until it had a honey-rich sheen, was being used to assist the figure to climb up a series of narrow steps until, shaggy and dusty, it stood upright in front of him.

'Well! A visitor! Welcome, sir, as you're the first to come here in years. Sit! Sit! Weigh down the reins with a stone. Does your horse need water? No? Do *you* need water? No! Or food? Please – sit on that stone. It's clean and safe, I swear to you.'

The gabbling figure was a small man who seemed even more dwarf-like because he was much bent and twisted by a disease that caused his joints to swell and his fingers and toes to twist. He wore a dusty, coarse homespun robe of brown wool. A twist of hide was tied around his gaunt waist to expose his hollow chest and grotesquely humped back. The man's body could have belonged to a dwarf or one of the small creatures that lived in the wild and wreaked mischief on humankind. Yet, the small man's face was very human, although it was worn and old. Arthur knew by the soft shine of the old man's washed-out blue eyes that he was some kind of hermit or outcast.

'My name is Arthur and I come from Britain, a country from far away across the great sea. I serve Stormbringer, the Sae Dene captain who has just destroyed the army of the Geat commander, Olaus Healfdene. Are you a Geat? What is your name, my friend?'

As asked, Arthur hunkered down on his heels so the small man could see him, eye to eye. Arthur deliberately forced his face into an expression of friendliness and curiosity without any of the caution or surprise he was feeling.

'Why! My name is Thorvald! Very grand, isn't it? I think I'm Dene, but who can tell? And what does it matter anyway? I've been here for such a very long time, fulfilling my duties to my master, that I forget the life I had before I came to the temple.'

'The temple!' Arthur exclaimed. 'What temple? There's nothing up here but those large stones.'

'Oh, no, Master Arthur. Can't you see the temple down there? It was here before my master came. And he said that his master was just one of a long line of priests who kept the altar clean and swept out the dusty corners. We can't have spiders in the shrine, can we? Would you like to see the temple?'

He's crazed from loneliness, or ... By the gods, how long has he been here? Arthur wondered, then smiled as guilelessly as he could.

'Show me, Thorvald. Whom does the temple worship?'

'Can't you guess, Arthur?'

Thorvald skipped down the steps with surprising agility, when Arthur considered the man's twisted feet. At the bottom of four stone steps, a short passageway of unmortared stone led to a conical room directly under the dolmen. Light slanted through the low doorway and marched towards a stone altar made of a single slab of crudely cut stone.

Arthur cautiously examined the room. The construction was coarse but very clever so the ceiling was a misshapen dome, yet the roof had all the strength of that architectural form. The only furniture was an altar, on which a statue of a man fighting a bull held pride of place.

The other objects in the room were a bowl of water on the floor near the entrance and Thorvald's sleeping pallet. He obviously lived here, as well as caring for the shrine. A broom of twigs leaned against the entry wall and a small box nested beside the sleeping pallet.

'Wash your hands, Arthur. Mithras expects every warrior to come to his house with clean hands.'

Somehow, Arthur felt the importance of obeying this harmless madman. What could it hurt to follow his instructions? The god of soldiers, Mithras, was a powerful deity who asked no evil from those who worshipped him.

'And now, Arthur, as the god watches, it's time for you to do those things that you were sent here to do. My master told me that someone was coming today. An owl and a raven came by turns into the sanctuary, so I knew you'd soon need my services. You are only the second man who has come to Mithras in sixty years.'

Sixty years? Dear God, how old can this man be?

'Who was the other man?' Arthur asked. 'Did he tell you his name?' Somehow, it seemed important to keep this eerie old man talking.

'I should remember . . . Was it wolf? No, that wasn't it! Bee wolf? No! Beowulf, that was his name!'

Thorvald was very pleased with himself, so Arthur was quite shocked to hear the name of this legendary hero spoken of as if he was a real person.

'But he *was* real, Arthur, very much so! He was a warrior who came to Mithras because he doubted himself. The god spoke to him and gave him what he needed.'

'Beowulf!' Arthur muttered.

'Come to the altar now, Arthur, and kneel before it. The god will show us what he wants you to know.'

The Briton reluctantly allowed himself to be led to the altar where he knelt awkwardly on the rough floor. 'You don't have to close your eyes, Arthur, for I know that a warrior is always careful.'

Thorvald knelt beside him and watched a finger of light on the wall. The silence was so thick that Arthur remained quiet, even when the stones under his knees began to cause him pain.

'You've been lost, Child of the Sword, lost for a long time.'

Arthur actually jumped to hear the voice that came from the priest's throat, a voice far deeper and more masculine than Thorvald's tenor-treble.

'You've been confused about your place in the world, especially here, but the time of confusion is over.'

Arthur turned to look at Thorvald's face, but his eyes were turned up so that only the whites were visible and his senses appeared to have fled.

'You must be thinking that I am a madman, but what you think today matters very little. Your page has already been written by the gods and only by denying yourself, as a man and as the foster-son of Bedwyr, can you change your fate.'

How could he possibly know Bedwyr's name?

'You will soon become the King of Winter and survive the disease that kills so many. You will be the ruin of many kings. You will return to your own lands, but nothing will be the same as it was, so you will carve out your new kingdom from Saxon earth and Saxon blood. And your kingdom will endure long into the future, although many men will think you are Dene or Angle. But you will not care, because you will save the world you know and love for the good of all your people. This goal is enough, Arthur.'

Despite himself, Arthur wanted to believe the Voice, but he had denied the worth of magic years before and he sensed that only a demon could know him as well as this priest.

'It is your duty and your fate to save Stormbringer from the Crow King, but you must always beware of corruption. Even the Red Queen will be ensnared, but you must remain clear-sighted. You are the Last Dragon, God's servant who is the ruin of kings and a master of the cold. If you stay true to the task that two fathers have bequeathed to the future, you will not fail in your appointed tasks, even though, in times to come, your deeds will be confused with those of your birth-father. Do not fear what was, for it can be again. But only if your heart remains true.'

'But I will see Britain again?' Arthur asked, with his eyes full of longing and his voice harsh with pain.

'You will see Britain again, even if you are corrupted along the way. The page is already written. Ask me no more now, for I have nothing further to say.'

But you haven't really said anything, Arthur's mind screamed in frustration.

Then, Thorvald's eyes returned to their normal position before closing into a deep and dreamless sleep. Try as he might, Arthur couldn't waken him. Eventually, to save the little man from harm, Arthur placed the slight form onto his pallet and covered him neatly with a threadbare blanket.

Despite arguments from his rational self, Arthur's heart had been touched by his experience. Perhaps that was why he took Olaus's torc from his tunic and laid it out as a gift to Mithras and to Thorvald on the centre of the altar where the light pooled brilliantly before dusk.

The return journey to the encampment was uneventful, and Arthur wondered that he had considered Mirk Wood to be wilder here than those places where Stormbringer's army had breached it. Nor was he a great distance from the site of the Geat camp. Before the last light had flickered out over the lake, he was sitting at Stormbringer's fire, and attempting to describe the hill, the dolmen, the shrine and the old hermit. For the first time in months, Arthur stayed awake and spent the evening drinking with Stormbringer, Hoel and Thorketil, talking strategies while Ole and a brace of young warriors listened with rapt attention.

The next morning, aware that they would be leaving Lake Wener on the following day, Ole and his friends mounted horses from the picket line and set off in search of the shrine of Mithras. Although they rode up and down the margins of Mirk Wood, they never saw the naked hill. Nor did they find any trace of the path that had led Arthur into the wilderness. Puzzled, they returned to the campsite and told Arthur that he must have been mistaken about the directions he had taken.

But both Arthur and Ole knew that there had been no mistake. The shrine had vanished, as if it had never existed.

And, perhaps, it never had.

POSTSCRIPT

The message came by ship as the Dene fleet was loading the last of the survivors from the battle of the Vagus River. Hoel's scouts had already reported that the north had settled once more, while the Geat forces that had massed along the borders had disappeared like smoke in a gale and returned to their own encampments.

Forty-seven ships were at rest in the cove when a very small vessel hove into view, its captain waving a scrap of woad-dyed cloth to indicate he was delivering an important message.

'Lord Stormbringer,' the captain yelled, as his boat nosed towards the beach where the Sae Dene commander awaited the arrival of the courier. The boat's master was little more than fifteen, a boy in the eyes of most men, but this young man could sail a small ship without assistance and he was blessed with a huge heart. His father and his brothers were dead, slain by their Geat enemies, and he would willingly risk his life to strike a blow against the men who had made his mother weep her heart out for the murder of her beloved kin.

Stormbringer stood four-square on the pebbled foreshore, holding a torch high above his head to light the twilight world of bustle as his men loaded the ships, including the string of horses which were regular sailors in these northern lands.

'Who calls my name?'

The small, elegant craft slowed and beached itself on a shoal of sand some fifty feet out from the sandy beach, requiring the young man to leap down into the waist-deep waters. Half-swimming and half-wading, he approached the Sae Dene and then shook himself vigorously to dislodge the worst of the water in his hair, just like a shaggy dog.

'Forgive me for the lateness of the hour, Lord Stormbringer, but I feared you would have departed before I could deliver my message.'

'Your name, young man?' Stormbringer asked.

'I am Erikk, son of Sven, son of Halvar, the Jarl of Halland. I am the last of my line, Lord Stormbringer, for my lands are taken back by the Geats and the land runs red with our blood.'

'You have my sympathy, Erikk. What is your message?'

'I was taken captive two weeks ago and expected to die. But I was plucked from my cage four days ago and taken to the hall where my father once delivered justice to our people. King Heardred of the Geats was there. He gave me this craft and a message for you. Dishonourable as it seems, I agreed to deliver his despatch because I'm free now, and able to kill Geats at will.'

'Tell me your message first, Erikk. Then, once I'm satisfied, I'll want to know everything you can tell me about the Geat king.'

Stormbringer stood easily on the pebbles as power radiated from every muscle in his body. Behind him, Erikk saw the looming form of a tall warrior with untamed amber hair that curled wildly. The eyes of the second warrior kept dragging him back to that huge form that made even Stormbringer seem insignificant. Who was he?

'Lord, please don't punish me for what I'm forced to say to you.' Erikk smiled nervously, so Stormbringer expected that the words from Heardred would be very insulting.

'Speak out without fear, Erikk.'

'King Heardred instructed me to tell you that he will kill the whole population of Blekinge, the province that lies on the south-east coast beside the great sea. It is the area that the Romans called Mare Suevicum. He hopes you will come to save the population and be trapped there but, if not, he will still do as he has vowed. The deaths of his warriors at Lake Wener demand his retribution.'

Before Stormbringer could respond, Erikk delivered one more message from Heardred.

'The king also instructed me to speak with a man whom he called the Last Dragon. For this man's impudence, Heardred says he will enslave those young children of Blekinge who aren't killed. He will then name them as beasts and inhuman, so that any and all crimes may be permitted on their bodies with impunity. They will henceforth be called the Dragon's Brood and will be regarded as monsters, beyond the help of men or the gods. They will be sold in the south to the Franks and the Saxons, where there is always a market for lost children. And so the Last Dragon will rue the day he chose to insult Heardred, son of Hygelac, and the King of the Geats, by killing his general.'

The silence that followed Erikk's speech was pregnant with menace. The threat from Heardred was appalling in its depravity. For his part, the Last Dragon, who had been standing behind Lord Stormbringer, turned away before his feral eyes could freeze the blood in Erikk's veins.

'I swear to you that we'll save Blekinge, Erikk. Meanwhile, you may sleep in my camp and join my crew.' Warm and strong, Stormbringer's hands cupped the boy's face and offered comfort and understanding. Yet Erikk's eyes continued to follow the tall figure of the Briton as he strode up the beach towards the camp and the torchlight.

'But will the Last Dragon forgive me for the intelligence I've brought him and the revenge that Heardred has sworn to inflict on the children of Blekinge?'

Stormbringer grinned without humour. 'You're safe from my dragon, Erikk. But I don't like the chances that the Geat king will be as blessed. For his vile threats, the Geat king tempts providence. To make war on children is despicable.'

Erikk thought hard on the matter and decided that, having met the Geat king and Stormbringer, he'd prefer to gamble on the Sea Dene's ability.

As for the Last Dragon? Erikk decide that he would be best placed to avoid the Briton. The man was obviously dangerous, and one of Fortuna's favourites.

But as Erikk would ultimately discover, fate never listens to frail humans. Nor does great suffering secure a future that is free of trouble and strife. The only way to reach absolute safety is through death, and Erikk wasn't ready for the grave.

Not yet . . . and not alone!

AUTHOR'S NOTES

What a task! After completing what I considered to be a large amount of research whereby I could plan the plot line for this novel, I started to map out my plan of attack and realised that I needed to carry out further research on the complex interrelationships between the tribes of Skandia. The further I delved into the history of the Scandinavian people, the more complex the personalities and hatreds of the period seemed to become. These complications were compounded by the inaccuracies and limited information available to researchers from the period between the fifth and eleventh centuries.

As an example of this, I had always believed the Black Death only came to Europe in the medieval period. I was therefore amazed to discover all the details of an earlier, equally destructive plague called Justinian's Disease that is virtually the same as the medieval version, except for the gangrene that attacked the nose, the lips and all the digits. Evidence from bodies of those who had suffered from Justinian's Disease and the Black Death has been compared by experts who have determined the two diseases were related and both were spread by lice that lived on rats.

The pandemic spread along the trade routes from Constantinople about AD 542. Some experts suggest that the collapse of the British resistance to the Angles, Saxons and Jutes was so sudden because they suffered huge losses during the passage of the plague. The Britons traded with the East, whereas their invaders, the Saxons, had fewer trading links with Constantinople.

Likewise, the disease gradually spread throughout northern Europe. The loss of life in the Frank kingdoms was significant as the disease spread all the way to the Dene, Geat, Swedish and Norwegian lands in the north. Once again, some experts postulate that the Viking advances of the eighth, ninth and tenth centuries into Britain, the North Atlantic, Russia and the Mediterranean, and all the lands between them, would have occurred earlier had the pressures on an expanding population not been abruptly and fatally solved.

My research into the Dene people was far more complicated than I ever expected, and I was surprised to discover that source material from the fifth, sixth, seventh and eight centuries was relatively limited in scope and was often vague in content.

When I became engrossed in my research for this novel, I was greatly amused to encounter references to a forest called Mirk Wood, and rulers with exotic names such as Frodhi, Frodo, Healfdene, Beowulf, and other romantic names from the pages of literature. My respect for J.R.R. Tolkien grew immensely once I became aware of the research he must have carried out to gain his insights into the northern cultures.

Likewise, I had never realized the complexities of the cultures that existed in the northern lands. To most readers, Vikings are all rather like Hagar the Horrible of cartoon fame, but the Dene, Geats, Saxons, Jutes Angles and the Norwegians possessed vastly different customs and cultures despite living in relatively close proximity to each other.

As a novice researcher, I was forced to scramble over many hurdles on my own journey with Arthur, Gareth, Germanus and Lorcan. At times, the sheer scope of their adventures left me feeling bemused. But, along the way, I came to realize the great spirit and abilities of those migrants who came from the Skandian lands to settle in the lands of the Franks and the Britons.

Of one thing I will always be certain, these heroes from the north will always remain close to my heart and will remain mysterious, god-like and alien.

I hope you enjoy your read.

M. K. Hume
March, 2014

GLOSSARY OF PLACE NAMES

Arden (Forest of Arden)	Warwickshire, England
Caer Gai Llanuwchllyn	Gwynedd, Wales
Cymru	The Celtic name for Wales
Dean (Forest of Dene)	Gloucestershire, England
Dubris	Dover, Kent, England
Gesoriacum	City in France
Gotland	Land of the Geat
Heorot	Hall of the Danish King
The Holding	Stormbringer's farm on Ostoanmark
Litus Saxonicum	The Saxon Shore. Loosely defined as the English Channel
Noroway	Norway
Opland	The western mountain regions of modern Norway
Ostoanmark	Modern Zealand
Reidgotaland	Part of Gotland
Reims	City in France
Soissons	City in France
Vestra Gautland	Part of Gotland

GLOSSARY OF BRITISH TRIBAL NAMES

Atrebates
Brigante
Catuvellauni
Coritani
Cornovii
Deceangli
Demetae
Dumnonii
Dobunni
Iceni
Otadini
Ordovice
Selgovae
Silures
Trinovantes